Jezebel

Harlot Queen of Israel

Chronicles of the Watchers
Book 1

By Brian Godawa

Jezebel: Harlot Queen of Israel
Chronicles of the Watchers Book 1
2nd Edition

Warrior Poet Publishing
www.warriorpoetpublishing.com

ISBN: 9798710913062 (hardcover)
ISBN: 978-1-942858-44-7 (paperback)
ISBN: 978-1-942858-45-4 (ebook)

Scripture quotations taken from *The Holy Bible: English Standard Version*. Wheaton: Standard Bible Society, 2001.

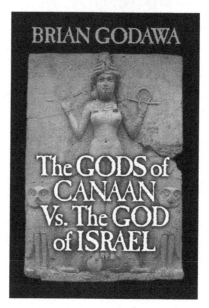

ACKNOWLEDGMENTS

Special thanks to Yahweh Elohim for the fearful symmetry of his narrative. And to my most awesome wife Kimberly, without whose loving support I would not be writing these novels. Also to my devoted readers who helped me to design the cover for this book as well as proof the text for me. I so appreciate your input. And thank you to my lovingly ruthless editor, Jeanette Windle, as well as to Dana Wilder, for her excellent editorial input.

I dedicate this novel to the godly women in our culture who stand up for Life and for godly masculinity in a culture of death and misandry.

NOTE TO THE READER

I receive commissions on all links to Amazon books in this book.

Jezebel: Harlot Queen of Israel is a standalone novel. But it is a part of the *Chronicles of the Watchers* series whose books all share what biblical scholar Michael S. Heiser has coined "the Deuteronomy 32 worldview."[1]

Rather than try to re-explain this worldview within the story of each novel, I will lay it out here in brief summary. For more detailed biblical support and explanation, I recommend reading my booklet, *Psalm 82: The Divine Council of the Gods, the Judgment of the Watchers and the Inheritance of the Nations (paid link).* It is the foundation of all three of my novel series, *Chronicles of the Nephilim, Chronicles of the Watchers,* and *Chronicles of the Apocalypse.*

Deuteronomy 32 is well-known as the Song of Moses. In it, Moses sings of the story of Israel and how she had come to be God's chosen nation. He begins by glorifying God and then telling them to "remember the days of old"...

> When the Most High gave to the nations their inheritance,
>> when he divided mankind,
> he fixed the borders of the peoples
>> according to the number of the sons of God.
> But the Lord's portion is his people,
>> Jacob his allotted heritage.
> (Deuteronomy 32:8–9)

The context of this passage is the Tower of Babel incident in Genesis 11 when mankind was divided. Rebellious humanity sought divinity in unified rebellion, so God separated them by confusing their tongues, which divided

---

[1] Michael S. Heiser, *The Unseen Realm: Recovering the Supernatural Worldview of the Bible*, First Edition (Bellingham, WA: Lexham Press, 2015), 113–114.

them into the seventy nations (of Gentiles), described in Genesis 10, with their ownership of those bordered lands as the allotted "inheritance" of those peoples.

But inheritance works in heaven as it is on earth. The people of Jacob (Israel) would become Yahweh's allotted inheritance while the other Gentile nations were the allotted inheritance of the *Sons of God*.

So who were these Sons of God who ruled over the Gentile nations (Psalm 82:1-8)? Some believe they were human rulers. Others argue for their identities as supernatural principalities and powers. I am in the second camp. In my *Psalm 82* book, I prove why they cannot be humans and must be heavenly creatures.

The phrase "Sons of God" is a technical term that means divine beings from God's heavenly throne court (Job 1:6; 38:7), and they are referred to with many different titles. They are sometimes called "heavenly host" (Isaiah 24:21-22; Deuteronomy 4:19 with Deuteronomy 32:8-9; 1 Kings 22:19-23), sometimes called "holy ones" (Deuteronomy 33:2-3; Psalm 89:5-7; Hebrews 2:2), sometimes called "the divine council" (Psalm 82:1; 89:5-7), sometimes called "Watchers" (Daniel 4:13, 17, 23), and sometimes called "gods" or *elohim* in the Hebrew (Deuteronomy 32: 17, 43; Psalm 82:1; 58:1-2). Yes, you read that last one correctly. God's Word calls these beings *gods*.

But fear not. That isn't polytheism. The word "god" in this biblical sense is a synonym for "heavenly being" or "divine being" whose realm is that of the spiritual. [2] It does not mean uncreated beings that are all-powerful and all-knowing. Yahweh alone is that God. Yahweh is the God of gods (Deuteronomy 10:17; Psalm 136:2). He created the other *elohim* ("gods"). These "gods" are created angelic beings who are most precisely referred to as Sons of God.

The biblical narrative is as follows. The Fall in the Garden was not the only source of evil in the world. Before the Flood, some of these heavenly Sons of God rebelled against Yahweh and left their divine dwelling to come to earth (Jude 6), where they violated Yahweh's holy separation and mated with human women (Genesis 6:1-4). This was not a racial separation, but a

---

[2] Michael S. Heiser, *The Unseen Realm: Recovering the Supernatural Worldview of the Bible*, First Edition (Bellingham, WA: Lexham Press, 2015), 23-27.

spiritual one. Their corrupt hybrid seed were called "Nephilim" (giants), and their effect on humanity included such corruption and violence on the earth that Yahweh sent the Flood to wipe everyone out and start over again with Noah and his family.

Unfortunately, after the Flood humanity once again united in evil while building the Tower of Babel, a symbol of idolatrous worship of false gods. So Yahweh confused their tongues and divided them into the seventy nations. Since man would not stop worshipping false gods, the living God gave them over to their lusts (Romans 1:24, 26, 28) and placed them under the authority of the fallen Sons of God that they worshipped. Fallen spiritual rulers for fallen humanity (Psalm 82:1-7). It's as if God said to humanity, "Okay, if you refuse to stop worshipping false gods, then I will give you over to them and see how you like them ruling over you."

Deuteronomy 32 hints at a spiritual reality behind the false gods of the nations, calling them "demons" (Deuteronomy 32:17; Psalm 106:37-38). The Apostle Paul later ascribes demonic reality to pagan gods as well (1 Corinthians 10:20; 8:4-6). The New Testament continues this ancient notion that spiritual principalities and powers lay behind earthly powers (Ephesians 6:12; 3:10). The two were inextricably linked in historic events. As Jesus indicated, whatever happened in heaven also happened on earth (Matthew 6:10). Earthly kingdoms in conflict are intimately connected to heavenly powers in conflict (Daniel 10:12-13, 20-21; 2 Kings 6:17; Judges 5:19-20).

So the Bible says that there is demonic reality to false gods. Just what this looks like is not exactly explained in the text of Scripture. But since those Sons of God who were territorial authorities over the nations were spiritually fallen Watchers, that makes them demonic or evil in essence. So what if they were the actual spiritual beings behind the false gods of the ancient world? What if the fallen Sons of God were masquerading as the gods of the nations in order to keep humanity enslaved in idolatry to their authority? That would affirm the biblical stories of earthly events with heavenly events occurring in synchronization.

Psalm 82:8 hints at the final judgment of these fallen gods when it links their disinheritance of the nations to Yahweh "arising" and inheriting the nations from them. He will literally take back their territorial rights and power.

The messianic connection is obvious and explained in more detail in my book, *Psalm 82*.

That is the biblical premise of the *Chronicles of the Watchers*. The pagan gods like Baal, Astarte, Asherah, and others are actually fallen Sons of God, Watchers of the nations, crafting false identities and narratives as gods of those nations. The ultimate end of these spiritual rebels is depicted in the series *Chronicles of the Apocalypse*. But for now, they plan, conspire, and fight to keep their allotted peoples and lands, all while seeking to stop God's messianic goal of inheriting all the nations (Psalm 2:1-9; 82:8).

One other word for those who share my high view of Scripture. My goal is to use the fantasy genre to show the theological reality of spiritual warfare while being faithful to the biblical text.

In the interest of focusing on the story of Jezebel, I had to skip over some other narratives that did not include her. I condensed and telescoped some events and people, but kept true to the essence of what was occurring. I had to use creative license occasionally. Otherwise, the story would be too long and fragmented for a novel.

I seek to stay true to the spirit of the text if not the letter. For instance, I cut out a large part of Elisha's ministry and telescoped the final events of Jezebel's demise with the end of Elijah's narrative because the focus of this novel is on Jezebel vs. Elijah (and Jehu). Elisha's ministry could warrant his own novel.

Thank you for your understanding of imagination and faith.

Brian Godawa
Author, *Chronicles of the Watchers*

TABLE OF CONTENTS

MAPS

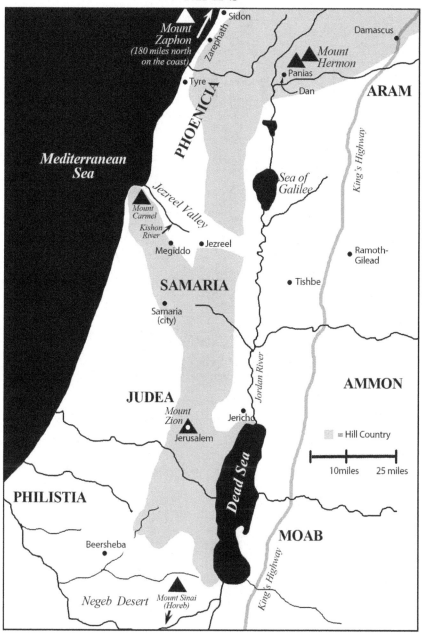

Mount Zaphon (180 miles north on the coast)

Sidon

Damascus

Zarephath

Mount Hermon

Panias

PHOENICIA

Tyre

Dan

ARAM

Mediterranean Sea

King's Highway

Sea of Galilee

Jezreel Valley

Mount Carmel

Kishon River

Jezreel

Ramoth-Gilead

Megiddo

SAMARIA

Tishbe

Samaria (city)

Jordan River

AMMON

JUDEA

Mount Zion

Jericho

= Hill Country

Jerusalem

Dead Sea

10miles   25 miles

PHILISTIA

MOAB

Beersheba

Negeb Desert

Mount Sinai (Horeb)

King's Highway

Enoch's Cosmic Geography of Sheol, the Underworld

(adapted from 1Enoch 17-19 & Kelley Coblentz Bautch,
A Study of the Geography of 1 Enoch 17-19 : "No One Has Seen What I Have Seen")

4 Winds & 4 Pillars
of Heaven & Earth

Great Rivers

River of Fire

Living Waters

Mt. Hermon

Fiery Beings

Mountain Reaching to Heaven
(*Celestial Storehouse*)

Chaos & Disorder
(*tohu wabohu*)

Tartarus

The Great Darkness

Valley of Water

Great Beasts

Prison House of Angels

Dark Mountain of the Dead

Wintery Winds

Cursed Valley (Gehenna)

Mount Zion

Tree of Judgment

Ends of the Earth

Chasm of Fiery Pillars

| 1 | 2 | 3 | 4 |

4 Hollow Places
1. Abraham's Bosom
2. Abel
3. the Wicked punished
4. the Wicked unpunished

Mountain of Water

Desert

Seven Mountains of Precious Stones

Chaos & Disorder
(*tohu wabohu*)

Sinai

Mountain of Fire

The Great Sea
Waters of the Abyss

4 Winds & 4 Pillars
of Heaven & Earth

PROLOGUE

Tohu Wabohu

The great beast came up from the depths of the sea. It rose like a king to its throne, the king over all the sons of pride. Its scales were impenetrable shields of war. Its teeth were terror. Its body iron muscle and sinew. Its heart as hard as stone. Its seven heads were the guards of the spiritual realm where it ruled.

The creature's purpose was lawlessness. To disrupt. To dismantle. To destroy the created order. It moved with serpentine ease through the black waters below as the dark sky above churned with swirling clouds and thunder.

It broke the surface. Its breath kindled coals. Its nostrils sneezed smoke, and a flaming torch of fire belched forth from its mouths with a fury that challenged the storm above. It was the sea dragon of chaos: Leviathan. Its destination was the Land.

The creature was there in the beginning after God created the heavens and the earth. Darkness was over the face of the deep until the Creator separated the light from the darkness, separated the waters above from the waters below, separated the land from the sea, other creatures from man, female from male. The heavenly host sang together. The Sons of God shouted for joy. The sea and its mighty denizen were tamed.

Leviathan was there at the Red Sea as well when Yahweh, the God of Jacob, established his covenantal order. With the roaring of the waves, the dragon was pushed back in the parting, its heads crushed, chaos held at bay. Its body was feasted upon in the wilderness of the heavens and earth of the Mosaic covenant, embodied in the tabernacle and written on tablets of stone.

But now Leviathan, the incarnation of chaos and destruction was back, resurrected by a supernatural call from the unseen realm. It headed toward the coastland where a city rose from the sea. An island city guarded by powerful ships and fortified by massive stone walls.

Tyre was the chief city of a confederation of coastal powers from Sidon and Byblos in the north all the way down to Mount Carmel in the south. This powerful trading confederation was Sidonia, also called Phoenicia by their Greek trading partners. They ruled the seas and grew rich with merchant trade from the wealth of nations. They had a cosmopolitan culture that drew the best from every trade partner on the seas, from Egypt to Greece and even as far as Tarshish. Their ancestry and bloodlines were mixed with all people groups as the Phoenicians intermarried with their trading partners from distant shores. Tyre's architectural structures were world-renowned for their sophistication and design. Especially their temples.

On the southern part of the island city, a stone temple to the god Melqart stood. Known as Herakles to the Greeks, Melqart was the god of Tyre and had been since the days of Lord Hiram's trading with the great king Solomon. He was also called the "Watcher" of Tyre, as gods watched over cities and nations as their territories. Melqart stood near his temple on the rocky shore with the goddess Astarte at his side awaiting the arrival of Leviathan. Melqart was muscular and striking in appearance with a bearded face and robed in a lion's pelt tunic. He grasped a massive club in his mighty right hand.

Astarte was considered the Queen of Heaven, the consort of the storm god Baal. She was voluptuous in her naked form with pale white skin and a hairstyle like that of the Egyptian goddess Hathor: black in color, full, but tightly coiffed to just above her shoulders, looking like its own headdress. A uraeus rose from the golden band around her head, another Egyptian symbol of royalty: a rearing cobra, its wings spread, ready for striking. Astarte's feminine traits were both seductive and deceiving for she was the goddess of both sex and war. She loved and she killed.

Unseen by human eyes and unheard by human ears, Melqart and Astarte and her guardian lion were silhouetted on the shore against the stormy skies. Sensing a surge of spiritual power, the gods gave one another a knowing look. The creature they had summoned was near now and they were empowered by its presence.

CHAPTER 1

My name is Jehu, son of Jehoshaphat, son of Nimshi, of the people of Israel, and I will tell you a story. It is a story of creation and fall. Of gods and men. Of kings and queens. Of miracles and lies. When future generations look back upon my day, they will wonder. But will they believe?

Will they believe stories of fire and brimstone? Of plagues and parting waters? Of fallen giants and falling walls? And if they heed not the warnings from heaven, what then will they believe? Will they gain the world, but lose their souls?

Listen to me now, and I will tell you a story of the rise and fall of the most powerful queen in the land, a woman who transformed her world and changed the course of history. Her name was Izabel of the Sidonians. She was born to Ethbaal, the high priest of Astarte, who became king of Tyre through a most common means of royal ascent.

Tyre, Phoenicia
874 BC

Ethbaal followed his king, Phelles of Tyre, through an underground passageway, protected by five armed palace guards. Ethbaal was thirty-four years old, in his prime, fit and disciplined as high priest of Astarte. At age fifty, Phelles was a fat, soft man of luxury whose family dynasty should have been over long ago. He was the last of four sons, who had previously slain his older brother to take the throne. His mere presence disgusted Ethbaal, but Phelles was king, and the high priest obeyed him.

3

Phelles had recently claimed his right to the Sacred Marriage, a fertility ritual where the king would copulate with the high priestess of Astarte as a symbol of marrying the goddess. This ensured good crops for the people and affirmed the sacred stature of the king as a member of the divine family.

What repulsed Ethbaal most was that this slobbering, lustful beast was giddy with anticipation because a new high priestess was to be anointed in a few days and he would soon have her.

Unfortunately, that high-priestess-to-be was Ethbaal's own daughter Izabel.

•••••

Izabel of Tyre was led through the streets by a procession of *qedeshim*. Qedeshim were male and female "holy ones." A male was called a *qedesh* and a female a *qedesha*. They were temple servants whose cultic responsibilities included both temple upkeep and prostitution. Qedeshim were very popular with the people.

The new high priest of Baal walked beside Izabel. His name was Hamilqart. He had been groomed for the position and now carried himself with a confidence of his worthiness. Eighteen years old, he was slim with a boyish face and the golden hair of his Greek ancestry. He had grown up with Izabel and had stolen her heart. They had been secret lovers for the past year, finding every hidden location they could to indulge their youthful infatuation with each other.

Izabel shared a glance with Hamilqart as they walked, trying to keep their regal poise, trying not to let their secret be apparent. But the truth was that Hamilqart looked much more desirable to her in the official uniform of the high priest: gold-gilded blue robe, gem-studded conical headdress, and carrying the sacred golden mace in his hand. Yes, much more desirable. She wondered when they might find a moment to be alone together again.

Izabel and her entourage arrived at the gate of the temple of Baal. Though Melqart was the patron god of Tyre, Baal was the Most High of the Canaanite pantheon and as such required his own temple. Since Astarte was Baal's consort, her new high priestess Izabel was to be Baal's own. Baal was also known as Hadad the storm god or Baal Shamem, Lord of Heaven—Baal for short.

His house was classic Phoenician in design, a long stone rectangular structure of ashlar masonry, huge stones cut to fit without mortar. It rested in the midst of a large courtyard with porticos around the perimeter. The actual temple was about seventy feet long, forty feet wide, and fifty feet high with two large bronze pillars at the entrance, where Izabel now stood.

A cadre of qedeshim surrounded her with shaving razors in their hands. She bowed her head, and Hamilqart poured oil on her, the anointing.

She had turned sixteen only recently, but she felt already a woman of age. Perhaps this was because of her sexual experience. Or because of what her father Ethbaal had taught her since her mother had died years ago. He had treated Izabel as he would a son, teaching her how to maneuver the politics of royalty and how to strategize and rule, but with an important difference.

It was more difficult for a woman than for a man in this world that men controlled. A woman had to be much more discreet and clever than her male counterparts if she was to achieve her goals. Her father had taught her well to use her feminine traits to her advantage and to use the system against itself. She'd even practiced some of those tactics on Hamilqart, who responded ever so predictably like a loyal puppy.

Izabel closed her eyes as the qedeshim shaved her head of all her long, dark hair. It would take years to grow back, and she felt the loss deeply. Her hair had been her pride. But the sacrifice was worth it for what she would receive in return as high priestess of Astarte.

She saw sadness in Hamilqart's eyes. He had worshipped her flowing hair. He stared at it lying on the stone porch as if he would never be happy again.

An offering of one ox and six sheep was performed by the priests on the altar in the courtyard. Then Izabel returned to the bath for her cleansing.

• • • • •

Ethbaal, King Phelles, and his guards came out of their underground passageway into a sacred shrine room for Astarte, Ethbaal's patron goddess. Astarte's temple stood near the house of Baal in the massive court surrounded by porticos. As consort of Baal, Astarte was privileged to have her own shrine within the temple complex, though smaller than Baal's, of course.

The guards remained outside the shrine as Ethbaal and Phelles were accompanied inside by four priests of Astarte. In the vestibule entrance, they all donned masks created for libation ceremonies. Ethbaal wore a cattle skull that had been altered to be worn over the priest's face. The others were artistic creations of leather, wood, and plaster. Phelles wore a bull mask, a symbol of Baal. The other priests wore various zoomorphic faces: a lion, a horse, a stag, and an ape.

They entered the inner sanctuary of the shrine in silence, their costumes looking like an eerie herd of anthropomorphized animals.

Incense was lit on the censers. Ethbaal carried the wine that Phelles would pour out to Astarte as a libation offering of preparation for his Sacred Marriage to the goddess.

An image of Astarte stood before them in the holy of holies. An eight-foot-tall white alabaster stone sculpture, she stood naked and voluptuous upon the back of a tamed lion. A serpent wrapped around her legs up to her waist. Full-bodied black hair replicating that of the goddess Hathor indicated Egyptian influence, and her eyes seemed to look down upon the masked priests and king with ghostly awareness. Ethbaal could feel that Astarte was here with them.

"Queen of Heaven," Ethbaal prayed aloud, "Our Great Lady Astarte, we bring the king before you to receive your judgment of his worthiness for the Sacred Marriage."

• • • • •

Stripping off her robes, Izabel descended into the steaming bath, a large ten-foot by ten-foot square filled with fresh water and surrounded by a portico of colonnades. Her bald head felt strange to her. She'd always had hair, and she now felt more naked than she'd ever felt in her life. It was unsettling.

Two qedeshim sponged her body clean. She thought of the large tattoo she'd recently received on her back of the sea dragon Leviathan. She still felt residual sensitivity from the ink needles piercing her skin. One of the servants poured soothing water down her back.

Looking into a double mirror positioned so she could see her back, Izabel admired the colorful image of a flowing serpentine body that ended in seven heads poised for striking, several of whose mouths flamed with fire. It inspired both beauty and awe, the very reaction she wanted to elicit from others in her life.

• • • • •

In the shrine room of Astarte, Ethbaal watched King Phelles take a plate of breadcakes a priest handed him and place it onto the small stone altar: a food offering. The king then took a deep drink of wine from the golden chalice he would use for libation to the goddess. Ethbaal knew the king was picturing in his mind the many ways he intended to sexually abuse Izabel in the Sacred Marriage rite. Ethbaal knew this because the king had told him often enough to make Ethbaal boil with anger.

Ethbaal kept his eyes focused on Phelles as the king poured the wine over the food offering, mumbling a prayer of thanksgiving.

The king broke off his prayer with a grunt. Dropping the chalice to the ground with a clang, he clutched at his abdomen and dropped to his knees, his expression one of excruciating pain.

Ethbaal had poisoned the king with hemlock.

The king looked up as he began to convulse, and his eyes found Ethbaal. No one moved to his aid. He wretched and vomit oozed from the mouth of the bull skull, an image unworthy of the mighty god Baal.

Surrounding the king, Ethbaal and the four other priests withdrew daggers from their dark robes. Ethbaal made the first strike, aiming for the heart. Phelles groaned in pain.

The others joined in by plunging their blades into the king's torso—over and over. The king fell to the floor, still convulsing from the poison as his life left his body. This small group of assassins looked like a pack of silent animals thinning the herd. It was a scene that struck Ethbaal as quite natural.

Ethbaal spoke mentally as if to the king's spirit, *You are unworthy of Astarte. You are unworthy of my daughter. You are only worthy of Hades.*

• • • • •

Izabel's body was dried from the bath. Her qedeshim then applied cosmetics to her face. Dark kohl around the eyes to emphasize them as Egyptians did. Ground beets to redden her cheeks. Metallic bluish eye shadow and red lip coloring.

As the servants carefully painted her, she stared at a small ivory carving by the large mirror. It was one of the most popular images in Canaan, called "the woman at the window." Framed by a square sculpted window with pillars

7

beneath it, the face of a painted woman with a Hathor wig on her shaved head looked out at the viewer. She represented the goddess Astarte. The image was also a popular reference to qedeshim as prostitutes in the service of Astarte, providing both fertility and life.

When the qedeshim were done with Izabel's make-up, they sprayed her with perfume made of frankincense, myrrh, and other rare herbs to incite the king's desire.

They hung gold earrings in Izabel's ears, the storm god's gold ring on her hand, the black hair of Astarte on her head, and lastly a purple robe of interwoven wool and cotton over her naked body. The Sidonians had become known throughout the entire world for their unique purple dye that was made from the murex shellfish found only off their coast. Its rarity and high price made Tyrian purple a symbol of power and wealth and a favorite of royalty.

• • • • •

Ethbaal stood on the steps of the royal palace before the people of Tyre to receive the crown. The murder of King Phelles had been kept sufficiently discreet, and since Ethbaal was of noble blood and well connected, he was the most popular choice for a new dynasty. It had taken but a day for the elders of the city to acknowledge his claim to the throne. Now here he was to receive it.

As Ethbaal's head was anointed with oil, the audience of Tyrians applauded with hope for a new era. He had planned and calculated for years to become the sovereign, and he was not going to waste one moment. He intended to create a lasting legacy that would cement Tyre's supremacy in the annals of history.

Now he was king of Tyre.

• • • • •

Veiled like a bride, Izabel was led on the arm of high priest Hamilqart through the streets. A group of singers went before them and she was followed by the current high priestess, now wearing humble white linen and carrying "the divine weapon," a golden axe. Crowds of Tyrians lined up to watch the procession all the way to the large pillared courtyard filled with hundreds of residents who watched a sacrifice of ox, sheep, and lambs upon the stone altar before the house of Baal.

As Izabel paused before the two large glorious bronze pillars at the top of the steps, the crowd cheered their new high priestess. She offered two golden figurines as an offering to the priests before entering the house of Baal.

Hamilqart escorted her through the tripartite building, three sections, each with a purpose. The first was the entrance. They walked over giant footprints, several feet long, engraved into the marble floor. These represented the god's own feet leaving an imprint as he entered into his house. Izabel noticed Hamilqart was walking at a delayed pace, noticeably slower than usual.

Then they reached the second room, the holy place of the temple, a long-pillared room where smoke from burning censers filled the air. Izabel felt herself get light-headed from the incense as she made her way up to the third section, the holy of holies.

In this section, a huge bronze image of Baal stood before a fire pit with burning coals in it. About fifteen feet high, the image of Baal in human form, a muscular male deity seated on a throne. He wore the conical-shaped *Atef* headdress common in both Egypt and Canaan. He also sported bull horns as a symbol of deity. He had long, braided hair and a long, squarely cropped beard. His hands were held out over the flames at his feet to receive the dismembered parts of the bull sacrificed on the altar in the courtyard.

The smoke that filled the temple obscured what Izabel could see. Had the image turned its head down to look at her? The drug-like effect of the incense must be producing hallucinations. She tried to clear her head just as her father, now King Ethbaal of Tyre, approached them.

Hamilqart squeezed her arm tighter as if he wasn't going to let her go.

"My daughter," Ethbaal said. "Welcome, my new high priestess."

He held out his hand to take her from Hamilqart. "I have waited too long for this moment."

"Yes, my father and my king." Izabel felt Hamilqart hesitate to release her. Looking at him through her veil, she saw eyes of sadness like a dog who had lost its owner.

Hamilqart finally released her.

Ethbaal grinned with pleasure. "Let us consummate the Sacred Marriage of king and goddess."

CHAPTER 2

In the spiritual realm, the storm god Baal watched father and daughter leave the holy place for the shrine of Astarte outside. Unseen and unheard by the human priests, Baal turned and sank his fangs into the bull sacrifice on the arms of his bronze image.

The sculpture was a good likeness of himself, though not entirely accurate. He did indeed wear the same conical hat and horns as well as the leather battle skirt. And he had the same long hair and tightly shaped beard. But, Baal found the face created by the human artisans was far less handsome than his own. And he was much more muscular than the image. They'd also failed to include Baal's weapon he wore strapped on his back; a mighty war hammer he'd named Yagrush, which meant *Driver*.

Well, humans are a feeble lot. They often don't get things right. Baal sucked more of the blood from the offering, feeling it surge through his being like his own life force. Sacrifices worked that way. When humans worshipped the gods, it gave those gods more power and control. Baal had been feeling stronger than ever. As Most High god of the pantheon, he'd already been allotted as his inheritance the Sidonians, Arameans, Philistines, and everyone who surrounded Israel and Judah. Now even that crawling infestation of Hebrews was descending further into idolatry and farther away from Yahweh, their allotted inheritance.

King David had almost wiped out the Canaanite pantheon with his successful campaigns to regain the land originally taken by that monstrous Joshua, son of Nun. The Hebrews called it conquest. Baal called it theft. But thank the gods for David's son Solomon, who had married so many pagan wives he'd become corrupt to the core, incorporating the worship of the pagan gods Astarte, Molech, Milcom, and Chemosh into his religion.

Because of that spiritual harlotry, Yahweh had split the House of David in two, crippling them as punishment. Which was just fine as far as Baal was concerned. He couldn't have asked for a better setup for victory than a divided kingdom. Rehoboam had ruled the southern tribes of Judah and Benjamin while Jeroboam had ruled over the northern ten tribes they now called Israel.

But both of them had also been "filthy idolaters" in Yahweh's eyes. Rehoboam had maintained the temple in Jerusalem, but he never tore down the high places, which were altars built in the surrounding hills as places of worship and sacrifice unto the gods of Canaan. He had even placed an asherah in the Jerusalem temple itself. Totems of the same name as the mother goddess Asherah, the asherim were wooden poles carved with images and crafted to look like a sacred tree of life. But they represented the goddess who had been worshipped as a wife to Yahweh by all twelve tribes for the last hundred years.

Jeroboam had been no better than Rehoboam. The leader of Israel in the north had forged two golden calves as images of Yahweh in direct defiance of Yahweh's own commands. He had placed one in the city of Dan in the north and one in the city of Bethel in the south. Jeroboam had also failed to destroy the asherim and high places all around Israel.

This fell right into the plans of Baal and the rest of the Watchers. Their goal was two-fold. First, take back the land of Canaan that Yahweh had stolen from their allotted inheritance. As the Hebrew authorities and their people were drawn away from devotion to Yahweh and toward Canaanite deities, those deities regained power within those territories. The authority of heavenly principalities and powers was reflected in earthly authorities and powers. On earth as it was in heaven.

The second goal of the Watchers was to destroy the chosen seedline of the Messiah, the one promised by Yahweh to ultimately crush the head of the serpent and inherit all the Land. That would be done by attacking the House of David, the bloodline of Messiah, down in Judah.

Since the Hebrews were squandering their inheritance, Yahweh's influence over them was waning, Baal and the Canaanite pantheon were waxing stronger than ever. The angels of Yahweh had become scarce in the land. They didn't show themselves much these days.

Baal came out of his thoughts just as the hands of the giant bronze image were moved with mechanical means by the priests. As the arms lowered, the sacrificial meat rolled into the pit of flames below. Sparks flew. Flames licked the statue, turning it red hot.

Now was the perfect time to strike with everything they had against Yahweh. Pulling out his war horn, Baal blew its supernatural call throughout the unseen realm, unheard by earthly ears, but very much heard by heavenly ones.

CHAPTER 3

The next morning, Ethbaal and Izabel walked along their favorite pathway above the sea cliffs near the royal palace. Below them, waves crashed into the rocks with relentless fury, chaos held at bay. But they could also see their harbor guarded by warships and full of merchant boats leaving with or bringing back items of trade. Metals of copper, iron and tin from the island of Cyprus. Linen and embroidered fabrics from Egypt. Spices, ivory, and ebony from Arabia. Horses and mules from the mountains of Urartu. Slaves from everywhere and to everywhere.

"Tyre is already the desire of nations," Izabel said. "Imagine the dynasty you could build."

Ethbaal demurred, "Damascus would not agree with you."

He was referring to the Aramean kingdom north of them and of Israel. Centered in the city of Damascus sixty miles inland at the base of the eastern Lebanon mountain range, the city was used synonymously for the kingdom because it was such a stronghold of power as well as being its capital. The Aramean king Ben-Hadad had caused much trouble for both the Phoenicians and the Israelites with his warmongering.

Izabel scoffed. "They busy themselves building armies while we become so wealthy we could buy Damascus."

"Their envy will no doubt turn to war," Ethbaal said. "That is why our only choice is to unite with Israel."

Izabel looked at him with surprise.

"We control the coast," he explained. "Israel guards the King's Highway inland. Separately, we have strength—but also weakness. Together, Damascus cannot defeat us."

A travel route from ancient days, the King's Highway was vitally important to the trade of all the nations of the Fertile Crescent. It ran from Egypt across the Sinai and up north through the Transjordan and Damascus all the way to the Euphrates River in Mesopotamia. Israel controlled the middle portion of the highway and thus controlled the access of Damascus.

Izabel scowled at the thought of such an alliance. "But Israelites are barbarians. Their religion is intolerant."

"Do not be so quick in your judgment, daughter. I have met their king, Ahab. He is more open-minded than you may think. And his people more inclusive than you give them credit."

"Do they not worship a single god?" She was incredulous at the simplemindedness.

"Yahweh," Ethbaal answered. "But he is not quite the bachelor you suppose. Israelites worship our goddess Asherah as his wife."

It sounded too good to be true.

He added, "And we could introduce them to Baal as well."

Izabel considered the possibility, but dismissed it almost as quickly.

"Then how could we trust such a double-minded people? If they betray their own god, they would certainly betray us."

"That, my dear daughter, is what marital alliance is for."

Of course. She should have seen it. Her father was always so good in steering her just where he wanted at the right moment he wanted.

"You could enlighten them," Ethbaal added. "Bring change. Progress."

Izabel turned sarcastic. "And unmolested economic expansion for Tyre."

"And why not?" he responded. "With much trade comes much tolerance. You would be the queen that unified our peoples and our gods."

Izabel's father was always so smooth with her. So manipulative. But he had a way of disarming her so that she didn't mind. She felt secure within his control. Still, the thought of leaving his protection and spreading her wings of independence suddenly became very interesting. He had taught her, trained her, prepared her to be a queen. She could never be his queen, but she could be the queen of another nation. That was the best a woman of royal blood could hope for.

Maybe she could civilize Israel. Maybe she could bring them into the modern age of iron.

CHAPTER 4

Mount Carmel

Thirty miles south of Tyre, the Mount Carmel peninsula jutted into the sea and rose to a height of seventeen hundred feet inland. This heavily forested mountain range marked a border between Phoenicia and Israel as well as Philistia in the south. Its northern corridor, the Jezreel valley, was a key travel route from the Mediterranean Sea all the way to the Jordan River.

Mountains were known to be sacred locations for deity, and Carmel was no exception. From ancient days, gods pitched tents on mountains to dwell with their people. They were points of contact between humanity and divinity. Baal had built a palace on Mount Zaphon in northern Syria. A significant holy place to the east is Mount Hermon, in the Lebanon range. It was where the fallen Watchers had descended from heaven as their mount of assembly in the primeval days of Noah. Mount Sinai in Arabia was where Yahweh had met with the Israelites and established his covenant. And Mount Zion in Jerusalem was where Solomon had built Yahweh's temple.

Mount Carmel had been a holy site to Israel. But the Canaanites had destroyed an altar to Yahweh there and replaced it with a high place dedicated to Baal, Lord of Heaven. A large open-air elevated platform made of stone; it was one hundred feet square with a horned altar for sacrifice. That holy monument was where Baal now stood in the unseen realm with his own divine council, called together for a mission. Astarte and Melqart were there along with Anat, Baal's younger sister, a warrior and fertility goddess.

Melqart responded first, trying to show leadership and outshine the goddesses. "I mean no disrespect, my lord, but the Hebrew judges eliminated Baal worship from Israel decades ago. How do you propose to return to power over them?"

The question angered Baal, coming as it did from the overly competitive Greek foreigner.

"Judges!" spat Baal, remembering those reprehensible Hebrew leaders. His scowl turned into a diabolical grin. "Gideon, Jephthah, Samuel, and the others are all dead and gone. Their independence and influence has died with them. Now, we are in a time of kings. The king of Tyre is mine. And the king of Israel will soon be mine as well."

Melqart bristled. Baal knew the hairy Grecian as patron of Tyre had a certain amount of ownership of the city. But he was not the head of the pantheon. Baal was Most High.

"But what about the archangels?" Astarte responded. "Will they not show up to protect the Hebrews?"

"Not where they lack the power," replied Baal. "Hebrews are hopeless idolaters. Their spiritual infidelity *is* our power. Both Judah and Israel engage in harlotry with every god and goddess they can find on every high place and under every green tree."

The others laughed.

He added, "Angels dare not show their faces where they lack authority."

Anat affirmed her brother. "It won't take much for you to regain your former glory. Especially with the impending wedding between Tyre and Israel."

"What do you care of weddings, Virgin Anat," Melqart grumbled.

Anat's eyes narrowed at the Tyrian king's insult. Her jaw clenched with anger.

Baal gave his sister a stern look that held her at bay.

Anat was loyal to Baal. She was also his consort and lover. She was considered young, svelte, and aggressive. In a strange twist of irony, she was called the Virgin Anat. According to the Baal mythology, she had earned the tongue-in-cheek title because of her "youth" and the fact that though she was a goddess of fertility, she could not conceive. As the story went, her frustration made her wildly violent. In some ways, fiction blended with reality in this spiritual world. A huntress of exceptional skill who rivaled the best of the warrior gods, she was often seen with her raven-black hair tied tightly behind her head for battle and her legs covered in the blood and gore of her enemies.

Say what the gods would behind her back, Anat had Baal's back, and he liked it that way.

Baal said, "Izabel, daughter of Tyre, will be marrying King Ahab of Israel in Samaria. Her father King Ethbaal has counseled her to bring my worship back into Israel. It will take time, but I am confident of its inevitability. And with it, my ultimate kingship over the Hebrew occupied territories."

Baal saw Astarte and Anat look maliciously at each other. He knew he was going to have trouble with what he said next. "I will be taking Astarte as my consort to Samaria. Anat will stay with Melqart in Tyre and Sidon."

"What?!" Anat blurted out. She jerked a look over at Astarte, who was staring back with a condescending grin. "I am the most loyal to you, brother. Yet you are taking that self-righteous twat?"

Astarte held her hand on her sword. "The little slut insults me?"

Anat dropped her bow and quiver of arrows on the ground, placing her hand on her own sword handle. "If the truth is an insult to you, goddess, then you are to be pitied."

"The only one to be pitied is she who underestimates the Queen of Heaven." Astarte drew her sword.

Anat drew hers. "And how will a queen command with her tongue cut out?"

"ENOUGH!" shouted Baal. They froze. "I will clip both your wings if you don't stop your clucking. Now put away your weapons."

They hesitated. Who would be the first?

Neither. Baal had to call it.

"Anat."

Anat pouted in a huff, but put her sword away. Astarte followed suit.

"There is no room for jealousy," said Baal. "We have a mission, and everyone has their part. I can't bring you all with me."

"Why not?" Anat whined.

"First off, the Mother is there, and she wouldn't tolerate it."

"The Mother" was a reference to Asherah, the mother goddess, wet nurse of the gods. In the Canaanite narrative, Baal was the Most High, but Asherah was his mother as she was mother to them all. And she had a stranglehold on the Hebrews unlike any other deity before her. Because of the unpredictable

17

changes of history, it was important that they not diverge too much from the narrative they'd constructed for the humans.

"Second," added Baal, "I chose Astarte because Izabel is the one who is marrying into Israel. And she is the high priestess of Astarte, not of Anat. The Queen of Heaven is also worshipped by the Hebrews." He looked at Anat again. "You are not."

Anat pouted silently. She couldn't argue with his logic.

He softened. "Still, you are my sister. You will always be my sister, my most devoted defender." Anat's eyes began to brighten. "And you are the one I trust most to represent my interests in my absence."

Anat gave a snide smirk at Astarte, who responded with a hiss.

Baal added, "If everyone cooperates, we will all be celebrating our allotment together instead of bickering over the scraps off Yahweh's table."

Looking over them all, Baal finally saw a team. A team ready to fight.

"A new day is dawning for Israel," he said. "It's time for us to take back our inheritance."

CHAPTER 5

Valley of Megiddo

The archangels Uriel and Gabriel stood watching a chariot race in the valley just below the city of Megiddo. This wasn't a spectacle for entertainment, but the testing of chariots built by the Rechabites, a nomadic tribe of chariot-makers employed by King Ahab to expand his chariot forces housed at Megiddo.

Turning, the angels walked back to the camp of the Rechabites in the nearby foothills. Uriel was the smallest of the archangels at five and a half feet tall with long, blond hair. He made up for his lack of height with his superior sword-fighting skills and a sharp wit. His companion Gabriel was just over six feet tall, muscular and dark-skinned with a bald head. The two of them had a long history of competition, but they were fiercely loyal to each other, and in their service to Yahweh. Their leader Mikael directed the seven archangels before the throne of Yahweh.

They walked in the unseen realm toward their destination. Like the gods, they too could allow themselves to be perceived by humans—or not—as the need arose.

Uriel was unusually quiet.

"Are you pouting?" asked Gabriel.

"I'm not pouting," complained Uriel. "I'm just disappointed with our assignment. I mean, let's face it, it's not boasting to say that you and I are the best warriors of the Seven."

"After Mikael," interrupted Gabriel.

"After Mikael, of course. Yet Mikael sticks us in Israel instead of with him in Judah."

Mikael was guardian of the lineage of David and had taken the archangels Remiel, Raguel, and Saraqael with him to Judah while sending Raphael with Uriel and Gabriel to Israel.

"What is so hard for you to understand, Uriel?" Gabriel responded. "The Remnant are equally important in both kingdoms. And that is who we are guarding."

It seemed like they had been given an actionless task in watching the Remnant while the gods of Canaan were allowed to grow in power over the Land promised to Yahweh's people. The Remnant were the few true followers of Yahweh within the corrupted twelve tribes of Israel. The archangels were split up to watch over them in both Hebrew kingdoms, north and south.

When Solomon, the son of David, had become king, he'd been compromised by foreign wives, eventually allowing idol worship into Israel that had taken root, leading to the current dilemma. The insidiousness of the idolatry lay in its syncretism, or blending of religions. The Hebrews hadn't exchanged their worship of Yahweh for the worship of Molech, Chemosh, Astarte, Asherah, and others. They'd simply added those gods to their pantheon. They worshipped Yahweh *and* the gods of Canaan.

To Yahweh, who considered his relationship with the Israelites as a monogamous marriage, this was spiritual adultery. They were married to Yahweh, but were acting like whores with the gods of the Canaanites, whom they were supposed to dispossess from the land. It had become quite common amongst the Hebrews to claim that Yahweh had a wife, Asherah. Both Israel and Judah had placed asherah poles in all the high places and even in the Jerusalem temple while continuing their worship of Yahweh as if nothing were wrong. Some of the most religiously devoted had become corrupted by this compromise.

This syncretism made Yahweh jealous with anger. He had proclaimed, "You shall have no gods before me," and he meant it. But the adultery was getting worse, the power of false gods over Judah and Israel was increasing. If it didn't get better, the archangels knew it would end in judgment as it had in the Torah for all adulteresses. Yahweh would kick his unfaithful wife out of his house and send her away.

But not all of Judah and Israel were so corrupted. As with Sodom and Gomorrah, there was a Remnant of pure followers who had remained faithful to their spiritual husband Yahweh.

The Rechabites were part of that loyal Remnant. Led by Jonadab, a fierce man of conviction, they were a guild of metal-workers and chariot-makers from the house of Rechab. Jonadab had known King Ahab's army commander, Jehu, when he was younger. But the two men had lost contact with each other over the years.

In response to Israel's increasing apostasy, Jonadab had withdrawn with his guild of several hundred men and their families into the wilderness. They refused to drink alcohol and lived in tents as a symbolic expression of the generation that had wandered in the wilderness, awaiting their deliverance from the apostasy poisoning the land.

Another group considered a part of the Remnant in Israel were the Sons of the Prophets. This was a school of those being trained in the ways of Samuel the prophet to lead Israel and Judah back to Yahweh their true spiritual husband. This school was presided over by a master whose name was Elijah the Tishbite. A few hundred of these men with their wives and families lived in homes carved into the cliffs just outside of Jezreel. The archangel Raphael was with them now.

"So is this all we're going to do?" asked Uriel. "Sit around and guard the Remnant? Why isn't Mikael on the offensive against the gods?"

"I think you're a bit too obsessed with battle and glory," answered Gabriel. "You know Yahweh has his reasons, and he doesn't always tell Mikael or us. Sometimes we just need to obey."

Uriel sighed. He knew Gabriel was right.

"Mikael is the prince of Israel," Gabriel added. "He is the chosen one to guard the seedline of Messiah through the lineage of David. He would not put that seedline in jeopardy."

"That seedline has been in jeopardy since the Garden," Uriel pushed back. "Need I remind you of the Nephilim in the days of Noah, or the Anakim and Rephaim who were finally eliminated in the days of David?"

No archangel needed to be reminded of that War of the Seed. It was the one perpetual war through sacred history of the Seed of the Serpent at enmity with the Seed of Eve. The ultimate goal of the woman's lineage was Messiah, the one promised to come through the line of Abraham and through Judah and David, who would crush the head of the Serpent. Unfortunately, that primordial prophecy also predicted that the Serpent would crush the heel of that promised seed. And it seemed clear to Uriel that they were experiencing that crushing right now before their very eyes as Yahweh was losing his inheritance through the spiritual apostasy of both Israel and Judah.

Gabriel spoke as if reading Uriel's mind. "To everything there is a season. A time to speak and a time for silence. A time for peace and a time for war."

"Well," said Uriel, "It looks like the time for war may be coming our way."

They were on a hilltop overlooking the Rechabite camp. He pointed miles into the distance, where only the eyes of an angel could see.

And Gabriel saw it: a caravan of Sidonian royalty from Tyre a hundred horses long making its way toward Samaria. They were led by an armed force of Israelite warriors. The train included an armored royal carriage that carried King Ethbaal and his daughter Izabel.

Accompanying that train in the spiritual realm were the Canaanite gods Baal and Astarte.

"Should we follow them?" Uriel asked.

"We observe and report and stay out of sight," said Gabriel. "Those are our orders."

CHAPTER 6

I have always understood marriage to be a symbol of the relationship with our Creator. Yahweh was said to have married his people Israel with the covenant of Sinai. He treated her as a bride with an everlasting love. He covered her with his protection. But he expected a purity of devotion in return. No compromise. Should Israel seek out the gods of Canaan, it would be harlotry, spiritual adultery against her husband, her maker.

Ahab was a king well-acquainted with compromise. He ruled over a kingdom divided between past and progress. He sought to negotiate peace over war. As commander of his armies, I, Jehu, sought to enforce the might of the crown for the glory of God. It was not an easy responsibility. I knew that my loyalty to both God and King was about to be contested.

Samaria

Jehu, son of Nimshi, led a contingent of two hundred soldiers guarding the Sidonian caravan of Izabel and Ethbaal as it trekked from Tyre to Samaria. He was escorting the royal travelers on behalf of Izabel's betrothed, King Ahab. The sixty-mile trip from the coast had given Jehu much time to think. This marriage alliance was a highly significant one for Israel, and Jehu knew it was going to change everything for them in both good ways and bad.

Brushing back his long, wavy brown hair, he scratched his tightly-cropped beard. He was a muscular warrior, but those muscles ached from the long ride, and he was looking forward to getting home to his wife. At just twenty-four years old, he held the exalted position of commander of the king's armies. His relationship with King Ahab had begun in their youth when Ahab was being groomed as the crown prince by his father, King Omri.

Omri had been commander of Israel's army before beginning his own new family dynasty of rulers in Israel through a military coup. He'd immediately started a campaign of fortifying the cities of Israel with bigger walls and a stronger army. His son Ahab continued this strong military policy for both Israel's interests and protection. He spent so much on military investment that civic development suffered from lack of attention and funds. Ahab took a particular interest in the chariot forces, which were based in the city of Megiddo not far away in the Jezreel Valley.

Jehu's father had been a chariot commander and had raised his son to follow his military path. From a young age, Jehu had shown much promise in both battle and strategy, so once Omri became king, he'd appointed Jehu to be Ahab's combat training partner.

The two young men had become fast friends. Jehu was a superior fighter to Ahab, but he'd always shown deference to the crown prince because of Jehu's high regard for authority. After all, the king was God's anointed one to lead the nation, and Ahab was heir to that kingdom. Jehu always knew his place and believed that Yahweh would one day provide the king who would ultimately unify the split kingdoms of Israel and Judah like a new David.

When Ahab was crowned, it was only natural that he'd appoint Jehu as commander of his army. Jehu was the king's most trusted advisor and servant with a fierce devotion to him. But Jehu was also devoted to Yahweh. It was Yahweh's prophets who anointed the king, and it was Yahweh's rule that Israel was supposed to enforce in the land. So the upcoming marriage with a Sidonian pagan princess was sure to create problems in Israel as it did in Jehu's soul.

There were clear military advantages to an alliance with Tyre, but the other gods the new queen worshipped was of deep concern to Jehu. Izabel was a Baal worshipper. Along with most of Israel, Jehu was no stranger to Canaanite gods such as Asherah and Astarte. He tolerated them because the king tolerated them. The king was God's anointed ruler, and it was Jehu's place as commander of the army to enforce that rule despite the king's flaws.

But Baalism was a unique danger to Yahwism. It was Baal, the Most High god of Canaan, that Yahweh dispossessed from the land. Israel had become compromised with other deities, appropriating them into her religious life. But none of those challenged the manifest superiority of Yahweh as Baal did.

It was clear to Jehu that a storm was on the horizon. An internal conflict that could lead to a war of gods and men. He prayed it would not. He had many times offered the king his counsel on the matter, but religion was one area where Ahab seemed more stubborn than others.

As they approached the city walls of Samaria, Jehu spotted the royal greeting party waiting outside the walls to escort them in, a line of a hundred cavalry and foot soldiers. The royal palace administrator Obadiah, graying already at age forty, rode ceremoniously at their head on a steed in royal regalia. Upon reaching the caravan, Obadiah turned his horse and assumed the lead. The horse pranced, escorting the entourage through the city gates.

Ahab's father King Omri had established the city of Samaria as Israel's capital, building the first royal palace there. Her population was several thousand. The city was built on a hilltop rising fourteen hundred feet above sea level in the midst of the hill country. It was protected by an impressive fortification that even surpassed that of Jerusalem, her sister kingdom in the south.

Samaria was sixty miles southeast of her new ally Tyre and one hundred miles southwest of her old enemy Damascus. Her key cities nearby were Megiddo and Jezreel, both in the Jezreel Valley to the north. Samaria sat in the highlands that split the west coast from the eastern Jordan Valley all the way to Jerusalem. Samaria was also the name of the entire region of that hill country, sometimes used synonymously with Israel as Damascus was used for the Arameans and Jerusalem for Judah, Israel's sister kingdom in the south. Samaria was considered both a city and a region.

The city of Samaria may have been the place of royal residence, but its culture and civic structures were as unsophisticated and rural as Tyre's were sophisticated and urbane.

Jehu knew Izabel of the Sidonians was sure to find the differences between the two cities a shock to her sensibilities, considering the finery and wealth she was used to in Tyre. He'd noticed the difference as soon as he'd arrived in Tyre to escort the wedding train to Samaria. The Sidonians were a merchant class of people who sought wealth and new things. They lived in buildings of elaborate cedar design on streets paved with stone that were constantly full of foreign traders from all over the world.

In contrast, the Hebrews of Samaria were a simple people. They lived in basic habitations of mud brick laid out on dirt streets. Loose animals wandered those streets and alleys, and there was no ornament or pride of place. The Hebrew people valued function over beauty, and the crown had put more money into military build-up than into civic infrastructure. Hebrews kept to themselves and were known to be untrusting of outsiders.

The marketplaces of Tyre were also well-organized in eclectic structures of sale by businesses of all kinds. They offered rich fabrics, exotic foreign foods, and highly artistic crafts of jewelry, metalworking, and blown glass. Meanwhile, Samaria's markets were chaotic bazaars of agricultural goods sold by farmers from their rickety carts filled with grains, fruits, nuts, and vegetables stored in simple and at times crude pottery.

As the caravan arrived at Ahab's royal palace, it seemed to Jehu that all the palace displays of wealth were eclipsed by Tyre's royalty. The palace grounds covered a few acres of space, about half the size of King Ethbaal's palace on the coast. And these marble pillars and walls lacked beautiful drapes and tapestries. No world-renowned Tyrian purple fabrics graced this palace.

The Sidonians and Israelites even looked like inhabitants of different lands in their personal appearance and dress. And that world of difference was on full display in the royal introduction of Princess Izabel at Ahab's palace.

His guard duties ended, Jehu quickly bathed and changed clothing in preparation for the royal welcome. By the time he'd arrived at the palace, a welcoming delegation had taken their places in the throne room to receive the guests of honor: King Ethbaal and his daughter, Princess Izabel.

As Jehu walked the long, pillared aisle to the throne, the contrast of the two sides of the royal guests was unmistakable. On his left were his fellow Israelites, dressed in plain robes and tunics, undyed, but clean with some color in their embroidered edges. They were festive, but not excessive. Their sashes were also wool as they mixed no fabric with linen. The men had full beards and wore small headdresses for such occasions. Standing separately behind the male section, the women wore humble head coverings with modest hairstyling and minimal jewelry.

On his right side, the Sidonians stood out like a burst of color, fabric, and precious metals. Men and women stood together. They all wore colorful tunics with brightly colored festive trimmings. Men tended to be clean shaven, but with long hair. Women had hair styled with full body, accented by extravagant hairpins. They wore an amount of jewelry considered scandalous by their fellow Hebrew participants. Multiple necklaces, bracelets of silver and gold, and exotic dangling earrings. Their cosmetics were distinctly Egyptian with dark kohl eyeliner and colorful eyelid shading. Sidonians were enchanted by all things Egyptian, the very world out of which the Israelites had fled their slavery.

As Jehu took his customary stance beside the king's throne, a wooden chair with simple gold trim and leather cushion, he could feel the tension in the room. He stood beside his seated king and observed the room. Though this event was sanctioned by both rulers, neither side knew exactly how to respond to each other's alien presence, so they remained quiet and waiting.

One year older than Jehu, King Ahab was a handsome young man, dark-skinned with a full, but shaped beard and wavy black hair. He was a warrior king who enjoyed occasional royal indulgences, tall and well-muscled, yet less physically impressive than Jehu.

The king threw his commander a smiling glance. The crowd began to chatter for just a moment before settling down as Ethbaal, king of Tyre, entered the throne room. He was dressed in the royal finest of his city. A purple satin tunic sashed with a golden girdle. A conical crown like Baal's. His beard tight and squarely cropped like an Assyrian king. His armlets and triple-layered collar were gold and Egyptian in appearance.

To Jehu, it was all garish and unappealing. But then the Sidonians were more progressive in their tastes. Maybe Jehu just wasn't informed on what the rest of the world was like.

Ethbaal was followed by a retinue of male servants, all bald with make-up and flowing linen tunics. They reminded Jehu of qedeshim, male prostitutes. Their profane presence in the throne room drew some huffs and murmuring of offense. Jehu saw Ahab shake his head with contempt for his people's intolerance. It was an example of the difficulty sure to come as these two contrary cultures united.

"King Ethbaal, welcome," said Ahab. He nodded with royal recognition.

Reaching the steps of the throne, the Tyrian king returned the regal gesture. "King Ahab, I present to you this dowry in good faith of the union of our nations."

Ethbaal clapped his hands, and another retinue of servants entered the throne room carrying a replica of a Sidonian merchant ship. About ten feet long and three feet wide with a single mast and glorious open sail, it sported the royal crest of Ethbaal: Leviathan, the seven-headed sea dragon. The boat was overflowing with Tyrian wealth. Colorful fabrics. Precious metalworks. Delicate glassware. And, of course, silver and gold.

The crowd gasped, then applauded. Ahab smiled broadly. There was enough wealth in that vessel to fund Samaria for the rest of the year. A financial boost Jehu knew the kingdom desperately needed, a need the king would never allow to be public knowledge.

The crowd quieted down, and Ethbaal continued. "May I now present to you the daughter of Tyre and Sidon: Izabel of the house of Ethbaal!"

All heads turned to see Izabel enter the room, escorted by attendants. A hush went over the audience. To Jehu, she looked like the goddess Astarte incarnate—very Egyptian in appearance, with dark make-up and black shoulder-length hair topped by a golden uraeus.

The princess wore multiple necklaces of precious metal and gemstones. Gold bracelets and armlets glittered from her bare arms. Her flowing white linen dress was accented with colorful Egyptian embroidered trimming. Her legs broke out through slits in the dress with scandalous sensuality as she walked. Her petticoat was tight beneath her breasts. She was clearly the desire of all men, the envy of all women. And Jehu saw Ahab smitten by her beauty. Enchanted by the high priestess of Astarte.

The Sidonian half of the room broke into applause as the princess approached the throne to bow before Ahab. The Hebrews were more restrained in their approval of the betrothed foreigner. It seemed to Jehu that every step of this new union was going to be fraught with suspicion or resistance to change.

Jehu knew that Ahab thought Israel was mired in tradition that stunted their ability to grow and meet the demands of a new world. But how much change was enough? Was change always good? Or could change actually be a bad thing?

Ahab stood and gestured for Ethbaal to join him. Making his way up the steps, the Tyrian king stood beside Ahab, equals in power. A new alliance for the future.

28

Ahab announced, "Fellow Israelites and our Sidonian allies, tomorrow begins the celebration!"

The crowd burst out with joyful applause. The wedding week had arrived.

CHAPTER 7

Izabel accepted Ahab's zealous attentions graciously as the king escorted her through the palace grounds. The pair was trailed by his bodyguard of six and a handful of regal servants from both families. There would be plenty of time later for engaging with the political concerns of her father and the celebratory interests of the populace. For now, there was value in getting acquainted with her betrothed before the festivities began.

As Ahab introduced Izabel to her new palace home, it was clear he hoped she'd be satisfied. She was not. But she hid the fact that her lifestyle in Tyre made Samaria look impoverished by comparison. Ahab had spent so much money on his military prowess that he'd neglected his duty for regal presence. That would have to change when she moved into this house.

They were currently walking through a hallway on their way to the garden outside. Unlike Tyre's palatial hallways, these lacked hanging tapestries and felt like cold, empty stone. Ahab was boasting of his garden's glory. He maintained a nervous monologue as though trying to fill uncomfortable silences.

"And I'm sure you will love our lilies and tulips. We are known for our most special roses from the Sharon Valley. Some are even purple like Tyre's own famous color."

As he walked and talked, Ahab kept his gaze focused on Izabel, not watching where he was going as he looked her up and down. His chatter was interrupted when he walked into a hallway pillar. As Izabel giggled, Ahab turned red with embarrassment. Then he burst out in hearty laughter, and she joined him.

"I'm sorry," he apologized. "I am staring at you and making a fool of myself."

"Not at all, my lord," she demurred.

"No, I am," he reiterated. "I just—forgive me, but you are a most stunning beauty to behold, Izabel. Distractingly so. You are like a Rose of Sharon. Delicate and radiant." He paused. "Yet, I suspect, with a touch of danger."

She felt herself blush now and tried to change the subject. "I am honored by your words of praise, my lord. May I confide in you a secret?"

His eyes opened wide. "By all means. I will stamp it with my royal seal. Death to anyone who breaks it!"

The seal of the king ensured protection on letters and correspondence under penalty of death. Izabel couldn't help but giggle again at his playfulness. The guard and servants remained far enough away not to listen in on their words.

"Well, if you must know," she said, "unlike some women, I am not fond of flowers."

"Oh. Well, in that case, I'll burn down the garden and replace it with a royal fabric shop to sew garments worthy of adorning your awe-inspiring form of splendor."

She laughed. "You flatter me, my lord. Your offer is tempting, but there is no need to dismiss the royal gardeners for my sake. Are your people accustomed to such dramatic changes?"

"I find my people rather resistant to changes of any kind," Ahab answered. "They are stuck a bit in our traditions. But fear not. That is why you are here. To help me open their minds. Challenge their intolerance." He smiled, then added with emphasis, "Within reason of course."

"Of course," she agreed. "Change always requires both reason and patience. I want to learn about your people's traditions and embrace them as my own."

"And I yours."

Izabel felt elation to discover her father was indeed correct. This Ahab was remarkably open and tolerant. Not to mention handsome and quite manly. She felt herself quiver with arousal at the thought of their impending consummation.

"Since we are done with the garden," he said, "let me show you something else."

Izabel smiled with anticipation as Ahab escorted her along, their dutiful guards and servants in tow. They walked, and entered a long flight of stairs in the highest tower of the palace. When they reached the top, Izabel found herself looking out onto the entire city of Samaria and beyond it the hill country of Israel.

Throwing out one hand with a flourish, Ahab smiled down at her. "This will all be yours as well."

Izabel hid her true feelings as she looked out onto the rolling hills, which were not particularly impressive to her. She longed for the sea.

Ahab pointed to the northwest. "Over those hills is the city of Megiddo. It houses my chariot forces. You will love the horses there. They are glorious."

He pointed to the north. "About twenty miles that way is Jezreel. I have a summer palace there. I think you will like it."

She thought it was not likely if it was anything like this palace.

He kept talking. "To the south about twenty miles is Bethel, the furthest reach of Israel's borders. Beyond that is Jerusalem in the kingdom of Judah."

Izabel had been surveying the city beneath her, which covered about twelve acres, looking for locations where she might eventually build a temple for her religion. His words became a perfect segue.

"Tell me about Jerusalem and her temple. I understand it is a sore issue for your people."

"Indeed, it is," Ahab said. "Israel has been at odds with our sister Judah since the death of King Solomon. We split into two kingdoms over claims to the throne."

"I understand such politics all too well," Izabel responded. As a federation of city-states, Phoenician cities struggled with each other for dominance and wealth. Currently, Tyre was the reigning power.

Ahab explained, "Judah of course controls the temple in Jerusalem. Though I'm working on diplomatic relations with her king Jehoshaphat, we of Israel still have only limited access."

"Why?" she asked.

"When the kingdom split, Jeroboam built shrines for Yahweh in Israel as competition with Jerusalem. One in Dan and one in Bethel, the northern and southern limits of Israel. He also instituted a new priesthood and set up golden calves for worship. It wasn't long before Yahweh's prophets began condemning both Dan and Bethel in the name of the one true house of God in Jerusalem."

"You haven't taken the shrines down," Izabel noted.

Ahab said, "No, I haven't. The prophets aren't my only concern. There are too many people in Israel who worship at Dan and Bethel for me to cause such consternation. A ruler must balance his interests."

It struck Izabel that Ahab was willing to defy his own prophets. He was no slave to fanatics. This could be useful for her. Maybe it wasn't too early to test the waters and see where he stood with her religion.

"Would you consider building a temple for Baal?"

Ahab's stare was not encouraging, but she persisted, "It might be a way for uniting our cultures."

Ahab frowned. "That would be a problem. Baalism is not an acceptable tradition in Israel."

Despite his frown, Izabel could see he didn't share his people's hostility toward her religion. She stepped closer to him. "Soon I will be your wife. And I will embrace your ways and be the queen you expect me to be—in every way." She said it provocatively, noting with satisfaction how his eyes filled with desire. "It would be an historic achievement of greatness if we were able to find a way for our traditions to co-exist without enmity."

"Indeed," he whispered as if enchanted by her words.

She added, "You would be considered the greatest king in the history of this land."

Reaching out, Ahab brushed some strands of hair that had fallen in front of her face. His hand trembled slightly. Izabel had captivated him with her presence. But she found herself just as captivated by his.

"You would then be the greatest queen in the history of this land," Ahab said, looking deep into her eyes.

She changed the subject back to him, "I have so much more I want to know about you, my lord."

"I have so much more to tell you. Let me show you the rest of the palace and city that you will soon rule—by my side."

CHAPTER 8

Izabel felt exhausted. The festivities for her marriage to King Ahab had lasted seven days. Feasting and dancing and meeting so many people, people she didn't care to remember.

But it was good for the people. For a brief moment in time, commoners forgot about the travails of their lives in a world of brutal nature and warring nations. They were just coming out of winter. The cold was waning, and blossoming almond trees gave hope for the harvests to come. Barley and wheat had been planted, and now the population awaited their growth with the help of the latter rains.

At least that is what Izabel had been told. She had traded in her merchant world on the coast for an agrarian one in the wilderness.

Those people had come from all around the cities of Israel to join with the Phoenicians in this celebration of unity between nations. On this seventh day, tradition dictated that the bride be taken from her parents' home and escorted to the bridegroom's home. Since Izabel's real home was sixty miles away, she had been staying with her father and their attendants in one of the residences of the royal palace.

But now she was paraded through the streets in royal procession, accompanied by singing and dancing minstrels. Wedding ceremonies were quite similar across the entirety of Canaan. But there were significant differences. For one, Hebrews were not quite as skilled as Sidonians in the performing arts. Theirs was the music of shepherds and farmers. To Izabel, their instruments and dance all bore a distinct rustic simplicity. She felt genuinely sorry for these hill-dwellers that they did not know the pageantry of an Egyptian procession, the fluid rhythms of a Manipuri dance of Krishna from India, or the passionate bacchanal of a Greek Dionysian orgy.

And she could see in some of their stares a resentment toward her. It was as if her presence shone a light on their own lack. Blaming her didn't seem fair. She would try her best to enlighten them.

34

Izabel listened to the words of the Hebrew Psalm written for her and being sung right now as she approached the king's residence.

> Hear, O daughter, and consider, and incline your ear:
>> forget your people and your father's house,
>> and the king will desire your beauty.
> Since he is your lord, bow to him.
>> The people of Tyre will seek your favor with gifts,
>> the richest of the people.
> All glorious is the princess in her chamber, with robes interwoven
>> with gold.
>> In many-colored robes she is led to the king,
>> with her virgin companions following behind her.
> With joy and gladness they are led along
>> as they enter the palace of the king.

As she reached the steps of the palace, a peculiar group of men caught her notice. Actually, a group of a dozen or so young men and boys dressed in cloaks made of sackcloth. They were led by an older man in his fifties dressed in a strange long-haired mantle and leather girdle with wild hair and a bushy beard—a hairy creature. His eyes watched Izabel. Steely, malevolent eyes. Like those of a madman. It sent a chill down her spine.

Shaking it off, Izabel ascended the steps into the palace.

Standing with the wedding party of witnesses, Jehu watched the palace full of royal family and attendants in joyful celebration. Izabel had joined her bridegroom Ahab beneath the wedding canopy. A Hebrew priest in white linen robe and headdress pronounced, "Let us rejoice in this unity of man and woman, of king and queen, of Israel and Tyre."

As he listened and watched, Jehu tried to discern what was going on behind the words and actions. King Ethbaal beamed, not with pride, but with a kind of cunning. The politics of the situation were inescapable. But just what were the Sidonian king's ultimate goals? Jehu didn't trust him in the least.

Now the Tyrian priest Hamilqart, dressed in his own colorful high priest garb, was stepping up next to the Hebrew priest. Jehu caught a peculiar, even intimate, look between Izabel and Hamilqart before the priest masked his expression. It wouldn't surprise Jehu that priests and priestesses might have more than professional familiarity between them. Was that what he had glimpsed here?

The very act of combining the two religions in one ceremony was offensive to the School of Prophets, currently protesting outside the palace. Would their zeal affect the broader populace or not?

They certainly had an effect on him.

CHAPTER 9

After the Sidonian parade of King Ethbaal and Princess Izabel had entered the palace, sixteen-year-old Elisha, son of Shaphat, continued staring at the closed gilded bronze doors. He was praying for Yahweh's judgment.

"Abomination," he muttered. He turned to notice his fellow students from the School of Prophets had already gone, leaving him behind. Pulling his sackcloth hood over his tightly shaven head, Elisha pushed his way through the crowd to catch back up with his master and fellow students.

The streets were filled with commoners engaged in their own parties and revelry to celebrate the wedding. The food was simple: bread, oil, olives, and nuts. And there was much wine. Musicians played instruments while both men and women danced in the streets.

Elisha suspected there was a world of difference out here from what must be going on inside the palace. At least in terms of wealth if not in terms of debauchery. Out here, he saw men playing drinking games, falling to the ground, brawling with one another. One man vomited perilously close to Elisha's feet. He hastened his pace to catch up with the others.

Elisha stopped again as a certain tent caught his eye. It was a tent of harlotry where lustful men paid painted women and followed them inside to indulge their fleshly hunger. Elisha felt his curiosity grow and something within himself flame up. He was somehow drawn to what he despised.

"Lord, forgive me," he muttered, turning to leave. He bumped into a pair of child beggars. They stretched emaciated hands towards him, their bodies in rags, their faces dirty and full of despair. Elisha's heart broke. No child should have to experience such suffering.

"Elisha!" The shout was from his master. Elisha quickly dug into his clothing to find a coin, dropping it into one small, skeletal hand before hurrying to join his comrades, his eyes blurred with tears of pain—and anger.

"Lord, may your justice roll down like waters," he prayed quietly. "And righteousness like an ever-flowing stream."

The group of students retrieved their horses from a stable and left the city. They had a fifteen-mile journey back to the School of the Prophets, their residence out in the desert wilderness away from the city's corruption and closer to that of Jezreel.

•••••

The banquet hall of the Samarian palace was closed to the public, but full of hundreds of royal guests from both Israel and Tyre. Izabel sat at a table with Ahab to sign their legal marriage document. Jehu sat beside the king. Ethbaal and Hamilqart sat beside Izabel. Assorted royal family and military leaders surrounded them.

When Ahab finished signing, he lifted up the papyrus for everyone to see and announced, "With this marriage, a treaty of alliance is secured between Israel and Tyre and all of Sidonia. And with it, mutual protection, shared wealth, and cultural diversity!"

The crowd applauded obediently.

Ethbaal added, "Now, let us drink upon it!"

Laughs and more applause filled the room as everyone lifted their cups and drank in deeply of the vine.

A group of twelve female Israelite dancers modestly dressed in dark, flowing gowns entered the room. A musical group of lyre, flute, and timbrel led them in the fluid movements of a Hebrew dance as the food was being prepared.

Izabel thought the dance charming, a kind of adolescent joyful fun. Simple, but she could detect an accent of Egyptian rhythm. At least the Hebrews learned something of value from their foreign captors all those generations ago.

The dancers left the room, and a new group of ten Tyrian dancers stood before them. Unlike their Hebrew counterparts, these wore barely anything in the way of dress, and what they did have on was transparent, exposing everything through a tantalizing veil. Izabel could hear gasps of surprise from some of the Hebrew guests of the wedding party. A few left the room.

The new musicians began to play. Their music was more percussive. Multiple drums, rattler-sistrums, and a gong. The heavy beat filled the room with a rhythmic pounding of desire. Izabel could feel it within her own body.

The dancers moved with erotic enticement more suited to a brothel than a wedding. But this was the Sidonian way.

These stodgy Hebrews will get used to it, She thought. *They may even learn to loosen up a bit.*

Izabel smiled at her new husband, who was watching her like a hungry lion. To her surprise, she had increasingly enjoyed his company during their week of betrothal. The more they spent time and conversed with one another, the more Izabel had discovered her father was right. Ahab was progressive, far more so than she had hoped. And they were deeply attracted to each other physically. The thought aroused her.

She returned his hungry stare with an alluring tease in her eyes. She could see him sigh with desire and move uncomfortably in his chair. Her father had taught her well how to capture the attention of a man.

The dancing had ended, dinner served, the participants full of food and drink. Izabel conversed with Jehu's wife Susanna at the main table of honored guests. About Izabel's age or perhaps a year or two older, Susanna was quite beautiful with black hair, dark skin, and penetrating light-brown eyes. But she chose to hide her beauty behind unimpressive attire. With minimal embroidery on her dress, a simple headdress, and modest amount of jewelry, the young woman lacked a royal presence.

Susanna answered the queen's question about how she and Jehu had met. "My father was an officer in the chariot corps at Megiddo with Jehu's father."

Now Izabel understood who she was talking to. She smiled and said, "Then you are well-acquainted with the military life. I hope you are not feeling abandoned with your husband spending so much of his time with the king."

"On the contrary, your highness. It is an honor to be married to a man of such loyalty and devotion."

Izabel wondered how simple this woman was. She said, "I suppose there are always your children to keep you company and assuage your loneliness."

"I have no children," Susanna replied. "Not yet. But we have only been married two years."

Despite her hopeful words, a sad expression crossed Susanna's face. Two years was long enough, Izabel was well aware, for some husbands to grow impatient. Maybe even turn to someone who might prove more fertile.

39

"Izabel," interrupted Ahab, "I have someone I want you to meet."

Izabel graciously turned her attention back to her new husband. Ahab gestured to a servant, who brought forward a young girl about seven years old with long, brown wavy hair and bright excitable eyes. She wore royal colors of blue and purple. As Izabel smiled at her, the girl giggled.

"My dear queen, this is Athaliah," Ahab introduced.

Izabel said, "Hello, Athaliah."

The young girl dropped her gaze shyly. "Hello."

"She is my sister," Ahab explained. "A daughter of the house of Omri, my father."

"Well, that explains her handsome likeness." Izabel ran her fingers through Ahab's wavy hair in comparison, noting the girl was lighter skinned than her brother.

He smiled and said, "I have a generous favor to ask of you, my love."

"Whatever you will, my husband."

"Athaliah is betrothed to Prince Jehoram, brother of Jehoshaphat, king of Judah."

Izabel knew what was coming. She'd been learning the politics of her new home and its relation to Judah.

Ahab continued, "The civil hostility between Israel and Judah has been long and exhausting. Jehoram is next in line to the throne of Judah. His match with Athaliah will bring a cease-fire between the northern and southern kingdoms."

Izabel finished Ahab's thought for him. "I would be delighted to help prepare her for her royal responsibility. I will teach her everything I know."

Ahab grinned with relief. "You, my lady, may prove yourself to be beloved of the patriarchs."

Drawing the young girl down onto the cushions beside her, Izabel looked into Athaliah's wide eyes with a warm smile and stroked her wavy hair with newfound affection. "Sit with me, Athaliah. I will teach you how to navigate this patriarchy with all the wit and wisdom at my disposal. We girls must stick together."

Athaliah smiled back, sweet and innocent, naively unaware of the unequal position she'd have to suffer in life as a woman—but also unaware that she was about to be educated how to rise above it and get her way despite it all.

Ahab and Ethbaal had been discussing the logistics of their new alliance. Sharing territories for armed forces. Exchange of money, goods and services. Leaning in across the table toward the kings, Hamilqart said, "Forgive my boldness, my lords, but Damascus will not be pleased with our alliance. Together we now control the dominant trade routes on land and sea. Surely they will want war."

Ahab turned to Ethbaal. "Your priest gives wise counsel. But I have already planned for such contingencies."

"How so?" asked Ethbaal.

"By this very hour, my diplomatic envoys should have reached Damascus for a meeting of minds to address our differences with King Ben-hadad."

"Oh, are you negotiating a treaty?"

Ahab smiled deviously. "No. His assassination."

Ethbaal's look of shock quickly turned into a grin of understanding. "I applaud you. Killing the Aramaean king will add some chaos into our enemy's camp and allow Israel and Tyre time to build a unified front."

As Jehu listened in on the royal discussion, he noticed a wine servant he hadn't seen before. Then several other servants he didn't recognize. Not that he'd know all the attendants brought in for a feast this size. But with his protective nature toward the king, he'd always made sure he knew by sight those tasked with serving the royal family. He'd have to reacquaint himself with any who might have been added in recent weeks.

He returned his attention to the conversation around him. The Sidonians were already addressing their religious differences. Not a good sign. They seemed too anxious to start poking at the hive of hornets he preferred to avoid.

Izabel told Ethbaal, "Father, my husband has explained to me that Israel has limited access to their temple in Jerusalem."

"My people built that temple for Solomon with Phoenician genius and craftsmanship," Ethbaal spoke up proudly. "Just say the word, my friend, and I will build you a temple in Samaria that will put Jerusalem to shame."

Ahab chuckled. "As much as I would welcome your generous gift, I was telling your daughter there can be but one temple for Yahweh. However, I think our city infrastructure could benefit from Phoenician genius and craftsmanship."

As Ethbaal raised his brow with interest, Izabel jumped in.

"Father, perhaps a donation from Tyre to rebuild Samaria and Jezreel would be a show of good faith toward your new ally—my new king," she ended with an affectionate look at Ahab. He grinned.

"Perhaps," Ethbaal said half-heartedly, no longer looking so enthusiastic.

In contrast, Ahab looked whole-heartedly happy. Leaning over, he kissed Izabel passionately. "Perhaps, indeed—my queen!"

Ethbaal complained, "I see you two are already quite united in your interests."

Izabel smiled at her father, then said to her king, "And perhaps a temple for Baal in Israel would be a powerful show of unity between our peoples."

The two men grinned at each other, effectively outdone by one woman.

It was at that moment that Jehu noticed the wine servant again. The man had been acting a bit too nervous, glancing too often at the king. Now standing just a dozen feet in front of the wedding party, he suddenly handed off his wine bottle to another servant, then reached into his cloak and pulled out a dagger.

Jehu reacted before he had time to think.

Rearing back, the wine servant launched his dagger at Ahab.

But Jehu was already there.

He pushed Ahab to the ground.

The dagger hit the commander in the left shoulder and went in deep. He grimaced in pain.

But he didn't stop. He pulled out the weapon, his blood splattering on the table, and flipped it around in the air, catching the bloody blade in his fingers.

With the skills of elite combat, he threw the dagger at the would-be-assassin.

It hit the wine servant in the left eye.

The man fell backward to the ground.

Screams from the crowd echoed through the hall. Partiers pulled away from the threat in the center of the room while others ran for the exit.

"Make sure he's dead!" Jehu yelled to the king's bodyguards, who swarmed the would-be assassin. He was definitely dead, his brain penetrated by the deadly accuracy of Jehu's throw.

Other guards sought to calm the crowd and bring back order. Several bodyguards joined Jehu to help lift Ahab from the floor. Izabel stayed close to the king's side.

"Apparently, my lord, the king of Damascus had the same plans of diplomacy for you as you had for him," Jehu commented dryly.

"Ah, but he didn't have my Jehu beside him!" With a grin, Ahab slapped Jehu's shoulder—his wounded shoulder. Jehu groaned in pain, protecting the damaged area.

Ahab withdrew in horror. "I am a fool! My apologies, Jehu."

Turning to Izabel, he said proudly, "My dear queen, take note. This man will be your rival for loyalty to both king and kingdom."

Izabel smiled at the light-hearted joke. But as she looked at Jehu, he saw in her eyes what could be a seed of jealousy.

Was it? Or was *he* the jealous one, knowing that the history and trust he'd shared with his king was about to be overshadowed by Ahab's new queen?

"Go home and heal, hero," Izabel said. "I will make sure our treasured king is protected in your absence." She cast a dirty look at the closest guard. "I will replace these bodyguards myself."

CHAPTER 10

Baal and Astarte arrived at the high place of Samaria, on a hill of its own just next to the city, across a small valley. The existence of high places on hillsides outside of cities had a two-fold purpose in Israel. First, to separate it as a holy place. Second, to relieve the moral tension of their violation of Yahweh's law prohibiting the high places. As with prostitution, it was better to have such activities done away from normal public observation so as to lessen the guilt of their moral inconsistency.

The gods walked through the sacred grove that surrounded the sanctuary and altar. Sacred groves consisted of a group of terebinth or oak trees, considered as holy instruments of communion with deity. They were also used as sacred beds for copulation with cult prostitutes. As the two gods walked through the grove, unseen and unheard by the humans around them, they watched Israelites under every green tree engaged in sexual coupling with qedeshim.

At this time before each harvest, Israelite farmers came to the sacred hill to beseech the goddess Asherah and participate in fertility rites. The worshipper would engage in sexual intercourse with a "holy one," a female qedesha, or sacred prostitute. They believed the sex act operated as a form of sympathetic magic, inducing Yahweh as the storm god to send the final rains that would ensure the fertility of their fields for the upcoming harvest.

The high place was a sanctuary complex consisting of a walled courtyard for worshippers, an altar, a platform with asherah pole, and rooms for the qedeshim. Various priests and qedeshim went about their duties, caring for the high place, disposing of bones from sacrifices, weaving tapestries for Asherah, and servicing paying customers.

Reaching the courtyard, Baal and Astarte ascended the elevated platform. Astarte admired the engraved stone incense altar and asherah. Both had images carved on them representing some aspect of Asherah. One engraving showed the goddess as Mistress of the Animals holding two lions in her hands.

Another showed her as the tree of life sustaining two goats. A third had a bull calf with a winged sun disk on his back, a reference to Baal, her offspring.

"She's making us wait," Baal huffed.

Astarte looked around. "Just remember, this is her territory. You can get further by respecting all she's accomplished here."

"*She* needs to respect *me*."

"There's my son." The voice came from below. Asherah had arrived. She conspicuously ignored Astarte. "I'm so sorry I'm late. I was preparing for the king and queen's Sacred Marriage rite. They're on their way, you know."

Asherah was a full-figured motherly presence. Buxom, but with the muscular arms of a battle maiden. Her long brown hair was pulled up tight into a bun beneath a golden crown that looked like a starburst on her head. She wore a simple Greek-style tunic lashed with a leather girdle. She was not an elaborate goddess, but pragmatic and matronly.

Baal got right to the point. "Mother, as you know, the marriage of Ahab and Izabel grants me authority over Israel. I have come to claim that position and implement my plan. I would appreciate your prompt support."

"No, it doesn't," she replied.

"Excuse me?"

"I said no, the marriage does not give you instant authority. You must earn it. As I have. I have a long tradition of being worshipped by the Israelites. You were kicked out in the days of Samuel."

Asherah's insolence was bold. Baal paused and reset his strategy. He could pulverize her quite easily. But she was right. She held much sway with this people. She required diplomacy.

"Well," he countered. "I'm back. And I'm here to regain lost ground. But I do have authority over this territory."

"So," Asherah hissed. "you can just tramp right in and take back control? Well, I have news for you, young man. It doesn't work that way." She gestured at Astarte. "What did you bring this one for?"

"I'm the consort of Baal," Astarte cut in. "Queen Izabel is my high priestess. I have the right to rule beside him."

Asherah laughed. "You forget one little thing, child. Ahab is the king of Israel. Israel's god is Yahweh. And I am his consort, Yahweh's Asherah."

To the surprise of both goddesses, Baal said, "You make a good point, Mother. People don't take quickly to an outsider with foreign culture."

Astarte huffed with disapproval. She didn't want to speak because she knew how violent Baal got and what he did to her when she talked too much.

Baal finished, "But lest we forget, you are Yahweh's consort in their worship, not in reality."

"Is that not where all our power comes from?" Asherah spoke with self-assured confidence. "Their worship?"

Then she shrugged as if changing her mind. "I will fully submit to you on one condition."

Baal looked first at Astarte with curiosity, then back at Asherah with interest.

Asherah gestured again at Astarte. "That you take me as your consort and send that one to Jerusalem."

"How dare you!" snapped Astarte.

Asherah raised her hands in deference to Baal. "Hear me out."

Baal's hand restrained Astarte from attacking. The war goddess could do great damage to the Mother.

Asherah continued, "Ruling Israel is not enough for your victory, am I correct?"

Baal nodded.

"You also need Judah. So, you need to eliminate the House of David, which is Yahweh's hope. No small task. Astarte worship is already well established in Judah, while Asherah worship is stronger in Israel. We would serve your interests best where we are loved most."

Baal raised his brow. Good point, indeed.

Astarte fumed. "Master, I can't believe you are considering this fat wench's offer."

"Shut up," said Baal. "I'm thinking." He paced past Asherah and behind her to look out upon the city of Samaria, his prize, towering on the very next summit of these rolling hillsides.

Asherah and Astarte kept staring each other down. They were about to explode into a fight that Baal with all his strength might not be able to stop. Though he might also find it entertaining.

He mused out loud as he turned and walked up behind Asherah. "There is something I must do before I make my decision. As you said, I need to earn my place of power."

Asherah turned to face him. Without warning, he punched her in her abdomen. It was a powerful hit. He had massive arms of strength. She collapsed to the ground with a grunt of deep pain. Getting behind her, he pulled her up and choked her from behind with his huge arm around her throat. She tried to pull his arm off, but it was useless. He was pure muscle.

Baal nodded to Astarte. She walked up to Asherah and punched the Mother in the face repeatedly until Asherah's nose broke and gushed blood.

Pausing, the goddess of war lifted her bloody fist up and pulled out a tooth that had been stuck in her knuckle.

She then grabbed Asherah's tunic and ripped it from her body, leaving the other goddess naked. Baal released his grip and Astarte followed through with a punch in the throat of her opposing goddess.

Baal let Asherah fall to the ground, choking over her crushed windpipe. He flipped her onto her stomach.

Astarte watched as the storm god violated his mother as warriors did to humiliate their defeated foes.

When Baal had finished his violence, Asherah sat up and positioned herself in an attempt to recover some dignity in the face of her shame and pain. Baal sighed with satisfaction and stood over the matriarch with pride. He could see Asherah understood him perfectly now. He had earned his power over her, and she was never going to stand up to him again.

Then he said, "Astarte, you will go to Jerusalem and conspire with Molech and Chemosh. Find a way to destroy the House of David."

Astarte rose up angrily. But after what he'd just done to Asherah, she held her tongue and her reaction. She wasn't going to let her temper get the better of her.

"Yes, my Lord," she forced out.

Baal addressed the goddess at his feet. "Asherah, you will stay here as my consort as you so wisely suggested. You will help me replace Yahweh in Israel's worship."

"Yes, Most High," Asherah croaked obediently.

"But first we will escort Astarte to Jerusalem."

"You don't trust me?" complained the war goddess.

"I expect you to earn my trust," Baal said. "And that is why I want to see for myself what we have to work with down there."

Astarte deferred to him with a bow and a look to the ground.

A royal human entourage drew their attention to the entrance of the high place. The king and queen had arrived at the sanctuary.

CHAPTER 11

Ahab and Izabel left their attendants outside the sanctuary and entered the courtyard of the high place. They knelt in prayer as priests sacrificed oxen and bulls on the stone altar that rose over their heads. Both king and queen were filled with burning desire to consummate the Sacred Marriage, the conclusion of their wedding week.

They were led to the asherah on the stone platform to offer prayers to the goddess for fertility and success. Burning incense from the altar rose into the sky in a lazy swirl. Izabel was taken by the beauty of the asherah that loomed before her. It was the body of a huge terebinth tree about four feet in diameter and twenty feet tall that had been shorn of its bark and branches. Stylized branches made of gold covered the top third of the pole. The goddess Asherah was likened to the tree of life, so this totem pole represented that identity.

The bottom two thirds of the asherah were covered with engravings of the narrative of the goddess depicted in the sacred texts. Izabel knew the Canaanite stories well. She had studied them since she was a little girl.

She picked out carved images of El and his consort Asherah as well as Baal and his sister Anat. The narrative rose from the bottom of the pole upward. First there was Baal contending for kingship over Yam, god of sea and river. Then Asherah supporting Baal's claim to the kindly father god, El, whom the Hebrews equated with Yahweh. Asherah pleading to be given as a ransom to Yam out of love for her son. Baal fighting and defeating Yam instead. Higher on the pole, Asherah was depicted persuading the reluctant El to allow Baal to build a house on Mount Zaphon. Lady Asherah knew how to manipulate her husband. Mother of the gods, consort of El, and a persuasive matriarch. She knew how to manipulate her husband.

Izabel also knew the story that wasn't carved into the asherah. Namely El's drinking party at a Marzeah Feast where the father god got dead drunk and Astarte and Anat had to find him a hangover cure. This event was a portent of Baal's ultimate rise to overshadow the father god as Most High of the pantheon. But Izabel would keep that to herself. For now, she rejoiced that the Israelites already considered Asherah to be the wife of their Yahweh. It was only a matter of time before they accepted Asherah's son Baal as well.

Leading a small chorus of priests and priestesses, a high priestess representing Asherah sang the lyrics to a Sacred Marriage liturgy.

> Let me invoke the gracious gods.
> Let them give a feast to those of high rank
>> in the wilderness of the end of the world.
> Greetings, king. Greetings, queen, priests, and qedeshim.
> El enticed his two wives,
>> Asherah and goddess Womb.
> Lo, this maid bows down. Lo, this one rises up.
>> This one shouts, "Daddy!"
>> And this one shouts, "Mother!"
> The organ of El grows long as the sea.
>> Yea, the organ of El as the flood.
> The organ of El is long as the sea,
>> Yea, the organ of El as the flood.

As the chorus continued its lilting lyrics, Ahab bowed and prayed before a *massebah*, a standing stone beside the asherah on the high place. Three other standing stones stood at the perimeter of the platform. Massebah were mostly limestone, phallic in shape, and as tall as eight feet. They were often erected in locations of theophanies, places where deities revealed themselves in one form or another. Other times, they simply represented the presence of the god. This massebah beside the asherah stood for Yahweh of Samaria. The three others for Yarikh the moon god, Shapash the sun goddess, and the rest of the host of heaven.

Izabel prayed before the asherah that she would please the king. She called upon the Mother goddess for fruitfulness and upon Astarte for sexual virility. She desired not only an heir, but all her womanly wiles to inflame the king's desire and influence him for the better. She knew men, and she knew that sexual satisfaction is what led a man to love. And love was surrender.

Ahab left votaries at the feet of Yahweh's stone and his asherah. Votaries were small ceramic figurines representing the king and queen that operated as stand-ins of their praying presence in the same way that images of gods were stand-ins for the god's presence.

The sound of thunder drew their attention to rain clouds moving in from the west. But Izabel and Ahab had finished their worship and offering rituals. Ahab returned to his bride, and the pair proceeded to the sacred chamber in the outer precinct of the complex for consummation of the Sacred Marriage rite.

The priestess representing Asherah would accompany them into their bedchamber and partake in the ritual. King Ahab would place his seed into Izabel, representing the goddess's womb, to insure the blessing of fertility for the royal family as well as for the land of Israel.

After their act of consummation, Izabel lay naked and satisfied in Ahab's arms on the plush bed of the sacred chamber. The high priestess had left to return to her duties in the sanctuary shrine. Izabel glanced around the room, furnished to please royalty with Phoenician tapestries, oak furniture, a huge roaring fireplace, and soft calf skins on the bed. She pulled the covering tighter as the flash of lightning through the window cast a glow in the room. The sound of thunder punctuated the calm of the pouring rain outside.

Ahab softly caressed her forehead, her cheek, her lips.

"My king," she said affectionately.

"Your husband," he corrected.

"My husband."

"My wife." His hand followed from her breast down to her thigh, worshipping her every curve. "Queen of Israel."

"Mother of your sons," Izabel replied.

She could tell he liked the sound of it. So did she. She noticed his eyes looked deeply vulnerable.

"Yahweh has blessed me with more than I ever imagined," Ahab said.

"And Baal has blessed me beyond my dreams," Izabel countered.

Ahab asked, "Do you think our peoples can find the same peace?"

"I think—" Izabel paused. "—my people would be most at peace with Israel if you built a temple of Baal."

"Ah, the temple." Ahab's attention was taken by the form of her hip. Izabel could see he was starting to get aroused again.

She kept him on topic. "Does our marriage not model tolerance and unity between both people and gods?"

Ahab sighed. He clearly didn't want to be talking about this right now. But she did.

"Many of your people already worship Asherah as Yahweh's wife. Well, Asherah is also Baal's mother, you know."

Ahab paused his adoration of her and smirked with amusement. "Now I'm being instructed in my own religion."

Izabel caressed his cheek, kissed him. "I mean no disrespect, my love. My concern is to be more inclusive. As more of my people immigrate here from Tyre, they will be a minority without a house for their god. A temple of Baal would encourage more cultural exchange between allies. Of course, we would force no one to comply. Everyone should be able to worship whichever god they desire. Or all gods."

He finished her argument from previous discussions. "Co-existence."

They shared a smile. The pair had talked of many things over the past week. Likes. Dislikes. Family background. Personal dreams. The religious schism between their people came up quite often.

"It might be too soon," he said. "Israelites will need some time to get used to the idea."

Izabel wouldn't give up. "We could build Baal's house in Jezreel, where the royal summer palace is, instead of Samaria. That way, Yahwists would have their city in Samaria, the capital, and Baalists would have theirs in Jezreel as subordinate. A compromise."

Ahab searched the ceiling, trying to picture it in his mind. "I can only imagine the curses from the Sons of the Prophets."

"Who?" Izabel asked.

"A school for prophets of Yahweh. Led by Elijah the Tishbite. He is a belly-aching troublemaker leading an intolerant herd of fanatics. They hate progress."

"Why don't you get rid of them?"

Ahab looked at his bride with shock. "What do you mean, get rid of them?"

Izabel sensed she'd trespassed into sacred territory. What she'd meant was to kill these fanatics. But apparently, she shouldn't admit that. "Well, you are the king, and you just said they're blocking progress. Can you not—?"

She searched for a more diplomatic approach. "—just send them to Judah?"

Ahab chuckled with amusement. "No, I can't send the prophets of Yahweh to Judah. They speak for Yahweh, Izabel."

"You mean the people *believe* they speak for Yahweh."

"Does it matter?" he complained. "The result is the same. Should I transgress that belief, I would be courting chaos."

Izabel wracked her mind trying to figure out another way. Any solution.

"Well, then," she concluded, "I shall have to meet this Elijah and his Sons of the Prophets. Perhaps we can come to an understanding."

CHAPTER 12

Susanna placed her breadcakes, fresh from the stove, on a plate and carried them to the shrine room. Her home was located just outside Ahab's palace in the wealthier district of the city. Here many city officials, elders, and landowners lived above the commoners and poor of Samaria. Though a large house with two floors, an atrium, and ten rooms, it was not as extravagant as one might expect for the commander of Ahab's army. Susanna's husband Jehu was a warrior and outdoorsman, son of a chariot captain, who cared little for the niceties or luxuries of his position. He sometimes lamented having five servants because it made him feel pretentious. But he never decreased the bodyguard of five soldiers outside their walled perimeter because it kept Susanna safe.

Their marriage had been a good match. Susanna didn't care about wealth or luxury any more than Jehu. Family was what she valued. Wealth could be gained and lost. Houses would be replaced by new owners. But children were a heritage. They would build the future. They would carry on the family legacy and the values Susanna taught them. Like an olive tree drinking living waters, a family grew roots deep into the earth and sprouted its branches to the heavens. Family lineage was how Israelites would ultimately possess their allotted inheritance, the Promised Land, as Yahweh had sworn in his covenant with Abraham. Children were a woman's strength in this world.

And that was what made Susanna anxious. She and Jehu had been married two years, and she hadn't borne offspring yet. It wasn't unheard of for a woman to take two or more years to conceive, but it also wasn't unusual either for men to take on other wives or concubines to ensure their progeny. Plenty of Susanna's friends had been pregnant within the first few months of their marriage. At Susanna's age of eighteen, some already had two and even three children. She felt lonely in this big empty house.

Family legacy was everything. If a woman did not give birth, she was worthless. And that was what Susanna feared. What if she was a worthless dead tree stump that could not bear fruit? What would be the purpose in living without children? To die and leave a mere shred of forgotten memories in the collective identity of her people?

Jehu had told her she worried too much. She overthought things. That it was still too early to conclude such fears and that she was causing needless anxiety. Children would come in Yahweh's time. He had no desire for additional wives or concubines. Her husband would often joke that if he was the king, he would quit because he couldn't imagine handling the many wives kings often juggled.

But Jehu was a man in a world ruled by men. And as much as she trusted his integrity and faithfulness, he hadn't yet been tested with the prospect of barrenness. Of lack of lineage. And the responsibility of childbirth was not upon him. As much as Susanna loved her husband, he could never truly understand her struggle as a woman in this world.

Jehu had found his worth in service to the king, God's anointed. But how would he feel if after a life of training as a warrior he was suddenly removed from his position and forced to be a farmer in the middle of nowhere? Susanna would comfort him with assurances of her devotion, but would it be enough? And what if he had no children to carry on the family heritage? Would his royal service not feel as worthless as hers should she not bear those children?

Jehu was right. She fretted too much. But she would take no chances or waste her time sitting around worrying. She would do everything she could to ensure a future family. She munched on mandrake root, considered to aid in reproduction. And she had also decided to increase her chances by appealing to the goddess of fertility, Asherah.

Susanna placed the breadcakes onto the small altar that stood before a foot-tall image of the goddess. Asherah was depicted in fired ceramic as a female figure whose feet blended into a pillar-like base. She held her full breasts up with her hands as an ode to fertility. Susanna had various other teraphim, red terracotta clay images of the goddess as well as an image of Bes, the bow-legged dwarf god with an ugly lion-like face and large phallus. His purpose was to avert evil, ensure fertility, and protect pregnant mothers and their birthing. It was always good to have more than one image or amulet for good luck because you never knew what would be enough. Susanna was hedging all her bets.

Her affinity for these gods was a sore spot with her husband. Though he was a Yahwist, Jehu allowed Susanna to have the shrine against his better judgment. It was a point of tension in an otherwise blessed marriage. When she'd first requested the shrine, he'd said no until she challenged him about his inconsistent behavior.

After all, King Ahab allowed the high places to thrive though they were condemned by Yahweh's prophets. The king also allowed the golden calves in Dan and Bethel. Asherah worship had become a widespread norm throughout all of Israel. And even though Jehu thought it a violation of Yahweh's exclusive claim on Israel, it was also Yahweh's word that the king was his anointed chosen one. So Jehu considered his obedience to his king as obedience to his god, despite the king's flaws. Jehu tolerated the lesser sin for the greater good. He often said that if everyone did what was right in their own eyes, chaos would reign like Leviathan the sea dragon.

Susanna had argued that Jehu's toleration of Israel's compromise hadn't been equally extended to his own wife, who simply wanted to try every possibility to ensure she could bear offspring for the good of Israel and the family lineage of Jehu. He'd finally let her put up the shrine, but it had become an issue of stress between them.

The truth was that most women she knew had Asherah figurines. It wasn't a denial of Yahweh's rule over Israel, just an accommodation to the needs of the female half of society who couldn't relate as easily to what seemed a distant male deity. Yahweh was a divine warrior father. And she worshipped him as the Most High. But people also needed a divine nurturing mother.

Susanna lit the incense housed on a lower tier of the altar. She adjusted two little clay votives of her and her husband that represented their constant petition before the images of the goddesses. She clutched an amulet around her neck and prayed. This was a copper good luck charm with an inscription reading, "I bless you by Yahweh of Samaria and by his Asherah."

Her prayer was interrupted by the sound of weeping. It was faint, behind closed doors at the other end of the hallway, but she could hear it.

Susanna's maidservant tapped on her door. "My lady, it's Galina."

"Thank you, Miriam." Susanna got up and left her family shrine, making her way down the hallway. Susanna's younger sister, Galina was fifteen years old, lighter-skinned than Susanna with brown hair, and seemingly her opposite in every way. Where Susanna was modest and proper, Galina was wily and impulsive. Where Susanna was cautious and organized, Galina took risks without thinking through the consequences.

In fact, Galina was staying with Susanna and Jehu due to the consequences of rash choices she'd made in the recent past. A year ago, Galina had gotten pregnant out of wedlock by the sixteen-year-old son of a traveling image-maker from the city of Dan. Galina had broken their father's heart. She'd been quickly married to the boy, and their father had been glad to send her off with the traveling merchant's family, expecting to never see her again. The shame was too great for a man of such high reputation in the military.

But just days ago, Galina had appeared at Susanna's house. Alone. Disheveled. Traumatized. And with a sad story to tell. She'd lost her baby in a miscarriage shortly after leaving Samaria. Worse, the entire family she'd married into had been murdered by marauding Aramean bandits. She alone had survived.

Galina hadn't gone into the details yet, only that her in-laws were all dead. She had nowhere to turn. She knew no one in Dan. Her father in Megiddo would never take her back. So Jehu and Susanna had taken her in without telling her father. Susanna deeply loved her sister and wanted to help her. But they had yet to find a way to do so that would redeem the shame hanging over Galina like a storm cloud.

Susanna opened the door gently to see Galina sitting on her bed sobbing, her eyes puffy and red, her face wet with tears. Her bedraggled hair had been cut short in mourning for her loss, but that didn't seem to stop Galina from making a mess of it.

This had happened once before, Galina suddenly weeping without warning. But only once. Her recklessness came with a corresponding toughness of soul. Susanna knew her sister would adjust to her harsh reality. She always did. This was just one of those moments when she was vulnerable.

Susanna couldn't imagine the terror of having her entire family of in-laws massacred by monsters. Sitting next to Galina, she placed her arm around her sister in comfort. "You are not alone, Galina."

"Not true," countered her sister. "I am alone. My husband and his family are all dead. And I am dead to my father and mother. I might as well be truly dead."

"Don't say such things. I love you. Jehu cares about you too. This can be your new home."

"I don't feel at home." Pulling up her knees, Galina buried her face into them.

Susanna said, "You need to give it time."

"How much time? Will I have to live in secret for months? Years? Father will never forgive me anyway."

Susanna's heart bled for her sister. Yes, she was experiencing the consequences of her decisions. But at what point was life's punishment enough? Could her sister not have a second chance at life?

She asked with genuine curiosity, "Galina, what can we do to make it better for you?"

As if on cue, Galina looked up at her. She might have been waiting for just that offer. She blurted out, "I want to join the palace court of attendants."

"What?" Susanna wasn't sure what she'd heard.

Galina's tears dried up as she spoke with a new enthusiasm. "Queen Izabel has made a public invitation to Israelite girls to be trained in a royal school for palace service in Jezreel. If Jehu vouched for my position, I'm sure they would accept me."

The suggestion had taken Susanna by surprise. She scrambled to gather her thoughts. "Galina, I understand you trying to run away from the world. But do you understand the world to which you are trying to run?"

"It would be a new life," Galina replied. "A second chance."

Susanna sighed. She wanted the best for her sister. And there was some truth to Galina's claim. It would be a new life with a new identity. But was this free-spirited girl capable of entering a life of service, even a prestigious service such as royal court attendant? She doubted it.

They were interrupted by the sound of the front door of the house opening.

Susanna said, "That's Jehu. Stay here. Let me talk to him. We'll see what we can do."

CHAPTER 13

When Jehu entered the house, he directed a servant to set a small ornate wooden chest onto the floor and dismissed him. He'd just returned from a meeting with his military captains at the palace. Jehu was always happy to return home, to see his wife, to experience the nurturing haven of her love.

Susanna met him just inside the door. "Husband, you're supposed to be resting. You could reopen your wound."

"I'm fine," he countered.

"Let me change your bandage. Come, sit down."

Jehu sat in a chair as Susanna removed his shoulder bandage and examined his wound. A physician had sewn the flesh together. But Susanna had a broad knowledge of herbs and potions, and she applied a special ointment that brought soothing in a way only she could accomplish. As she wrapped his shoulder with a fresh linen cloth, he already felt better.

"The king owes you his life," she said.

Jehu grunted with pain as she moved his arm. "Susanna, my loyalty to the crown is not conditional. He is God's chosen king."

"The king's foreign queen provides little to be loyal to."

Within their home, Susanna felt free to speak her mind to her husband. This was their refuge from the power and lies outside. She was his helpmate, and he welcomed it.

"Nevertheless," Jehu responded, "Izabel is his queen. And we are their subjects."

Susanna added the phrase he always repeated, "Obedience to authority is obedience to God, despite the authority's flaws."

Jehu smiled. "You are a good student of my aphorisms. And an even better lover."

Kissing her, Jehu felt his wife melt in his arms. He refused to register the pain in his shoulder because it was worth the touch of her body against his. Her lips to his lips. Her soul to his soul. Susanna was his true refuge.

Jehu had explained to her often enough his conviction about the nature of authority and God. When Saul was king of Israel, David had received more praise in public song than Saul. After David defeated Goliath, people sang "Saul has struck down his thousands, and David his ten thousands." An evil spirit of rage had possessed Saul, and he'd sought to kill the son of Jesse, who'd been rightfully anointed by the prophet Samuel to become Israel's next king.

Despite this, David had refused to hurt King Saul, even in self-defense. Twice he had the chance to kill Saul, and twice he had refused because he knew the king had been anointed to his current position by Yahweh's authority—regardless of Saul's current spiritual state of unrighteousness.

The first time had been in the forest of Engedi when David and his mighty men were hiding out in a cave. Not knowing of his enemy's hideout, Saul had chosen to relieve himself in that very cave. Instead of executing the wayward king, David secretly cut off a corner of his cloak, trying to demonstrate to Saul that he wasn't the king's enemy. When questioned by his men, David told them, "Yahweh forbid that I should do this thing to my lord, the Lord's anointed, to put out my hand against him, seeing he is Yahweh's anointed."

A second time, Saul had madly hunted David in the wilderness of Ziph. This time David and one of his officers snuck into Saul's camp at night. Once again, David had refused to "put out his hand against the Lord's anointed." Instead, they'd taken a jug of water and spear from the head of Saul's bed, again trying to prove to Saul that David wasn't his enemy.

But the balance of loyalty to both king and god came to a final expression in Saul's death. A young soldier had chanced upon Saul dying in the aftermath of a battle. When the king pleaded with the man to put him out of his misery, the soldier complied, then brought Saul's crown to David, rightful heir to the throne. David had that soldier executed for killing the Lord's anointed.

The principle of loyalty to the crown despite the king's own wickedness was a loyalty to higher authority. The authority of the Lord's anointed. It was a conviction Jehu sought to live by. But the conviction had brought much trouble in his life as King Ahab was not all that different from King Saul.

Susanna interrupted his thoughts, "What is that?" She pointed to the ornate wooden chest by the door.

"A gift for you. From our foreign queen you so distrust." As his wife's cheeks reddened in embarrassment, he added playfully, "Shall we see what Izabel has given her disloyal subject?"

Within moments, they had the chest on the table, and Susanna was opening it with curiosity.

She reached in and pulled out a foot-tall bronze image of a goddess, a slender female with a starburst for a crown.

"Astarte," said Jehu with disdain. "Queen of Heaven, goddess of fertility."

"I told the queen that we had no children," Susanna explained.

"Yet," Jehu emphasized, then went on, "Izabel was a high priestess of Astarte in Tyre. I suppose it is her way of offering support."

Susanna demurred, "Or condescension."

She watched him for his decision on what to do with the gift. Conflicting loyalties to God and crown came into play once again as Jehu said with resignation, "We can't turn down a gift from the queen. Just keep it out of my sight."

Placing the image back in the box, Susanna closed the lid and changed the subject again. "Galina told me of the queen's public solicitation for palace attendants."

"I heard of it."

"Galina wants to join and for you to vouch for her."

After a moment of silent incredulity, he protested, "She is not a burden to us. Why would she want to do such a thing?"

Galina's voice came from behind them. "The queen wants to give girls like me a better opportunity in life."

They turned to see Susanna's sister now standing at the entrance to the room.

Jehu said, "Do you think you will be anything more than a servant to royal privilege?"

Galina replied, "Like you are to the king?"

"Galina," Susanna scolded her. "You disrespect my husband, our lord."

She was as quick to repent. "I apologize."

Jehu had felt the sting of Galina's comment. The girl had a singular talent of using his own principles against him.

"Queen Izabel is a strong woman," Galina continued. "I want to be like her."

"So you want to be queen," Jehu responded sardonically, knowing his words would expose her childish fantasies.

He added, "Yes, Galina, I am a servant of the king. And you have no idea what it means to work for the crown. What it will cost you." He thought of his daily struggle of dual loyalty to both God and king.

Galina's expression was defiant. "So it's okay for you, but not for me."

"I'm sorry, but the answer is no."

The girl burst out crying again. Angry crying. She ran back up the stairs to her room.

Susanna gave Jehu a look as if to say he could have been a bit less harsh. She followed the girl to her room. This time Jehu did as well.

When he arrived at the doorway, he saw Susanna holding the crying Galina. When she quieted, Susanna said to her, "We can't replace the family you lost. But you are still my family."

Galina looked up at her and said, "And I can't replace your want of a child."

Susanna looked at Jehu. He didn't know how to respond.

But then his wife said a brave thing to her sister. "Perhaps we are each other's answer to prayer."

"I know you are trying," said Galina. "But I feel more at home with the Phoenicians." It was the first time Jehu had heard the girl say it. But it made sense. She had always seemed like an outcast in her own family, her own people. And in a way, Tyre and all of Sidonia was a collection of people more at home with other nations.

"Matthew's hometown of Dan was close to the city of Tyre," Galina went on.

Matthew was the name of her dead husband. Her look focused off into the distance, recalling what used to be.

"His clan were image-makers. But they sold their images in all the towns around. My favorite place to go to market was Tyre. It was a beautiful city with boats that brought things from all over the world. Wonderful, strange new things. Matthew's father studied the crafts of Egypt, Greece, Cyprus. They sculpted terracotta images of Asherah. They forged metal statues of Baal, Anat, Astarte. Matthew even worked in stone."

She stopped for a moment. A dark look came over her before she continued. "One day Matthew's father was hired to fix the golden calf in the sanctuary of Dan. It had been accidentally damaged. It was a high honor for him to work with the sacred image of Yahweh. So he brought all of us with him: Matthew, me, Matthew's three siblings. While he worked on the image, we cleaned the holy place, the standing stones, the asherah, and the sacred utensils of the priesthood. And when he was done, we all got to help polish the bull calf."

She paused again, shaking her head with awe. "I had never seen a more beautiful image in my life. As image makers, they had created many bull calf representations of Baal, but this one for Yahweh was different. It sparkled. It seemed to glow with the presence of Yahweh. Matthew's father told us the story of how Yahweh delivered the Israelites through the golden calf at Mount Sinai. Moses's brother Aaron forged the bull, and it led them through the wilderness into the Promised Land."

Jehu had heard different versions of that story, so he couldn't be sure which version was true. All he knew was that since the great split with Judah, the Israelites worshipped Yahweh through the golden calf images in Dan and Bethel. They were the king's way of countering the Jerusalem temple cult.

Galina swallowed. Her voice cracked with emotion. "When we were leaving the high place, a prophet of Yahweh came up to my husband's father and cursed him. He said that he and all his family would suffer for his spiritual harlotry. That night, we ate a feast with the family clan in a farm outside Dan. We were attacked by a gang of Arameans. They killed all the men and boys, then forced themselves upon the females. When they were done, they killed all of Matthew's clan."

She choked up, holding back tears. "If I hadn't hid beneath the bodies of Matthew's parents, I wouldn't be here. But now I wish I had never survived."

Susanna reached out to Galina and held her tightly. "Yahweh has a reason for saving you, sweet sister. He has a purpose."

Galina replied into her shoulder, "What kind of purpose could there be to such suffering?"

Susanna's silence appeared to be no comfort. Jehu offered the only hope he had in this iron world of brutality. "The Sons of the Prophets say that a righteous king will come, a Son of David. He will bring the house of Israel and the house of Judah together. He will put all to rights."

His young sister-in-law looked at him with honest doubt. "When?"

Jehu had no answer. He wasn't even sure he believed what he'd just told her.

Galina asked, "Who are these prophets?"

CHAPTER 14

Outside Samaria

Fifteen miles north of Samaria, the School of the Prophets was located in the cliffside of a ravine a hundred feet above the valley. From below, it looked like a small town carved from the rock with winding paths and plenty of rope ladders to and from residences and meeting places. It housed several hundred people, including prophets, their families, and students.

There was only one access route up a winding dirt path to the rocky village. The prophets and their students preferred to be isolated and self-sufficient. Below them in the valley was a large field for growing grain and a small vineyard for wine. They had their own storehouses of food and water to sustain them through difficult times. Everyone wore simple wool robes to complement their simple lifestyle.

They also had dug several classrooms out of the rock for teaching students who sought to become prophets. The classroom in which young Elisha argued with his teacher felt more like a cave than a class. Fifty-odd other students gathered around him, which fed his energy. He liked the attention, and he didn't mind standing alone against the crowd.

Or in this case, against his teacher, Micaiah son of Imlah, an elder of sixty with gray hair and beard. The students remained clean-shaven until they rose to the office of prophet, whereupon they would grow a beard as a sign of their calling.

Elisha had felt that calling, and he wasn't going to waste his education. He was having a hard time accepting his elder's argument for patience in light of the turn of events in Samaria.

He spoke with conviction. "At that despicable wedding of our king to that whore of Baal, I saw abominable idolatry. I saw our people drunk on their own depravity. Where is justice? I say we rise up and slay the idolaters."

Micaiah was being very patient with him. "Yahweh will send a deliverer, but I see him as one who suffers, as did Moses in the wilderness."

"We have suffered enough," complained Elisha. "It is time to raise an army. Like Joshua. Look at the Rechabites. They are devoted to Yahweh, and yet they are armed."

The other students murmured with scandal at his pretension.

Micaiah replied, "The Rechabites are chariot-makers for the king. It is their job to make tools of war. They are required to defend themselves."

"And sometimes they protect us," Elisha countered. "Do we only wait until we are attacked? Is not a good offense also a good defense?"

Micaiah sighed with frustration.

Elisha turned and said, "What say you, Master?"

Elijah the Tishbite sighed thoughtfully on his wooden stool. He had been quietly watching the exchange. The students went silent. As headmaster of the school and respected prophet, his presence conveyed an aura of holiness. In his fifties, with greying black hair and bushy beard, he was not impressive in worldly terms. But his voice commanded with authority. When he spoke, people listened as though he were a military general. Though his actual troops were a couple hundred neophyte young men.

"Elisha," he said thoughtfully, "you have a hunger for justice. That is good." A murmur of praise came from the students. "Yet you ask not what Yahweh requires." Excitement turned once again to silence. "Without God's judgment, what is human justice?"

Elisha was speechless. Micaiah leaned in and half-whispered to Elisha, "Naked power. The strong oppress the weak."

"Thank you, Micaiah," said Elijah. "But I would prefer our students ponder the questions than parrot the answers."

Micaiah bowed in apology.

"Class is dismissed."

The students filed out of the cave.

"Elisha," came Elijah's voice behind him. "Come with me."

Prophet and student walked toward a garden that overlooked the valley. Elijah slung a hairy mantle onto his shoulders and fastened it with a leather belt. The mantle was dirty-white and made of the silken long hair of an angora goat. It was a prophet's mantle, used only by a master prophet of Yahweh.

And it stank. Elisha wrinkled his nose with aversion.

"Smells obnoxious, doesn't it?" chuckled Elijah. They arrived at the edge of the garden. The two of them looked up into the night sky at the full moon, which illuminated the vast plains before them.

Elijah said, "The prophet's mantle is not one of sweet-smelling lies."

Elisha responded with concern. "I think you consider me rebellious, master."

Elijah smiled. "I consider you zealous. But sometimes a misplaced zealotry."

"Are we not to be zealous for Yahweh?" demanded Elisha. "Zealous for righteousness?"

"What did your father teach you about righteousness?" Elijah responded.

This was a sore spot for Elisha. His father and mother had both pleaded with him not to join the School of Prophets. They wanted him to stay and take over the family farm. But he'd been determined to do something more with his life. Growing crops and raising animals seemed like a waste of time to Elisha.

"My father is a good man," he confessed. "He taught me the value of integrity and moral character. He is faithful to my mother. He works hard farming the land. Harder than anyone I know. But his simple life has no effect on the world. He plows his field, and the world changes around him."

Elisha paused, thinking sadly about his parents and their lives of struggle. "I want to change the world."

"Hmm," responded Elijah. "So Yahweh promises a new world to come, and you want to be the one to bring that world in with your sword ablaze."

Elisha nodded. "With the fire of God."

"Why don't you join the army?"

"Because the army is a tool of the king. And our king is unjust and ruled by his harlot wife."

Elijah said, "You should have learned more from your father."

"Are you saying I should have stayed a farmer?"

"I'm not sure you have what it takes to become a prophet."

Elisha's heart dropped. Was the master trying to get rid of the student?

Elijah continued, "God has called some to be warriors, others to be farmers, and still others to be prophets. But God desires all his people to have honorable integrity and upright moral character. Yes, Yahweh cares about our world. But he also cares about the individuals who make up that world. The calling of a warrior is to fight. The calling of a prophet is to speak God's truth."

Elisha felt chastised like a young child. He protested, "But why can we not do both?"

"Yahweh's Word is the only sword a prophet is to bear," countered Elijah. "We trust him to fight for us."

Elisha sighed. He knew there was no argument against this.

Elijah concluded, "If you can't accept this, you shouldn't be studying to be a prophet."

Did the master want Elisha to quit? Or was he just challenging his student to get more serious.

Elisha stepped back in sudden fear as a flock of crows approached. They fluttered around Elijah, and several landed on the prophet's mantle as if called.

Pulling some seed from his pockets, Elijah fed the birds from his hands. Elisha was curious at the strange interplay between man and avian. But he didn't know what to make of it, what to say. Maybe he shouldn't say anything. Maybe he talked too much.

Elijah said, "The new queen of Israel has bid me to audience. I am bringing a group of students. I want you to go with us."

"Me?" Elisha looked at the prophet with surprise. He'd just been challenged to quit the school, and now the master was suggesting he stay?

"Yes, you. But I do want you to listen this time. And keep your mouth shut." Elijah looked at the youth with a grin. "Can you do that for me? For Yahweh?"

His smile disarmed Elisha, who looked to the ground humbled. "Forgive me, master. I will obey."

CHAPTER 15

Jerusalem

Baal, Asherah, and Astarte made their way to the southern hill of the Mount of Olives where Solomon had built the high places for Astarte, Milcom, and Chemosh. They stopped at the temple of Astarte to partake of the blood sacrifices being offered. They kept themselves concealed in the spiritual realm, unobserved by the humans in the temple. A large stone platform and temple grounds overlooked Yahweh's temple on Mount Zion.

Because of these high places, the Mount of Olives had been nicknamed the Mountain of Shame by intolerant Yahwists. To Baal, they were self-righteous hypocrites considering they had an Asherah in the temple of Yahweh. Not to mention that even now as he stood on the hill, he could see the high priest carrying the Nehushtan into the temple grounds while Judeans circled it with worship.

Nehushtan was the bronze serpent on a pole that Yahweh had told Moses to make during the wilderness generation. The story was told that Yahweh had sent fiery serpents to bite the Israelites because they had complained against Yahweh. Thousands had died for their rebellion. Moses had created Nehushtan as a means of salvation. If a bitten Hebrew looked upon the bronze serpent raised high, he would be cured of the deadly bite.

Unfortunately for Yahweh, the image was kept and ultimately became an object of worship by the Hebrews. Their circumambulation around it right now created a wave-like effect of people who dissolved their individual identities into the singular mass of oneness with each other and the image. Baal laughed at how easy it was to enslave Judeans to false gods.

Those self-righteous Yahwists also called Astarte "Ashtoreth." It was another of their insulting plays on words, where they inserted the vowels of the word "bosheth," which means *shame*, between the consonants of Astarte's

69

name. The result was *Ashtoreth*. The altar of burnt offering they called
"topheth" or "tophet" for short, which meant "firepit of shame." The prophets
and the few fanatics who tried to push their solo, bachelor god were fortunately
not influential enough as to have much impact on the people.

Chemosh, the Moabite deity, was nowhere to be found around his high
place. Baal wondered if he might be with Molech in his valley. Milcom was
back in Ammon for some reason. Baal looked at the temples of the other gods
and resolved to have his own house in Jezreel completed as soon as possible.
But Queen Izabel was only now laying the foundation and had so much more
to go. It would take a year to finish it.

Baal turned to Asherah and Astarte. "Let us go to Gehenna."

Gehenna was another name for Molech's Valley of Hinnom on the
southwest side of the city walls. Yahwists called the valley cursed because it
was where the Hebrews made their sons and daughters pass through the fires
of Molech.

As they travelled down into the valley, Baal announced, "By the way, I
have sent for Anat to meet me back at Jezreel."

"Why?" asked Asherah. "Am I not enough for you?" She spoke with the
fearfulness of an abused wife.

"My sister and I are very close," he said. "No one can replace her loyalty."

Astarte's silence barely contained her resentment.

"Or her passion," Baal added. That passion was both sexual and violent.
No one was as bloodthirsty as Anat. Her lithe, graceful figure belied her speed
and skill with a blade. She used two *khopeshes*, Egyptian sickle swords, to
reap the heads of her enemies. After battles, she would bind those trophy skulls
to her back along with severed hands as a girdle.

Baal's most delicious memory of Anat was when she had transformed
into a heifer and he coupled with her seventy-seven times. She had bathed
herself with sky-dew and rubbed ambergris from a sperm whale all over her
body. At least that's how the myth went. And Baal reveled in the narrative. It
was a narrative that empowered the bestiality of the Canaanite culture. Sex
with animals to reflect the gods. Sex with everything, or anyone, *except* one's
husband or wife was the ultimate goal.

"Anat will meet us back in Samaria when we return," he said to Asherah.
Hopefully, this would make Asherah mindful of her behavior, enough to not

betray him back in Jezreel and also make Astarte jealous enough to inspire her work here in Jerusalem.

As they walked through the Valley of Hinnom, Baal was a bit envious of Molech's personal residence. Molech was an Ammonite deity of the underworld. He lived in a maze of underground tunnels beneath their feet. Valleys were sites of transition between the land above and Sheol below. In the three-tiered cosmos, mountaintops were the transition between the heavenly and earthly realms, so valleys at the base of mountains functioned as entry points into the underworld.

In this particular valley, Judeans engaged in mortuary rituals, ancestor veneration, and fire sacrifices to Molech. In the Valley of the Rephaim, just west of here, Judeans performed Marzeah Feasts to call upon the divinized dead kings, called Rephaim. It was also the place where King David had wiped out the giant clan by the same name. These valleys were charged with spiritual energy.

As they approached the stone tophet on the hillside, Baal noticed that Molech was nowhere to be seen.

Strange. Molech was quite territorial. Why was he not here to greet the three of them?

The three gods stopped. All sound of desert creatures had gone silent. Baal suddenly felt a presence. Not a human presence, a supernatural one. They were being watched—or more accurately, hunted.

Before he could reach for a weapon, a dozen dire wolves burst out of the brush. The gods were large beings, nearly seven feet tall each. But these wolves were twice the size of a man, making formidable opponents. Two launched themselves at Baal. A third jumped Asherah.

Baal pounded one of them, crushing its skull. But the other tore at his arm, ripping into the flesh. Baal yelled in pain. Though the gods could not die and were unbeatable by humans, these wolfen monsters were not of this earth. And heavenly creatures could cause enough damage to incapacitate a Watcher—and cause pain. Heavenly creatures felt pain just like any other creature. Though they had flesh with supernatural qualities, it was nevertheless flesh and therefore required healing or regeneration.

Asherah stumbled heavily as a wolf bit deep into her calf. But she managed to draw her sword and cut off the wolf's head. A second one she skewered through the belly.

Baal grabbed the throat of his biter and ripped its esophagus out. The creature released its grip on his arm, leaving torn and bleeding flesh.

He pulled his hammer out with his good arm and swung. It connected with a fifth wolf's body and launched it howling in pain a hundred feet away, its body crushed by the force. In the hands of Baal, that hammer could unleash untold devastation.

Asherah and Baal backed up against one another. They had dispatched five of the wolves rather quickly, but were now surrounded by seven other snarling monsters ready to pounce.

It was at that point that two questions rose to Baal's mind. First, these dire wolves were supposed to be Molech's underworld hounds. Why were they attacking Watchers? Secondly, he had realized that Astarte was not with them anymore. Had she fled to call Molech and Chemosh for help? Or had she betrayed them?

Just as suddenly as they'd attacked, the pack of wolves all stopped in their tracks, turned and fled the scene as if called away—or frightened.

Baal turned to see four archangels standing behind him. The dire wolves had fled at the approach of Mikael, Saraqael, Remiel, and Uriel.

"What are you doing here?" Baal blurted out.

Because of the Hebrews' apostasy and corresponding strength of this territory's principalities and powers, the archangels hadn't been seen or heard from in the land for a long time. Yahweh was losing the battle for the Promised Land as his people empowered other gods by worshipping them. But now four archangels were here to attack two legally justified authorities. According to the Mosaic covenant, Baal and Asherah had every right to be here.

It seemed like overkill to send four archangels, the mightiest host of heaven.

"Greetings, god of broccoli," quipped Uriel to Baal. "You have an appointment with Mot."

Blond haired Uriel was smaller than his fellow archangels and often used his sharp tongue to compensate. His clever insults, referencing Baal as the god of vegetation or storm, had a way of sticking in Baal's craw. Yet Uriel was not to be underestimated as he wielded a sword in each hand.

Mot was the Lord of Death, Keeper of Sheol in Caananite lore. An appointment with Mot was an appointment with death. Now Baal knew why

Yahweh had sent four archangels and why they were in Gehenna, a valley of the underworld.

Well, I'm not going down easily! Baal swung his hammer over his head, ready to pound. "Come and take us, godlickers!"

Asherah held her weapon ready for the fight.

The angels drew their swords. Mikael and Uriel paired off against Baal, Saraqael and Remiel against Asherah.

Baal used his hammer head to block the thrusts and parries of his opponents. Sparks flew as heavenly metal clanged with heavenly metal.

Asherah fell back under the relentless attacks of her opponents, her wounded calf clearly giving her trouble.

They were being separated.

Baal got a lucky swing in and disarmed Mikael. His sword went flying from his hands. As the angel went to retrieve his weapon, Uriel used his two swords with nimble dexterity to hold Baal at bay.

Glancing over, Baal saw that Asherah wasn't keeping up with the swordplay of Saraqael and Remiel. She screamed in pain as one of them cut her arm clean off.

Removing his dagger, Baal threw it, hitting Remiel in the shoulder. The angel faltered and Asherah got in a good cut on his chest. He stumbled backward. But that was when Saraqael caught her off guard, plunging his blade into her abdomen. Dropping her sword, she fell to the ground, gasping.

Saraqael and the wounded Remiel had now joined the runt Uriel against Baal, who swung his war hammer, keeping them back. If the mighty Baal were to land a blow on any one of the archangels, they'd be smashed into angel meat.

Just then, Baal felt his hammer arm cut from behind him. His muscle lost its strength, and the hammer fell from his grip to the valley floor.

Mikael had retrieved his sword and had launched a surprise attack.

Baal backed away, holding his throbbing arm wound.

The angels lined up against him. Four armed archangels against one unarmed Watcher. They slowly advanced together.

Baal backed up, desperate for a strategy.

Then he realized the angels had stopped and he was a good fifteen feet from them. Should he run?

He suddenly understood what the angels were doing. They were getting out of the way.

As the ground tremored beneath him, Baal lost his footing. A twenty-foot diameter of ground around him began to sink like a hole.

And he was in the middle of it.

"Damn you, Yahweh!" he yelled. The yawning jaws of Mot were opening to swallow him whole.

The angels had tricked him and called upon the Lord of Death. He was going down into the pit, and there was nothing he could do to stop it.

He plunged into darkness.

Asherah came back to consciousness on the desert floor, greeted by the glowering face of Anat, who was shaking her awake. It was night. The moon lit up the desert with an eerie glow. Her heavenly flesh wounds had almost fully healed. Her arm had been returned by Anat and had regenerated.

Asherah sat up with a grunt. "Where am I?" They were not in Gehenna.

"We are in the Valley of the Rephaim," Anat said impatiently. "What happened? Where is Baal?"

Asherah croaked out, "The jaws of Mot took him. It was a trap. Four archangels sabotaged us before we could enter the city."

"Why did Mot not take you?" Anat asked suspiciously.

"I don't know. But it had to have been done in collusion with the archangels. But why in Hades would Mot work in collusion with the archangels? It doesn't make sense."

Anat drew her two sickle swords from her back. "And you failed to protect your lord."

Asherah backed up on the ground. "What are you going to do?" Hacking her enemies to pieces was not uncommon for the warrior goddess.

"What do you think, moron?" said Anat. "I'm going down to bring him back."

With that, the goddess turned and started her journey north.

Asherah knew where Anat was going: the Gates of Sheol.

CHAPTER 16

Jezreel

Izabel and Athaliah walked through the summer palace that King Ahab had built in the city. Located twenty miles northeast of Samaria on the southern edge of the Jezreel Valley, Jezreel was a strategic location that guarded the roads from Samaria into the valley. Situated on a high hill with a view of the plains, it operated as a kind of second capital. Like Samaria, its fortifications were impressive, and the two cities were similar in size and population.

Jezreel was rustic in city planning and architecture. Izabel considered it indistinguishable from Samaria. These Israelites didn't have much variety to their public or private spaces.

That was all going to change.

Izabel brought Athaliah up to one of the four high towers that fortified the palace corners. From there they could see the entire city spread out below. The palace and its grounds. The surrounding mudbrick residences and dirt streets. A high place, just outside the city walls. And in the distance, ten miles west, the Mount Carmel mountains which continued to the sea.

Below them, the city was alive. Phoenician artisans, architects, and builders of every kind flooded the public roads and palace grounds. Massive loads of stone were being carted through the gates for structural enhancements.

"Athaliah, my people will bring a beauty to this city you have never seen before," Izabel said to her seven-year-old companion, as a teacher would to her pupil. The girl was quite smart for her age. "Marvelous Phoenician architecture. Glorious Egyptian sculpture. Tapestries from Greece and Asia. Take notice of how the design and beauty can affect the very heart of the people. The way they see the world."

Izabel knew that art and architecture were the incarnation of values and ideas. It was her goal to help change the Israelite culture by importing the best of the world.

"Will we be living in Jezreel now?" Athaliah asked.

"For a while," replied Izabel. "I persuaded the king to build a temple of Baal here and to establish a new priesthood to serve this region. With his approval, I get to oversee the building."

Athaliah scrunched her face inquisitively. "How did you do that?"

Izabel had been schooling Athaliah in the religion of her people, its differences with Israelite religion, and how to overcome those differences through compromise.

The queen smiled. "Remember, the king is my husband. I know him very well, and he wants me to be happy. So I made sure he knew how unhappy I was."

"What did you do?"

"I became very sad. I told him I felt there was no place for me here. I was lonely and felt excluded. If we wanted our nations to be real friends, we needed to make it easier for my people to come to Israel and feel welcome. You will find, Athaliah, that a husband wants to have logical reasons for his decisions. But we women have the power of our emotions. We can override logic with feelings. So even though I gave him some reasons, what it really amounts to in the end is that if I'm not happy, he's not happy."

Athaliah appeared to think it through. She was a fast learner.

Izabel added, "And when he agrees to things that make me happy, I will then make sure that I make him feel very happy."

"What do you mean?"

"I will explain that to you when you're a bit older. You will also learn that men are more driven by their desires than by logic, though they don't like to admit it."

"Where is the temple going to be?" asked Athaliah.

Izabel pointed to a large open field area filled with workers marking out boundaries, hauling stone, and breaking ground.

"That, my dear princess, will be a grand and glorious temple for Baal, the Most High."

"I thought Yahweh was the Most High."

Izabel smiled. "Come."

She led the young girl down the tower back out into the courtyard. "You know of Asherah, the wife of Yahweh?"

"Yes," Athaliah said. "We worship Asherah at the high place."

"Well, Baal is Asherah's son. So let me tell you a story of Baal building his house on Mount Zaphon in the far reaches of the north."

Izabel told her the epic story of Baal's victory over Yam and his desire to build a temple on his holy mountain. But the queen substituted Yahweh's name for El as the father god whose approval Asherah manipulated to help Baal build that house. She also told stories of Anat, the mighty warrior goddess, saving her brother Baal from his own follies. And then how Anat and Astarte, Baal's consort, had to find a cure for the father god's drunken hangover.

"So you see, Athaliah, behind every god is a goddess who is the true hero of the story." Izabel paused for a moment to let this sink in before drawing her analogy. "Kings and men are like gods: vain, selfish, violent, and given to excess of appetites. It is we women who tame them and guide them. But we must do so without drawing attention to ourselves. They must always believe that our ideas are their own original thoughts. We cannot be perceived as telling them what to do."

"Why not?" asked the curious Athaliah.

"Because then they will take our heads."

Izabel saw the girl's eyes go wide. She leaned in with a whisper. "Which is why we must be discreet about what we tell each other."

Athaliah repeated what Izabel had been teaching her from the start, "Our sisterhood."

"Our sisterhood." Izabel's smile drew one in return from Athaliah.

Izabel and Athaliah had arrived in the garden atrium amidst flowers and foliage. The high priest Hamilqart met them, accompanied by a female court liaison and an entourage of a dozen male qedeshim, servants of superior physical prowess.

He bowed, "My queen."

Izabel looked at the high priest curiously. "Yes, what is it?"

"King Ahab asked me to deliver these qedeshim to you, should the king ever be—" Hamilqart sought for the right words. "—unavailable for your desires."

Izabel stared coldly at Hamilqart. The priest couldn't look her in the eye. He averted his gaze downward.

Izabel noticed that Athaliah was watching closely every nuance of the exchange.

She spoke like a patient, but firm mother to a disobedient son. "Hamilqart, I am devoted with my whole heart to the king. I have no need for such indulgence. Never present these to me again. Do you understand?"

Hamilqart bowed. "Your highness. I will inform the king."

He led the male qedeshim away.

Izabel turned to the woman who was with them. "Court liaison."

"Yes, my queen."

"Where are the royal concubines?"

•••••

Ahab marched down the hallway to the concubine residence of the palace. Bursting into the main entrance, he found Izabel and Athaliah overseeing the final removal of furnishings and ornaments. His expression seethed with anger.

"Izabel, what have you done with my concubines?"

Izabel gave Athaliah a quick glance. She had just been explaining this very thing to her. Now the girl would see theory born out in practice.

She turned to Ahab with a conciliatory demeanor. "My love, they are all safe. I have made them my court attendants."

"Your attendants? Izabel, I am the king!" Her husband looked like a pouting man-child.

"And I am your queen. How can we rule a people with integrity if we can't rule our own appetites?"

"Solomon had hundreds of wives and concubines," Ahab protested.

"Is that what you want? Illegitimate sons fighting for your throne and dividing your kingdom?"

Ahab looked flustered. As though he knew she was right, but didn't want to admit it. And she was so right!

But he was desperate. "I will still keep my sons. I already have seventy of them, and they are not going to lose their royal privileges."

Izabel smiled lovingly and drew near to him, wrapping her arms around him.

"Of course, you will, my love. But now it is time for *us* to build a family dynasty. Let my womb be your field to plow."

Ahab looked at her suspiciously. Izabel knew he loved her so deeply he wouldn't hold his doubt for long.

Still, his concern was simple. His needs were simple. He said, "Do you swear full devotion to my pleasure?"

She smiled like a mother and stroked his cheek like a lover. "Trust me, my husband. I will please you more than you have ever been pleased, and in ways you've only fantasized."

She could see his eyes widen, his pupils dilate with excitement.

"And let me not delay in proving it to you right now."

Izabel spoke to the girl while still staring into Ahab's delirious eyes. "Athaliah, meet me in the palace kitchen in ten minutes."

She led Ahab toward an inner room, winking secretly at Athaliah as if to say, *Watch and learn, my little sister.*

Izabel would teach Athaliah the details of this lesson in later years when she was ready for it.

CHAPTER 17

Elijah and Micaiah walked with a group of students from their school in the highlands to the city of Jezreel. It was a journey of about five miles. Elisha and the six others followed their mentor prophets up the hill to the city.

Before entering the city, they stopped outside the high place. Like the high place outside Samaria, this one was also amidst a grove of trees. Standing at the small fenced perimeter, they could see priests offering incense on the platform altar, which was surrounded by standing stones. A large asherah loomed twenty feet high over the altar. Like Samaria, there was also a small complex of rooms used by the priests and qedeshim as they performed their duties.

The students had all been well taught about these forbidden altars and how Yahweh had condemned them. Elijah's purpose in stopping here was to pray for Yahweh to raise up a king who would finally destroy these altars and shrines of depravity throughout the land, and cut down the asherim, and burn the groves. But alas, that hope for a righteous king didn't seem likely to be fulfilled anytime soon.

One of the male qedeshim strolled within earshot of the students and shouted, "Free services to students and virgins! I promise, no babies!"

The young man was their age, bare-chested with a female skirt, long hair, and female cosmetics. He was deliberately defying the Torah on so many counts it made Elisha nauseous. Not only was prostitution immoral, but men were not allowed to lie with other men as one would with a woman. Men were also forbidden to dress as a female. It was against nature, defying God's separation of gender at creation itself. Rebels like this knew God's righteous decree and that those who practiced such things deserved to die. But they still behaved with brazen audacity and boasted about it—all because the king allowed it. Elisha wanted to jump the short fence and strangle the Sodomite with his bare hands.

Glancing over, he saw Elijah staring at him as though the prophet had read his mind. The master spoke to the rest of the students. "In your righteous desire for justice, do not forget the lovingkindness of our God, who will not turn away any man who repents of his wickedness."

Elisha knew the master's words were intended for him. He wasn't comfortable with having been called to task.

Elijah walked on toward the city without more conversation. Sighing, Elisha followed with the rest of them. He thought about the sacred prostitutes and priests of the high places. Could such servants of demons repent? Yahweh had drowned the world for its evil in the time of Noah. Joshua had been commanded to wipe out the Anakim clans of Canaan. But now both Israel and Judah had become so apostate it seemed Yahweh would surely judge his own people at last.

The Jezreel gate soon loomed above the Sons of the Prophets. The city walls were forty feet high, and to one side of the gate, Sidonian workers had already set up one of two sculpted gate guardians transported from Tyre. These monsters were Egyptian-style cherubim, thirty feet tall, made of limestone. Winged lion bodies painted with bright Egyptian colors were topped by human heads wearing an Egyptian hairstyle. The cherubim were supposed to guard the entrance to the city, but Elisha considered them harbingers of evil.

The students followed the prophets, crossing on a drawbridge over a water filled moat, to enter the city. These city defenses were rare and unique in Canaan; only Megiddo, further west in the valley, had so much protection.

Passing through a guarded six-chambered gate into the city, they made their way through the local marketplace. The streets buzzed with commercial activity and overflowed with Sidonian workers hired to transform the city into a Canaanite abomination.

The sound of distant thunder stopped Elijah in his tracks. The rest of the group stopped with him to look at the darkening sky above. The rains would soon be here, and the people would have to close up shop and halt their construction. A perfectly normal occurrence during the rainy season.

At that moment, Elisha noticed fear in Elijah's face. Under the long, hairy prophet's mantle, he could see his master's left hand trembling.

Inching close, Elisha asked in a hushed voice so as not to be heard by the others, "Are you afraid, master?"

Elijah shoved his hand under his cloak. But he wouldn't lie. "Very much."

"But you are God's prophet."

"And I am human," replied the bearded old man. "Only fools are fearless."

He turned and continued toward their destination.

Elisha noticed a stall in the marketplace. Its wares were hundreds of terracotta figurines. There were votives for worshippers. Images of Asherah and Astarte. Amulets and other magic devices. The owner shouted, "Images of Baal, Asherah, and Astarte for sale!"

A hawker across the way shouted the same. Another nearby yelled, "Cakes for the Queen of Heaven!"

There were a dozen of these idol workshops in the marketplace with their sales goods. All this open idolatry was equivalent to spitting upon the covenants of Yahweh. It enraged Elisha.

He exploded, grabbing the closest shop table and heaving it over with a shout. The figurines crashed to the ground in pieces. The owner yelled at him, "My gods! My gods! What have you done?"

Elisha felt the scruff of his cloak grabbed, and he was yanked away. It was Elijah, angrily pulling him along.

Elisha looked at Micaiah, who only shrugged with a grin. He couldn't disagree with Elisha, but he wasn't about to defend him either.

• • • • •

Izabel sat next to Ahab on their thrones. Before her arrival, there'd been only one simple wooden chair with golden trimmings. She'd quickly replaced it with two new ornate thrones of Phoenician beauty and craftsmanship placed side by side. The thrones were carved from the most exquisite Ethiopian ivory. The cushion seats were covered with the finest silk from Asia. Below the armrests were carved cherubim sphinxes, leonine bodies with wings and human heads, covered in gold. Throne guardians on earth as it was in heaven.

Athaliah stood in a place of honor beside the queen. Hamilqart, the new high priest of Baal for Jezreel, stood behind her. Jehu, the commander of Ahab's armies, stood behind the king.

Izabel recognized the disheveled old man approaching her with another even older man and a half-dozen clean-shaven young lads in sackcloth robes.

She remembered seeing the prophet's glare from the crowd at her wedding parade. She'd never forgotten those penetrating angry eyes.

Now he didn't seem so mysterious. He actually looked a little silly and theatrical with his mantle of long-haired angora goat fastened with a leather girdle. His bushy beard and wild hair reinforced a sense of detached eccentricity. And these so-called Sons of the Prophets looked like beggarly children. A line of armed Sidonians on either side of the throne room ensured this motley group was no threat to her safety.

Izabel grabbed the chance to speak before Ahab could. "Elijah the Tishbite, welcome! And your students."

Bowing, Elijah said subtly, "King Ahab, Queen Jezebel."

Izabel tilted her head with curiosity. She hadn't heard her name said that way before. Leaning over to Ahab, she whispered, "Is that a Hebrew dialect?"

Ahab glared angrily at Elijah, then whispered back, "I'll explain it later."

Elijah motioned with his left hand toward his older companion, standing to his left. "This is my colleague, Micaiah, son of Imlah."

As the prophet dropped his left hand, Izabel noticed it was trembling. With a glance at her, Elijah quickly hid it in his cloak. Izabel directed a good-natured smile to him, then around the rest of the group. "No need to be anxious today. This is a friendly gathering."

Their stiff stance gave no evidence they believed her. She gestured behind her. "This is my high priest, Hamilqart. And his temple guards." She gestured to the armed soldiers staring at them from both sides, thinking with amusement how few of them it would take to cut this small band of boys into dog meat.

One young student, the closest to Elijah, was staring at Izabel with a look of intense hatred. He had tightly shaved black hair and distinctly bushy eyebrows. An angry little mouse. She looked back at Elijah and spoke.

"I have been encouraged by our king to gain your endorsement for a new temple I would like to build in this city."

Elijah said, "You are already building it."

"True enough. But my desire is to build a bridge between our cultures, not a wall. Many Tyrians have migrated here already."

Elijah spoke with suppressed anger, "Yahweh is a jealous god."

"And I would gladly build him a temple, but it is forbidden."

The prophet had no patience for this doubletalk. "Samaria's high places are an abomination. And so is that House of Baal."

Finally, Ahab jumped in, complaining like a little boy. "Solomon built high places in Jerusalem. And he worshipped Baal."

"Yes," Elijah said. "His pagan wives influenced him."

He was still looking straight at Izabel. Glancing over, she saw her husband roll his eyes. Anger rose within her.

The prophet continued, "And that is why Yahweh split the kingdom. There can never be unity with evil."

Ahab sighed with frustration. "Elijah, must you be so—extreme?"

Izabel held her hand out to calm Ahab. She spoke to Elijah. "My dear prophet, I understand your conviction. I really do. And I have great respect for Yahweh. I am not demanding that anyone worship Baal. And I will not attack your religion. I am merely offering diversity and inclusion. Freedom to choose."

Elijah stared at the king. Ahab complained, "What are you looking at me for? I've given her charge of this project. She is your queen."

The young bushy-eyed student blurted out, "Yahweh is your king!"

Elijah hushed him, "Elisha."

An awkward silence permeated the throne room. Izabel would not be mocked. She said to Elijah, "And from where did this student learn his manners?"

Elijah flashed a damning stare at the young acolyte, and the older prophet, Micaiah, pulled him back, humiliated.

Then Izabel heard the caw of ravens. A moment later, three of them fluttered into the throne room right up to the prophet, landing on his mantle as if he were a sorcerer. She shook her head, unimpressed.

Elijah spoke boldly. "O queen, this Baal of Tyre, he is a storm god? He controls the weather?"

Izabel raised her chin with pride. "He rides the clouds with thunder." She thought of her god's glory, how the Most High Baal brought both provision and judgment in the storm.

Lowering his head, Elijah squeezed his eyes tight as though praying.

Or maybe he is hearing voices in his head like a madman.

As the silence dragged out uncomfortably, Izabel looked at Ahab and Jehu for explanation. Ahab shrugged. Jehu remained stoic.

Finally, the madman spoke, "As Yahweh, the god of Israel lives, before whom I stand—there shall be neither dew nor rain these years except by my word."

Elijah turned and immediately left the throne room, his pupils and fellow prophet followed close behind.

Izabel felt herself flush with anger. *How dare he!*

"Arrest him, Jehu," she ordered.

But Ahab put his hand up to stop Jehu.

Izabel snapped, "Are you going to let that self-righteous fanatic treat the throne with such contempt?"

"I'm sorry, my love, but Elijah is the head prophet of Yahweh, and Yahweh is the Most High god of Israel. Prophets are supposed to be his mouthpieces."

"Supposed to be," Izabel mocked. She felt herself shake with rage. This was insolence. What kind of religion allowed such disrespect of the crown? In Tyre this hairy-mantled fool would have been beheaded on the spot!

Izabel immediately realized the threatening potential of mobs that could arise and follow this troublemaker. A man who attacks the king with his tongue would surely next attack with a sword. She had to figure out what his weakness was.

Then it came to her. "And what is the confirmation of a prophet of Yahweh, my love?"

It took Ahab only a moment to consider. "That his prediction holds true."

She smirked with satisfaction. Israel was in its rainy season. "So if the prophet claims it will not rain, but it does rain, what would that make Elijah?"

Ahab was now beginning to follow her reasoning. "A false prophet, I suppose."

"And what is the punishment in your law for false prophets?"

A slight grin spread across Ahab's face. "There you go again, instructing me in my own religion."

They both knew the unspoken answer to the question was "death."

As he shared a knowing smile with her, Izabel noticed that Jehu, standing stiffly behind Ahab, didn't appear to appreciate their humor.

"By the way," she added, "you were going to explain the Hebrew pronunciation of my name as Jezebel."

It wasn't uncommon. Different dialects would speak names differently depending on their language. But in this case, Ahab didn't look very happy with the pronunciation. The smile left his face.

"It's a wordplay," he said. "A subtle insult."

"Insult?" Izabel repeated. Once again, she felt the heat of rage kindled inside her.

"In your language, Izabel means 'Where is the prince?'"

Izabel nodded. The phrase was a form of calling upon Baal.

"Well, the Hebrew pronunciation as Elijah used it, Jezebel, means..." Ahab lowered his voice so the servants would not hear it. "There is no prince, but dung."

Instead of exploding, Izabel remained silent. Better to turn her vexation into strategy. She'd enact her vengeance after the rain—when that braying old goat was stoned as a false prophet. Or maybe she'd cut off his head, herself.

Turning to Athaliah beside her, Izabel spoke softly. "When bad people are mean to you, you must not let them make you mad in public. You will look weak and create mistrust in your subjects. There is always time later for a proper response. Let's go see how Baal's house is doing. Be sure to bring a cover for the rain."

But there was no precipitation outside. The clouds had dissipated, the skies had cleared, and the coming rain which had appeared imminent never arrived.

CHAPTER 18

Mount Hermon

The sacred grotto of Azazel at Baal-Hermon lay sixty miles northeast of Jezreel in the foothills of Mount Hermon, barely three miles from the city of Dan. Anat had traveled the distance with ease, her hateful thoughts focused on Mot and what she was going to do to him. She had no fear of the guardian of Sheol. He was huge in stature, and his captivity was strong. No human could escape his grasp. But Baal and Anat were not human, and Anat had helped Baal defeat Yam and tame Leviathan. She carried with her the mighty bow of Aqhat; built by the divine craftsman Kothar-wa-Kahasis. She was equipped with weapons and a vengeful fury to rescue Baal, her treasured brother and lover. She wasn't going to let him be a prisoner in that godforsaken pit for long.

Anat arrived at the red rock bluff of the sacred grotto. Spring waters poured from a cave in the cliff, the source-waters of the Jordan River. The face of the bluff was covered in engravings and shrines to Azazel, god of the *seirim*. Having the torso of a man and the legs of a hairy goat, the seirim were called satyrs in Greek. Hebrews called them "goat demons."

Azazel was a hero to all the Watchers. He had been a co-leader with Semyaza of the ancient ones, two hundred Watchers who fell to earth in primordial days at this holy mountain, Hermon. They'd rebelled against Yahweh, bringing power, sorcery, sexual freedom and war to mankind. They'd been punished at the Flood for their revolution, and Azazel had been bound into the darkness at a wilderness location they called Dudael.

Humans had built these shrines and cast the huge golden image of Azazel that guarded the interior of the cave. Anat marched past the statue toward her destination deep inside.

She soon arrived at her goal. The Gates of Sheol was a large chasm in the ground that opened up like the jaws of Mot. The Greeks called it Hades.

87

Vapors rising from below would intoxicate humans, resulting in death if overexposed. They had no effect on Anat.

Drawing her dagger, she raised it to her face and sliced a gash down both cheeks. She gritted her teeth at the pain, letting the blood flow freely over her jaw and down her neck. Then she opened her garment and applied the dagger to her chest, raking her flesh from collarbone down her breast several times like plowing a field. More blood flowed over her body and onto the ground. This was her mourning rite as her heart went out to Baal.

She muttered the liturgy of her mourning. "'Baal is dead. Where is the Prince? After Baal I shall go down into the underworld.'"

She stared down into the darkness. It was deep. Immeasurably deep. All light and sound were swallowed up into black silence. Far below in the depths of that murky unknown were the waters of the Abyss.

She jumped.

CHAPTER 19

Samaria
1 Year Later

The drought continued throughout all the land for a year. Its devastating effects were everywhere: Samaria, Jerusalem, Tyre, and Damascus. Crops were ruined. The people suffered with sickness and disease. It even began to affect those of us connected to the royal palace. With my position as commander of the king's armies, my family would not starve. But we felt hunger under the rationing as did everyone.

Despite this austerity, the king continued his lavish building projects in Jezreel and Samaria. Queen Izabel completed her temple of Baal in Jezreel and was now residing in the city to oversee its grand opening and operations—forcing King Ahab to spend more time with her in Jezreel and less in Samaria.

I saw the king change. Whether it was to please the queen or his strategic ally Tyre, he began to promote the Baal cult and integrate it into the life of Israel. What could I do but support the crown as God's anointed? The truth was that we were all so weakened by the drought, weakened in our faith, that we welcomed the new hope of salvation offered by the foreign god of the Sidonians. Because of Baal's relationship to Asherah, perhaps he was not so foreign to our religion after all.

Sitting with Susanna and Galina in the atrium of his home, Jehu looked thoughtfully at his sister-in-law, now a young woman of sixteen. "And you still feel the same way after all this time?"

"It's all I want to do with my life," Galina answered. "I dream about it."

The girl had just relayed another public royal invitation from Queen Izabel for Israelite girls to join the royal palace court in Jezreel. Galina's desire hadn't subsided. During the past year, she'd convinced Jehu and Susanna to let her become head mistress over their household servants. She'd wanted to learn the skills of domestic service in the hope that the need for more royal palace attendants would arise again.

And arise it had. As the king's presence in Jezreel increased, so did the need for more royal attendants. Queen Izabel had apparently chosen to spend most of her time there because of its nearness to the House of Baal.

Susanna was tearful at her sister's decision, but resigned to help her rise above her predicament. She'd been preparing emotionally for this day. She and her sister had spent much time together over the past year. But Galina had constantly reminded her she didn't really belong here. She felt more at home with the queen's Sidonian culture.

"At least she'd be well taken care of in this drought and famine," Susanna reminded her husband.

Indeed. The royal household was always the last to experience the suffering of the people.

"They would be taking us down to Jezreel for training," Galina added eagerly. "They said we could communicate with family after the first year."

Jehu sought clarification, "And this is for the summer palace court, not for the temple or as the queen's own personal attendants?"

While he didn't like the idea of Galina being so near to Izabel, being part of the royal court was a great honor, and a way for Galina to start anew. But the temple would involve service to Baal, and that he wouldn't permit for a member of his household, regardless of his duty to support the king's decrees.

"Just the summer palace court," Galina assured.

Jehu sighed. He'd said no a year ago, thinking Galina would forget her crazy ambition and that would be the end of it. But trying to guide this stubborn young lady was as difficult as training a mule. She had a determination about her that rivaled Jehu's own. And maybe getting a taste of the discipline involved in training for the royal court was just what that stubborn nature needed.

"All right, then," he said reluctantly. "I will put in a word with Obadiah, the palace administrator, since he will be organizing the choosing of girls for the queen's invitation."

With a yelp of joy, Galina jumped up to hug Susanna. Jehu hadn't seen her so happy the entire time she'd been with them.

His pleasure in Galina's happiness faded as he noticed his wife surreptitiously wiping tears from her own eyes. Was it the thought of how far away her sister would be? That they couldn't communicate for a year?

Or was her sister's opportunity to start a new life an unhappy reminder that Susanna had now completed her third year of marriage without having conceived a new life of her own?

CHAPTER 20

Jezreel

Izabel and Athaliah stood before the large blue veil of the holy of holies in the house of Baal. It was embroidered with images of the host of heaven. As Hamilqart pulled back the veil, Izabel let out a sigh of gratification with the image of Baal now towering before them.

This was a perfect replica of the image in Baal's temple back home in Tyre. Made of bronze, seated on a throne, fifteen feet tall, with conical headdress, horns of deity, and square-cropped beard. His hands were held out before him to accept offerings for the fire pit at his feet.

The entire temple was a replica of Baal's house in Tyre, which was almost a duplicate of Yahweh's house in Jerusalem. It was one hundred feet long by fifty feet wide, intentionally larger than Yahweh's house at ninety feet by thirty feet. This new temple for Baal was a grander house for a grander god.

The inner temple contained the standard tripartite interior of entrance, holy place, and holy of holies. This was surrounded by a portico of colonnades and temple rooms, which were in turn surrounded by a larger outer courtyard with a stone altar and large bronze laver for worshippers.

Preparing for the temple opening just two days away, priests were busy polishing large bronze censers, located in the holy place and used for burning incense. With a grumble of dissatisfaction, Hamilqart hurried over to supervise their work, leaving Izabel and Athaliah momentarily alone.

"Temples are the heavens and earth of the cosmos," Izabel explained to her now eight-year-old charge.

For the past year, Izabel had brought Athaliah with her everywhere, teaching her everything she could in preparation for her eventual marriage to the prince of Judah in Jerusalem.

"What do you mean?" Athaliah asked.

"The courtyard outside with the altar represents the earth," Izabel explained. "The bronze laver on the back of the bulls is the sea, the chaos our god controls. We call him Yam. The two bronze pillars at the entrance of the temple are the pillars that hold up the heavens and earth."

The queen pointed to several lampstands around them in the holy place. They were shaped like trees with branches that held candles. "See how the lampstands are shaped like almond trees with blossoms."

Continuing on, she motioned to the pillars lining the outer perimeter of the temple. "Notice the pomegranates engraved around the bases. And the lilies up on the capitals at top."

She gestured to the furniture around them. "See the palm trees and flowers, so detailed here in the wood. What does all this imagery remind you of?"

Athaliah thought for a second. "A garden?"

Izabel smiled with approval. "We are in the garden of God." She turned and pointed to the massive floor to ceiling curtain, known as the veil. Athaliah followed her. "The Phoenician blue is the sky. The host of heaven represent the cosmos. And behind it all is the Most High god, Baal, Lord of Heaven."

Izabel gestured toward the towering bronze image. "He resides in his holy of holies, the garden from primordial days."

"It's beautiful," Athaliah blurted out. "I feel like I'm in Eden."

Athaliah had been taught the Hebrew stories of Moses. Izabel was now teaching her the Phoenician stories of Canaan. These stories were not so different from the Israelite tales on the surface, but featuring different gods and teaching different theology.

"It is beautiful, my dear. And you must remember this beauty. Carry it with you to Jerusalem. It will help you understand that temple. One day when you become queen, you can convince the king to build a house for Baal down there. And it will be beautiful as well."

Izabel could see in the younger girl's eye the imagination of innocence dreaming of the future, of the pomp and fantasy of royalty, of the romance of marriage and family. Smiling with satisfaction, Izabel caressed her very pregnant belly. She was ready to give birth any day now.

• • • • •

A line of young Hebrew girls entered a passageway to the new temple of Baal. Galina was one of about forty girls, ranging in age from eleven to sixteen, who followed Hamilqart, the high priest of Baal. Galina considered him quite attractive with his blond wavy hair and friendly looking face. And now he was bringing them to the temple for final approval. He'd warned them to be respectful as they were going to meet the queen. They were the chosen ones, picked from a much larger group of girls who'd applied for the chance to become attendants in the royal court.

Finally, the queen would be choosing some of them to join her own personal court. Galina had intentionally omitted this detail when asking Jehu to sponsor her application. She knew Jehu would not have allowed her to participate had she been completely forthcoming with all the details, so she simply hadn't told him.

Galina felt her stomach flutter with anticipation. She was about to meet the queen in person!

Exiting into the courtyard, the girls filed over to the entrance of the temple where Queen Izabel stood with her sister-in-law, the princess Athaliah. They'd all been briefed by Hamilqart on everything they needed to know so they wouldn't say or do anything embarrassing before the queen.

When they reached the queen, the girls bowed in unison. She welcomed them with a warm smile. Queen Izabel moved with grace despite being heavy with child, and she hoped it would be a prince. Galina prayed a quick prayer to Asherah in hopes she would be chosen. What a privilege it would be to attend the queen and witness the royal birth.

Queen Izabel went down the line, examining each of the girls, checking their teeth, and looking them up and down. She spoke to the high priest as she did, but so quietly Galina couldn't follow their words until they drew close.

"I don't mean to put a damper on the grand opening of the temple, your highness," Hamilqart said. "But it hasn't rained since Elijah prophesied."

The queen looked perturbed. "I don't need to be reminded."

Examining a girl two places to Galina's right, Queen Izabel pulled her from the line and gestured for another priest to escort her away.

"The people are restless," the high priest went on. "Whispers and rumors."

"And what do they whisper?" the queen responded.

"They say the king and queen are decadent."

Queen Izabel stopped right before Galina to look at Hamilqart with concern. Galina felt herself trembling. This was the moment that could change her life. She wanted desperately to be chosen, certain that if she were not, her life would not be worth living.

Galina's trembling grew worse as the queen examined her. Noticing it, the queen turned her concern to Galina. "There is no need to be fearful. You are exactly what I need."

She smiled warmly and moved on. Galina was no longer trembling, but frozen with delighted astonishment, her thoughts buzzing through her head. *Exactly what I need. Queen Izabel of Israel just said that I was exactly what she needs! Thank you, Asherah. Thank you, Yahweh.*

As the queen moved on down the line, Galina could hear her return to her conversation with the high priest, but she was too caught up in her own ecstasy to pay attention. She was going to be an attendant in the court of Queen Izabel! The queen who'd told her she was exactly what she needed!

"They have reason to be angry," the high priest continued on. "People see excessive government spending. Their taxes have increased. And with this drought, they are suffering. It will make them critical of the crown."

"Do you think they will revolt?" Queen Izabel asked.

"I think that a gesture of welfare would inspire gratitude in the people," Hamilqart answered.

Izabel stopped her examination, clearly giving thoughtful consideration to the high priest's words. Then she dismissed the girls with a wave to the accompanying priests.

"Get them cleaned up, dressed in proper clothing."

As the line of girls was led away, Galina wondered what delicate and ornate dress royal attendants wore. It would certainly be Sidonian. Colorful and vibrant. Would it include silk?

As Izabel and Hamilqart watched the girls being led back to their rooms, Hamilqart clarified with the queen, "They are all to be your attendants, then?"

"No," she said. "Temple prostitutes."

CHAPTER 21

Izabel and Athaliah sat inside the royal litter, carried on poles by servants. It was a Phoenician-style carriage of oak with gilded gold and velvet purple curtains. She looked through the latticed windows at the streets of Jezreel. They witnessed scenes of tragedy. More hungry beggars than she'd ever seen before. The drought was wreaking havoc on the population. There were no children playing in the streets, only lifeless residents with dead eyes watching her pass them by.

Izabel felt a sudden movement in her womb. At least the child she was bringing into the world wouldn't have to experience such adversity, since the royal family never lacked food or drink. Still, Hamilqart was right. She knew her image would suffer if she didn't do something to portray herself as caring about the plight of her new people. And she wanted to image herself as the ideal queenly example for Athaliah. Calling out to her footmen to lower the litter, she held out her hand to Athaliah. "Come, child."

Stepping from their luxurious transport, Izabel gestured imperiously to one of her guard detail. "Hurry to the palace and command Obadiah to join me."

She began to walk away from the litter, holding Athaliah with one hand and protectively cradling her belly with the other. Shouldering the litter, her bearers dutifully followed while her remaining guards spread out, awkwardly attempting to carry out their duty of shielding the queen from the press of jostling pedestrians.

Izabel and Athaliah advanced down the dirt street. The sun seemed to have overbaked everything, the parched misery emphasized with unending clouds of dust that arose from every footstep. Residents watched their queen with surprise as she passed them by, walking in their midst, treading their dirt, getting her royal finery sullied with the grime of the streets. At first they weren't sure it was her. Once they were sure, some started following her. They were weary of the dry misery, but curious to see what their queen was doing. This was unprecedented. Royalty simply didn't do this sort of thing.

Izabel could see Athaliah was fearful of the commoners. "My dear, these are our subjects. If we remain in our palace, we are distant and unseen. People don't love what they cannot see. We want them to trust us completely. If they feel we are near, that we care, they will love and obey." Athaliah listened, as always.

They eventually arrived at the destination Izabel had chosen, one of the city food storehouses not far from the palace. This was guarded by a contingent of soldiers, at least thirty of them. In such times, these were the commodities that had to be protected.

Obadiah, the palace administrator, arrived. A loyal elderly servant of the king, he was also a devoted follower of Yahweh, and for this Izabel despised him. As far as she was concerned, Obadiah was an unwanted and intrusive influence on the king. He supported the fanatical Sons of the Prophets as well as the Rechabites and had been vocal in expressing his prejudices against Baalism. Izabel had tried to replace him as palace administrator when she first discovered the virulence of his religious exclusivity. But Obadiah had a long history with Ahab and had garnered the king's trust, so she'd have to wait and catch him in a compromising situation if she was to get rid of him.

Pulling out a massive silver key ring and selecting the appropriate key, Obadiah obeyed Izabel's instructions to open the side door of the store house. Izabel motioned her guards to remain outside as she entered with Athaliah, following Obadiah. Inside was a large group of compartment stalls filled with wheat, barley, and corn. Her eyes quickly adjusted to the dim interior and scanned for the main gate. Split into upper and lower halves, this divided door would work well for distributing food.

She signaled for Obadiah to open the upper door, leaving a barrier to keep the gathering crowd from entering, then ordered her guard detail, "Bring sacks of each grain to the gate."

Leaving them to carry out her orders, she walked outside and called to the procession of people that had followed her, "Go tell your families to bring bowls and sacks to receive extra rations of food."

The crowd looked at each other as if unsure what she'd said. Then one man shouted, "The queen is offering free grain!"

With that, the crowd scattered to gather containers, some even running in haste. Obadiah emerged beside Izabel. "Your highness, are you sure you want to do this? If the people become entitled, they may mob us and pillage the stores. Then none of us will have any food left. This is a risk for you and our future prince."

"Have some faith, Obadiah," Izabel told him with a smile. "A mother cares for the welfare of her children. Mother Asherah cares. Does not your father god also care?"

Obadiah abandoned his objections. She added, "A grateful citizenry is a loyal and obedient citizenry. The House of Baal opens in two days, and they will surely come to show their gratitude. And Baal will answer their prayers with the dew from his brow."

A mob of people was now racing toward them. Izabel and Obadiah retreated behind the gate.

"Scoop out grain for the citizens," Izabel told the guards. "Fill their bowls, pots, and pitchers."

As the guards obeyed, Izabel shouted out to the jostling crowd, "Baal loves you and cares for you! He feels your pain! He brings the abundance of the field!"

Someone in the crowd yelled out, "May the Queen of Heaven bless Queen Izabel!" Other voices responded with hearty approval.

The crowd grew quickly. Hungry residents pushed against the gate, causing it to creak under the pressure.

"Calm down!" Obadiah yelled out. "Do not press in! There's plenty for all!"

It was then that Izabel heard the sound of shouting beyond the hungry crowd. Was a riot breaking out? Looking over their heads, she spotted the madman Elijah standing on a wooden crate in the middle of the street. He was cursing.

"Woe to you, Israel! Spiritual adulterers! Turn from your lover Baal and his harlot, Jezebel! Seek Yahweh's face or you will burn up like chaff!"

"How dare he." Izabel felt her insides begin to churn with outrage. She was not going to let this purveyor of hate poison the public against her.

Holding out her hand to Athaliah, she ordered four of her guard detail to accompany her. As they exited the side door, the guards wielded swords and cudgels to clear the way for her and Athaliah. As the crowd scrambled out of their way, Izabel could hear the madman still screaming.

"Hear O Israel, thus saith the Lord: 'Your father was an Amorite and your mother a Hittite! You were rejected and cast into the open field. But I came and rescued you. I cleansed you, I covered you in your nakedness. I put fine clothes and jewelry upon you. And when you came of age, I married you myself with an everlasting covenant. But you, O Samaria, and your sister, Jerusalem, uncovered your nakedness and played the whore with every nation that passed you by. You had sex with every foreign god on every high place and under every green tree!'"

"Despicable," muttered Izabel. *These prophets are obsessed with sexual metaphors. They're secret perverts.*

As they reached the street where Elijah screamed and ranted, Izabel saw others with the prophet whom she recognized from a year ago in the palace. His sycophantic so-called Sons of the Prophets. She'd never forgotten those troublesome meddlers.

There were also four Rechabites surrounding Elijah like bodyguards. Izabel recognized the largest of them, an imposing muscular man with long hair. Their leader Jonadab. These Rechabites were not only Yahwist extremists, but Ahab's chariot-makers and therefore protected by the king. Izabel considered them particularly dangerous.

Elijah finished his rant, "And so Yahweh has brought this drought upon us as judgment for our sins, for the harlotry of Jezebel and her abominable gods!"

Izabel burned with righteous indignation. *The gall of that cretin attacking me with that insulting name, Jezebel. Calling me a harlot. I should have his tongue cut out.*

Elijah's audience parted for Izabel and her guards, leaving her face to face with her accuser. The prophet stopped speaking at her approach. Her stride was like that of an angry mother, the child Athaliah's right hand grasped tight as she was nearly dragged along.

Izabel wanted to order her guards to arrest the entire lot of Yahwists. But she couldn't afford to have them in a scuffle with Ahab's favorite Rechabites. There would be hell to pay when the king found out. Far better to simply gain the support of this mob.

"People of Israel, I am your queen!" Izabel calmly addressed the crowd with authority, "This man has called down a curse upon you. He claims

Yahweh brought this drought and suffering. That Yahweh scorches the earth, kills humans and animals, and turns the environment into a wasteland. Well, I don't condemn Yahweh! I condemn only those who preach hatred in the name of Yahweh!"

Scattered cheers broke out across the crowd. Her ploy was working.

"He preaches bitter gall. I give you food. He promotes a religion of fear, but which of us offers you compassion?"

"Queen Izabel!" several cried out.

"Jezebel!" a heckler yelled.

The heckler was drowned out by the crowd. The people shouted their support for Izabel. Cries of affection and praises for the queen rang out.

She looked at Elijah with a smile of satisfaction. The madman and his godlickers picked up their wooden crate and left. The Rechabites left with them. She had emerged the victor in this confrontation. Though she knew there would be more to come.

Izabel smiled down at Athaliah. "That, my dear, is how you deal with bullies. You stand up to them, and they run like cowards."

Turning back to the gates, she yelled out to those who could hear her, "Free food for all! Come to the temple opening and give thanks to Baal!"

The crowd cheered and pushed their way closer for more free grain.

CHAPTER 22

Sheol

Anat lost track of how long she'd been down in Sheol. Time was not the same in the underworld. When she'd first jumped into the chasm in the cave of Azazel, she hadn't been sure what she would encounter. She'd fallen for a long distance before hitting the black waters of the Abyss. She'd sunk into the depths for another long distance before breaking through into the underworld. When she did, it was like falling from a ceiling of water hundreds of feet down into a parched land of death.

The Land of Forgetfulness. Picking herself up, Anat looked around her. As far as she could see was a desert wasteland of sand and rock studded with dead looking, upside down trees. The grotesque twisted dry rot added emphasis to the death and absence of life in this place, ugly and gnarled roots stretched upward instead of leafy branches. The underworld was dark and silent save for a hot dry wind that whistled around her with the sound of moaning masses. It burned her lungs.

This was where the dead descended to wait for their judgment. No human could escape Sheol's grip. But Anat was a Watcher of divine origin who could traverse between the lands of the living and the dead with a certain amount of freedom. She could see through the underworld darkness, and she knew where she was going: the city of Mot, called simply the Pit.

The geography of Sheol corresponded to the geography of the world above, so she knew roughly where she was. She began at the foot of a large mountain that rose up into the watery ceiling. This was the underworld foundation of Mount Hermon, guarded by fiery beings. Just as the Jordan River began as a stream from Mount Hermon, in the underworld the great rivers of Living Water and of Fire began here. These rivers flowed to the west, all the way to the Dark Mountain of the Dead where the Hollow Places kept the human dead, including the righteous located in Abraham's bosom.

Directly south was the underworld foundation of Mount Zion, also rising up and into the ceiling of the Abyss with its cursed valley of Gehenna beside it. Further south were the Seven Mountains of Precious Stones, which included the Mountain of Fire, Sinai. All this had been written down in Enoch's vision.

Anat headed east, and would continue east beyond land. An island in the *tohu wabohu*, the sea which encircled the expanse of the underworld, was her destination. She had come to rescue her brother Baal from Mot, the Lord of Death. She had the bow of Aqhat in her hands and her two sickle swords on her back. Setting her forehead like flint to the east, she began to run.

Her footsteps sounded in her ears as she travelled the long journey through the dead landscape. The ground moved beneath her feet as she jogged. Like something was pushing up at her from below.

Pausing for a moment, she looked back in the direction she'd come. She saw the hands first, breaking the surface of the ground. Then heads and full bodies appeared, rising up from the landscape. They were humanoid with bony rotted flesh. Where their face should be was just a large mouth full of teeth. Chomping teeth.

Shades! she recognized with horror. *The living dead!*

These were souls whose individual identities had faded in death until they'd simply become part of a horde of eternally hungry creatures—who were now coming after Anat. Being a Watcher didn't protect her from these underworld entities. These things could do real damage to her.

Placing her bow on her back, Anat withdrew her two swords. Her swords cut through the air, slicing the nearest shades in half... but those bodies continued toward her in broken yet determined movement. These things would not be stopped easily. She adjusted her attacks and discovered that only decapitation seemed to incapacitate these living dead.

Swinging wide and repetitively, she cut down dozens of them at a time. But they kept coming. Hundreds of them. And behind them thousands more.

Thousands upon thousands.

Like underground bats hearing their prey, they must have heard her footsteps on the ground above them. She couldn't stay and fight. She had to run or be overtaken by the horde. But already it was too late. She was now surrounded. Their clawing hands and chomping mouths pressed in toward her like a tightening circle of hunger.

Anat panicked. For the first time in millennia, she felt trapped, overwhelmed. There were no gods to help her. She was all alone and overwhelmed by enemies. What strategy could be used against mindless ravenous corpses? She didn't have the strength to kill them all. Their numbers were like the sand of the seashore.

One of them got close enough to take a bite out of her shoulder. Spinning around, she cut the shade in half. The pain penetrated her body like a lightning bolt.

Then a thought struck her. She'd seen a certain defensive move performed by the archangel Uriel that had impressed her. Like her, he too had double swords. What he'd done with them was something she'd taken note of and practiced a few times herself. Of course, she'd never admit where she learned the move since archangels were despicable and unworthy of such praise. But his move was effective.

This was her last chance. Holding her swords out on each side of her body, she begin to spin them and then began rotating her body. She became a deadly double windmill of blades, rotating and devouring everything within reach. She added a directional movement to her spinning and began to progress. The blades created a swathe of shades cut to pieces. She moved forward, still spinning, cutting her way through the gauntlet that had been created. Heads, arms, legs fell to the ground in piles around her.

Once she had sliced and diced her way through the surrounding shades, she slowed and finally stopped her spinning. Her body was covered in the gore of her enemies and she was slightly dizzy. But she'd done it. She had broken through. The underworld desert was wide open before her.

Replacing the swords on her back, she took off running to the east. The shades were hungry creatures, but lacked her speed. They couldn't keep up so long as she kept her pace.

By the time she was out of their range entirely, she'd come to the shore of the *tohu wabohu*. The sea marking the perimeter of the underworld stretched away from her in an endless black expanse. A single island, miles out in the sea, was visible with her supernatural vision. This was the Isle of the Dead where she would find Mot and his captive Baal.

"My brother, here I come," she muttered and dove into the black waters.

CHAPTER 23

Jezreel

Galina awoke to the sound of the priestess matron clanging a small handbell. Yawning, the girl looked around at the forty other young female initiates on their bed mats in the long room. It was hard to sleep in a strange new place with a bunch of strangers. However, Galina's sleeping troubles stemmed from what the priestess matron, a stout older woman with graying hair and cold temperament, had told the girls the night before.

It seemed there'd been an overabundance of Israelite young women volunteering to be palace attendants. So Galina's group had been assigned lodging at the Jezreel high place across the hill from the palace. She found this turn of events troubling and wondered how they could be trained for palace service while residing at the high place?

The matron, whose name was Devorah, had explained that they were in the holy sanctuary of Baal and Asherah so the girls must behave reverently. It seemed strange to Galina that the matron spoke of Baal and Asherah instead of Yahweh and Asherah. But of course, Queen Izabel had built a magnificent temple to Baal here in Jezreel. So it made sense for Baal to be the patron principality of Jezreel even while Yahweh remained patron deity of Samaria.

In any case, Galina trusted the queen. And she felt comfortable with Asherah. The goddess was originally a principality of Tyre, and Galina had always loved all things Phoenician. There was something comfortable about the fertility goddess, something Galina could identify with. In contrast, Yahweh had always seemed cold and distant. Like most men, he was harsh and demanding, while Asherah was warm and accepting, a nurturing mother figure.

The girls rolled up their bed mats, went to the latrine, and washed themselves up. They were then led to the assembly room of the temple complex. The space was large, designed to hold more than a hundred people.

The nervous chattering of young girls quieted down when the priestess matron introduced the high priest Hamilqart to the room. Today he was dressed in bright colors of satin and linen, and he spoke with authority. "I welcome you to the sanctuary of Baal and Asherah. Your service to the gods will be a signet of honor and respect that you will carry for the rest of your lives."

Service to Baal and Asherah? Galina wondered uneasily. *What about service to the queen?*

Hamilqart continued, "I announce to you Queen Izabel's command. Your training will not take place at this temple. The king and queen have arranged an exchange program of goodwill with our sister nation Judah in the south. You are to be part of this diplomatic mission of peace. You will travel to Jerusalem, where you will be trained in your duties of palace attendants. You will represent your queen in the court of King Jehoshaphat, and when the princess Athaliah weds the prince of Judah, you will accompany her as her attendants."

The girls burst out in chatter. Some of the girls, like Galina, were disappointed while others tittered in excitement. They would become attendants to a queen. Maybe not to Izabel, but at least to Izabel's sister-in-law.

"Quiet down, girls!" Matron Devorah snapped.

Once silence was restored, the handsome high priest continued, "Scribes have written letters which will be distributed to your families, detailing your honorable appointment."

Since attendants in training weren't allowed to see family for the first year, a letter would have to suffice for the news. Galina knew this was the nature of a royal court, rules for everything from the way one dressed and acted to the way one communicated with one's family. She'd have to get used to rules.

Jehu and Susanna would be sad to hear Galina was being moved so far away. Then again, surely they'd be happy she was in the holy city Jerusalem. And she'd be serving a future queen of Judah, even if not the queen she'd dreamed of serving.

Anticipation warred with resignation as Galina and the other girls followed Matron Devorah to pack and prepare for their travel. She already felt out of place in Samaria, and Judah would be even more Hebrew and less Phoenician than Samaria. The Jerusalem temple was Phoenician in design, and they worshipped Astarte there. But it wouldn't be the same as Queen Izabel's court.

Still, the distance might prove beneficial as Galina attempted to start a new life far away from the one she was leaving behind. And since she could do nothing about it, there was little point in dwelling on her disappointment.

• • • • •

The forty girls with their few belongings and some ten or so additional young boys were loaded into carts pulled by donkeys. A contingent of soldiers on horseback guarded the caravan as they embarked on their journey. But they hadn't traveled far into the Jezreel Valley when Galina realized the caravan was headed northwest.

Jerusalem was south.

Gripping tightly to the side of the swaying cart as it moved slowly along the dirt road, Galina managed to catch the gaze of a soldier on horseback. "Excuse me, sir, why are we going this way? Is not Jerusalem to the south?"

The soldier smirked and shook his head. "You're not going to Jerusalem, little girl. You're going to Tyre."

Shock washed over Galina like a tidal wave. Around her girls gasped and began to chatter.

"But the queen said we were being brought to Jerusalem to be trained for the royal court."

"The queen told you that herself, did she?"

Galina paused. "The high priest of Baal told us."

"Well, he lied. Get used to it, little girl. You're being brought to Tyre to become qedeshim, holy servants of Asherah."

The high priest had lied to them? Galina felt dizzy with confusion. Why would he lie? Or was this soldier lying now?

Galina knew qedeshim were temple servants, not palace attendants. They engaged in holy duties like cleaning the sanctuary, weaving garments for Asherah, and other liturgical obligations. But they also performed fertility rituals with men. Young she might be, but she'd been a married woman and knew only too well what that meant.

Shivering with fear, Galina prayed to Asherah for protection. What had she gotten into? Was she escaping one life of shame only to enter a new one?

But after a short while, she began to reconsider. She was going to Tyre, the city where she felt most at home. The city of her heart. The trading center of the world, where all people and all gods were accepted and none were hated. Tyre of Phoenicia was what had drawn Galina to Queen Izabel in the first place. Now she was going to the queen's original home. Perhaps it wouldn't be that bad after all. Perhaps her life was about to become better than she had ever dreamed.

CHAPTER 24

Abel-meholah, by the Jordan

Elisha's hometown was a small village in a farming region just sixteen miles southeast of Jezreel. One of the larger farms was owned by Elisha's father Shaphat, who owned twelve yokes of oxen for tending his fields. The drought had hurt them all, but thank God for the Jordan River, from which Shaphat had cleverly dug canals for watering his fields. Like other farmers, his crops had been damaged from the drought, but not so much as to threaten the family with starvation.

The bountiful meal Elisha's mother Judith had just served her son and Elijah felt like a dig to Elisha. He thought it implied that if he had just stayed home and followed in his father's footsteps, he wouldn't suffer as others did in this drought and would have ample provision.

Elisha still did not understand why Elijah had determined they must visit his family farm. The purpose of the original trip had been to denounce Queen Izabel, but afterward they had traveled half of the night and most of this day on this out of the way journey. And all because his parents continued to express concern over Elisha's choice to join the School of Prophets. Elijah had observed significant growth in his student, yet Elisha seemed haunted with his parents' concerns and these unresolved matters were affecting his continuing development and interrupting his prophetic calling.

Well, if Elijah thought a visit with Elisha's parents would calm their worries or change their mind, he had less insight than a prophet of God should have. As they ate their meal of quail, corn, yams, and figs, Elijah appeared clueless as to the subtle family powerplays around him. Shaphat and Judith spoke of their rural life and how they saw their life on the land as a blessing from Yahweh.

Shaphat mused, "When Yahweh gave Moses the Law, he said that if his people obeyed his commands in the Promised Land, we would reap his blessings." He recited from Scripture, "Yahweh will make you abound in prosperity, in the fruit of your womb and in the fruit of your livestock and in the fruit of your ground, within the land that Yahweh swore to your fathers to give you."

"But he also said if his people didn't obey him, he'd curse us and strike us with diseases and famine," Elisha contested. "What we are experiencing is a sign from God that our entire nation needs to repent of idolatry. I want to speak to the nation, not live and die in obscurity on a farm in the middle of nowhere."

He broke off at the hurt expressions that rose to his parents' faces.

Turning to Elijah, Judith managed a feeble smile. "As you can see, Shaphat raised our son to have strong moral convictions. Even as a young child, he was passionate. Sometimes to excess. I trust the school is teaching him how to channel those passions properly."

Shame and irritation struggled in Elisha. He loved his parents. He really did. But he still couldn't understand how they could be so satisfied with their insignificant life.

Elijah spoke to Shaphat and Judith. "I thank you for your hospitality. And I appreciate your concerns for Elisha's welfare. You are right. He is an excessively passionate young man." He looked at Elisha with a smile. "But he's also one of the strongest, sharpest students I've had at the school. You should be proud of him. He shows great promise."

Hearing such praise from Elijah, who often chastised Elisha, made the student feel worthy of his master. Not too long ago, Elijah had questioned whether Elisha had what it took to be a prophet. This was progress.

Judith said, "The farm has great promise too."

Elisha butted in, "Mother, I told you, I must seek my calling from God." He held himself back from launching into another round of unending argument.

Shaphat asked a question of Elijah, "Do you think my son will prove himself and become a prophet of Israel?"

Elijah glanced without expression at Elisha. "That remains to be seen. But he does show promise."

Promise, promise, promise! To Elisha it was an annoying word that seemed merely an excuse to put off a decision. He was impatient with the process and with the promise. Time was running out for Israel. Action was needed.

Shaphat concluded, "Well, son, just know the farm will always be here should your schooling prove too difficult."

Elisha glanced at his master as if to say, *See what I mean?* In his estimation, Elijah was far too patient with Elisha's parents.

But Elijah merely replied, "I pray this drought won't prove too difficult for the rest of your harvest. God has rewarded you greatly for honoring him."

When the meal had finished, Elisha was relieved to discover Elijah had no plans to extend their visit overnight. After cordial goodbyes, master and student made their way down the farm lane to the road that would lead back to the school. If they pushed their pace, they could be back at their cliffside refuge for tomorrow's evening meal.

Elisha's parents stood outside watching their son's departure. As a curve of the road placed them out of sight, Elijah looked over at his student. "You know, you are blessed to have a father and mother who love you and dote on you."

Elisha grimaced. "And now I have you to dote on me as well."

Elijah just smiled at the sarcasm. "When you are older, you will appreciate the nuisance of doting parents."

It didn't take a prophet to understand that Elijah was talking about himself. Elisha knew that his master's parents were long dead, but Elijah never mentioned his family. It seemed the prophet preferred to keep his past hidden and thus remain a mystery to those around him.

But it appeared even this man of mystery had family regrets and missed his parents.

"So the master wasn't borne to earth on the wings of cherubim," Elisha commented dryly, "but had parents like everyone else."

He knew how to draw a smile to the old prophet's face. And he enjoyed doing it now.

Elijah shook his shaggy head. "I hope you don't plan on telling jokes the entire way. It's a long walk."

But the twinkle in his eye belied his mock frown as he lengthened his stride, forcing Elisha to scramble to catch up.

CHAPTER 25

Jezreel

Standing at the top of the stairs, at the entry to the new temple of Baal, Izabel looked out over the temple courtyard. Already hundreds of Israelites had gathered, and more were streaming in, not only from Jezreel and Samaria, but the entire surrounding countryside.

Tonight, was the first service in the newly completed temple. There would be a seven-day temple dedication ceremony beginning with a first sacrifice and many festivities. She looked over at her father Ethbaal, who stood with her at the top of the steps. They shared a smile. He had brought a company of Phoenician dignitaries from Tyre to celebrate her accomplishment.

Beside her, King Ahab grinned. "I am proud of you, Izabel. You have brought sophistication and enlightenment to my nation."

Ahab whispered in Izabel's ear, "I must admit I doubted that my people could be awakened from their slumber of ignorance. But you have proven me wrong, my queen."

She held her pregnant belly with pride. The child had been quite active lately and was due to arrive within a week or so. If a son, he would be heir to the throne of Israel.

Standing behind the king next to Obadiah, Jehu watched the queen carefully. Building a temple of Baal was an offense to Yahweh. But the king had approved it, indeed encouraged it, and the king was God's anointed one. He ruled and the queen ruled beside him. Not everything an earthly ruler did was righteous, but his authority must be obeyed. Corrupt authority could be a blight on any people. But if the people didn't obey authority, society would crumble into lawlessness and destroy itself from within.

Yahweh had placed Ahab and Izabel on the throne. Disrespect of that throne was disrespect to Yahweh. Respect for the office didn't always coincide with respect for those who held it.

Jehu felt the sting of the conflict within himself, and that sting became a bite when he noticed the prophets of Yahweh outside the entrance to the temple court. He could barely see them at this distance, but he knew what they were doing. These were not the students. These were the prophets themselves, about a hundred of them. And they were declaring condemnation upon this temple and the worship of Baal.

Jehu saw Izabel notice them as well. The Yahwist prophets had been doing this for the past year, and she'd increasingly allowed her frustration with them to show. The king's respect for Elijah held the queen in restraint. But Jehu could see that her patience had come to an end.

"Do you see them outside the gates again?" Izabel complained to Ahab. "They seek to spoil even this beautiful celebration of your achievement, of your kingdom and rule." She pandered to the king's ego as if all this was not her own achievement and ambition.

"They're deplorable. Intolerant religious bigots. We talked about this at length, husband. They've been doing this for a solid year, sowing division and condemning *your* rule. You promised me that if this kind of thing happened again, you'd let me send a message to the people that this kind of rebellion will not be tolerated."

Ahab considered her words sheepishly and finally nodded with reluctance. His respect for the prophets had crumbled with Izabel's flattery. He loved Izabel and she had become a master of influencing her husband.

Izabel turned and her eyes sought out Hamilqart. The High Priest stepped forward to receive the queen's instruction. She spoke in a low voice, "Send your temple guards immediately to the prophet's school and destroy it."

"Shall I imprison the prophets?" Hamilqart asked.

"No. Kill them all. And send a team of assassins to the Rechabite camp as we planned."

Though her words had been spoken quietly, careful listeners in the royal entourage had overheard. Jehu and Obadiah glanced at each other in shock. Jehu knew Obadiah to be a trustworthy man of Yahweh. He ruled the royal household with justice and fairness. And he held Elijah and the School of Prophets in high regard.

As the king, queen and high priest moved out of their earshot and into the temple for preparations, Obadiah muttered to Jehu, "You heard her."

Jehu nodded.

"You heard her command the slaughter of the prophets of Yahweh. Are you going to let that happen?"

"The king approved," Jehu replied. "I will not defy him. He is the Lord's anointed." It was David's own reply when confronted with the injustices of King Saul.

"And what of the prophets?" hissed Obadiah. "Are they not the ones who anoint Yahweh's king? Are they not his mouthpiece?"

"God raises up prophets, priests, and kings," Jehu shot back. "And he brings them down as well."

"Yes. And does he not also use us men for the taking down? He also commands the protection of the innocent."

"What you imply is treasonous, Obadiah."

"Let me ask you a question, Jehu. When obedience to God is considered treason to the king, what authority do you think a man should obey?"

Jehu became agitated. He had no good answer.

"Well if you won't do something, I will," Obadiah said grimly and marched away.

Jehu watched him, considering what Obadiah might be planning—and the consequences of trying to warn the prophets.

But Jehu knew the might and skills of Jonadab and his Rechabites. What exactly was the queen planning with her secret assassins?

CHAPTER 26

The activities surrounding the dedication of the temple of Baal had kept Obadiah occupied and unable to do anything about the queen's threats. Now the sun hung low on the horizon as he raced his horse toward the School of the Prophets. Scattered trees and large boulders in the desert cast long shadows across his path like a sun dial counting down to total darkness.

This was the road the prophets and their students would have taken back to their residence in the cliffs of the Carmel mountain range about five miles south of Jezreel. But Obadiah had no idea how far they might have gotten by the time he'd been able to sneak away from the Baal festival. He had to find them before Hamilqart's armed temple guards did.

Nor was there any telling how far the guards were behind Obadiah. He wasn't even sure when they'd left. Could he get to the school in time to warn its residents? Would they run and hide, or would they stand their ground and die? He prayed for the former. But he feared the latter. Elijah was a stubborn prophet.

Or had Obadiah miscalculated, and the temple guards were actually ahead of him? He prayed to Yahweh to protect his Remnant.

$$\bullet \bullet \bullet \bullet \bullet$$

The captain of the temple guard led a hundred armed soldiers from the temple of Baal on horseback toward the School of the Prophets. Hamilqart had sent his own guards to do the job because Izabel didn't trust the royal armed forces. It was already late in the day, so likely they would arrive just at dark, which would make the massacre more difficult. People could hide better in the dark. On the other hand, the darkness of night would cloak their advance and provide cover until they were upon their prey.

Tracks on the ground showed that a group of about a hundred people had passed this way earlier. These were no doubt the prophets who'd been in the city earlier agitating against Baal's temple and were now heading home. The captain of the temple guard unit pondered the potential of slaughtering those rodents while they were still on the road as an easy massacre. Then they would eliminate the remaining Yahweh pests at the school.

• • • • •

Jehu raced his horse along the western road to Megiddo. His mind was running equally as fast as he considered the risk he was taking in riding to the camp of the Rechabites to warn them of the coming assassins.

Obadiah's courage had been a rebuke. The palace administrator was risking his life to warn the Sons of the Prophets. Which had made Jehu realize he had to warn the Rechabites. The temple guards Izabel was sending against the prophets had been approved by the king. But the assassins on their way to Megiddo were not. Jehu had seen that order given out of the king's hearing. Theirs was a secret mission known only to the queen—and her henchman Hamilqart. The Rechabites were protected favorites of the king. The queen would be risking her own life if she openly killed those who made King Ahab's chariots and tools of war.

So Izabel must have decided instead to secretly assassinate key religious leaders of the Rechabites as a way to send a message. A dangerous risk on her part, but it just might work. By killing only the religious leaders, she'd get her vengeance on those preaching against her without crippling their vital industry. And if secret assassins were responsible for their deaths, she wouldn't be implicated. Jonadab and his metal-workers would know who was responsible, but unable to prove it. And so a clear message would be conveyed. Either stop their condemnation of the queen and of Baalism or face deadly consequences. The Rechabites would know that the king had failed to protect them.

Jehu had known Jonadab since their youth. The son of Rechab had taught the son of Nimshi how to ride a chariot. But when Jehu had been commissioned to become crown prince Ahab's training partner, he and Jonadab had lost contact. When Jehu became Ahab's army commander, he'd re-established that contact with his old friend as he worked with the Rechabite guild to increase the king's chariot forces.

Jonadab was also a devout Yahwist. The entire guild of Rechabites lived as nomads in tents on the outskirts of Megiddo because they felt as aliens and sojourners in their own land due to the increasing idol worship. Their purity of devotion to Yahweh affected even Jehu. He struggled increasingly in his own conscience with his loyalty to a king whose rule was so marked by corrupted religion: a syncretistic worship of Yahweh alongside the gods of Canaan.

At times Jonadab and his Rechabites seemed excessive in their religious expression. And at times they seemed a necessary catalyst of reform.

Whichever the case, Jehu had to get to them before the assassins did.

•••••

Night fell around the hundred prophets as they followed the road from Jezreel into the foothills. They'd proclaimed Yahweh's judgment at the grand opening of the temple of Baal, and there was nothing more they could do, so Micaiah was leading them on the five-mile journey back to the school.

They'd been discussing among themselves whether or not Queen Izabel would retaliate because of their stance, so when they heard the sound of approaching hooves, most of them scattered into the underbrush edging the road.

The hooves proved to be a single horse and rider.

Micaiah stepped forward to meet him. "Obadiah!"

"Micaiah, you're all in danger!" Obadiah shouted. "A party of armed temple guards is on the way right now with orders from the queen to destroy the school and kill all of you."

The prophets reacted to the news with various degrees of murmurings and expressed concerns. Kill all of them? The queen ordered it? Why? But what about King Ahab?

"You must hide," said Obadiah.

"We must tell our brethren at the school," countered Micaiah.

"I know a cave not far from here where you'll be safe," Obadiah said. "Let me show you. Then I'll ride on to the school to alert them. I will be much faster than you could manage on foot."

Turning to the others, Micaiah commanded, "You heard the man. We must move quickly for the sake of our brethren."

Obadiah offered the old prophet a hand to help him onto the horse, but Micaiah shook his head. "No, I would slow you down. Take Amos here. He is young and can return quickly for us once you've shown him the way."

A younger prophet barely out of his teens clambered onto the horse behind Obadiah, holding tightly to the palace administrator's waist as Obadiah galloped on down the road toward the secret cave.

A few minutes into the ride, Amos raised his voice hesitantly over the horse's hoofbeats. "Why are you, an official of King Ahab, helping us? Will you not be hanged if you are found out?"

"I am helping you because I serve Yahweh first," Obadiah said. "And since you won't be informing on me, who could know what I have done?"

He yanked the horse to a stop near an embankment. "See that outcropping that rises above the ridge? Just a hundred feet to the right behind a patch of juniper is the entrance to the cave. You will find a spring inside that will provide water. I will bring you food as I can."

As the young prophet slid from the horse's haunch, a realization struck Obadiah. "Elijah was not with you. Where is he?"

The young prophet shrugged. "He didn't leave the city with us. I heard him tell Micaiah he was heading east toward the Jordan River."

CHAPTER 27

Jezreel

Izabel cried out, "Husband, it is time!"

She was standing inside the foyer entrance of the temple just over the gigantic footprint of Baal impressed in the stone at her feet. The stone was now wet with the birth water that had broken in her womb.

She considered this an omen of her son's spiritual importance.

Ahab gestured for some guards to help carry her back to the palace. Thank Baal they could take the underground tunnels out of the temple without distracting from the festivities. The sacrifice was about to begin in the outer court. The temple dedication would have to continue without them.

• • • • •

The squad of a hundred temple guards approached the base of the cliff where the School of Prophets loomed a hundred feet above them, peacefully unaware of their presence. No one had seen the armed force arrive in the dark of night.

They started their way up the inclined path toward their unsuspecting quarry.

• • • • •

Six shadowy human figures looked down from the hillside above the Jezreel Valley. The Rechabite camp spread out before them under the moonlight. Few fires remained lit. Hundreds of tents were quiet with sleeping families. A handful of guards watched the perimeter.

The six shadows were Izabel's personal assassins, the best of her guard for the temple of Baal. To remain invisible, the silent denizens of darkness dressed in black and wore no armor. They carried long daggers for assassination and scimitar swords for combat. Combat was unlikely on this mission, as their task was to strike unnoticed and melt back into the night like serpents of doom. They had been given intelligence on the location of

118

Jonadab, leader of the tribal guild, as well as five key elders who were the guild's most outspoken Yahwists.

They slithered down the mountain toward their targets.

• • • • •

Izabel screamed in pain. She was naked and squatted on her birthing stool, a chair that had no seat, only arms. She was surrounded by a company of handmaids and midwives. One of them wiped Izabel's sweat with a sea sponge while another knelt at her feet with linen-wrapped hands and pillow to receive the baby when it came out.

Izabel had never felt such pain. She'd been warned of it, but you could never really understand it until you experienced it. And she was experiencing it now.

This little creature in her womb had better do right by her when he ruled—for all she was suffering and all she'd have to do to raise him. And if a girl, the princess would have to work twice as hard in this world of men, just as Izabel had.

The queen had never cared much for children. But a woman's worth in this world was her ability to bear offspring. She was fulfilling her duty and would use the responsibility to her advantage by teaching her children her ways just as her mother had done with her.

Men were too busy controlling the world to bother with bringing up their children, which left women stuck with the lion's share of the responsibility. But if children are the future, then the one who rocks the crib is the one who truly rules the world. At least her children would have a far better life than ninety-nine percent of the rest of humanity.

But none of that mattered right now. The only thing that mattered was the horrible pain shooting through her body. She cursed the maid for sponging her too much. Everything was irritating and annoying in this pain.

She clutched her small palm-sized image of Bes, the lion-faced bow-legged dwarf god of fertility. It was something she could focus on. Someone she could pray to.

Bes, grant me a boy of my heart. Grant me a son of Baal.

• • • • •

The temple guards had traversed the path up the cliff and had crashed through the simple gate of the mountainside School of Prophets. They threw torches onto thatched roofs, lighting them on fire. As prophets and students awoke to the chaos, many were quickly slain with swords, axes, arrows, and spears. Some attempted to flee, others scrambled to hiding places and deep within the caves.

• • • • •

The courtyard of the temple of Baal was full of Israelites. The Baal epic had been read describing the story of Baal's rise to the headship of the pantheon of gods and his desire to build a house for his name. His house had been built on Mount Zaphon at the pleading of Asherah and Anat with El. This grand new temple was another House of Baal, a spiritual satellite of that heavenly one.

Dressed in his linen robes and conical high priest's headdress, Hamilqart sacrificed a goat and lamb on the altar, then they had the broken bodies carried before him into the temple to present before Baal.

He was amazed at how easily the Israelites had taken to Baal worship. But this temple was not so different from the Hebrew temple in Jerusalem, a similar design and purpose. People are quick to accept that which is already familiar. These rituals and the celebrations were simply for Baal instead of Yahweh, and they hardly seemed to notice. Give the masses a celebration, and you could indoctrinate them into anything. There was more to introduce to these backwards people, but there would be plenty of time for that in the future. For now, they needed to get used to the fact that Yahweh was not the only male deity around here anymore.

• • • • •

Izabel nearly fainted from the pain of delivering, but her midwives kept her conscious, rubbing her muscles and sponging her skin. The midwife kneeling before the birthing stool announced that the baby was crowning. She could see the child's head begin to emerge.

Between contractions, a handmaid coached Izabel in her breathing. The queen pushed and grunted; her eyes locked on an alabaster statue of Asherah placed strategically in her line of vision.

Lady Asherah of the Sea, Mother of the gods, consort of Baal, please help me.

Finally able to push, she felt herself being stretched immensely as the head emerged. The pause of waiting for the next contraction seemed interminable, but she was ready when it came. She pushed again. Relief! The baby emerged. It was out. It had felt to her as if she were passing a large melon through her body, and she wanted never to do it again. She looked down.

The midwife at her feet wiped the newborn baby with linen, the placenta still attached to the umbilical cord.

"It's a boy, your majesty!"

"Praise Baal!" she shouted in reply. "He has given me a prince to rule the kingdom."

Overcome with a deep wave of emotion, she began to weep.

• • • • •

In the holy of holies at the temple of Baal, Hamilqart placed the slaughtered firstborn goat and sheep into the bronze arms of Baal. The fires in the pit below were stoked. The animals began to burn, first the hair and then the skin sizzled over the flames. The high priest prayed to Baal on behalf of Izabel, who was at this moment giving birth. He prayed for a safe delivery and even more so for the health and safety of Izabel, whom he still loved with all his heart.

The arms of Baal were lowered, and the sacrifices rolled into the flames below with a shower of sparks and puff of smoke.

Hamilqart couldn't help but throw a request of his own into his prayers. He asked that Baal would someday bring Izabel back to him. That she might return to him… for companionship, for intimacy, for all the pleasures they'd shared before.

He still loved her so.

• • • • •

In the School of Prophets, temple guards were now going door to door in the residences of the cliffside village, hunting down prophets, wives and children and cutting them down without mercy. The holocaust of fire was increasing. The burning structures and landscape forced the innocents from hiding places out to the waiting swords of their murderers.

A group of twelve soldiers stumbled over to a large cave. It was packed with prophets and their families hiding out there. The guards hacked them all to pieces.

Blood flowed in the streets as the heavens went dark and the stars fell from the sky.

•••••

In the Rechabite camp outside Megiddo, the handful of guards who had been patrolling the perimeter were silently dispatched by the assassins' blades. The six figures then spread out through the camp, unseen and unheard, seeking their designated targets. They had planned their raid to be synchronized so that all six leaders would be dead before any alarm would be sounded.

•••••

Ahab entered the bedchamber with young Athaliah at his side. Izabel had been cleaned up and now lay in her bed. The baby's umbilical cord had been cut and tied, its body rubbed with salt, water, and oil. It now lay swaddled tightly in a cloth in Izabel's arms.

"My king," Izabel said at the sight of Ahab. His apprehensive expression turned to joy. Approaching, he leaned over the bed to see the child. "A son! I have an heir. Thank Yahweh."

"Thank Baal," Izabel corrected him. "It is not by luck that the birth of our child coincides with the very day of dedication of Baal's temple."

Ahab was too intent upon seeing his son to hear everything she was telling him. He reached for the child. Izabel handed him gently to Ahab, who couldn't keep his eyes off the boy or stop smiling.

"He's beautiful," he exclaimed.

"His name is Jehoram," said Izabel. "Joram for short."

Ahab continued to gaze at the newborn's face, caressing his skin ever so softly. "Welcome young prince Joram to your kingdom. There is much you will need to learn. But there is plenty of time for that."

Izabel suddenly noticed that Athaliah was hanging back. She patted the bed. "Come, sweet girl. Come see your nephew."

Athaliah sidled closer, a pouting expression marring her pretty young face. Izabel realized right away what was going on. She reached her arms out to the girl.

"Athaliah, come to me and give me a hug. I've missed you."

Athaliah obeyed, but her hug felt tentative. Izabel pulled her back to look into her eyes. She said with firm conviction, "My dear girl. There is no need for jealousy. You are still my ward, and your future is my utmost concern. Do you understand?"

The girl peered back into the queen's eyes, and Izabel glimpsed a bit of trust return.

"This is simply the way of the world. One day you will bear children and will have to give them your love and attention. You will learn that each one will have their own special personality as well as their own special purpose in this world. When we give our love away, it never runs out. The more we give our love the bigger our heart becomes."

Athaliah smiled reluctantly, but this time she gave Izabel a full hug.

Holding her close, Izabel whispered in her ear, "One day your little nephew here will be king of Israel. And you will be queen of Judah, which is just as important. He will never take your place. Never. Do you understand?"

She smiled. "We're a sisterhood."

Their special shared-saying fueled Athaliah's confidence and restored brightness to her expression.

Athaliah wanted to be just like Izabel.

· · · · ·

Obadiah raced down the road. His detour to show Amos the hidden cave had taken precious time. Was he still ahead of the temple guard? He could only hope. The secret caves were a blessing from Yahweh. With ample water inside the prophets would survive safely hidden until he could return with food supplies.

How long could they hide out there? Obadiah couldn't guess. All he knew was that he had to protect the servants of Yahweh from the queen's searching eyes and be willing to accept the consequences if he was discovered.

He kicked his horse into a faster gallop, praying he wasn't too late to warn those still at the School of Prophets.

But when he came within view of the cliffside school, he saw the glow of flames and smoke billowing into the sky from the ruins, and he knew his worst fears had been realized.

The temple guards had caught the school unaware and the people would be dead by now. Riding any further would just be throwing his own life away, and the hidden prophets were now dependent on him for food and supplies. Brokenhearted, Obadiah turned his horse around.

As he urged his tired horse into a fast trot, he choked up with pain for all those young students who would never get a chance to live a full life. They'd sought to honor Yahweh, and they'd been rewarded with death. Not to mention the wives and children residing at the school, some of whose husbands and fathers were likely among those heading now to the secret cave. They would be waiting for news of their loved ones even more eagerly than for supplies.

But first Obadiah had to get back to Jezreel before his absence was noticed and his secret deeds uncovered.

• • • • •

In the Rechabite camp, all six assassins had found their target tents. They had drawn their blades and finished counting in their heads to the agreed-upon number so that all might strike at the same moment.

The assassin at Jonadab's tent opened the flap as quietly as he could. He knew his team members were doing the same thing right now all around the camp at their assigned victim's tents.

They would enter and quickly cut the throats of any sleepers inside before slipping back out into the night to reconvene at their hiding place on the hillside.

Entering, the assassin spotted two adults in the dark on the bed, Jonadab and his wife asleep beneath the covers. Moving swiftly to the larger, he paused for a moment before pulling the covers back to finish his task.

When he did, he froze in surprise. The bodies beneath the covers were not human but straw dummies made to look like sleeping victims.

The assassins had been tricked. Someone had warned the Rechabites.

A torch appeared at the entrance, flooding the tent with its light. Scrambling to his feet, the assassin saw his target, the muscular Jonadab, holding the torch instead of laying in the bed. Standing beside him was another official he knew from Jezreel. Jehu, son of Nimshi, commander of Ahab's army.

Queen Izabel's secret assassins disappeared from the face of the earth that night. She would never know what happened to them, for she could never risk King Ahab discovering her murderous plot.

CHAPTER 28

As the sun rose and lit the day, Elijah and Elisha stood in the midst of the smoldering ruins that had once been the mountain village. The blackness of everything seemed to mock them. Elisha watched his master closely for what he would do next. Staring off into oblivion, the older prophet looked like a statue of dread, his only movement his trembling left hand.

Before them were thirty dead prophets and students, their bodies impaled on poles stuck in the ground. It was too horrible for Elisha to look at. He knew these men. They had lived together, studied together, prayed together. As the shock of the horrible scene began to settle, the two men methodically searched the ruins and caves with the hope of finding survivors.

There were none.

All they'd found were more dead prophets, students, wives, and even their children burned alive in the residences or hacked to death—everywhere. There had been no safe place to hide.

Overwhelmed, Elisha felt his strength wane and his knees began to buckle. Kneeling on the ground, he couldn't stop weeping. Nor could he stop asking Yahweh, "Why? Why? Why?!"

Elijah finally spoke. Elisha stopped his blubbering to listen.

"It is me she was after. They died because of me."

Elisha tried to console his master. "Even if you had been here, Jezebel would still have killed everyone."

Elijah's expression eased as though taking some comfort in Elisha's reassurance. He mused out loud, "We must leave. But where can we go?"

Elisha responded with firm confidence, "Back to my father's farm." The student had become the teacher.

• • • • •

Stretched out beside Izabel, Ahab cradled Joram in his arms while Athaliah sat quietly by the queen's bedside. After hours of labor and the excitement of new birth, exhaustion had caught up with Izabel and she still slumbered.

She was awakened by the creaking of Ahab shifting position on the bed and the sound of voices. Opening her eyes, she saw the high priest of Baal standing at the foot of her bed.

"Whatever it is you desire so urgently, Hamilqart," Ahab huffed, "now is hardly the time."

Struggling into a half-sitting position, Izabel said groggily, "My love, please, let him speak."

Stepping forward, Hamilqart glanced nervously at Ahab before murmuring discreetly, "Your highness, we will hear no more from the prophets of Yahweh."

Ahab's eyes went wide, then narrowed. "What have you done?"

Hamilqart shifted to bow deep before the king. "I obeyed the queen's orders, my lord."

Ahab looked to Izabel, who added, "With the king's approval, of course."

The king now looked flustered. Izabel knew he hadn't thought through the implication of his order when she'd goaded him to authorize it. He clearly hadn't realized the action would be so quick—or extreme.

Ahab sighed.

Izabel looked back at Hamilqart. "And Elijah?"

"They didn't find him, my queen. But they interrogated some of the students before they were executed, and we know where he is."

All sleepiness left her as anger rose within. "Why are you still here, then? Send a search party and bring me Elijah. *Now.*"

"Yes, my queen."

Hamilqart spun on his heel and left the queen's bedchamber.

Izabel returned her gaze to Ahab, his stunned expression a blank mask, he offered no protest over how she'd carried out his poorly considered consent. The queen smiled inwardly. Achieving her objectives was proving easier than she'd hoped.

• • • • •

126

Jehu sat at the dinner table with Susanna in their home. Too disturbed to eat, he'd left his food untouched on the plate. A servant poured him more wine. Taking the goblet, he downed it with irresponsible speed.

As much as he wanted to protect his precious wife from the horrible truth, he could not.

"Queen Izabel murdered the prophets of Yahweh."

"Dear God," Susanna exclaimed. "Did the king know?"

"She manipulated his approval."

Jehu waited until the servant had left the room before leaning forward to say quietly, "She didn't find them all. Obadiah has managed to hide a hundred prophets."

He took a deep breath before confessing even more quietly, "The queen also sent assassins to kill the religious leaders of the Rechabites. But I was able to warn them in time and they are okay. The assassins were killed."

Susanna carefully set her wine glass down, her beautiful features displaying both shock and fear. "Does the queen have any idea you were involved?"

"No, I am confident she doesn't." Jehu looked into the depths of his wine glass. "But this means Obadiah and I have committed treason against the crown."

Susanna leaned forward to touch his hand. "No, don't say that! You performed allegiance to your God."

Jehu's dual loyalty to God and king was tearing him in half. He shook his head somberly. "The queen may not know. But we cannot hope my actions will remain concealed. If she learns it was me, I will be executed. And you would no longer be safe either."

But Susanna would have none of his gloomy predictions. "Then we must ensure she does not find out. And you did the right thing, Jehu. We must trust Yahweh."

Jehu was having a hard time, trusting God felt hopeless. Yahweh had seen fit to allow the destruction of the School of Prophets and the slaughter of all those innocent faithful believers.

He said, "Galina is being trained to attend the palace court of that harlot queen." It was what the prophet Elijah had called Izabel. "I no longer trust her safety there. We must bring her home to Samaria."

"That is not necessary," assured Susanna. "Galina is safe enough. I received a letter from the palace just today. She has been sent with an entourage of other girls to Jerusalem in a diplomatic exchange. Galina is going to be on the palace court of Athaliah when she marries into Judah."

Jehu wasn't so sure that was good news. "You may never see her again."

"But she is safe, away from Queen Izabel. And for that I rejoice."

"But you are not safe if the queen discovers my betrayal," he countered.

"She won't find out. You obeyed Yahweh. That is what matters."

"I feel as if I serve two masters," he said.

Susanna reminded him of his own words, "But you have not lifted your hand against the Lord's anointed."

CHAPTER 29

Abel-meholah

When Elijah and Elisha departed the devasted school, they mounted up on two horses they'd found roaming. The destination was Elisha's family home. They had traveled through a longer less-worn path for safety reasons. It was the following day when they reached their destination, but what lay before them was not a welcoming sight.

Elisha was the first to spot smoke drifting into the sky from the location of his family's farm. As his father's wheat fields came into sight, he saw they were now blackened stubble. Then he saw flames still jumping from the thatched roofs of farmhouse and outbuildings.

"Nooo!" he screamed, kicking his horse into a run toward what was left of the farmhouse. "Nooooooooooo!!"

Reaching the farmhouse, he jumped off the horse and raced toward the front door. Straw mixed into the adobe bricks had blackened in the intense heat, but the walls still stood. Grasping the metal door latch, Elisha felt his flesh burning. He didn't care. Gripping more tightly, he pulled with all his might.

The door flew open, and he was blown backward by a gush of hot air.

Elijah was beside him as he peered through the smoke and flames to see his parents' bodies hanging by their necks from the ceiling.

Then the rafters collapsed, igniting a new inferno. Elijah pulled his young student out of range. There was nothing to be done but stand and watch while the fire consumed itself.

Elisha had no more tears left. He could weep no more.

Only as the flames died down did he begin to feel the pain in his right hand. Searing pain. Looking at his palm, he saw that it was badly charred from the metal door handle. The blistered flesh was black and red. The pain was so great he passed out.

When Elisha came to, his master had just finished bandaging his burnt hand in a linen wrap.

Elijah helped Elisha onto his mount, leading the student's horse by the reins well away from the farm into a sunbaked wasteland, where he built camp for the two of them.

Unable to do more than collect a few thorn bushes for firewood, Elisha grimaced at his hand. But his raging hatred was far greater than the pain.

"I will kill that godless whore for what she has done."

"Vengeance belongs to the Lord, Elisha," Elijah responded calmly.

"But Jezebel has taken everything from us."

Elijah didn't back down. "We still have our lives."

It angered Elisha that the prophet could be so passive in the face of injustice. "My father was a good man. He obeyed God. This was his reward?"

"I will be your father now."

"My father is dead. The Sons of the Prophets are dead. Why did Yahweh allow all this? Why did he not save his servants?"

Elijah looked defeated. "I don't know."

"What kind of God do we serve?" complained Elisha.

Elijah replied, "A God we cannot make in our own image."

"A God who permits such slaughter of his holy ones?"

"A God who chooses for his own holy purposes whom he will save."

That didn't sit well with Elisha. He wanted action. He wanted passionate purpose, not resignation. "Jezebel seeks our lives. What will we do?"

"We will hide."

"Is it our calling to be cowards?"

Elijah sighed before explaining. "Sometimes, Elisha, protecting your own life enables you to later protect others."

That sounded a bit too passive and self-preserving to Elisha. Had the old prophet lost his courage? And with it his authority as Yahweh's prophet in Israel?

"Where will we go, then?" Elisha demanded.

Elijah contemplated their future. "The one place Jezebel would not think to look for us."

CHAPTER 30

*As I continued my commander's duties serving King Ahab, the
queen continued her search for the prophet Elijah. She could
not find him or the hundred other prophets that Obadiah had
kept hidden from her grasp. It was only later that the story of
Elijah's escape and hideout would be told. And when I heard it,
I knew it was a foretaste of redemption for God's people.*

City of Zarephath

In the heart of Phoenicia, Elijah and Elisha approached the walls of a harbor
city which was located exactly between the twin cities of Sidon and Tyre.
Rumor had it that this had been a vacation spot for Jezebel's family when
Ethbaal ruled in Sidon. A prosperous trade based city, this was Elijah's chosen
place of refuge.

"I cherish the look on Jezebel's face when she discovers we hid out in
her vacation palace," said Elisha.

Elijah countered, "The point is not to be discovered at all, if you please."

Elisha smiled. Elijah added, "And we won't be staying in the palace."

"Where will we stay?"

Elijah looked ahead at the looming city walls. The gates were open, and
people were coming and going into the city to do their business. He pointed to
a woman and her son not far from them, gathering sticks. "We'll stay with
them."

Elisha followed the direction of Elijah's gesture with confusion. It wasn't
like his master to be impulsive. He watched Elijah approach the woman and
boy, then finally trotted to catch up with him.

131

The pair looked poor with tattered robes and wretched sandals. The woman was still young, a few years older than Elisha, while the boy looked to be about five years old. Like most little boys, he'd gathered more than he could handle. He tried to save the sticks as they fell out of his hands, but they all tumbled to the ground, leaving their gatherer with a pouting look. Elisha smothered a grin, not wanting the child to think he was laughing at him.

Elijah spoke to the woman. "Greetings, my name is Elijah, and this is Elisha."

The suspicion she expressed on her face, fell away as her gaze moved to Elisha. She seemed to brighten, almost smile. She was quite beautiful beneath her poverty.

"My name is Dido," she responded hesitantly. "And this is my son Abibaal."

"May we call upon your family for hospitality?" Elijah asked.

She chuckled as if he were mad. "Sir, I am a widow. I am gathering sticks to make a fire to cook the last of my food, and then my son and I will die."

So Sidonia had been hurt by the drought as well. The two travelers weren't the only ones facing difficult times. Observing her skeletal frame and tattered robes, Elisha felt a pang of pity.

"My companion and I are prophets of God," Elijah replied.

"Which god?" she questioned.

"Yahweh. And he says to give us the last of your food."

What in the world? Elisha stared at his master in disbelief. This time the prophet had outdone himself in presumptuous crazy claims. *What is he doing?*

Dido looked as incredulous as Elisha felt. She glanced at her son, still pouting from his stick disaster. Then with just as much unpredictability, she handed her bundle of sticks to Elijah. "Pick up my son's sticks and follow me."

Taking the bundle in his arms, Elijah said to Elisha, "You heard her. Pick up the boy's sticks."

Elisha picked them up, favoring his burnt hand as he did so. The boy stared at the bandaged hand. With a conspiratorial grin, Elisha handed the lad a few sticks, so he'd feel useful.

A few quick steps and he caught up to his master, who was following the woman back to the city gate. He hissed in Elijah's ear, "What are you doing demanding this woman's last food?"

Elijah gave him a wry look. "Yahweh is clearly not speaking to you yet."
Elisha rolled his eyes, but followed obediently through the city gates.

The streets of the city reminded Elisha of Tyre. Classic ashlar-style brick with cedar wood roofs. A large harbor for merchant trade ships. An eclectic marketplace of goods from all across the Mediterranean.

Dido's neighborhood was a poor one. Widows struggled without a husband to care for them and the children. As they walked the poverty stricken streets, there were beggars who slept in alley ways, and Elisha spotted rats lurking in the shadows. During droughts and famine, sicknesses seemed to follow rodent infestation while urban neighborhoods became filthy garbage piles. So God's judgment had indeed hit all of Phoenicia.

The widow's house was a small one tucked away at the end of an alley, looking very much like a builder's afterthought. The door creaked and was difficult to move, but the young woman was clearly used to this. Leaning in, she forced it open, then motioned the two men to enter. The boy didn't follow, but scampered up an outdoor staircase that led to the flat roof.

Once inside, Elisha was impressed with how clean the place was despite its sparseness. A pair of bed mats lay rolled up against the far wall. The only other furnishings were a small blackened hearth, a few bits of pottery and wooden dishes on a shelf, a rickety table and bench, and a woven basket that held a few wooden utensils and a single long knife.

Moving towards the hearth, Dido said, "There is an upper level chamber where you may lodge as you need."

Elisha noticed that though she addressed her words to Elijah, she kept stealing glances in Elisha's direction. Following his master's lead, he placed the gathered sticks neatly near the hearth.

Elijah looked around. "Where is your flour and oil?"

"You mean what's left of it." Dido lifted a pottery pitcher from the shelf and set it on the table. Next to it, she set a small wide-necked jar. "You are welcome to it. I suppose one small ladle of oil and handful of flour would not have kept us alive anyway."

"Are you sure that's all you have?" Elijah asked her in a challenging way. "Perhaps you'd better check again."

Dido's face clearly expressed her thoughts of how silly the question was, then said to Elijah, "I may be poor, prophet, but I'm not stupid."

Elijah repeated his challenge. "Perhaps you'd better check again."

Certain that her visitor was a mad man, Dido removed the jar's lid, then tilted the jar to show him. As she did so, flour spilled out of the top. Yanking the jar back, she looked inside.

From where he stood, Elisha could see it was filled to the brim with flour.

"How did you—?" Dido was so stupefied she couldn't finish her question.

"And your oil?" Elijah prodded, grinning.

The woman's eyes went wide with excitement. Reaching for the pottery pitcher, she lifted it from where she'd set it on the table. This time it was clearly heavy for her. Pulling off a small cloth draped over top and spout, she looked inside.

"I had just a spoonful of oil!"

"Not anymore," said Elijah.

Walking over to Elijah as if in a trance, Dido fell at his feet and cried out, "You ARE a prophet of God!"

Eliah's huge smile was evident beneath his bushy beard. "Get up, good woman. This jar of flour and jug of oil shall remain full until the day that Yahweh sends rain upon the earth."

Dido couldn't stop smiling or crying. She blurted out, "You can stay as long as you like!"

Heading for the door, she added, "I will prepare the upper room for you." She pointed to Elisha's bandaged hand. "And then I will help you with that wound. I have some skill with injuries. I pray you find Zarephath to your liking."

Elijah stopped her in the doorway. "Our identities cannot be discovered."

Her smile grew wide. "Whatever do you mean? You are my uncle and cousin visiting from Ugarit."

With that, she rushed outdoors. As she disappeared up the staircase toward the flat roof, Elijah turned to Elisha. "You see how she looks at you."

Elisha brought an expression of confusion to his face as though he'd no idea what Elijah was saying.

"Remember, she is a righteous widow, and we are her guests," Elijah said. "She must be treated with propriety and respect."

"And when did Yahweh tell you to remind me of that?"

Elijah grinned. "When you were not listening."

CHAPTER 31

Sheol

Anat raised her body out of the water and quietly stepped onto the sand of the shore. She swam through the waters of the Abyss for miles before arriving at her destination, the Isle of the Dead, where Mot resided in his City of the Dead, better known as the Pit.

From where she stood catching her breath and resting for strength, Anat could see the entire island was the black rock of a volcano top rising out of the sea. It looked dormant with no smoke rising from the summit. No sounds of life as there would be up above on the earth. And no vegetation whatsoever. Everything about this place was death.

Anat spotted Mot's boat in the rocks nearby and just beside it a pathway up the mountain. She started up the path, thankful she hadn't taken off her sandals to swim as the coarse, black basaltic rock beneath her feet would have quickly shredded her flesh.

Remaining alert for attack by any sentries, Anat hiked up through jagged-edged boulders of igneous rock. A couple hours had seemed to pass by the time she made it to the rim of the volcano. Mot must not have anticipated her arrival since she'd come upon no traps or guards. She still maintained the element of surprise.

She could now see that the volcano was an ancient one that had exploded or collapsed in the distant past, creating a wide-rimmed mouth about a mile in circumference. However dormant, there were plenty of vents from which steam escaped all around the basin floor, creating a heavy fog that gave an eerie impression of unknown depths lurking below. Peering down into the caldera, Anat could barely see Mot's City of the Dead nestled in the folds of hardened magma on the basin floor several hundred feet below.

She began her descent, climbing down the rocky ledge of the throat rather than taking the single road that circled down the other side. That route would surely be guarded, making her an easy target should she be foolish enough to follow it.

Though even this direct descent was child's play compared to Tartarus where the ancient ones had been bound at the Flood. That was a dungeon sealed by Yahweh and surely impossible to breach or escape from.

No, this wasn't Tartarus, and Anat wasn't afraid of it as she was of that ancient underworld prison. In truth, she was angry and was going to make sure Mot experienced the fullness of her judgment in wrath. He would never try this antic again when she was done with him.

Reaching the bottom, Anat made her way through the steamy atmosphere to the city at the center of the basin. Though called a city, it wasn't a place of buildings and residences, but an expansive array of huge monolithic rocks jutting toward the sky like pylons or gravestones. They looked as though they'd exploded from the floor by some force of sorcery below the earth. Within their perimeter were the prison pits of Mot.

A pair of giant lamassu, animal human hybrids with human heads and winged bull bodies, guarded the entry to the city. Anat had no fear of these creatures, but she would not risk the element of surprise. She elected to find another entry point. There was no telling what Mot might do to Baal if he thought his captive was about to be freed.

Grabbing the rough edges of the frozen molten wall, Anat climbed it like a quiet spider. She paused at the top to survey the labyrinth which lay ahead. It was engulfed in fog, so she quickly studied it before leaping down. The maze which lay ahead was a Gilgal formation. Gilgals were megalithic monuments of concentric stone circles set up with a tumulus, or burial mound, in the center. In the surface world, the cult of the dead often utilized this type of labyrinth. Anat knew Baal would be in the center of the pattern, buried in the tumulus as Mot's prisoner. Following the maze-like walls to the next gateway, she made her way to her target.

Before long, she arrived at Mot's underworld throne room. The center circular area prominently displayed Mot's polished black basalt throne atop the tumulus. But Mot was not upon it.

"You were expecting a royal welcome?"

Anat turned to face the voice behind her. It was Mot, the underworld god of death. Standing eight feet tall, he was a decrepit-looking creature, his skin pale and worm-like with inordinately long, bony fingers on each hand. His face was skeletal and fleshless without nostrils. He had rotting skin with deep, sunken eyes and a monstrous mouth full of teeth on putrefied gums.

"Greetings, little sex tart," he said. "Have you come to pleasure me?"

Anat looked like a schoolgirl next to his monstrous form. But Mot was clearly not aware of her skill as the goddess of war. She drew her sickle swords from her back.

"What do you desire, Virgin Anat?" Mot repeated.

It was the question of a gatekeeper. The wrong answer of which would result in serious suffering.

She said, "O Mot, give up my brother."

"You want the storm god, do you?" he mocked. His hearty laugh echoed throughout the caldera around them. "I seem to remember approaching Mightiest Baal and taking him like a lamb in my mouth. Like a kid crushed in the chasm of my throat. And you have come to me with your little blades to rescue him?"

Anat didn't respond. She was calculating her moves.

He ranted, "I will rape your every orifice seventy times and then give your broken body to your brother at the bottom of his cell as his only food to eat. Bow before your Lord of Death."

Mot raised his hand as if to beckon her. But it was a trick. He was using sorcery to make the megalith behind Anat fall upon her. She sensed the danger and rolled out of the way as the fifteen-foot-tall multi-ton stone crushed the ground at her feet.

But it did not crush her.

He gestured again, and Anat dodged another falling stone.

And another. She was too quick for him. Another advantage of her smaller size.

"Here's your little tart!" she yelled, dodging and rolling out of the way of the stone dominoes.

Dust clouded the air from the crumbling rocks. This dark black basalt haze obscured her small form from the beady, sunken eyes of her underworld nemesis.

Losing track of her, the beast bellowed with a howl that made the megaliths around them rattle. In this underworld, Mot was a mighty god.

But every god had a weakness. Mot's pride had blinded him like the dust in the air.

Anat came up behind him on one of the fallen stones. She had one sword now firmly in both hands. Launching off the rock, she hit him with everything she had in her. The sword cleaved him in two from head to sternum.

She withdrew her sword and finished the task. His two halves fell to the ground in a mess of blood and gore.

Anat stood over his helpless form, breathing heavily from her exertion, her lips twisted in a bloody grin.

She muttered, "Filth is the land of your inheritance."

Mot, like all the unearthly flesh, could heal from any wound. But the worse the injury, the longer it would take. And Anat was going to make sure it would take a long time for him to heal from the devastation she wrought.

She took her time.

She cut him into pieces and then burned them in a fire.

When the pieces of his body had been thoroughly charred, she took a large stone and ground the blackened bits to powder.

She then sowed the ashes and pieces in the dead ground at the heart of the Gilgal in that deep crater.

Let his servant toadies find him now and piece him back together again!

Yes, she would make an example of the deity who dared capture the storm god and mock the goddess of war— no one would underestimate this sexy tart again.

Walking over to the tumulus, Anat moved the stone over the entrance. She entered the tomb and began to dig for Baal's body. Now that Mot's binding spell had been released, the storm god's strength would return.

She reached him a dozen feet below the surface. Pulling himself out of the dirt, he shook his head. "My sister! What took you so long?"

"I expected some gratitude," she complained.

In truth, Anat knew her brother would never show weakness. After all, Baal was the Most High god of the pantheon. Gratitude wasn't fitting for a king.

She added, "Let us get you back to the overworld so you can bring the rains and break Elijah's damned drought."

139

"That is easier said than done," he replied. "I am going to need Ayamur and Yagrush."

These were the names, translated as Chaser and Driver, of his two mighty weapons, a spear and a war hammer. Used by the storm god to overcome Sea and River in the Baal epic, they'd been confiscated by the ruler Zimri-Lim long ago and were securely stored in the city of Terqa in Syria. Baal had retrieved his hammer. But when the archangels trapped him in Mot's jaws, they'd surely returned the hammer to its guarded location.

"Well, let's get moving, then," said Anat, "before our earthly subjects die of thirst waiting for you."

CHAPTER 32

Jezreel
Two Years Later

It was in the third year of the drought that hope was lost for my people. Pestilence and disease were widespread with the famine. Damascus bandits roamed the highways stealing what little food was being shipped between desperate cities. Queen Izabel had stopped sending scouts to look for Elijah because all hands were needed to protect the few food stores left. Little mail was being sent on the dangerous roads. Susanna and I had not received word from Galina in Jerusalem since she'd left Jezreel. We prayed for her continued safety. We prayed for the future of Israel. We needed rain. Some cried out to Yahweh. Others cried out to Baal. The weakest, both young and old, were dying by the day. Without rain we were all going to die.

Jehu marched down the long palace hallway to the king's bedchamber, followed by Hamilqart and two palace guards. Inside, he could hear the sounds of giggling and laughter. He knocked on the door.

"What is it?" the king's angry tones bellowed from the other side of the door.

"My lord, forgive my intrusion, but I have urgent news of the king of Damascus, Ben-hadad II." Unfortunately, the successor to the king Ahab had assassinated had continued both the name and policies of Ben-hadad I. They remained in opposition to Israel.

Ahab opened the door. Half-naked and holding a goblet of wine, he looked visibly perturbed.

"This had better be supremely urgent, Jehu, because I am seriously engaged."

Ahab wriggled as a slim female hand reached from behind the door to tickle him. He chuckled, the agitation leaving his expression.

"Apologies, your highness," Jehu said woodenly, keeping his eyes on the distant wall. "But another caravan with food for Jezreel was pillaged by Damascus bandits."

The king's face turned sour again. "Curse Damascus!"

The queen emerged from behind the door. She wore a translucent gown which concealed nothing. Jehu averted his gaze in respect, but he noticed Hamilqart's unrestrained stare. Ahab was too preoccupied to notice.

"More of our people will starve," Izabel said. "This cannot go on."

"I'm being pushed into a war I do not desire," Ahab added morosely.

"Let me go to Tyre," Izabel suggested. "I will beseech aid from my father."

Ahab's angered face relaxed. "Excellent idea, my love." He turned back to Jehu. "Jehu, you will accompany her as bodyguard with a contingent."

"My lord, you are far more deserving of the commander's attention," Izabel interjected diplomatically. "A squad of temple guards should be sufficient for my security."

Jehu knew that wasn't her real reason for rejecting his escort. The queen despised Jehu, and he returned the sentiment, yet they'd managed to keep their animosity from the king. Still, it was no secret Izabel favored the guards from Baal's temple for her own protection. They were Sidonian after all.

Hamilqart certainly looked pleased with the change of plan. Temple guards meant he would accompany her.

After a moment's consideration, Ahab said to the high priest, "Guard her as you would the king."

Hamilqart bowed. "With all my heart, your highness."

The drunk king was oblivious to notice the subtext occurring right in front of his face. Izabel and Hamilqart had managed to keep their past relationship concealed from the king.

Jehu was relieved and grateful to Yahweh. Guarding the queen was the last thing in the world he wanted to do.

"I will bring Athaliah with me," Izabel added.

Jehu kept a scowl from rising to his features. The queen took the king's sister everywhere, infecting the young girl's mind with Canaanite ways that would undermine the kingdom in the south with the same poison she was spreading in the north. Jehu wouldn't be surprised if Athaliah was in the room with them right now, hiding behind a curtain, learning how to control the king through bedroom tactics.

CHAPTER 33

Tyre

Galina awoke from a deep sleep. She could swear she'd heard her name whispered. Rubbing blurry eyes, she looked around the dark room, lit only by moonlight streaming in through the windows. Who could it have been?

Galina was in the bedchambers of the qedeshim of Astarte. There were about twenty women in this room and others in nearby chambers. No one else appeared to be awake. Laying her head back down, she looked up into the dark cedar ceiling. She fought back an urge to cry when she thought of all she'd been through. Stroking her belly, she wondered whether the child in her was a boy or a girl. She'd managed to hide it well for several months, but was beginning to show. So far, she'd been able to explain it to the other girls and matron as weight gain. But she wasn't sure how much longer that would last.

The life of a qedesha was a hard one. In addition to all the temple duties, they were also called upon for sacred prostitution. Her first experiences had nearly broken her. She'd been abused, beaten, and forced to engage in unspeakable acts by some patrons of the goddess. Like demons, the memories still tormented her.

In her earliest youth before reaching womanhood, Galina had been taught that sexual congress was a beautiful act of unity between a husband and wife that built a family and strengthened the tribe. But her life experience told her something very different. The lustful hunger of men seemed so excessive that she wondered if God had played a sick joke on all women.

To survive as a temple prostitute, she'd found a way to mentally remove herself from her situation and play along with whatever sick or perverted fantasies were demanded of her. She often felt as if she were leaving her body and floating above herself, watching what was happening as a spectator.

She had considered suicide to escape her miserable situation, but once she'd found out she was pregnant, she'd changed her mind and found purpose in living, if only for the sake of protecting her innocent child. It somehow made her feel as if she were redeeming her ruined and worthless life.

Since most of the men who used her were married, she'd come to see marriage as a fraud, a delusion created to control women. Men just couldn't control their own desires, so what good was their covenant promise to anyone? They were like animals following their instincts, slaves to their lusts.

Qedeshim were made to eat herbal concoctions of a sorceress that were supposed to keep them from getting pregnant. Whenever these failed and a girl got pregnant, they were given additional herbs that would force a miscarriage. The qedesha would be back to work within a few days. Children were an inconvenient consequence for sacred prostitution. They had to be eliminated.

Keeping her baby secret was her one act of defiance in this temple that used and exploited her. It was the one thing she could control. At least until now. Soon she could hide her condition no more. She was facing a crossroads. What would she do? What *could* she do?

She could run away. But where would she go with such shame covering her and her baby? There would be no place for her in any of the cities of Israel where the hypocritical men were no different than the men of Tyre. As an unwed mother she would only move from sacred prostitute to street harlot in order to care for the child.

Perhaps the time had come to give up and announce her pregnancy, take the herbs, abort the baby, and return to the good graces of the temple. This was her only home. What else could she do? She could never return to her sister in Samaria. She could never face her after a second life of shame.

She felt her baby move inside her.

"Galina," a voice whispered.

It sounded as though right next to her, soft in her ear. But there was no one awake nearby. Galina raised her head again to look around the room.

Then she spotted two figures standing at the far end of the room. One was the white alabaster Asherah statue. The other was the bronze Baal. But they were not statues. They were living beings.

145

As the pair moved from the window into the moonlight, Galina could see they were holding hands. Asherah had a Hathor wig and jewelry adorning her naked body. Baal wore his battle skirt and conical horned hat of deity. A large lion stood protectively beside Asherah, its hair ruffling as it glanced around the room as though seeking whom it could devour.

These beings are alive!

Despite her confidence and clear vision, Galina found it hard to believe what she was seeing. Had she fallen asleep again? She rubbed her eyes, hoping she would awaken. But when she opened them again, she froze in fear.

Floating a foot above Galina's prone frame, face to face, body to body, was Asherah. A snake slithered around the goddess's neck. Asherah looked Galina over with cold, black reptilian eyes. Galina couldn't move. Was she in shock, or was she being held down by a force?

Then the voice whispered inside her ear again. This time Galina knew it was Asherah's. But her lips didn't move. "Your child is ours. All the children of Israel are ours."

Galina felt herself break out in a cold sweat. Her whole body tingled as if warning her of danger. She closed her eyes tight, wishing the goddess to go away.

When she opened her eyes, Asherah was gone. So was Baal and the lion. Galina was all alone again in a room of sleeping qedeshim.

What had the goddess meant that Galina's child was hers? And all the children of Israel? Had this been a vision? Galina felt a dark and ominous dread.

In the morning, Galina rose with the others, washed, and prepared for breakfast. The priestess matron, a kindly older lady who had treated Galina with sympathy since her arrival here, called the girl aside and led her down the hall to the sorceress. When Galina saw the sorceress's measuring look, she suddenly understood what was going on.

"Galina, I know you are with child," the matron said. "You must take these herbs so you can miscarry. In a day or so, it will be as if it never happened. And you can get back to your normal life. A gift of the gods."

Galina contemplated the matron's words and her own destiny. The matron added, "It's your only choice."

The sorceress, a tall, scrawny woman with one off-color eye, held out a small cup. Galina's vision became suddenly hyper-aware of the room. She saw the cup in the woman's hand. She saw the shelves of drugs, potions, and herbs behind her. She saw the table, messy with experimentation, and a large waste container beside the table for failed tests.

Grabbing the cup, she said, "I was ashamed to tell you. I didn't know what to do. Am I in trouble?"

"Of course not, my dear," said the matron. "It has happened to many of your sisters. And it will happen to you again. It is just part of the risk of what we do in service to Asherah. Now drink the potion and retire to your room. You will feel sick for a while, but that is necessary for the body to expel the toxic waste in your uterus."

In the temple of Baal, babies were toxic waste in the uterus.

Suddenly, the sound of trumpets out in the streets turned everyone's heads to the window.

Galina moved with instinctual reaction. She dumped the cup's contents into the waste container as the women were looking toward the window. When they looked back at her, she held the cup to her mouth and mimicked drinking the potion. She'd been told it was bitter herbs, so she scrunched her face as if tasting the bitterness. Faking a gag, she handed the cup back to the sorceress.

The matron said, "That was the announcement of the arrival of Queen Izabel of Israel. We must attend to the royal events. Go back to your room and rest. You can get back to work in a day or so."

"Yes, mother," said Galina. And she left them for her room.

Everyone had been planning for the royal visit. There was to be much celebration and an important sacrifice.

Galina had been planning as well. If she decided to escape the temple, this might be her only opportunity, but it was definitely the only chance for her baby.

CHAPTER 34

Zarephath

Elijah and Elisha walked through the city streets to Dido's home as the time of the evening meal was fast approaching. Pestilence ravaged the city. God had protected the prophets from sickness and disease, but the boy Abibaal was very ill. He lay on a pallet in the small home awaiting death.

Elisha complained to Elijah as they walked down the street. "We have been with her these two years. Yahweh miraculously keeps her food jars full, as you promised. And yet now her son may die? It doesn't make any sense. Why won't the Lord simply heal his sickness? Why would he provide miracles to keep us alive, only to let him now die?"

Elijah stopped and glared at Elisha, who just kept on rolling out the questions that bothered him. "Why does the Lord make a drought that brings suffering to both the wicked and the righteous? How is that justice? What is the point he is trying to make?"

"I have a question for the Lord too," Elijah said. As Elisha stopped to listen, the old prophet finished, "Why won't he grant me peace and quiet from you?"

Elisha's countenance fell. Apparently, he would continue to hear no answers from his master.

Elijah said, "Let me see your hand."

Elisha raised his hand, now healed as much as it could be from that burning door latch at his parents' home. Scars across his inner knuckles still caused pain when he opened his hand too much. He lifted it for Elijah to see.

The master spread open Elisha's palm and asked, "What do you feel?"

"Pain."

"What does the pain remind you of?"

"My parents."

"Your purpose," Elijah added.

Elisha nodded agreement.

"So if it healed completely, what would you be left with to remind you?"

Elisha didn't answer. The point was made. Of course, he remembered his parents and the events. But it was the pain in his hand which brought them to active thought on a regular basis. Scars kept the memories from fading away.

He asked, "How do you hear the voice of Yahweh?"

Elijah rolled his eyes in mock irritation, "It is getting more difficult with all your chattering."

With a smile, he moved on.

When they arrived at their residence, they headed up the outside staircase to place their cloaks in the small upper chamber that was now their home. But they hadn't reached the roof when they were interrupted by Dido's wailing cry from the room below.

Rushing downstairs, they found her weeping over the still body of her son. "You are too late! He is dead! My Abibaal is dead!"

Elisha followed as Elijah moved to take a closer look at the boy. His eyes were wide open and unmoving. His skin had the white pallor of death, and no breath issued from his mouth. His life had left him.

Kneeling beside the weeping woman, Elisha moved to help her stand. "Come, Dido."

Her sobs were so deep she gasped for breath between them. She had loved Abibaal dearly. As Elisha led her away from her son's bed mat, with an arm around her back, feelings he had long suppressed and thought banished came flooding back.

Ever since the two men had become part of Dido's household, Elisha had felt an attraction to the young widow. And he had no doubts she felt the same for him. With a price on the head of every prophet of Yahweh, his master above all others, Elisha was well aware how dangerous it could be for Dido to become too personally involved in his life. He wanted to protect her, so he'd done all he could to keep a cool distance and avoid being alone with her.

But he'd come to love her son and had turned his attention to spending time with Abibaal, playing and teaching him how to become a young man. Which had only endeared Elisha even more to Dido.

Now the mere touch of his hand on her sent a shockwave of desire through him. It was embarrassing and revolting to him that in a moment of her intense suffering, he could feel such attraction.

He had tried to ignore these feelings, to suppress them. But now they had roared to life inside him. Perhaps he didn't have the spirituality it took to be a prophet of God. Maybe he was just a man of flesh after all.

Then why was he so sure he'd been called by Yahweh to this life? Was this God testing his resolve?

Reality pulled him from his thoughts as he felt Dido bolt away, running back to the bed mat. Picking up her son's body in her arms, she turned accusingly on Elijah. "What have you against me, O man of God, that you have come to me only to bring my sin to remembrance and cause the death of my son?"

Elijah's gaze was filled with deep compassion. Holding out his arms, he commanded calmly, "Give me your son."

As if in a trance, Dido stopped her sobbing and handed him the boy. Elijah carried him out of the room and up the stairs to the roof. Elisha followed silently, leaving Dido alone with her tears.

Entering the upper chamber, Elijah laid the boy's body on his own bed mat.

"What are you doing?" Elisha spoke aloud the question racing through his mind.

Elijah didn't answer. Raising his face and arms to the ceiling, he cried out, "O Yahweh, my Elohim, have you brought calamity even upon the widow with whom I sojourn by killing her son?"

Elisha stood there watching in dumbfound stillness. So Elijah didn't always know what God was doing either!

Elijah proceeded to stretch himself out over the boy's body. He prayed something under his breath Elisha couldn't hear, then pulled himself up and looked down upon Abibaal's lifeless body. No movement. No breath.

Stretching himself out again over the boy, he prayed again, then raised himself up.

A third time he stretched himself, and Elisha heard his words. "O Yahweh my Elohim, let this child's breath come into him again."

When Elijah pulled himself up off the boy, he awaited the answer. But none was forthcoming. The boy was still stone-cold dead.

Elisha looked at Elijah, the old man's shoulders dropped in apparent disbelief that there was no change in the boy. He had been so sure of Yahweh's answer.

But at that very moment, the boy snapped up as if out of a nightmare, choking and gasping for air, a healthy color quickly returned to his flesh.

The boy looked up at Elijah, who had a big grin on his face. Elisha felt his whole body burn with excitement.

Yahweh had raised Abibaal from the dead!

"Come," Elijah said to the boy. "Your mother has been waiting for you to awaken."

Looking confused, Abibaal glanced at Elisha, who gestured with a smile for him to obey the prophet. The three of them went down the stairs and entered the main chambers.

But Dido must have heard something happening because she was already standing at the door, her mouth open in silent awe and her eyes wide with shock.

"Abibaal! My Abibaal!" Running to her son, she grabbed him in her arms, lifting him off the ground, twirling around with him, kissing his forehead.

"See, your son lives!" Elijah said.

"Yes, he does," Dido cried, setting the boy down. Abibaal rushed over and hugged Elijah like a father. Dido said to him, "Now I know that you are a man of God and that the word of Yahweh in your mouth is truth."

With that, she turned as though heading for the street, pulling Abibaal along by the hand.

Elijah turned, concerned. "Where are you going, Dido?"

"To tell the world. Everyone must know!"

They followed her outside. Elijah commanded, "Dido, no!"

She stopped.

"You must tell no one."

"But why? Why would Yahweh want a miracle to be kept hidden away?"

"It is not the right time."

Elisha suddenly noticed there was a flood of people at the end of the alley, making their way down the street with donkeys, carts, and horses. He stepped forward to intercept a middle-aged man who had just emerged from the neighboring house, dressed for travel with a staff and carrying bag. "Where is everyone going?"

The man said, "Have you not heard the announcement? Queen Izabel is visiting Tyre. There is to be a public gathering and announcement on the morrow."

Elisha looked at Elijah. "Is she still looking for us?"

"I don't know," answered the prophet. "Let's go find out."

Find out? They'd been in hiding from that wicked queen for three years, and now Elijah just wanted to traipse right up to her in Tyre and find out if she was still after them?

The crazy notions of Elijah never seemed to end.

CHAPTER 35

Tyre

Izabel led Athaliah along with Hamilqart and some guards to a clifftop overlooking the Mediterranean Sea. Her father Ethbaal was nearby, looking out onto the horizon as he contemplated statecraft or religion or some other topic of importance. He'd often taken Izabel here to be alone with nothing but the sound of waves crashing below them. He always said he could think more clearly here than cooped up in the palace.

Leaving the high priest and his guards, Izabel walked over to her father with Athaliah following. He turned as if aware of their presence. A smile spread across his austere face, and he held his arms open wide. Izabel ran to him and embraced him. And kissed him. On the mouth as was their family custom. It was a deep kiss, as was father and daughter's personal custom.

Ethbaal said, "I have missed you so, my daughter."

"And I you, my father. Terribly so."

The king noticed Athaliah standing at a distance. "I see you brought your lovely ward."

Izabel held out her hand for Athaliah to join them. The little girl bounded up like an excited puppy. "I am teaching her everything. As you taught me."

"Excellent. So Judah will also one day become enlightened."

Ethbaal looked past her to Hamilqart, who had remained at a distance, watching them with intensity. "I see your blood hound remains ever-vigilant in his devotion."

Izabel smiled. "He remains crucial to my plans. Father, we have much to catch up on."

Ethbaal gestured. "Come, let us walk."

As they strolled along the cliffside, Athaliah stayed close behind, listening to everything spoken.

Izabel said to her father, "I am afraid my journey is not without self-interest."

Ethbaal replied, "If it was, I would consider my training of you a failure."

They shared a smile. Then Izabel sobered and told him the bad news.

"Damascus bandits are pillaging Israel's caravans. We are starving to death, father."

Ethbaal considered her implication, then said, "Ahab has a capable army. Has he done nothing?"

"Fighting a war is direct," she answered. "Playing hide and seek with desert rats is not so simple. Father, please contact Ben-hadad and have him call off his bandits. For me?"

He looked at her. "That would risk Ahab discovering my secret treaty with Damascus, your sworn enemy." Ahab had never discovered Ethbaal's double-dealing with Ben-hadad. Izabel had made sure of it.

"Then at least give us provisional aid." Izabel worried she was sounding desperate. Never sound desperate in negotiations with a king, even if the king was your father.

"My dear," Ethbaal said, "I would gladly grant you resources, but this drought has affected us all. Baal does not seem to hear our cries."

"I am not asking for charity."

"Admirable," he replied.

"But," she said, "a life-sustaining loan would surely increase Ahab's indebtedness to Tyre. A debt that will grow with time."

"Cunning," he mused.

"As for waking the gods to stop this drought," Izabel finished, "I am here for a sacrifice of appeasement."

"Ingenious!" he concluded.

• • • • •

Qedeshim helped put the finishing touches of make-up on Izabel's face in her preparation room at Asherah's temple. She looked into the mirror with satisfaction, then placed her hand on her ivory carving of the Woman at the Window and prayed to Astarte for blessing.

Izabel was wearing the headdress of high priestess, a lovely purple conical ateph with a uraeus on the front and ostrich feathers on the side. The high priestess represented the goddess, so she wore the crown of deity.

A towel wrapped around her, she stood up and faced Hamilqart. As they looked into each other's eyes, she felt the flame of years past rise within her. She dropped the towel to the floor to receive the high priestess's robe.

She saw the gaze of his eyes hunger for her body, but he dared not touch the queen without invitation. She turned around, and he slipped the purple satin robe on her. Hamilqart stood behind her as she looked at herself in the mirror.

"This will be like old times when we served together."

Izabel shook her head. "Times have changed, Hamilqart."

He turned her around and leaned in close to her face. "Izabel, do you deny what we shared together? What we *were* together?"

He had become bold. It was what she had liked about him.

"You tell me times have changed," he continued. "That you have no interest in past appetites. But I don't believe you."

She turned back around toward the mirror, pulling herself away from him.

"We shared god, body, and soul," he went on. "That doesn't just vanish because you are queen. Tell me it doesn't."

She didn't want him to see her emotions and vulnerability. "I've already told you what must be."

Hamilqart moved right up to her back, leaning his face to her ear. When she didn't wince or withdraw, he whispered with passion, "I know you too are haunted by the memory of our love. Why limit yourself from what the king need never discover?"

He turned her around to face him again and knelt down on one knee, kissing her ring. "I will do anything for you." His voice cracked. "If I cannot have you, I will die."

Izabel hesitated to look him in the eyes, fearful of what he might see in hers. She sighed. "Hamilqart, your obsession is flattering."

She kept him wondering and moved over to the table to pour wine into a pair of goblets. "And you have helped me solve a problem."

She offered him a goblet. Saw his curiosity. He drank deeply.

She told him a story. "When I was a child, I had an older sister. Her name was Elissa. She was Ethbaal's first-born. She shared everything with me. We were inseparable. Blood-sisters. Then one day a calamity arose in Tyre. I don't even know what it was. I was too young to understand."

She noticed Hamilqart had turned pale and sweaty. She continued, "And then my father took my sister away. He sacrificed her to Baal to save the city. That was when I first learned human sacrifice was our custom in the face of great adversity. At that moment, I feared my father and his god. But when I grew and understood, that fear became my strength when I realized that power is built upon the sacrifice of love."

Hamilqart was now feeling so light-headed he had to sit down on the chair.

She said, "You say if you cannot have me, you will die."

He could barely focus on her or her words.

"You are a first-born, Hamilqart, are you not?"

Terror slowly dawned in his eyes through the drug induced stupor. The poisoned goblet slipped from his palsied hand, striking the floor.

Confident that all was now as she had planned, she turned away and placed the tiny vial of black henbane on the table.

Darkness swallowed him as he fell to the floor.

CHAPTER 36

Izabel walked through the temple of Baal with Athaliah at her side, showing the young girl the beautiful display of Tyrian craftsmanship that their own temple in Jezreel was based upon. They joined the Tyre high priest of Baal and his retinue of priests on their way to the sacrifice. Now ten, the young girl had finally been deemed old enough to watch the celebration up close.

Izabel wore her high priestess garments, her ateph still fixed firmly on her head. Athaliah was dressed as a priestess in a white linen robe with her hair beneath a skull cap. In contrast with Izabel's four golden necklaces, the girl wore a simple necklace of beaded pearls.

They walked from the priest quarters through the holy place and out to the temple gates, where a vast audience from the coastal cities of Phoenicia had assembled to plead to the storm god for mercy in the face of the drought and famine. The crowd was less than Izabel had expected, but she quickly banished any negative thinking. So many had already died while others were so broken from their suffering that the numbers were simply less. Only a few thousand instead of the crowd of ten thousand she remembered from years ago.

But faith and hope were alive as the crowd cheered the arrival of the high priest and high priestess. They were to offer a *Mulk Adam* sacrifice to Baal in order to save their people from the drought. It was Phoenician tradition to sacrifice first-born children of royalty at such dire times like this in order to appease the gods and plead for mercy.

·····

The qedeshim quarters inside the temple of Astarte were empty. Everyone was serving in the celebration—everyone except Galina, who got up from her bed mat and grabbed the small sack of food and necessities she'd hidden in preparation for this moment. Opening the door to the chambers, she looked both ways down the hall. Empty. Nothing but the sound of distant drums pounding away at the temple of Baal. She slipped out into the hall and made her way to her planned destination.

• • • • •

The drums pounded out a heavy beat in conjunction with the hypnotic rhythm of other instruments as Izabel approached the altar. She saw the supine form of Hamilqart laid out on the altar in a simple sacrificial white robe. He would be the first offering.

Following the high priest up the steps, she approached the altar stone. Hamilqart came out of his groggy, drug-induced stupor. Looking around, he discovered his predicament.

A small part of Izabel, deep in her heart, felt pity for the man she was about to offer up. As he'd argued earlier, they *had* shared gods, bodies, and souls. He *had* been a great comfort to her in her youth.

Now he would be a comfort to her future. This sacrifice would solve two problems for her: the drought on the land and the jealousy in her marriage. Hamilqart's relentless desire for her was becoming increasingly apparent and would threaten her relationship with the king. She could not let it continue.

• • • • •

Galina moved swiftly down the empty street toward the public stables. Dressed in the simple robe of a qedesha, she fought to maintain a controlled pace and calm appearance. Her plans would be instantly ended if someone were to observe her and sense the desperation of her flight.

She made it inside one of the stables and breathed a sigh of relief. Now to find a horse for her getaway. The only two places she knew well in life were Samaria and Dan. Neither seemed a great choice. Samaria would mean returning to her sister with new shame upon her previous shame. She hadn't listened to Jehu and Susanna, and now look where she'd ended up. She was unforgivable.

Dan was no better. It was the hometown of her husband's family. But they'd all been killed, and it was unlikely she would find others there that would accept her. Dan might as well be any foreign city. Right now, all she could think of was that she had to get away, no matter what. If she died in the wilderness, so be it. Maybe she deserved that anyway.

But what about her innocent child inside her? Should he suffer for the sins of his mother?

As she began to search the stables for a suitable horse, her nervous energy seemed to transfer to the animals. Skittish behaviors and a general restlessness seemed to move through the stalls as she sought the right horse for her escape ride.

She found her. An Arabian mare, strong and beautiful, who seemed calm at her presence. Petting the animal, she whispered, "Girl, we will rescue each other from this city."

Galina was looking around for the horse's saddle when she was interrupted by the voice of a guard. "What have we here... a pretty little qedesha in my stable. A gift from the gods for our pleasure!"

She turned to see not one, but two guards watching her from the stable entrance. Grabbing her sack, she ran in the opposite direction.

The guards gave chase.

•••••

A dozen priests lined up behind Izabel at the altar. Athaliah watched from the temple steps. The percussive drums ended and a large choir of priests and priestesses began to sing a beautiful operatic chorus. As Izabel moved close to Hamilqart, the voices increased in intensity and glory. The crowd below joined in the singing.

This was beautiful, fitting praise for Hamilqart. He would be missed. His loving affection. His sexual vitality.

Izabel looked down upon her high priest, helplessly tied up and staring at her with frightened, shock-filled eyes. Struggling with the ropes, he pleaded, "Izabel!"

Ignoring his plea, Izabel raised a large ornamental sacrificial dagger above her head and prayed to the skies with a loud enough voice for the entire audience to hear. "O Baal, we sacrifice this first-born child of Tyre to end this drought and save our lives!"

Hamilqart froze. He now called out to her from his broken heart. "Izabel."

She plunged the knife down.

•••••

159

Galina ran into a civic building. She didn't know what it was. She didn't care, the pursuing guards were closing in on her. She didn't know where to go or where she could hide. She could only think that she'd been discovered and now was not going to escape the city. She was going to lose her baby to this monstrous system that had betrayed her.

• • • • •

Out on the altar of Baal, heavy drums returned and competed with the exultation of the crowd. Elijah and Elisha stood incognito in the audience. They'd traveled to Tyre to see for themselves the evil horror they now witnessed. This was what it all led to, what idolatry led to: human sacrifice. Judah already had the bloodguilt of passing their sons and daughters through the fires of Molech. Now Israel would become seduced by this spiritual harlot queen into the same abomination. It was only a matter of time.

Elisha was close enough to see the orgasmic pleasure in the queen's reaction. Her chest heaved. She raised the bloody blade above her head again to the cheers of the mob around them.

The abomination was only beginning.

• • • • •

Galina exited the back of the civic building she was running through. She found herself in an alley full of trash. It was a dead end. She'd run herself into a corner. She heard the guards not far away, trampling through the marble hallways toward her.

They would be upon her in seconds.

There was one way out of the alley and it was blocked by a donkey-drawn cart overflowing with rotting garbage. Galina felt vomit rise in her throat at the smell, but thanked Yahweh for this opportunity.

She climbed onto the pile and burrowed her way beneath the stinking refuse. She was barely out of sight when she heard the footsteps arrive at the alleyway and stop. She heard the male voices complaining about the stench and then about losing their quarry. Then nothing.

Had they gone?

She heard footsteps approaching the cart. They must have figured out her ploy. She prepared to be discovered.

But footsteps were different. And they climbed onto the cart's front seat. She heard curses and the crack of a whip. It was the garbage collector. The donkey brayed, and the cart pulled out of the alleyway on its way to the garbage dump outside the city. She was saved.

· · · · ·

Priests carried the corpse of Hamilqart into the holy of holies of the house of Baal. They laid his body on the outstretched arms of the bronze image and stoked the fires in the pit below. The mechanical arms moved downward, and the body rolled into the flaming pit.

Back on the altar of Baal, Izabel cried out, "Mighty Baal, hear our prayers and stop this calamity of drought!"

Elisha saw the line of several dozen noble women below the altar, holding infants in their arms and the hands of young children beside them. They wore their best clothes as a sign of their status. Purple satin, embroidered linen, jewelry of precious gems and metals. It was the offspring of the noble caste that would most satisfy this bloodthirsty god.

Elisha could see the faces of the parents, a mixture of hope and fear. They really believed that what they were doing would appease the gods, but they were terrified to give their children up. It struck Elisha that when a people did not worship Yahweh, their true creator, there was no end of possibility to the evil they would perform. No atrocity too grim they would not justify. This was the consequence of turning away from the Creator.

A mother handed her two-year old child to the high priest, who carried the poor victim up to the altar to be received by other priests. The toddler was place upon the stone of sacrifice. Its cries could barely be heard above the crowd.

Jezebel raised her knife again, her eyes full of delirious ecstasy.

Elisha turned away. He couldn't bear the sight. As the crowd cheered, he couldn't help but think of the lives of countless children who'd been offered up for the idolatrous convenience of this wicked culture. How could mothers do this to their own children? How could a people believe that this was a sacred right? Elisha's body felt the chill of spiritual wickedness all around them. And he knew with certainty, despite his failures or personal struggles, regardless of what the enemies of Yahweh might do to him, he would embrace his calling to be a prophet like never before.

He looked over at Elijah, who said with a solemn face, "It is time to return to Samaria."

CHAPTER 37

Samaria

Ahab gripped his sword tight and lunged at Jehu. The commander blocked the king's every move with relative ease. Jehu was a master of the sword, and Ahab was no match for him as a sparring partner. They had first paired up for combat practice many years ago in their youth, and the king trusted Jehu completely. Ahab liked the challenge and desired to improve his sword skills, but ruling a nation rarely allowed time for serious training.

Jehu returned Ahab's volley with some restrained thrusts that Ahab managed to block. "Good, good! Keep your guard up even on the offense. See my eyes."

But Ahab could barely keep up. He appeared exhausted to Jehu. He launched into a last burst of desperate swinging, trying to overwhelm his opponent.

The commander sent Ahab to the ground as a lesson in impatience. He placed his sword point at the king's throat. "Desperation provides opportunity for betrayal."

The thought suddenly intruded into Jehu's mind how easy it would be to take his defeated opponent's life with just one simple plunge.

Ahab caught his breath. "Your loyalty is only outdone by your skill, my Jehu."

Jehu pulled the blade. "My skill is at the service of my loyalty, O king."

"Well then," quipped Ahab, "help your king up or suffer my wrath!"

With a smile, Jehu helped the king up. They walked over to a servant who held a water jug and a tray with two cups.

Ahab said, "I want you and Obadiah to help me look for more water sources outside the city walls."

"That is not something you should be doing, my lord. Leave it to us."

163

"Nonsense," said the king. "My people need water. It's something I can do to actually help them rather than sitting on my throne barking out commands."

"Yes, my lord."

The servant poured water into two cups and handed them to Jehu and Ahab. The king took a long drink before directing a hard look at the steward. The man looked fidgety and nervous, though that wasn't unusual for those who found themselves in the presence of the often-intemperate king.

"Your name is David, is it not?" Ahab asked.

The steward twitched with apprehension and his voice became unsteady. "Yes, your highness."

"Obadiah tells me he caught you siphoning water from the palace and selling it to peasants in the city."

The servant glanced at Jehu, then down to the floor.

Ahab demanded, "Did you do this?"

The servant couldn't look him in the eye. He shook with uncontrolled fear. Ahab shouted, "Answer me!"

"I was trying to help friends and family, my lord," the steward confessed.

Ahab disagreed. "You were exploiting your privilege for profit."

"I won't do it again, your highness. I swear on my life."

Ahab set his cup back onto the servant's platter. The man's shaking hand could barely keep the water jug from spilling.

Without warning, Ahab plunged his sword into the servant's belly. Platter, jug, and cups crashed to the floor, spilling the water everywhere. A low grunt escaped the servant's lips as terror filled his eyes. As the king withdrew the sword, the man collapsed clutching his fatal wound.

Ahab said to Jehu, "It appears desperation does indeed provide opportunity for betrayal."

Jehu didn't disagree. In the midst of a drought that was killing the populace, stealing from the royal rations was treason. Though the king might have been more merciful in his punishment. A gut wound was a slow, painful way to die.

Behind him, Jehu heard a woman's voice respond to the king's comment.

"Well, then, my king had better renew his servants' loyalty oaths."

It was Izabel. She had returned from Tyre.

"My queen of heaven!" exclaimed the king. "How I've missed your sassy presence."

He went to embrace her. Jehu looked down on the dying servant, blood pooling on the floor around him as he moaned in agony. Gritting his teeth, Jehu thrust his sword into the heart of the young man, killing him quickly before walking over to the two royal lovebirds, who were indulging in a passionate greeting.

"It is good to be home," Izabel said.

"It is good to have you home and alone to myself," Ahab responded with another fervent embrace. He looked around with feigned surprise. "Where is my sister? And your high priest? They seem to follow you like two shadows."

"Your sister has gone to her quarters to rest from the journey," Izabel responded calmly. "As to Hamilqart, he will not be returning. He is dead."

Surprise flashed in Ahab's eyes and before he could find his words, Jehu's questions voiced his own thoughts, "Dead? How did this happen? When?"

"He was executed after he tried to seduce me."

"What?" shouted Ahab.

Izabel answered her husband in a calculated, smooth voice, her head turned slightly toward Jehu with accusation flaring in her eyes, "A man of divided loyalties is not to be trusted."

Jehu felt her words piercing like a sharp dagger. Was the queen speaking of her erstwhile high priest, or did she have suspicions of his own conflicted emotions?

Ahab shook with rage. "I would have cut out his heart and cast him into the fire."

Izabel smiled and stroked Ahab's cheek. "Then you and I are of one mind, my love, because that is exactly what I did."

Ahab calmed and said, "Jehu, the queen and I must spend some time together reacquainting ourselves. I will meet you later with Obadiah to find that water, and curse Deber and Resheph!"

Deber and Resheph were the gods of pestilence and plague.

Ahab escorted his queen from the room. Jehu nodded in acknowledgment as they walked away, passing the lifeless servant on the floor. Jehu's eyes landed on the corpse as he mentally replayed the conversation.

CHAPTER 38

In the valley west of Samaria, Jehu and Obadiah oversaw the search for new water sources. A dozen men worked with divining rods, attempting to sense the pull of underground water. The kingdom urgently needed new wells with new sources of water. After three years of drought, most of the wells in the cities were running low or already dried up. Desperation was rampant among the residents. Ahab was losing control. If they didn't find more water soon, the king might find himself barricaded in the palace protecting himself from his own citizens.

Jehu saw two cloaked figures approaching at a distance. He quickly mounted up to investigate the newcomers. Drawing his sword, he kicked his horse and galloped toward them, looking around for a surprise attack.

When he arrived at the figures, he stopped and called out, "Identify yourselves! This is the territory of King Ahab!"

As the two new arrivals pulled down their hoods, Jehu recognized the prophet and his student.

"Elijah, what are you doing here? The king has just recently sent new scouts to all the nations seeking you."

Obadiah's voice behind Jehu added, "The queen will have you killed if she knows you are here. And no doubt kill Jehu and me for not turning you in."

"Fear not, good men," Elijah said. "Trust in Yahweh."

Jehu said, "Obadiah is right. If I do not arrest you, I will be executed for treason."

Elijah said, "Then arrest us and bring us to the king."

Jehu stood there dumbfounded. He wanted to object, but could find no words.

Elijah went on, "The king will not allow me to be killed."

"But the queen will," Obadiah countered.

Jehu agreed with the palace administrator. "Ahab serves two masters, Yahweh and Baal. There is no telling which he will obey."

"And how many masters do *you* serve, Jehu?" inquired Elijah.

The question pierced Jehu. His heart raced. How? How could the prophet know of this battle that raged within his soul?

Elijah's next words snapped Jehu out of his quandary. "Fear not. I don't even think the queen will want to kill me when she hears my offer."

Offer? thought Jehu. *What could he possibly offer?*

* * * * *

"Prophet, you *are* mad!" Izabel's words echoed in the throne room.

Jehu had brought Elijah and Elisha to the king. For the moment, the prophets were still safe and alive and granted audience. They stood boldly representing Yahweh, surrounded by fifty prophets of Baal which lined the room.

Ahab was incredulous. Jehu was incredulous. Everyone was.

Ahab shook his finger at the prophet. "You are the troublemaker of Israel."

He took a deep breath to calm himself. After a moment to consider further, he turned to Izabel, "Perhaps this is a good thing. It could settle matters once and for all. What do you say, my queen?"

Jehu watched carefully the exchange between king and queen. She had far too much influence over him in Jehu's opinion. And then he saw it, a slight trembling in Elijah's hand. The elder prophet moved his arm casually behind his back, as though nothing were amiss.

Izabel's eyes blazed in undisguised hatred for the two prophets of Yahweh. "Challenge accepted!" her words rang out, full of confidence. The king smiled at his wife. Victory was at hand.

She said, "We will meet at Mount Carmel in one week, as you requested. You with your prophets, I with mine. And the king will see which god answers our sacrifice."

Jehu saw Izabel's grim lips turn slowly into a smirk as she added, "But I am concerned that winning the contest will not settle the dispute permanently. So I propose that the prophets who win execute the prophets who lose. Winner kills all."

Ahab let out a breath of excitement. "Oh." The king tended to be drawn to spectacle with morbid curiosity.

Elijah swallowed, then bowed. "My king. Yahweh's will be done."

The prophet and his student turned and walked down the long throne room in silence.

Izabel was near giddy with overconfidence as she spoke quietly to the king, "Mount Carmel is Baal's holy mountain. I have four hundred and fifty prophets of Baal and four hundred prophets of Asherah who eat at my table. All the prophets of Yahweh are dead. Elijah is alone. My dear husband, soon Israel will be freed from fanatical religion."

Could that possibly be true? Jehu wondered, *or was Izabel's fanatical religion about to replace Yahwism and control the nation?*

CHAPTER 39

Terqa, Syria

Baal and Anat approached the town of Terqa on the Euphrates River in Syria. The moon and stars overhead lit up the landscape with a blue haze. They had returned from Mot's Pit in Sheol and were on their way to get Baal's weapons, Chaser and Driver, from the temple of Dagon in the city.

With those two weapons, Baal would be able to bring storm upon the land again. Yahweh had suppressed the rain through Elijah the prophet, and it was making the storm god look bad. Baal needed to reassert his power over his inheritance. But it wasn't going to be easy.

In the days of King David, Baal had betrayed Dagon to the archangels, who imprisoned him in the earth. Another Watcher had stepped in to assume the identity of the missing Dagon. But he knew what Baal had done. Holding onto Baal's weapons of power, Chaser and Driver, was part and parcel of keeping that assumed identity intact. This new Dagon had doubtless heard about Anat's successful rescuing of Baal and the storm god's plans to regain control over Israel. So Baal and Anat fully expected to meet the vengeful deity head on.

Terqa was a large city with walls and a moat. Unseen and unheard by the few humans around them, Baal and Anat climbed the double gate entrance and strode right up to the temple of Dagon in the center of the city.

The goddess Ishara stood at the entrance to the temple. She was the wife of Dagon and a fertility deity like her husband. But, she was also a war goddess and carried a double-headed mace.

"So, you're answering the call of Queen Izabel to Mount Carmel, are you?" she said derisively. "Going to show Elijah who the true storm god is?"

Baal and Anat shared a glance of confusion. They had been in Sheol a long time and didn't know what she was talking about, but they didn't let on.

"Call your husband," Baal responded. "I've come for Chaser and Driver."

Ishara barked, "I don't need my husband's approval. The weapons are staying in his temple. Go back to Canaan with your incestuous slut of a sister."

"Are you going to let her talk about me like that?" Anat said under her breath. She drew her sickle swords and began to twirl them in an intimidating fashion.

Baal surmised that Ishara had been referring to some kind of contest between Elijah and Izabel and their gods. He was going to need his weapons more than ever.

He muttered, "I will teach this bitch goddess who is the Most High."

The sound of large wings in the air, caused Baal and Anat to see who else approached. Two goddesses landed nearby, their leathery wings quickly folded up and rested behind their backs.

Ishtar and Ereshkigal were sisters, the Babylonian Queen of Heaven and Queen of the Underworld respectively. They were mighty Mesopotamian divinities, and they looked ready to do battle. Both wore their horned helmets of deity and body armor. Ishtar carried a scimitar and was followed by a lion, her daemon guardian. She was an ancient warrior with more experience than Anat.

Ereshkigal was the dark, powerful wife of Nergal, the underworld god of plagues. She was not Baal's equal, but she carried Chaser, his mighty spear.

Baal had never been on the receiving end of Chaser's heavenly fire.

Three gods verses two, and Baal without his weapons. The odds were not looking good. But the ladies of the opposition sure looked good to Baal. He would rape them after he defeated them, it would make the victory even more satisfying.

"Where are your husbands?" he insulted the goddesses. "Should you not be home pleasing them?"

"And where is your consort Astarte?" countered Ishtar, remaining calm despite Baal's taunt. "Is she cuckolding you?"

"Why do you oppose us?" Baal's voice rang out. "Return my weapons and we will leave. You need not suffer." A cackling laughter rang back and Baal found his patience evaporating.

The goddesses laughed. It sounded like cackling to Baal. He was becoming impatient.

"Come and take them, big boy," Ereshkigal suggested.

Baal said to Anat, "Sister, it's time we show these river rats our family unity."

"Are you so sure of your family?" said Ishtar. "Where is Astarte?"

Baal paused at the comment. What did she mean—*are you so sure?* Why did she keep bringing up Astarte? Was she referring to Anat's rivalry with Baal's consort? Did she not know that Baal had sent Astarte to Judah for his purposes?

Ishtar made a move toward Anat. Her daemon guardian ran toward Baal. The great cat pounced on her prey.

He rolled in the dirt with the great feline. The king of beasts against the king of gods. The monster's muscular strength was impressive, its teeth and claws razor sharp. Baal grunted with pain as the lion swiped at his chest and leg, leaving two bloody sets of gashes.

When the lion moved to claw him again, Baal was faster. He maneuvered to the side and grasped the mane, pulling himself onto the back of the cat. He reached around and grabbed the upper and lower jaws in his mighty bare hands.

With a shout, Baal pulled open the jaws of the great lion. The beast growled from deep in its throat. It tried to resist, but Baal's strength was mightier. The loud sound of bones cracking ended with Baal ripping its mouth asunder. Ishtar screamed with pain as her daemon companion suffered in Baal's hands. The lion whimpered and fell to his feet as Baal's war cry rang out in triumph.

Anat used that moment of Ishtar's weakness to launch a forceful attack of her double swords upon the goddess. Ishtar was a skilled warrior, but Anat was a whirlwind of youthful fury, and her two swords swung with speed and precision at the goddess. Her rapid succession of strikes had been skillfully countered by Ishtar, but the Babylonian goddess was barely keeping up. Anat continued her furious attack and had Ishtar backed up against the stairs.

Standing up, Baal grimaced in pain. He was losing a lot of blood from his wound. But he focused his hatred upon Ereshkigal. He could still rip her apart as well.

Anat's youthful speed and passion had been overwhelming to Ishtar. But Anat felt herself slowing down. Her strength was ebbing. She had burned up her energy too quickly. Ishtar noticed the fatigue of her opponent and mustered a rally. Using technique over passion, she began to turn the tables on her foe. Ishtar was in no hurry. She was strategic. Anat became defensive with her blades.

Before Baal could reach Ereshkigal to grab her, she held Chaser to the sky. With a surge of power, it drew fire from heaven like a lightning rod. She pointed it at Baal, and released the powerful strike. Baal was blasted back, surprised by the intensity and force she had managed to wield against him.

Forcing Anat back, the Babylonian goddess managed to disarm Anat of a sword, leaving her with only one. Anat continued to battle on as her own fears flared in the knowledge that she might not be able to turn this around.

Baal was flat on his back in the dust. He could still feel the energy of the blast he'd received surging through his body, making his mighty muscles freeze in seizure.

And before he could gather together his strength, he saw Ereshkigal standing over him in victory, his own spear pointed at him, ready to finish him off.

Anat's emotions swirled to new extremes as she glimpsed Baal's precarious position. The thought of losing him superseded the idea that her own failure was inevitable. Distracted, she tripped. She fell and lay on the ground, vulnerable and open. Ishtar stood above her, sword raised for its victory plunge.

Just as Baal's vision and strength were coming back, Ereshkigal raised the spear for her final thrust into his chest. He knew he could not escape the pending strike.

Then Baal saw her jerked back as if by a supernatural force. The underworld goddess landed in an explosion of dust several yards away, the spear no longer in hand.

Baal looked up to see Mikael the archangel standing above him.

He looked over and saw Ishtar skewered by the two swords of Uriel, who within seconds had the goddess cut down and on the ground.

What in the cosmos are archangels doing here? Are they going to fight us too?

Baal saw Mikael withdraw his sword from Ereshkigal's sternum.

Then, quick as a wink, the two archangels disappeared.

They'd left. And were nowhere in sight.

Was this a trick?

Baal and Anat looked at each other, wordlessly searching for an answer. She shook her head. No idea. Two archangels had just helped Baal and Anat defeat Ishtar and Ereshkigal. Then they'd fled without explanation.

This was not the time to try and puzzle out the mystery of what happened.

Snatching up his spear Chaser from where it had fallen, Baal said, "This is our opportunity."

They sprinted toward Dagon's temple. There was still Driver to retrieve. Anat's movement of retrieving her sword while running appeared effortless. She felt energized again, prepared to face Ishara. Was Dagon inside with her? Were they running into an ambush?

But Ishara and Dagon would not be fighting them today.

Their decapitated bodies lay in the temple courtyard.

Anat finally voiced the question hounding them both. "What in the heavens is going on around here?"

Baal's mighty shoulders rose and fell in a shrug. "This day is full of surprises. Our allies fighting us. Archangels defending us."

"What's next?" Anat asked. "Yahweh throwing us a party?"

"I don't have time to ponder paradoxes," Baal replied. "I need to get Driver, and I need to get to Mount Carmel before it's too late."

The war hammer would be hidden in a secret passageway in the temple sanctuary. But as he followed his memories to Driver's hiding place, Baal couldn't stop thinking about what Ishtar had blurted out at him. It sounded like an enigmatic code. *Are you so sure of your family? Where is Astarte?*

What did that mean? What did Ishtar know about Astarte? Had Baal's own consort somehow betrayed him? He would have to find out later. Like he'd said, he had no time to stop and ponder. They were needed at Mount Carmel.

CHAPTER 40

Mount Carmel

The early morning sun cast long shadows and bathed the Mount Carmel peninsula in a blanket of orange. On the southwest side, a caravan of a thousand Israelites made their way in the dawning light up the mountain to the high place situated a thousand feet above the valley. Ahab had called on the people to gather and witness this contest of the gods. Elijah was to stand off against the prophets of Baal and Asherah to see whose god would answer the call when they sacrificed.

Izabel sat with Ahab in their closed traveling carriage as they led the caravan up the mountain pass. Ahab was asleep, snoring like a pig. Izabel could stand the obnoxious noise no longer.

She shook him. "Husband, wake up."

He coughed and sputtered, opening his bleary eyes. "Are we there?"

"No. But your snoring is offensively loud."

"Oh, sorry."

"I've been thinking," said Izabel. "When this contest is over and Elijah loses, we need to discuss giving Baal a more exclusive position in Israel. What do you think, my lord?"

Ahab smiled. "I think you are relentless, woman. But your point is well taken. This is a moment of truth. A crossroads."

The carriage stopped. Izabel felt impatient. She opened the curtain to see Jehu on his horse beside them.

"Why have we stopped again, commander?"

Jehu said, "We have arrived, my queen."

"Is Elijah here?"

"Not yet."

"I wouldn't be surprised if he doesn't show up at all."

Izabel whipped the curtain shut.

The gathering crowd of Israelites massed on a large flat field before the high place, a stone open-air platform with an altar in the center. The people made themselves comfortable as they awaited the promised spectacle. Above the fray of commoners, Izabel stood and watched the valley below. Nearby, servants labored to erect the royal tent. Near the high place, they set up two portable thrones for the king and queen to observe the contest.

Squinting, Izabel spied two lone figures far below, hiking their way up the mountainside. She turned to her new high priest of Baal, an older bearded Tyrian man named Hannibal. "Assemble the prophets."

• • • • •

Pushing upward on the mountain path toward their destination, Elijah and Elisha heard the sound of ram's horns.

"That's the call to assembly for their prophets," Elisha said.

"I know, I know," Elijah answered irritably, pausing to catch his breath.

Elisha looked at Elijah's left hand. It was trembling again. The prophet hid it in his cloak with a scolding look. "The bane of old age returns."

"You didn't have it when we were safe in Zarephath."

Elijah pushed past him without responding.

• • • • •

The Night Before

Baal and Anat had run the whole way from the Euphrates River in Syria to the Jezreel Valley in Israel. They were supernatural, and they were faster than horses. But they were not all-powerful. They were created beings with limitations, and even they had to rest to regain their strength. This was their fourth day, and they had a mere forty miles to go to the summit of Mount Carmel. They would rest for the night and make the last of their trek tomorrow, renewed for the heavenly contest.

Watchers did not sleep in the human sense. They would enter into a trance-like state that approximated sleep, but was more like disembodied access to the spiritual realm. As Baal lay in that state under the moon in the valley, he was alerted to a feeling of being sexually aroused. But why?

Looking around, he saw Anat nearby. She was caught up in her own ecstatic trance. He looked out and saw a large terebinth tree in the distance. A figure sat up against the tree. He sensed it wasn't an enemy. It was a woman— a naked woman. Her words seemed to whisper in his ears, she called for him to come to her. He stood up, immersed in the haze of his trance-like state. He moved quietly past Anat as she slept on, through the brush and bushes toward the ever-beckoning figure at the tree.

He'd also left Chaser and Driver behind.

Arriving at the foot of the large tree, Baal recognized the enticing woman: Lilith the night creature. She was indeed naked in all her voluptuous beauty. Legend had it that she was the first wife of Adam, but had been kicked out of the Garden for being assertive and unwilling to submit. In truth, she was a Watcher. Like all "female" gods, she was a male who'd mutilated his body to fabricate the form of a goddess. They were all playing roles after all.

Baal didn't care. She enticed and his body was responding. All he wanted now was to satisfy his sexual urges. It didn't matter who or what. Lilith would do. He would force her if he had to.

"What do you want me to do?" she asked him in her enchanting whisper.

His eyes locked onto her, while an Anzu bird cawed overhead. He took off his clothes. His breathing became rapid. His thoughts focused on one thing.

He barely noticed the dark shadow of movement around the base of the tree. He could only see, hear, and smell what he wanted to take. And he moved to take her.

She gasped with her lips barely opened as if frightened, but also excited. As if she wanted to be ravaged.

At least that was how he imagined it in his mind. In his fevered, enchanted mind.

Before he could lean in and even touch her, he felt his body wrapped in a coil that climbed his torso.

The spell broke!

It was a huge serpent. Its black coils were pure muscle. Even Baal with all his strength couldn't release himself from the vise grip that bound his entire body and squeezed the breath out of him.

Lilith said in her haunting voice, "Meet my little friend, Ningishzida."

With each exhale, Baal felt the coil tighten, making his breathing more and more difficult.

Lilith grinned, a blood-thirsty smile. Her fangs descended and gave her mouth a venomous appearance.

The serpent opened its mouth wide over Baal's head.

Baal blacked out.

• • • • •

Elisha and Elijah arrived at the plateau of Mount Carmel. Jehu greeted them, and escorted the prophets onward with a small guard of ten soldiers. The Israelites watched in silence, eager for the showdown to begin. They walked up to the high place, the area designated for sacrifice.

The stone platform was several hundred feet square with a stone altar at the center. A wooden asherah had been erected beside the altar, a five-foot diameter faux tree standing thirty-feet high. Its golden branches up at the top glinted in the morning sun. Hundreds of prophets of Baal stood in quiet formation, filling the platform.

Elisha looked over and saw the king and queen on their portable thrones. Jehu led the prophet to stand before them.

Elijah bowed before the king and Elisha bowed with him.

Jezebel seized the opportunity to speak first. "Welcome to Baal's mountain, Elijah." She looked around as if seeking for others, then said, "And where might the prophets of Yahweh be?"

Elisha glared at her with hatred in every fiber of his being. She had murdered the prophets of Yahweh years ago.

Elijah responded to her, "O Queen Jezebel, I see you brought your prophets of Baal. But where might the prophets of Asherah be?"

Her face flushed with anger. Elisha knew her rage was pricked by the way Elijah pronounced her name. The young protégé would be sure to continue that practice when he began his own prophetic ministry.

Jezebel's mouth twisted into a snide smirk, "Since this is a pissing match between male gods, let them fight it out. We women and goddesses will take the opportunity to observe —and enjoy the entertainment."

Elijah said, "Then where is Athaliah? Surely you want her to learn from this important event."

Jezebel hissed, "Prophet, I do not want to hear her name on your tongue again, or I will cut it out. Do you understand?"

Ahab spoke quietly to her, a hint of warning in his tone, "Izabel, you know full well he is not threatening Athaliah."

She sat back in her throne, and with a sarcastic voice said, "Forgive my overzealous devotion to your family, my lord."

Ahab rolled his eyes.

Elijah bowed. "My lord and lady." He gestured to Elisha to stay put and walked over to the high place.

He mounted the steps, and when he did, the prophets of Baal began to chant in low voices, "Elyon Baal, Elyon Baal, Elyon Baal."

It meant Baal Most High. It was a theft of Yahweh's title of El Elyon, God Most High, a reference to Yahweh's incomparability with the gods. Ignoring their chant, Elijah walked boldly up to the front and middle of the platform, facing the audience.

He waited. At a cue from the high priest of Baal, the chanting stopped.

Elisha saw that Elijah had hidden his hand in his cloak again. He worried for his master.

But when Elijah spoke, his voice seemed to fill the area with a strong presence that surprised Elisha.

"People of Israel! How long will you serve two masters? Wavering in loyalties, and hopping between two different opinions? If Yahweh is God, follow him. If Baal, then follow him!"

The people were stone-silent after hearing the prophet challenge them. Was Elijah serious? Did he really mean it? Would he let them worship Baal without condemnation?

As if on cue, the Baal prophets began their low chant again. "Elyon Baal, Elyon Baal, Elyon Baal."

Elijah waited impatiently until they stopped. He then resumed, "I, even I only, am left a prophet of Yahweh, but Baal's prophets are four hundred and fifty men."

Elisha felt slighted at his remarks of the prophet being alone. But of course, Elisha was not yet an ordained prophet, so technically, his master was right.

Elijah continued, "Let two bulls be given to us. Let Baal's prophets choose one bull for themselves. Let them cut it in pieces and lay it on the wood, but put no fire to it. I will prepare the other bull and lay it on the wood and put no fire to it. Then you call upon the name of your god, and I will call upon the name of Yahweh."

He paused dramatically. Then his voice raised several octaves. "AND THE GOD WHO ANSWERS BY FIRE, HE IS GOD!"

Elisha overheard Jezebel's contemptuous comment, "Oh, he is so theatrical."

The prophets of Baal now burst out loudly, "Elyon Baal! Elyon Baal! Elyon Baal!"

"Cunning!" Elisha heard Ahab respond to Jezebel above the chanting. "He chooses a bull, the symbol of Baal, as the sacrifice."

"Soon Elijah will be on that altar stone," Jezebel replied furiously.

The synchronized chant of the prophets continued on, "Elyon Baal! Elyon Baal!"

Elijah stepped down off the platform, and the high priest of Baal gestured to his prophets. They rearranged themselves on the platform, leaving a clear circle of space around the stone altar.

·····

Baal came back to consciousness. He didn't know how long he'd been out, but the sun was already rising in the morning sky.

He felt wetness on his face and wiped it. Blood. He was covered in blood, but not his own blood. At his feet were the chopped coils of the black serpent Ningishzida, as Lilith had called him. He'd been hacked into pieces.

Anat sat against the tree, waiting for Baal, her two sickle swords dripping with gore.

Baal rubbed his head. "What happened?"

"I rescued you again," Anat said with disgust. "That serpent swallowed you whole. I had to cut you out."

It was all coming back to Baal now. He'd been enchanted by Lilith. Seduced by her wiles.

Anat added, "I was going to do the same to your little whore, but she was rescued by the Anzu bird who flew away with her. You should have heard the wench shriek when I sliced her precious pet into pieces."

He said, "Well that's another unfulfilled fantasy you're going to have to fulfill for me."

She shook her head with contempt. "When are you going to learn? Your appetites and lusts make you such an easy target. What would you do without me, 'O Most High'?" She pronounced his title with sarcasm.

Baal coughed getting his breath back. "That's why you and I are a team, sister. Family are the only ones you can trust."

She looked up in the sky. It was nearly noon.

"Well, you just may have missed your chance to prove yourself worthy of your title, storm god. Let's go."

• • • • •

The prophets of Baal had selected two bulls from the herd brought up the mountain. Leading one to the top of the high place, they now surrounded it ceremoniously. Dozens of prophets thrust their swords at the same time, killing the bull almost instantly. It fell to the ground in death. They butchered the animal, dividing it into large pieces and placing those upon the horned altar, beneath the asherah.

The platform was covered with bull blood. Blood dripped from the altar and from the priests who had cut and carried the animal. The priests seemed to revel in the sticky red mess. Circling the sacrifice, they began to chant in syncopated dance.

Hours passed. The prophets of Baal continued their singing and dancing. But nothing happened. Their music became more dissonant and bizarre sounding to Elisha. Some of the prophets had fainted from exhaustion. Others were moving in delirious epileptic-like seizures and spoke in foreign tongues. Elisha decided that they'd become possessed by *shedim*, demons of the wilderness.

He and Elijah had been resting in the shade of a tree, watching the madness. But it had been hours, and nothing had happened. By the sun's height, it must be close to noon. The sky was bright, no clouds in sight. No fire from heaven.

Elisha watched as Elijah got up and walked over to the thrones.

Ahab was snoring. Izabel jabbed him awake.

Elijah announced, "O Queen Jezebel, where is your prince, Baal?"

She refused to answer him with anything other than a hate filled glare.

He turned to the prophets and shouted, "Cry aloud for he is a god! Is he busy musing over philosophy? Maybe he is taking a piss! Or better yet, on a journey in the underworld? Perhaps he is asleep and must be awakened!"

He turned back to Izabel, who seethed with hatred, looking ready to explode. But she answered in a steady voice, "You dare mock me."

"No, your highness," Elijah demurred. "I am merely inquiring—with a bit of poetic license." He knew that his digs were pointed exploitations of the Baal mythos.

Izabel arose from her throne. She stormed over to the bloody platform. The liturgical movements of the priests slowed as she approached, then stopped as she took center stage.

Grabbing the sacrificial dagger from the high priest, she held her hand up into the air. She placed the knife in her palm.

Elisha had joined Elijah by the thrones. He heard Ahab mutter, "No, don't. Please, Izabel."

The queen pulled the blade across her palm, gritting her teeth with the pain. Her blood now dripped onto the platform. She shouted, "Prince Baal, we rend our skin! We plow our chests and backs and draw our blood! Where are you, O Prince?"

Her action propelled a surge of new hope and activity among the prophets of Baal. Confident that she had inspired the god, she stepped off the platform. They all drew their daggers and began to follow her lead, re-enacting the ritual, cutting their cheeks and chests, raking their arms and backs. Some of them pulled out scourges and began to flog one another. Blood now flowed like rain from their veins onto the stone platform. The music started up again with its strange rhythm and percussion.

Izabel returned to her throne. Ahab handed her a cloth, and she wrapped her wounded palm.

• • • • •

Baal and Anat were almost to the high place. He could hear the sounds of music and the cries of prophets calling out to him.

Peering into the distant crowd, a particular figure caught Baal's attention. Moving around the edge of the crowd, watching the spectacle that unfolded, the man moved in a guarded fashion. It was an archangel. Then Baal saw another of the heavenly host further along the perimeter of the high place. And another. All seven of them, Baal suspected. This was too important of a contest not to send them all.

He gripped his spear Chaser and considered reaching for Driver, which was strapped to his back. He know the odds were against him. It would be a war to fight his way through a wall of archangels intent on keeping him away. There was no time to waste, he quickened his pace.

"This way," he called to Anat. "Hurry!"

This was his mountain, after all. He'd stolen it from Yahweh long ago, destroyed Yahweh's altar, and replaced it with his own. He also knew the caves and tunnels dug by the Phoenician priests.

Baal led his sister to a small cave opening in the side of the mountain. They didn't need light in the dark tunnel since their supernatural eyes could see here as easily as down in Sheol. They trotted quickly up a long tunnel that led to the high place.

As the end of the tunnel neared, Baal stopped Anat. He could feel the energy in Chaser surging in his hand. Sometimes the power of the thing became unwieldy. Today he'd need all the power he could get.

Arriving at a doorway, the siblings stopped to listen to the prophets still shouting and bleeding their lives out. "Where is the Prince? Where is Baal? Elyon Baal, Elyon Baal, Elyon Baal."

Baal could hear his followers were losing heart. Well, he would fill their hearts. He would answer their prayers, bring the rains, and curse Yahweh.

He kicked open the door. They exited out into the priests' holding pen to one side of the high place. Baal stepped out onto the platform in the unseen realm. No humans could see or hear them. The prophets of Baal continued shouting. It was past midday. They were falling like flies from exhaustion and blood loss.

But he was here. Baal had arrived.

He and Anat moved to the altar. He saw the archangels move in from their stations around the perimeter, but it was too late to stop him now.

Raising Chaser to the heavens, Baal bellowed out with a shout that only the gods and angels could hear. It rang through the heavenlies to the ears of Yahweh himself.

But nothing happened.

Baal gripped Chaser tighter, shaking it with intent to draw down the power.

But nothing happened.

No power flowed.

No fire came down.

Nothing happened.

He looked about him. The archangels had not actually moved from their prior positions.

He looked at Anat, who appeared to have figured out what was going on.

She shook her head. "What did you think would happen? Do you actually believe you control the weather?"

Baal dropped to his knees, staring his delusion in the face, his own face.

"Yahweh is the Creator," his sister scolded. "*We* are the Watchers. He establishes the boundaries of our inheritance, every power we have in the spiritual realm he has granted us—as well as our limitations. You were a fool to think Yahweh would allow you to call down fire from heaven and make *him* look like a fool. You had better wise up, brother. I think the gods of Canaan want to replace their defeated king with a queen."

He watched her turn and walk away.

Her words resounded in his ears. Baal had become so caught up in his own narrative, he'd believed his own lies. And he'd missed what was happening right in front of him. Her words had said it all: *The gods of Canaan want to replace their defeated king with a queen.*

It all became clear to him. He gathered himself back to full composure and then ran after her.

In the earthly realm, it was now Elijah's turn. The prophets of Baal had finally stopped their rituals, worn out and dispirited.

Elijah led Elisha to the ground in front of the altar platform. The two of them gathered twelve large uncut stones, then built an altar to Yahweh. A trench was dug around the altar. It seemed so humble in the dirt next to Baal's mammoth monument of masonry.

Elijah slaughtered his bull. Its body was cut into manageable pieces and placed upon their humble altar. Elisha stepped away at the completion of the labor and Elijah began speaking quietly to Yahweh.

As Elisha watched Elijah pray, Jehu whispered into his ear, "You are not alone. Your allies are amongst this assembly."

Elisha looked around him at the masses of Israelites, a thousand of them. He had been so focused on Elijah he hadn't realized. A well-built man with long brown hair and a square jaw stepped up beside Elisha. He nodded, a quick and silent greeting.

Jehu whispered, "This is Jonadab, leader of the Rechabites. He has brought many of his clan, and they are prepared for Yahweh's victory."

Elisha knew this would be their moment. He heard Elijah shout, "Pour out the water on the burnt offering!"

They had drawn the water from the Kishon Brook below. Four Israelites carried a large pot each and poured water over the bull and altar. It ran down and filled the trench.

Elijah shouted, "Do it a second time!"

The Israelites looked at each other, then went and filled their jugs again. When they poured the water out again, they were told to do it a third time.

When they had finished, the altar was thoroughly drenched and the little trench was like a small moat of water around the altar.

Elisha watched Jezebel and Ahab, deeply interested in their reactions to what Elijah was doing. Ahab's eyes were wide open with excitement. Jezebel appeared ready to explode with rage.

Finally, Elijah held up his hands and prayed aloud before all the crowd, "O Yahweh, God of Abraham, Isaac, and Israel, let it be known this day that you are God in Israel and that I am your servant and have done all these things at your word. Answer me, O Yahweh, answer me, that this people may know that you, O Yahweh, are God, and that you have turned their hearts back to you!"

Kneeling, the prophet bowed his head.

Elisha looked in the sky. There was nothing. Would Elijah be made a fool of as the prophets of Baal had been? Did his master really hear the word of the Lord? Or had he been deluded by his own legends?

The sound of crackling thunder drew Elisha's eyes back up into the sky that seconds before had been bright blue. A small and distinct swirl of darkening clouds had suddenly appeared. The cloud mass seemed to be increasing. It was only a matter of moments before it grew into a massive thundercloud, blocking the sun.

It was a swirling mass of fury. Elisha felt his mouth frozen open.

Then it happened.

The sound of thunder crackled in the air as a surge of lightning from the sky burst downward to touch the earth – right in the center of the altar for Yahweh. This was no ordinary lightning.

Fire from heaven burned up the sacrifice and the wood and licked up the water in the trench.

As quick as it had begun, it ended. The sun returned as the cloud disappeared. There was no evidence of the bull or the wood, just stones that glowed red like hot coals upon the scorched earth.

The entire crowd of Israelites and prophets of Baal stood in a jaw-dropped silence.

The voice of king Ahab broke the silence, "That was awesome!" The king clapped his hands with the glee of a happy child. "Elijah, you've outdone yourself!"

The crowd of stunned Israelites, began to fall to their knees and proclaim the greatness of Yahweh in praises. Elijah looked over at Jezebel, who glared back with burning rage.

Elijah shouted to the crowd, "Seize the prophets of Baal! Let not one of them escape!"

As these words rang out, the stunned prophets of Baal quickly regained their senses. They scattered, running chaotically in every direction to escape.

Hundreds of Rechabites in the crowd pulled out their swords. The rest of the Israelites followed suit. They chased the prophets, who were now scrambling for safety down the mountain.

Elijah made his way through the confusion to stand before the thrones of the king and queen.

Ahab was grinning wide and smiling. "Elijah, you did it! You won the contest! We must celebrate with a feast!"

"Yahweh won the contest, your highness. I am a mere mouthpiece. I suggest you return to Samaria before the rains become severe."

"Rain? Is it going to rain?" The king stared up into the sky, once again bright blue. "But your servant has been up to the summit seven times and hasn't seen a thing."

Elijah gestured for the king to come near. He turned and pointed out onto the horizon. There in the distance, a little cloud like a man's hand was rising from the sea. Lightning flashed within the cloud, followed by distant peals of thunder.

The sun was setting. The tiny cloud appeared to grow in the far distance. Elijah had spoken, and now the rain was finally coming.

"Come back with me tonight to Jezreel," said Ahab. "Dine with us!"

Ahab's gaze remained upon Elijah as he held up his finger before Izabel to keep her from speaking. Elisha thought she looked ready to explode. But she obeyed the king.

Elijah said, "I will run before your chariot, my king."

Ahab's expression indicated that was an odd offer, but he shrugged. "As you like." He slapped Elijah with joviality and turned to Jehu. "Make sure the prophets of Baal receive their due."

"Yes, my lord," said Jehu.

The king walked toward his chariot with Jehu following behind.

But Jezebel stood up from her throne, glaring at Elijah like a serpent ready to strike.

Walking right up to him, she spoke in a hush of restrained fury, "You cling to your swords and your religion, Elijah. As surely as I am 'Jezebel,' so may the gods cut me into pieces if I do not make your life as the life of my prophets by tomorrow's end."

With that, she turned and left him.

Elisha saw Elijah's hand trembling. She had mocked his insulting name for her, embracing it with defiance. Jezebel. The spectacular display of miraculous intervention had served only to harden the heart of the queen.

Elijah said, "I will obey the king. Meet me back at the school in a few days." As Elijah departed, Elisha turned to see Jehu on his knees before the altar of Yahweh. His body heaved with sobbing. He was broken before Yahweh, confessing and repenting and praising the God Most High.

When Elijah was out of his sight, Elisha pulled open his cloak to reveal a sword he'd hidden there for this moment. He hadn't told Elijah because he knew it would have gotten him thrown out of the school. Prophets were not to bear the sword. But Elisha would not miss this opportunity for which he'd prayed for years. Damn the consequences. He wanted action. He wanted vengeance upon the prophets of Baal who'd murdered the prophets of Yahweh. He wanted to change the world *now*. Holding the sword's handle tightly with mounting rage, Elisha took off down the mountain after the prophets of Baal.

CHAPTER 41

It was that night on Mount Carmel that I, Jehu, son of
Nimshi, realized the true nature of my own compromise. I
could no longer serve two masters. I had seen with my own
eyes the deliverance of Yahweh from the power of Baal. I
now knew with certainty that Jezebel would have to be
stopped. But the war of gods and men was only beginning.

Thunder overhead pierced the night. Rain descended upon the mass slaughter of the prophets of Baal by the Kishon Brook. Elisha marched along the creek-side, cutting down every prophet he could find. Lightning flashed, lighting up the scene with an eerie vision of shock and awe.

He buried his sword in the back of a fleeing Baalist. Glancing over, he saw Jehu as well as Jonadab and his Rechabites taking down Baal prophets.

Victims screamed and ran. Some fought back. But it was futile. The Israelites overwhelmed them, hacking, impaling, bludgeoning.

Elisha felt possessed by a force of anger.

Was this righteous anger?

Vengeance is mine, says the Lord.

The massacre went on into the night.

The rain poured down. Sheets of rain. Rivers of blood.

When the massacre was over, Elisha stood in the stream, surrounded by death. He'd been trying to wash off the blood, but realized he was standing in a stream of it. A headless corpse floated toward him. He watched as it drifted away.

There were so many dead. Bodies heaped upon bodies. Impaled. Beheaded. Limbless corpses strewn about like waste. Four hundred and fifty dead prophets of Baal, judged.

But Elisha now saw himself differently as though he stood outside his own body, looking down upon himself and what he'd done. What had he become in his zeal for revolution and violence? All his claims of justice and desire to take up the sword now mocked him.

He had violated his calling as a prophet.

Dropping his weapon in the water, Elisha fell to his knees and wept tears of grief. He was not a prophet, after all. Just an angry fool consumed by his hatred, overtaken by a spirit of revenge instead of the Spirit of God.

It was time for him to return home.

Samaria

The streets of the city were flooded from the rain. Citizens danced with joy, splashing in the muck and water. Jars were lined up gathering as much from the heavens as possible. Water—everywhere was water. Three years of deadly drought had finally come to an end. So many had suffered. So many had died, even with prayers on their parched lips. But now waves of rain washed away death with a baptism of life.

Jehu arrived back in the city with his contingent of men. They had followed Ahab's orders and ensured the thorough destruction of the prophets of Baal. It had been a bloody slaughter, but the rains had washed away most of the blood as they traveled home.

Leaving his horse in the stable, he entered his house.

Inside, he found Susanna seated at the dining table, crying. To his surprise, his wife's sister sat beside her. Dressed in a simple tunic, she looked careworn and older than the eighteen years he knew her to be.

"Galina!" he exclaimed.

She looked up at him and attempted to smile at his pleasant greeting. But something was wrong. Galina's eyes were as reddened with tears as his wife's.

When she stood, Jehu understood why. His sister-in-law was visibly pregnant.

"I'm sorry. I'm so sorry!" she repeated.

Jehu sat down heavily in a chair. "What happened in Jerusalem? We had not heard you'd remarried."

Galina took her seat again. The sadness of her expression touched his heart. He glanced at Susanna for illumination. She sighed heavily before revealing to Jehu what Galina had not.

"Jehu, Galina was not recruited for the palace all those years ago. She was forced to become a qedesha in Tyre."

That explained the pregnancy. Jehu felt a righteous anger rise up inside his chest.

"Jezebel," he growled. It was the insulting pronunciation the prophet Elijah had given the queen's name. Jehu had never forgotten. Now he uttered it with all the hatred in him.

Susanna added, "The letter we received telling us the palace attendants were being sent to Jerusalem was fabricated so that no one would come looking for them."

Galina raised her head and looked directly at Jehu. "When I became pregnant in the temple service, I was told to kill my child in the womb. They said it was my only choice as a servant of Asherah and Baal."

A darkness fell over Jehu's countenance as his gaze turned to Suzanna. *Asherah. The goddess to whom Susanna prays for a child. How violent the contradictions of this world. Death in the name of fertility.*

"But I couldn't kill my child," Galina went on. "And I hated what they'd made of me. So when Queen Jezebel came to Tyre, I used her presence as a distraction for my escape. I wasn't going to come here, I couldn't face you. My shame was too great." She choked on her words before continuing, "But in the end, I had nowhere else to go." She held her belly. "I only came for the sake of my little one."

"Galina, what was done to you is not *your* shame," said Jehu, his voice firm and certain. "It is Jezebel's."

"I came here hoping you'd allow me to be your servant. I will do anything to provide for my child."

Susanna reached over to embrace her. "My sister, you are no servant. You are family."

Jehu was already calculating. "Galina, you are indeed as my own sister. And we will care for you and your child. But you cannot leave this house. You are a fugitive of both Tyre and Jezebel. If you are discovered, you'll be returned and punished."

Galina gasped and proclaimed. "If I am discovered, *you* will be punished."

Jehu clenched his jaw. "Then so be it. I no longer fear the queen. And I will never choose king over God again."

CHAPTER 42

King Ahab was dressed in a colorful costume of Baal, complete with horned conical hat, battle skirt, and club. He wore thick make-up. Men wearing make-up was among the strange cultural differences between his wife's country and Israel. But Ahab tried to be open-minded. And it helped make him feel more like the role he was playing. Such role-playing was becoming more frequent.

"Where is my Queen of Heaven?" he growled playfully.

He looked beneath a table spread out in the lounge area. He checked behind a marble statue of Herakles. She wasn't in either place.

He went into the bed chamber, calling out, "Astarte? Where is my Astarte?" He added with roguish impatience, "I demand my consort!"

Ahab turned to see Izabel in her nightgown and bandaged hand. But she wasn't playing along. She had an angry scowl.

"You mock me?"

"What do you mean, mock you?"

"I had to suffer through the slaughter of Baal's prophets and priests, and now you dress up as Baal to flirt with me? It's a slap in my face."

Ahab's shoulders drooped. "My love, I didn't intend it so."

She wouldn't listen. "And then you bring that filthy, self-righteous Elijah into our palace to feast with you and become your religious advisor? He is sleeping in our home!"

Ahab became firm. He sometimes needed to be. "My dear, he did win the contest."

She ignored his reasoning. "I will not tolerate it. I am your queen."

The king scratched with frustration at his beard. This was happening more often now. Whenever his beautiful wife didn't get her way, she became unreasonable. This felt like a recurring battle that he could never win.

"Why can't everyone just get along?" he blurted out.

"You fool," Izabel hissed. "Yahweh and Baal cannot *get along*."

"Why not?" he protested. "Replenish your prophets."

She straightened herself, her body physically displaying her stiff resolve. "Oh, I *will* replenish the prophets. And until I do, you will just have to—" she gestured to his club, "—beat your club without me. I will be sleeping in the queen's bedchamber. Goodnight."

He made one last weak whine. "Izabel!"

But she just marched away, leaving him alone with his club and costume, feeling like a court jester.

Ahab walked over to a table with refreshments on it. Picking up the wine, he poured himself a full cup and drank deeply.

Once outside the bedchamber, Izabel stopped where she would be unobserved. Her whole body shook with frustration. Her goals had been blocked at every turn. Her breathing was labored, her eyes squeezed tight. She gasped for air, sobs were threatening to unleash and she was on the verge of crying with frustration. She slowly forced the feelings down and suppressed those emotions of weakness.

She felt as though she'd been sacrificed on the altar of a backwards patriarchal system of oppression. A religion that refused to change with the times. That chose to remain stuck in the archaic past of the stone age.

This was a new age of iron. And she wanted to be a queen of iron. But it felt as if everything had come crashing in on her.

• • • • •

Elijah stood in the palace bedchamber to which he'd been assigned. He stared out the window into the moonlit night. The rain had stopped. For now.

Pacing over to his bed, he picked up the plush feather sleeping cushion and tossed it onto the floor. It had been decades since he'd attempted to sleep on anything that decadently soft. He sat down on the hard floor.

A plate of food sat on a nearby table along with a goblet of wine, but he couldn't eat. He thought of the feast they'd celebrated upon his return with the king from Mount Carmel. Ahab had celebrated Yahweh's victory and been vocal in his support of the true god. But had he repented? The king was fickle and easily manipulated by the queen, so Elijah had to wonder how long this faith in Yahweh would last. Jezebel hadn't been at the feast for obvious reasons. But when Ahab had asked Elijah to stay for a while in the palace to give him spiritual direction, Elijah had felt he couldn't turn down the offer.

An almost paranoid sense of impending doom had settled over Elijah. Just the day before, he'd faced down Baal's prophets and witnessed the glory of Yahweh lighting up the night. He'd seen Jezebel humiliated.

Yet now, after all that great victory, Elijah felt frightened of the future. He just couldn't shake his fear.

A soft knock at his door drew his attention. Straightening up, he called out, "Enter."

As the queen entered his bedchamber, Elijah rose to his feet in respect. Jezebel was wearing her royal night robe and had her hair down. She looked more approachable as if something had changed in her.

"Elijah," she whispered.

He prepared himself for some kind of verbal attack. But she gave him none. Instead, her eyes teared up.

"I have come to apologize for my insolence."

Elijah couldn't believe what he was hearing. Shock ran through his body like lightning. Could this truly be Jezebel speaking?

She continued, "Mount Carmel was my shame. And the more I think about it, I cannot escape the fact that my pride blinded me from seeing what was so obvious."

She stopped after choking a bit on her words. She appeared to be holding back a torrent of tears.

"Please forgive me, Elijah. Please allow me to pledge my full allegiance to Yahweh and to you, his true prophet."

Elijah was speechless. Was this really happening? Had the wicked queen truly repented?

Then she opened her gown. It dropped to the floor, leaving her completely naked except for the white bandage wound around her left hand.

"I offer my body and soul in the service of Yahweh."

Elijah didn't look down at her body, but kept his gaze on her face. He swallowed with difficulty as he glimpsed the triumph in her eyes. This was a trick. She was trying to seduce him into violating his covenant with Yahweh.

He grabbed his mantle, ran for the window and jumped, crashing through the wooden slats and rolling down the roof.

"ELIJAH!" Jezebel screamed after the prophet.

She ran to the window just in time to see Elijah escaping down the ledge into the night. She pulled her dagger from behind her back. She had affixed it close to the Leviathan tattoo, ready to strike him like the great sea dragon would have.

But her plan hadn't worked. Not tonight.

She cursed and yelled out, "Guards!"

• • • • •

Elijah rolled off the roof, falling a full story to the ground. Thankfully, a patch of ornamental shrubbery at the bottom broke his fall. He pulled himself out from the branches, scraped, but with nothing broken. Thankfully again, he hadn't begun undressing for sleep, and his hairy mantle had kept him from being scratched by thorns.

Several bobbing torches revealed a group of guards racing around the corner of the palace wing in his direction. Elijah used the dark cover of night to sprint as noiselessly as possible toward a grove of citrus trees that were part of the palace gardens.

The guards paused under the window through which he'd escaped, waving their torches over the trampled branches and leaves where he'd fallen. From above them, Elijah heard Jezebel's angry orders. "He isn't there! Spread out and find him! He is an old man! He can't have gone far!"

As the torches split up and fanned out, Elijah took off in a run. But he soon lost the cover of the citrus grove. And while in adequate physical shape for his age, he was still aching from running in front of Ahab's chariot all the way from Mount Carmel. God's Spirit had given him the strength for such a feat, but the aftermath had left him exhausted.

He wove his way toward the entrance gate, ducking under cover each time a torch drew close. It was a dodge and dart game of hide and seek, and with one exhausted prophet against many guards, it was a game Elijah couldn't keep up for long. Maybe it would be safer to slip back inside the palace and find someplace there to hide.

Then salvation arrived. Actually, it was two stable boys leading a half-dozen saddled horses. They passed close to where Elijah had ducked behind a bush.

Elijah didn't hesitate to seize his opportunity. Moving noiselessly between two horses, he grabbed the nearest bridle and pulled himself into the saddle. Yanking the horse's head around, he kicked its flanks into a gallop and headed straight for the palace gates. The next great danger now was if the gates had already been shut for the night.

But they were not. It appeared they'd been opened again to permit an exterior perimeter search. Nearby, additional guards were mounting another group of saddled horses.

Elijah slipped low over the horse's neck and encouraged the animal to peak speed through the open gate. By the time the guards had scrambled into their saddles behind him, he was gone into the night—to God knows where.

$$\bullet \bullet \bullet \bullet \bullet$$

Crashing into the king's outer chamber, Izabel found Ahab still in his Baal costume, but not alone. Despite the late hour, his commander Jehu and a handful of captains had joined the king. They were all huddled around a table covered with maps and crafted miniatures of chariots, soldiers, and other war pieces used for battle planning. Izabel stopped in surprise, clutching her nightgown tight in a show of modesty.

The rumble of discussions silenced as the men caught sight of the queen. Ahab took a big gulp from his goblet of wine as he looked her up and down. "Izabel, so you've decided to join me after all."

He turned as serious as possible, considering the ridiculousness of his attire. "But it seems I can't play tonight. I've had word that Ben-hadad of Damascus is moving upon us with his armies for war. We must make immediate plans. Where is Elijah? I want his counsel."

Izabel eyed the king coldly. "Elijah has fled the city."

Her husband's mouth gaped open. "What?"

"Your so-called prophet tried to rape me." She saw his face register shock. "When I called for the guards, he escaped."

She quickly glanced at Jehu, attempting to read his reaction. He had not quite managed to mask his skepticism.

Ahab set down his goblet gently upon the table. He then lifted the table and threw it across the room. It crashed, maps and pieces flying all over. The wine splattered everywhere.

Ahab yelled out, "Can I trust no man with my wife?!"

The drunken and enraged king stumbled over to one of the captains. The captain, a big, muscular man named Medad, froze in fear as the king drew a dagger and raised his hand to stab it into the captain's neck.

Jehu stopped him mid-plunge.

Ahab shouted, "Jehu, do you defy your king?"

Jehu slowly lowered the king's arm and blade. "No, my lord. I protect you. You were about to kill a captain who will help you defeat Ben-hadad."

Ahab mumbled something in humiliation, then ordered, "Ready the chariots. We will ride out to meet Ben-hadad at midday."

Glancing over at Izabel, he offered a placating gesture, and said, "And I want a search party for that dung beetle prophet. Bring him to me."

Stepping forward, Izabel replied promptly, "Allow me to organize it, my Lord. Focus your attention on the war." As she spoke, she felt moisture on the bandaged palm and realized that her hand was bleeding again.

The king looked at her with a sad, unfocused gaze, then turned to a servant. "Bring me more wine."

CHAPTER 43

Jezreel

Baal sulked on his throne in the holy of holies of his temple. He couldn't believe he'd been such a fool. He'd been lied to and manipulated by those around him, and he'd been blind to it all.

Why hadn't he seen it? How could he have been so blinded it took Ishtar's slip of the tongue to open his eyes? *Are you so sure of your family? Where is Astarte?*

The words of Anat flooded back to him and his anger swelled, she had been correct. He was a slave to his appetites and his pride. He'd come to believe he was everything his mythology had constructed. He was the head of the pantheon, the most powerful of the gods of Canaan. He had his own house built on Mount Zaphon, and now he had one in Israel as well. He was usurping Yahweh's power over his people. He was the storm god! He controlled the weather! He had the power of lightning, thunder, and storm!

Reality had revealed the truth: he could not bring a drop of rain if he wanted to. Anat was right. Yahweh was the only true storm god. The whole contest had been one big set-up to make Baal look impotent. To contest his kingship over the land. And that must be why the archangels had helped him and Anat to defeat the goddesses in Terqa. To make sure Baal made it to Carmel for his consummate humiliation.

What a deluded fool he'd become. And his sister had supported him all these years because of the status and power it gave her. She'd rescued him from Mot and Lilith. But that had only made him need her more. She couldn't become king of the gods, but she could become everything but.

And then there was Astarte. She'd been Baal's consort, but now he couldn't help but wonder if she actually was the betrayer as Ishtar had hinted.

Did Astarte want to be more than his Queen of Heaven in Judah? Did she want to be Queen of All?

He'd believed it was his decision to send Astarte to Jerusalem. But now that he thought back, he realized it was Asherah who had suggested it.

Asherah, whom he'd believed he'd raped into submission, had maneuvered herself to become a favorite of the Hebrews. Come to think of it, every high place with an altar to Baal also had an asherah pole. When he'd been swallowed by Mot in the Valley of Hinnom, he'd been with Asherah and Astarte. Had Asherah betrayed him for how he'd humiliated her? Was the Mother goddess helping Astarte take his crown?

Goddesses. They were the cause of all Baal's problems. It was goddesses who'd complicated his rule in Israel. The goddesses Ishtar, Ishara, and Ereshkigal had hindered him in Terqa and delayed the retrieval of his weapons. The goddess Lilith had seduced him in the Jezreel Valley. They'd all been trying to keep him from Mount Carmel. To discredit his rule. They must have been helping Astarte in her secret ambitions.

The irony was that Baal *had* been discredited, but not by them—by Yahweh himself. Baal had played the fool and had lost his hold over Israel. Now the goddesses were jockeying for power to become Queen.

Goddesses were all bitches, and he'd never trust any of them again. He would use them for his pleasure or his own ambition, but he'd never trust a single one of them. They were all manipulative usurpers, jealous of the rule of greater gods like himself. They deserved to be held back—and beaten if need be.

Ishtar's slip of the tongue was his strongest evidence that Astarte was the queen of his betrayal. *Are you so sure of your family? Where is Astarte?*

He'd go to Jerusalem and find out for himself. He would recruit Molech and Chemosh to help him regain his power.

CHAPTER 44

Abel-meholah

Elisha stood still, staring at the blackened ruins of his father's old farm. It had been years since the tragic events, this was his first return and he was awash with memories. Now he was back for good. He looked out on the fields, trampled and dead.

He walked into what was left of the farmhouse, just the foundation stones, a few scorched timbers, and crumbling, blackened mud brick.

Picking up a black chunk of wood that had been a rafter, he carried it out of the house, then made his way back inside. It was going to take a lot of work to rebuild this farm and make it fruitful again. But he was looking forward to it. He wanted to build and grow, not tear down. He wanted to feed life, not death.

Elisha needed the daily demands of the farm to keep his mind planning and his body working. He needed to keep his new life different and distant from the one he'd left behind.

Wilderness of Beersheba

The hot desert sands radiated heat and baked Elijah as he stumbled. It had been a journey of over seventy miles from Samaria in the north to Beersheba in the south. But he had left Beersheba and had been wandering in the wilderness for days.

The sun was without mercy. The heat made him dizzy and burned his lungs. All around him was an endless sea of sand and rock. It made him think of *tohu wabohu*. The wilderness of Azazel.

Sunburned and delirious, his lips parched and cracked, Elijah couldn't decide if he was running away from Jezebel or his own fears. How could he have seen Yahweh's mighty works and then find himself in fear of another human, no matter how powerful she was? What kind of a prophet was such a coward? He'd condemned the Israelites for hopping between two masters. But he was no different. He was hopping between the two masters of faith and fear.

Elijah remembered and pondered over the history of his people back at the Red Sea. How the Israelites had been guided by the pillar of cloud by day and the pillar of fire by night. How the sea had piled up to let them cross on dry ground, then crashed down on the Egyptians in a tsunami of judgment. The Israelites had seen the plagues. They'd eaten manna, bread from heaven. They'd seen the fire and smoke and lightning and thunder on Mount Sinai. Yet still they'd cast the golden calf and worshipped it. After everything Yahweh had done to care for them, they had still longed to return to the food and security of their slavery in Egypt.

As a prophet, he had denounced the people and rulers for unfaithfulness to Yahweh. His words were full of conviction and proclaimed judgments. But he was no different than those fickle people. He was just as much a coward. And now he wanted to die.

Through his hazy vision, Elijah spotted a desert broom tree. It was shrub-like with wide-spreading leafy branches. Here, in the middle of nowhere, the shade of the tree beckoned, and Elijah crawled beneath the branches to rest.

"It is enough! Now, O Yahweh, take away my life, for I am no better than my fathers."

Collapsing, Elijah felt the breath leave his lungs. All the pain left his body. He felt himself lift off the ground as though floating.

Then he saw himself lying beneath the broom tree. He was somehow looking at himself dying.

A whispering voice interrupted his observations and thoughts. It spoke with quiet authority.

"Elijah."

Was it Yahweh calling him home?

"Elijah, rise."

Rise to heaven?

A third time, "Elijah, rise and eat."

Elijah felt a touch on his chest and suddenly experienced himself being sucked back into his body. He awakened, coughing, sucking in air— burning-hot air.

A man stood at his feet. A small, blond man in warrior's armor with two swords on his back. The prophet had no doubt this stranger was a supernatural being.

"You're small for an angel."

"That's what they all say," the messenger replied with a grin. "Until they fight me."

The angel knelt down beside the prophet and lifted Elijah's head as he held a jug of cool water to his lips. Blessed, cool water filled his mouth and the prophet swallowed greedily. He gulped until his thirst was quenched. He lie back, still dizzy and observed. The angel placed the jug on the ground and reached for a large cake of baked grain.

The angel broke off a piece from the cake. He held it to Elijah's mouth. "Eat, for the journey is too great for you."

"What journey?" asked Elijah, pushing away the food.

"To Horeb, and the mountain of Elohim."

"Are you commanding me?"

The angel didn't answer. Again, he held the food to Elijah's mouth. This time Elijah ate. It tasted sweet, almost melting in the mouth like honey cakes. Was it possible this was what manna had tasted like?

Then he heard the sound of ravens cawing around him. The sound increased as though the ravens were right by his ears. His vision blurred again, and the angel faded into blackness.

When Elijah came to, he could feel once again the aches and pains in his body, his dry throat. Had the angel just been a hallucination?

Then he saw a raven perched on his stomach with a piece of bread in its beak. It dropped the bread on Elijah's chest. Another raven fluttered by, depositing a second piece of bread.

Lifting up his head, Elijah saw a flurry of ravens all dropping pieces of bread at his hands and feet. He laughed and sat up.

Gathering the bread together, he ate it.

Then he saw the clay jug beside where his head had rested. As before, it held water. Drinking deeply, Elijah replayed the angel event. He was supposed to go to Horeb.

Yes, I think I will go back to the origin. To Horeb. To Mount Sinai.

Now that is going to be quite a hike.

CHAPTER 45

Jezreel

Izabel stood at the window looking out into the night. Because war with Damascus loomed, she had moved from Samaria to the summer palace in Jezreel. She preferred being here anyway. Baal's house was here, and it made her feel more at home.

She heard the sound of the door opening and a soldier's armor clanking. Turning, she saw Ahab enter, his armor was filthy with dirt, blood, and the grime of battle. She surmised that the muck which covered him was just another reflection of his piggishness.

Making no move to greet him, Izabel demanded, "What news from the battlefield?"

Ahab walked over to the table and poured himself a cup of wine. He guzzled it noisily, allowing excess to spill from his mouth. When he finished, he belched like a pig with a self-indulgent smile. "We routed Damascus."

He began taking off his armor, piece by piece. The tension between king and queen had continued to rise ever since Mount Carmel. Something irreparable had happened there. She'd been humiliated, and he hadn't defended her. He'd taken Elijah's side, if only for that brief moment in time. But it was a significant moment when she'd needed him the most. After all, Ahab was no stalwart for Yahweh. He was only attracted to power. And it had been real power on display at the top of Mount Carmel. He, and the people, still worshipped Baal and Asherah, perhaps just with less vigor.

For Izabel, that day at Mount Carmel had been the beginning of their division. Her bitterness about it had only grown and festered in the subsequent days and weeks.

She asked coldly, "Did you capture Ben-hadad?"

"Yes, but I released him." He'd taken off his helmet and breastplate. Now he unleashed his sandals.

"Mercy for your enemies?" Izabel questioned snidely despite the relief she felt. Her father Ethbaal would have been furious had Ahab executed Tyre's secret ally.

Ahab dropped his battle skirt. "He will raid our caravans no more. And Damascus will now be an ally of Israel and Tyre. We must all be united against our growing enemy in the north, Assyria."

"The endless wars of gods and men."

"Yes," he said, ripe with implication. "We tend toward violence when things are taken away from us."

Pulling off his tunic, the king stood completely naked before her. It was a challenge. Would she dare turn him away after a victory of such prowess?

She walked past him toward the door. "Take a bath. You're filthy. A feast is being prepared in your honor. You must bask in the glory of this great victory."

As she turned to close the door, she saw him pour another cup of wine.

• • • • •

The banquet tables were overflowing with meat, vegetables, and drink. Quail and partridges were garnished with dates, figs, and olives. There were pomegranates and melons, butter, cheeses, nuts of all kinds from almonds to pistachios. A delicious and delicate young calf had been herbed and roasted whole for the main course.

Reclining at the table with Athaliah, Ahab, Jehu, and other captains from the battle, Izabel hid her disgust at the sight of her husband eating like a wild boar. With a mouth full of food, he boasted of his exploits.

"We encamped opposite each other for seven days. The Arameans filled the valley with their numbers. I tell you; Israel was like two flocks of goats in comparison."

His hearty laugh drew agreement from Jehu and the other captains.

"But I knew we would win."

His young sister's eyes were wide with excitement as she asked breathlessly, "How did you know?"

Ahab turned a crumb-laden smile on Athaliah. "Because a prophet had told me I would. He said Yahweh would give the multitude into my hands. Ben-hadad was arrogant—overconfident. He had proclaimed that Yahweh was a god of the hills, not a god of the valleys. The fool. When we enjoined them in battle, we struck down a hundred thousand men in one day!"

Izabel assumed the king to be exaggerating. As he often did. As most men did when boasting of their victories. But Jehu was reacting as though the story was completely true. Sycophant.

Ahab continued his story. "The rest of their troops fled into the city of Aphek. And I jest not, a wall fell on them, and tens of thousands more were killed. A wall! Like the walls of Jericho all over again. I tell you; Yahweh is on my side again."

Izabel despised when Ahab told his overblown stories, and she hated it even more when he gave Yahweh credit for any so-called miraculous events. She tried to change the subject. "What of King Ben-hadad?"

"Well, that is another surprise. That rascally weasel had hidden deep inside the city. But when I approached his location, lo and behold, the king and his servants came out to me dressed in sackcloth with ropes on their heads, begging and pleading for mercy. He was pathetic."

"Did you execute him?" Athaliah asked eagerly.

Ahab turned another fond smile on his young sister. "No. I couldn't bring myself to do so. After all these years of warring with him, I found myself pitying the poor bastard. Especially when he offered to give back all the territories he and his fathers had taken from Israel along with a generous offer of markets for our goods in Damascus. It was then I realized it would be a far greater advantage for Israel's interests to have a submissive economic ally than a subjugated foe. So I made a covenant with him."

The king looked thoughtfully into the distance as he added one more thought. "Oddest thing, though. When we captured Ben-hadad, I discovered he had only been pirating our supply caravans and leaving the Tyrian caravans alone."

Izabel stiffened. Maybe it would have been better after all if the king had executed Ben-hadad. At least her father's secret treaty would have died with him.

Raising eyebrows as though surprised, she asked, "Did he say why?"

205

"Only that he lacked intelligence on Tyre because his spies there had been caught and executed."

Relieved, Izabel affirmed the lie. "That makes perfect sense. Besides, Israel is a greater threat because we control the King's Highway."

Jehu had been listening carefully to the conversation and the queen felt certain he was less than persuaded.

Ahab replied, "You would tell me if you knew your father had a secret treaty with Ben-hadad, would you not?"

Izabel acted insulted. "Have I ever withheld anything from you, my king?"

"In the bedchamber," he grumbled.

She switched to a completely different tone, a seductive one. "Well, my husband, perhaps you will be glad to know that in your absence I've replenished my priesthood as you suggested. And you know what that means."

Ahab stopping eating. Looking at her lustfully, he swiped the back of his hand across his mouth. He was practically drooling with anticipation already.

Izabel glanced at Athaliah, who watched with knowing interest. The queen had explained to the young girl how male nature worked, and the king was responding perfectly, according to Izabel's predictions. Izabel had withheld marital relations since that night so long ago, when all her Baal prophets had been murdered after losing to Elijah. Now, it was finally time to reward her trained dog, to throw the king a bone.

Her satisfied thoughts were interrupted as Jehu suddenly shouted, "Get back, my lord!"

Looking up, Izabel saw a one-eyed man in a ragged cloak standing in the middle of the banquet hall before them. Jehu had already thrust himself in front of the king, guarding Ahab from another assassination attempt.

Ahab arose and firmly pushed the commander aside. "It's okay, Jehu. I know this man. He's the one who prophesied my victory."

But this time, the one-eyed prophet bore words not so friendly to the king. Pointing his bony finger at Ahab, he yelled, "Thus says Yahweh: 'I have devoted Ben-hadad of Damascus to destruction. But because you have let him go, therefore I shall require your life for his life and your family for his family."

Izabel gestured to a nearby palace guard. Stepping behind the prophet of Yahweh, the guard drew a dagger across the one-eyed man's throat.

The prophet fell to the ground, clutching his neck and bleeding out onto the floor.

Ahab barked, "Izabel, why did you do that?"

"He threatened your life and the lives of your family."

The guard dragged the dead man out of the room.

"He was a prophet, not a warrior," Ahab complained.

Izabel was ready with her response. "The prophets of Yahweh are like rodents. You get rid of one and another replaces it. They just keep coming back."

She stared accusingly at Jehu. "The real question is how he got through our security?"

She could see her question bothered Jehu. He said, "I will investigate it, your highness."

"And what about your family, Jehu?" she asked. "Are they safe?"

He gave her a hard look, only too clearly understanding her implied threat. "Yes, my queen. You need not concern yourself with my family."

Izabel caught Ahab's ignorant glance. The king had no clue what was actually being said between the two of them.

"On the contrary, commander. I do concern myself. With you and *all* your loved ones."

Izabel was indeed threatening Jehu, and the king could not see it. Jehu understood her message perfectly. Finally, she would take charge and get this "loyal servant" removed. She just knew he schemed and manipulated matters, it no longer mattered if she could prove it. He was too cunning to get caught. So her intent was to make the commander think he'd miscalculated somewhere, anywhere. That fear might cause him to make a real mistake. Then she'd be there to catch him.

CHAPTER 46

Jehu burst into his home on a mission. He called out, "Susanna!"

She wasn't in the lower level. He knew exactly where she'd be. Climbing the stairs to the second level, Jehu opened the door to the shrine room.

Susanna was on her knees, the images of Asherah and Astarte laid out before her. She rose hastily to her feet. "What's wrong, Jehu?"

"You and Galina must pack quickly. I need to send you away from here. I must keep you safe."

"Why?" Susanna asked fearfully.

"Jezebel has threatened my family. It was implied. But it was real nonetheless."

"Does she know about Galina?"

"Possibly."

"How?"

A voice came from behind him. "Asherah told her."

It was Galina. She'd been listening to them. She stared at the images of Asherah in the room.

"What do you mean Asherah told her?" Jehu demanded.

Galina looked at Susanna for approval, dread in her eyes. Then she swallowed. "I haven't told you about my encounter with Asherah in Tyre. I had a vision of her one night when I was awakened. I saw Asherah and Baal together. The goddess spoke to me."

She broke off with a shudder, holding her belly protectively.

"Go on," Jehu urged. "What did she say?"

Galina's face was ashen as though in a trance. "She said, 'Your child is ours. All the children of Israel are ours.'"

Jehu felt a shiver go down his spine.

Galina concluded, "That was when I knew. Asherah is not the wife of Yahweh. She is the mother of Baal. And Baal demands human sacrifice."

Jehu ground his teeth furiously. "I'm going to kill her! I'm going to kill Jezebel."

"Don't say that!" Susanna protested, "You'll be executed."

"I don't care."

Susanna took a slow, deep breath to calm herself. When she spoke, she hoped her husband would reconsider. "And what would the king do to us then?"

Jehu looked from his wife to his pregnant sister-in-law, fighting to bring his anger under control. Then he announced, "In any case, I am sending both of you to Jonadab in the camp of the Rechabites. Tonight."

Galina immediately barked out, "No!"

Neither Jehu nor Susanna needed to ask why. But Galina said it aloud anyway. "I am not returning to our father's clan. Not with the shame that he still holds over me."

Jehu looked at Susanna, who appeared torn. They'd managed to avoid raising the subject of his wife's family until now. But Jehu knew there was no other option. He addressed Galina with firmness.

"Your people are strong in the art of war. The king holds them in high regard because they supply the best weapons and chariots, they are protected and strong. The queen even fears them. She tried to assassinate the Rechabite leaders a few years ago. They escaped her treachery only because I warned them. They are in my debt and their encampment is the only place in all of Israel where you will be safe."

Galina's expression was unyielding. "I will be rejected like a leper. I'd rather face Jezebel's wrath."

"And what of your child?" Jehu countered. "Are you prepared to make the babe face that wrath as well?"

Galina went silent, Jehu pressed on. "You will stay with Jonadab. He is the general of the clan, a good man I've known for many years. Your father will not dare oppose him or defy his protection over you."

"How long will we stay?" Susanna asked fearfully

"At least until Galina has had her baby. Then, if things have settled and you are no longer in danger, you will be able to return home. Now go quickly and pack your things."

209

As the women packed for their journey, Jehu stood in the shrine room thinking over everything Galina had just told them. And he recalled everything he had learned about holiness and loyalty to Yahweh.

He looked at the alabaster Asherah and the clay figurines. The stone carving of the deity Bes. Walking over, he picked up the Asherah, raised it above his head, and smashed it to the floor in pieces. A holy anger welled up within him. He swiped the clay images to the floor in more pieces. He slapped the tray of breadcakes for Astarte into the air. They went flying. He pushed over the incense altar. It too crashed to the floor in pieces. Only the menorah was left standing, untouched.

His chest heaved with heavy breathing, not from exertion but fierce intensity. Looking up, he saw Susanna and Galina at the doorway, watching him. Their expressions said they understood and agreed. Yahweh was a jealous god, and they'd been unfaithful to him for long enough. There would be no more cavorting with foreign gods in the household of Jehu. Those gods could not co-exist with Yahweh. Yahweh was life and everything good, the other gods demanded death and brought misery.

Jehu had selected four of his most trusted warriors to escort his wife and her sister to the Rechabite camp. Jonadab would protect these women. Their belongings had been packed into a small wagon large enough for the two women to ride.

Allowing one of the soldiers to lift her into the wagon seat, Galina asked Jehu what Susanna was too afraid to ask, "What will you do now?"

"I must right the wrong choices I've made."

Jehu kissed Susanna. She clutched him, not letting him go.

He whispered into her ear, "You can come back when it's safe."

Susanna's eyes pooled with unshed tears. Her love for Jehu would carry her through this time apart from him. She would be strong. She made no sound as he helped her into the seat beside Galina.

Moments later, under the midnight moon, the small caravan slipped out of the city and into the darkness.

CHAPTER 47

Ahab stumbled down the hallway to his bedchamber, spilling wine from his goblet with each faltering step. The feast was over, and he was anticipating his reward. He'd waited too long for his wife to return to him.

Bumbling into the room, he shut the door, then looked over at the bed. A female shape stood there in the dark, not quite lit by the oil lamps in the room.

He squinted his blurry eyes to see more clearly. The female shape was Izabel dressed in her Asherah costume. In other words, naked except for jewelry and a headdress. Her body was made white with make-up.

"Ahab." He could swear he'd heard the queen call his name in a sing-song voice. But he didn't see her lips move. He responded with a smiling growl.

He stepped back as what seemed to be a large snake slithered across her torso and up her body. Then a lion stepped out beside her.

Frightened, Ahab shook his head and rubbed his eyes.

Suddenly, the animals were gone. He set his wine down. "I am done drinking for the evening."

Ahab did his level best to walk a straight line across the room, direct to his queen. When he got within grabbing distance, she pulled out a dagger and placed it at his throat, stopping him in his tracks.

"Ah, ah, ah," she teased. "Take off all your clothes first."

"Yes, my goddess."

Grinning, he pulled off his robe and tunic. He felt like he was sobering up quickly. Though he had a hard time with his sandals.

He finally got everything off, his clothes strewn about him on the floor. Ahab stood naked and full of pride before his painted goddess.

She said, "You've been a good boy. Waiting so patiently for your treat."

But her dagger stayed extended out toward him. He started to push it gently aside to move closer, but she flicked it back, giving him a minor cut on his hand. He looked at the blood and sucked on the lesion. Why wouldn't she put the blade down? He started to sense danger.

She said, "Get down on your hands and knees."

He smiled. It wasn't danger he was in for. It was a role play. The poor thing sometimes needed to experience dominance in their sexual play to compensate for her frustrated ambitions in the real world. He didn't mind. As long as he got his.

He got down on his hands and knees. At least this felt more stable than on his drunken feet. He looked up at her. Now what?

She smiled. "Bark like a dog."

He chuckled. "Are you serious?"

She didn't move or change her expression. She was serious.

"I said bark like a dog, or you won't get your treat."

He barked. "ARR ARR!" He chuckled at himself. He barked again, "ARR ARR ARR!"

He looked at her for approval.

She said, "Howl."

He howled. "AARRROOOOOOOOOOOO!"

She smiled and commanded him, "Good boy. Now you're going to do exactly what I tell you."

What King Ahab didn't know was that young Athaliah was watching everything from behind the curtain of the bedchamber balcony. Izabel had told her to be quiet, to observe, and to learn how easy it was to manipulate a man through his weakness for sexual indulgence. Every step he was willing to take, no matter how small, could be used to draw him deeper into the web of control. Men were only the stronger sex physically. Emotionally, they were pathetic morons. Slaves to their appetites, they'd give up happiness, riches, even their power for a momentary spasm of sexual gratification.

Athaliah had to learn. A queen should know how to rule over her king.

CHAPTER 48

Outside Megiddo

Susanna looked up at the vast sky filled with stars and wondered about life and destinies of man. She pondered how all people, the righteous and the wicked, were at the mercy of Yahweh. She sat beside her sister, holding her hand. She could feel Galina's fear. She gave a gentle squeeze of reassurance to the clammy, damp hand which gripped hers tightly.

Jehu's warriors had brought them safely to the Rechabite camp in the Jezreel Valley near Megiddo. They now just waited. One of their escorts had gone to meet with Jonadab, the son of Rechab and the leader of the Rechabites. He would deliver Jehu's protection request.

Sentries manned a line of fires around the camp perimeter. The encampment had grown significantly since Susanna and Galina had lived here as children. And there was increased security. The times were more dangerous now. But the Rechabites were a mighty clan, and her husband trusted them.

One sentry stood near the wagon, a small man with blond hair. He looked peculiar, almost out of place wearing an unusual armor and just seeming somehow different to Susanna. He smiled, a reassuring type of smile, and nodded in a deferential greeting.

"What is your name, soldier?" Susanna asked.

"Uriel, ma'am." He added, "You are safe now. Yahweh protects his Remnant."

Susanna found his reply strange, as though he knew what they were going through. And what did he mean by Yahweh's Remnant?

At that moment, a hearty familiar voice drew her attention. "Susanna, welcome!"

Turning her head, Susanna saw the large, brawny figure of Jonadab, son of Rechab, striding toward them. He offered Susanna a helping hand as she stood up, then turned to help Galina. His square jaw and muscular frame had always been impressive to Susanna. They complemented his strong leadership.

"Your husband's message says that you need a safe place to stay. I owe him my life, so it is my honor to have you as guests and extend our protection. You are our kinsmen."

Susanna put her arm around Galina and drew her forward. "Do you remember my sister Galina?"

Jonadab looked at Galina with surprise. "Yes, though I didn't recognize you at first. You were still a young girl the last time I saw you. Perhaps twelve, thirteen? I was gone to war when you left to be married."

He added, "I must say you have grown up well into womanhood." He coughed, suddenly stumbling over his words. "I mean, you're much taller and, well, filled out, and—" His words trailed off.

"My sister has suffered much tragedy, losing her husband and his family—and much more."

"Susanna," Galina warned in a low voice, turning her face away as though with embarrassment. Susanna gave her a reassuring squeeze. She would never betray the true nature of her sister's shame.

Though shame was not what Jonadab saw as he smiled at the younger sister. The Rechabite leader's gaze was glued to Galina. In his eyes she was the former duckling now transformed into a beautiful swan. But the momentary spell broke as he comprehended what had been said. His voice filled with compassion as he bowed to the younger girl and said, "Forgive me. I am deeply sorry for your loss. And with a child on the way."

"That is another story for another time," said Galina, keeping her face turned away from the handsome leader.

"Well, I'm sure we will have plenty of time to hear it." Jonadab gestured for the two women to follow him. "Come, let us give you a comfortable place to sleep. I have decided to house you on the other side of the camp from your father."

His last statement made clear Jehu must have explained some of their dilemma in the message the guards had brought. As the two sisters turned to gather their belongings, he added, "And leave your bundles. My men will bring them."

Susanna said, "You are too kind, Jonadab."

"It is my pleasure and privilege to be of service to the house of Jehu," he replied. "He has been of great service to our people. May Yahweh guard you and watch over you. We will be his hands in doing so."

Galina gave Susanna a worried look. Susanna knew the fear that clouded her sister's thoughts right now. Just what did the Rechabite leader know of her family? It wasn't a huge clan, and word traveled fast. Had her father broadcast the circumstances of Galina's runaway marriage and subsequent shunning? What about her current pregnancy that was clearly questionable? The Rechabites were a devout clan of Yahwists, concerned with holiness. They condemned Israel because of the people's acceptance of Canaanite gods. The same gods Jehu had just removed from their own home.

Remembrance of those smashed figurines gave Susanna hope that perhaps she and Galina both could start afresh in their new temporary home. She silently prayed the psalm she'd memorized and prayed so many times to convince her of that hope:

> Yahweh is merciful and gracious,
> slow to anger and abounding in steadfast love.
> He will not always chide,
> nor will he keep his anger forever.
> He does not deal with us according to our sins,
> nor repay us according to our iniquities.
> For as high as the heavens are above the earth,
> so great is his steadfast love toward those who fear him;
> as far as the east is from the west,
> so far does he remove our transgressions from us.
> As a father shows compassion to his children,
> so Yahweh shows compassion to those who fear him.
> For he knows our frame;
> he remembers that we are dust.

But would the Rechabites remember that mankind was all dust? Would they forgive as God forgave? Would they display mercy and grace?

Or would they end up rejecting Galina as unclean and Susanna for being her sister?

Susanna suddenly noticed a warrior walking beside her as they trailed in Jonadab's footsteps. The same blond warrior she'd seen upon their arrival. The small man leaned in and whispered, "Fear not, wife of Jehu. Though Yahweh seems distant and difficult to find, yet he is near."

A tingle went down Susanna's spine at the man's words. He spoke as if he could read her thoughts. She glanced over to see if Galina had heard him, but her sister was engrossed in a conversation with Jonadab.

Susanna glanced back at the small warrior. But he'd once again disappeared.

Within a few paces, Jonadab stopped a short distance from a tent. This must be where the sisters were to stay. Two soldiers placed the bundles of their belongings inside the tent.

Then Susanna spotted the two figures standing in the tent entrance. She grabbed Galina's hand, and the two stopped silent in their tracks.

It was their father and mother standing in the torchlight. The couple, now in their forties, wore faces that bore the pain from years of familial alienation.

Her father began walking toward them first, trailed by their mother. Susanna prepared herself for the worst. She fully expected the old scene to replay, they would spit upon their younger daughter and curse her before ripping their clothes and turning their backs to storm off to their own tent in righteous indignation.

Then she saw it, the reflections of light in the tears. Her parents were crying as they approached.

Her father opened his arms.

Galina burst out with sobs and tears flowed.

She ran to him.

As they met, she fell at his feet, weeping and clutching his sandals.

He immediately pulled his youngest daughter to her feet, kissing her and hugging her.

Susanna joined with their mother, and the four of them held each other, sobbing.

"I'm sorry, Father," Susanna could hear Galina babbling through her tears. "I am so sorry."

"You have suffered enough, my child," her father muttered back. "My daughter."

216

It was the one thing Susanna hadn't expected. Forgiveness.

Rather than trying to hide her shame behind lies, Galina would have the chance to start a new chapter of life, freed from the past by forgiveness.

Susanna looked at Jonadab's smiling face. He had orchestrated this moment, and she would be forever grateful to him. It felt like the world's entire weight had just rolled off Susanna's shoulders.

"You will come back home with us," she heard her father say.

They made their way through the camp to their parents' tents. But Susanna's heart was not fully convinced that the past would not rise again. As they walked, she pulled Jonadab aside to discuss with him.

She said, "This is only a start. Galina has a long hard road ahead of her."

He replied, "Your sister is in need, and I intend to help your family. She will deliver her baby, and we will find her a husband to care for her and raise her child. She is—" He paused as though searching for appropriate words. "—young, healthy, and certainly attractive enough. It will not be difficult to find a willing man."

Susanna wondered if perhaps one of those "willing men" might be Jonadab himself, he seemed almost entranced with her sister. If so, Galina would be a second wife in his household. But that was acceptable enough, especially with Galina's history. At least she'd be cared for and ensured an inheritance.

But there was more on Susanna's heart than her sister. "I am also worried for my husband, Jonadab. I believe he is in danger from the queen."

The warrior leader smiled. "Let me tell you a story about your husband."

She listened, with every ounce of hope, to his story about the man she loved with all her heart and soul.

"When we were young, I remember seeing his skills with a chariot and a sword as well as his wit and wisdom. I knew that Yahweh's favor was upon him. On the day Jehu was chosen to be the training partner of the crown prince Ahab, I knew I would not see him much any longer. I thought his royal duties would consume him. He smiled and told me, 'Is your heart knit to mine as my heart is knit to yours?' I nodded, yes, and he said, 'Well, then, we will see each other again when it is Yahweh's will. And together we will do great things.'"

Jonadab paused, looking up into the night sky. "And now here we are together in the service of Yahweh and the king. Trust in Yahweh, Susanna. Your husband will do great things."

Susanna's eyes dampened as she thought of her beloved, his character, and his love for her. She already missed him. His strong, comforting embrace. His passionate kiss. The heat of his breath upon her skin. She prayed that their time of separation would not be as wide as it had been between these two friends.

She didn't have the patience of Jonadab, let alone Job.

CHAPTER 49

Jerusalem

Baal and Anat looked out upon the Valley of Hinnom outside the southwestern walls of the city. They were waiting for the right moment to make their move. In the unseen realm, Astarte stood with Molech on his Tophet of sacrifice.

The valley was full of Judeans from the city and surrounding area. They were there in solidarity to keep the Tophet and high places of Astarte, Milcom, and Chemosh from being destroyed. King Jehoshaphat of Judah had gone on a rampage of reform, tearing down the asherah in the temple of Solomon and executing the male temple prostitutes as well. The bodies of several dozens of them hung from the city wall for everyone in the valley to see. The people had risen up in protest against the king's actions and were calling out to Molech to stop the violence and destruction.

A high priest stood at the Tophet. His robe of Amorite design was embroidered with golden thread and blue in color to represent the waters of the Abyss that led down to Sheol where Molech was supposed to reside. The altar stood in the middle of a large open-air stone platform similar to those on other Israelite high places.

Raising an infant in the air, the high priest prayed to the underworld deity. The child was the son of a nobleman in the city. Three such infants were being offered on the high place this day. One after the other was raised and prayed over before being taken into the shrine of the holy place to be passed through the fires of Molech.

They wouldn't be slaughtered on the altar before the people. The priesthood had learned that when worshippers saw the public act of ending a child's life, no matter how sacred the act was, it caused problems. Some people were troubled by the violence of the sacrament and would spread their doubts and fears, they called the child innocent and the ritual a gruesome cruelty. Of course the people had no problem with the act of sacrificing a goat or a lamb. Slicing the throat of an animal didn't bother anyone, but slicing the throat of a human child for the same purposes seemed to inflame some of them. They were still indoctrinated by the Mosaic belief that humans were made in the image of God.

To avoid these messy social problems, the high priest had the children carried from the stone platform into the holy place of the shrine. Unseen by parents or the public, the child was slaughtered and placed in the arms of Molech. This bronze statue had outstretch arms, extended over the flames, very similar to Baal in his Temples at Tyre and Jezreel.

Molech's image here had a bull's head on its seated human form. Most parents refused to think about what it truly meant to place one's child into the loving arms of Molech.

Molech and Astarte followed their human servants into the structure. Inside, each child was first swiftly and compassionately killed with the sacrificial dagger, then cut into pieces and rearranged in Molech's bronze arms. The flames of the pit were stoked, and the child was burned in sacrifice. Unlike Baal's image, Molech's arms did not lower. The priests simply waited until the flesh was burned off the body, then put the bones into an urn and buried them in a crypt beneath the temple shrine.

As the three babies were being made to pass through the fire, Molech breathed in deep the pleasing aroma of the sacrifice. His body seemed to expand, his muscles becoming larger with each breath. When he opened his eyes, he saw Baal and Anat staring him down, both of them with weapons drawn. Anat was armed with her two swords, Baal his war hammer.

Astarte moved to draw her sword, but Molech stopped her. He spoke to the Canaanite deities without fear. "I would welcome you into my house, but it appears you have hostile intentions."

Molech's raspy underworld voice annoyed Baal.

Astarte said, "Would this surprise visit have anything to do with your recent defeat and complete humiliation at Mount Carmel? I've heard you've become quite the recluse as a result of it."

Anat glared at the Queen of Heaven as if ready to cut her to pieces.

Baal said, "I see the qedeshim hanging from the walls of Jerusalem and the burning of your asherim. So I can only conclude you are quite familiar with the humiliation of intolerant Yahwism as well."

Astarte replied, "That will all change when Jehoram becomes king of Judah."

"Or is it Athaliah, his betrothed queen, whom you think has the most potential, O Queen of Heaven?" Baal suggested snidely.

She smiled. "Spare me your male machismo, storm god. I suffered long enough under it as your consort. Now, it's my turn for power and influence."

Baal demanded, "Is that why you conspired with the goddesses to entrap me in Sheol and hinder my return?"

Astarte shared a look of surprise with Molech, then laughed. "Is that what you think? That I plotted your debasement with other goddesses? Oh that poor little fragile ego of yours. Have you stopped to consider just who benefits the most from your failure?"

Baal kept listening. She wasn't taking the credit.

"Whose prophets were not on Mount Carmel that day? Who convinced you to send me down here to be out of the way? Who has lost her priesthood and images in Judah while retaining them in Israel where you are discredited?"

Baal looked at Anat, then back to Astarte. He said reluctantly, "Asherah."

Astarte gestured with open hands of agreement. "Now, you're thinking. That is why I am glad the asherim have been removed from Judah. I detest the Mother as much as her son."

Baal said, "Astarte, your disrespect for me is considerable. Perhaps I should take you back with me as my consort and put you in your place."

Anat's expression flashed with anger and displeasure. Astarte said sarcastically, "I'm sorry, but you'll have to go through my new lovers." She gestured behind Baal and Anat.

They turned to see Chemosh and Milcom standing silently behind them, weapons drawn, eyes focused. They were the high gods of the Moabites and Ammonites. Both were brawny. Milcom had a full beard and bald head while Chemosh's head was covered with multiple horns. Both wore the warrior armor of their nation. Singularly, each was lesser in strength than Baal. But together and with Molech, they could take the Canaanite storm god.

"I want to show you something," Molech told Baal and Anat.

Brother and sister followed Molech and Astarte through a priest's door down some stairs into a subterranean chamber carved into the bedrock of Jerusalem's valley floor. Baal saw hundreds if not thousands of small urns stored in niches that had been cut into the chamber walls. He knew what was in the containers: the blackened bones and remains of the child sacrifices made to Molech on the Tophet above. Sacrifices that empowered the deity.

Thousands of them.

Molech said to Baal, "You know I've always respected your strength, storm god. But if you had this many child sacrifices for you in Jezreel, how strong would you be?"

Baal caught the subtext. Human sacrifice gave a god great power. This underworld maggot was warning him that he and his sister had not come prepared to face the power of the gods and goddess of Judah. If he tried, he might experience another humiliation that would sink him even deeper than he already was.

Astarte reiterated, "Judah is an ally of Israel, not her enemy. We have no quarrel with you. But who would benefit most from your failure?"

Asherah. It had to be Asherah. Queen Izabel had introduced Baal as Asherah's escort, replacing the old Yahweh with vibrant young Baal. But Asherah sought to undermine Baal and replace him as the primary deity.

Baal looked at Anat and considered things for a moment before turning his attention to Molech and Astarte. "I accept your offer of peace. I will return to Samaria. And when I have regained my power, I will not forget the respect you have shown me here."

"Oh, good!" Astarte said. It was another sarcastic jab at him. "Now, if you'll excuse us, we have an orgy to attend."

CHAPTER 50

Horeb

Elijah had traveled for forty days and forty nights in the wilderness. He had long since lost his way and truly did not know where he was anymore. But he followed the ravens.

During this journey he had consumed only water. It wasn't a fast. The angel had told him he would journey on the strength of that last meal alone, and that promise had held true.

Yahweh had once again miraculously provided.

And now Elijah stood before the mountain of God in Horeb. Mount Sinai. It loomed before him with supernatural meaning. Elijah had returned to the origin. He could see the top of the mountain was still black from the fire of Yahweh's theophany at the cutting of the covenant with the Israelites. This was truly a holy site, and it filled Elijah with awe.

Emotion overwhelmed the prophet, and he fell to the ground overcome with weeping. He didn't know why. Was it for all he'd endured these past years? Was it for the people of Israel, who remained unfaithful to their husband, Yahweh? Was it for the fear he felt unable to relinquish? Was it for the reputation of Yahweh himself in this brutal iron world of suffering and evil?

A holy psalm came to his mind. A psalm of David. It was one he'd memorized, recited, and cherished for years. Now he felt that he was experiencing it.

> The earth is Yahweh's and the fullness thereof,
>> the world and those who dwell therein,
> for he has founded it upon the seas
>> and established it upon the rivers.

Yahweh's establishment of the covenant at Sinai had always been understood as the creation of a cosmos, the heavens and earth, embodied in the tabernacle. The temple was now the sacramental symbol of that cosmos. As the true storm god, Yahweh had conquered Sea and River—as Baal and other gods only claimed.

> Who shall ascend the mountain of Yahweh?
> > And who shall stand in his holy place?
> He who has clean hands and a pure heart,
> > who does not lift up his soul to what is false
> > and does not swear deceitfully.
> He will receive blessing from Yahweh
> > and righteousness from the God of his salvation.
> Such is the generation of those who seek him,
> > who seek the face of the God of Jacob.

Elijah felt so unworthy. He did not have clean hands or a pure heart. Only Yahweh could make him clean. Only Yahweh could atone for his sin.

And one day Yahweh would send an Anointed One, Messiah, the King of Glory, the second Yahweh from heaven, to tear down the Gates of Sheol and conquer death itself.

> Lift up your heads, O gates!
> > And be lifted up, O ancient doors,
> > that the King of glory may come in.
> Who is this King of glory?
> > Yahweh, strong and mighty,
> > Yahweh, mighty in battle!
> Lift up your heads, O gates!
> > And lift them up, O ancient doors,
> > that the King of glory may come in.
> Who is this King of glory?
> > Yahweh of hosts,
> > he is the King of glory!

Ahab was no king of glory. And Queen Jezebel could not shut that glory out. One day Messiah would come.

As the sun set, Elijah began his ascent in search of a place to camp. He found a cave halfway up the holy mountain and made a small fire.

As he stared into the flames and embers, he heard a voice. "What are you doing here, Elijah?"

He looked up to see a being standing in the flames without being consumed. The being was dressed as a warrior in leather armor with a sword. But this armor was all white and his hair was white. It was the Angel of Yahweh.

Elijah dropped his head, discouraged, and complained, "I have been very jealous for Yahweh, the God of hosts. For the people of Israel have forsaken your covenant, thrown down your altars, and killed your prophets with the sword. I, even I only, am left, and they seek my life to take it away."

Elijah heard nothing, no response. He raised his head and looked up at the figure in the fire, and he felt suddenly overwhelmed and ashamed at his own words.

Then the angel spoke. "You are not alone. Go out and stand on the mount before Yahweh."

With that, the angel was gone.

Obediently, Elijah went to the mouth of the cave and stepped out onto the mount.

He saw the moon and the stars of God in the sky, lighting the cold, empty wilderness all about.

He felt a breeze hit his face. The breeze became a blast of wind so that Elijah had to steady himself against a rock. Then the wind became a whirlwind. Was this the pillar of cloud that had led Moses and the Israelites here?

The whirlwind now spun on the desert floor below. It grew and became furious, the sound was a continuous rumbling and roaring of wind. He felt the mountain quiver and tremble. The whirlwind began to climb the mountain, tearing up everything in its path, breaking rocks and boulders into pieces. It approached and passed right by in front of Elijah and then simply vanished into the ground.

And Elijah knew—he just knew—*that Yahweh was not in the wind.*

What did it mean? Before he could figure it out, the ground began to move. The basin rocked and swayed as an earthquake rattled and shook everything. Elijah fell to the ground and watched as a huge crevice opened. It split massive boulders and divided a hill as it travelled. The whole desert was rolling and shaking from deep underground.

Then it stopped.

And somehow, Elijah knew again *that Yahweh was not in the earthquake.*

Down on the desert floor, he saw a pillar of fire burst out of the crevice that had been caused by the earthquake. The flames swirled in a cyclonic motion as it travelled on the desert floor. Like the pillar of fire that had led the Israelites?

It too vanished, and Elijah was left with the certain knowledge *that Yahweh was not in the fire.*

What was going on? Why were all these miraculous displays of power lacking the presence of Yahweh? Were they not the very kinds of dramatic events that Yahweh had used in the past to deliver his people? To show them that he was God and no other? Elijah had called down fire from heaven to prove Yahweh's superiority over Baal. Why would Yahweh divest himself from these symbols and signs of his power?

And then Elijah heard all sounds cease. The noises of the night, the insects and animals, the sounds from the breeze moving across the land, these all vanished, and there was nothing but sheer silence. Elijah felt as if he were all alone in the cosmos and that Yahweh too was absent.

At first he felt terror. But then a strange calming presence.

Yahweh was in the silence. His voice was not in the presence of power, but in its absence, in the silence. It was a complete inversion of everything Elijah had understood about his Creator. It seemed to mock his ministry, his entire life.

Wrapping his face in his cloak, Elijah stepped back into the entrance of the cave. He remembered the thoughts that had gone through his mind forty days and nights earlier as he lay dying in the wilderness of Beersheba. He recalled the many miracles Yahweh had done for the people of Israel. The pillars of cloud and fire. The Red Sea deliverance. The fire on Mount Carmel. And then how the Israelites had always fallen back into idolatry despite it all.

Yahweh was not denying those acts of deliverance or regretting them. Rather, he was illustrating that the heart of man was so depraved it would always twist everything into power and glory instead of truth and goodness— and beauty. Maybe the whole point of this was that no matter how loud

Yahweh shouted, or how low he whispered—or if he didn't speak at all—only those with ears to hear would listen to him.

He heard a whisper ask him again, "What are you doing here, Elijah?"

He didn't see the messenger, but he knew the heavenly being was there. He answered into the air, "I told you, I have been very jealous for Yahweh, the God of hosts. And I alone am left."

The voice whispered, "You are not alone. I have left seven thousand in Israel, all the knees that have not bowed to Baal and every mouth that has not kissed him. Go, return on your way to the wilderness of Damascus. And when you arrive, you shall anoint Jehu the son of Nimshi to be king over Israel. And Elisha the son of Shaphat you shall anoint to be prophet in your place. The one who escapes from the sword of Damascus shall Jehu put to death. And the one who escapes from the sword of Jehu shall Elisha put to death."

Elijah had heard the Word of the Lord and he would obey.

CHAPTER 51

*Life is a storm cycle of God. First you see darkened clouds.
Then rain, lightning, and thunder attack the land and its
inhabitants. But when the storm leaves, the land gives birth
to the fruit that nourishes all life. Until the next storm.*

*At the appointed time, Galina gave birth to a boy she named
Daniel. Jonadab the Rechabite, who first had pitied
Susanna's sister, fell in love with her. He married her and
gave her a home with his family and clan. Jezebel's hostility
toward me subsided, and Susanna returned home to me.*

*After some years when Athaliah had turned fifteen and come
of age, she was sent to Jerusalem to marry prince Jehoram,
son of Jehoshaphat the king of Judah. All of Jezebel's
designs had come to fruition. Her sons, whom she had
raised, would one day inherit the monarchy of Israel, and
Athaliah, her ward whom she had instructed, would one day
become queen of Judah.*

Jerusalem

Izabel accompanied Athaliah to the temple precinct on Mount Moriah. They
had recently arrived in a caravan from Samaria in preparation for the wedding
between Athaliah and the prince.

This was to be the climax of everything Izabel had worked for with the
princess. She had spent all these years mentoring and imparting her own
strategic view of how to rule. How to rule as a queen. How to rule a people.

How to rule a husband and king. How to use the patriarchy to a woman's own advantage. How to subvert and fundamentally transform the nation.

Kings like Ahab and Jehoshaphat considered their legacies to be rooted in their sons who would rule after them. But Izabel knew she had managed to shape and mold her sons in her own image. She considered Athaliah to be part of her legacy as well. Through her, Izabel would bring progress and change to Judah's ignorant and barbaric religion of intolerance just as she was doing in Israel.

The two women entered through the southern gates into the outer courtyard, hundreds of square feet surrounded by porticoes and priestly chambers. In the center of the court was a raised stone platform, large enough to contain the temple of Solomon and the sacrificial altar area.

"It's beautiful," said Athaliah. "Yahweh's high place is just like the temple of Baal."

"Phoenician design," said Izabel. The platform looked about two hundred feet long and a hundred feet wide with a temple that took up two thirds of that space. A rectangular tripartite temple with two large bronze pillars at the entrance. They wouldn't be allowed to go inside to see where the ark of the covenant sat between the cherubim in the holy of holies. Only priests could enter there.

Here in the temple courtyard, the two women looked around at the fixtures. To the left of the temple was the enormous molten sea, a swimming pool sized bowl on the backs of twelve oxen, which represented Yahweh's power over chaos. Behind them were various lavers and basins for washings. To the right was the stone altar of sacrifice and a fenced-in courtyard for the animals.

"I see the asherah has been removed," said Athaliah. There was only a hole next to the altar where the asherah pole had previously been planted.

"But see Nehushtan?" Izabel pointed to a bronze pole with a graven serpent on it standing before the stairs of the temple. She'd taught Athaliah the story of the image, how viewing it had saved people who'd been bitten by poisonous snakes, and how to properly worship it.

"When you become queen, you can restore the asherah pole to its place and even build a temple of Baal."

"But Jehoram won't be king until his father dies," Athaliah pointed out.

"You'll have the time to know Jehoram and shape him, so that when he does become king you will have his favor. And, he will become co-regent with his father shortly, which means your husband-to-be, and you, will have influence soon enough."

Athaliah hugged Izabel. "Thank you for all you have taught me."

Izabel hugged her back tightly. "We have been a sisterhood, you and I, have we not?"

Athaliah smiled. "We have."

Izabel placed her hands on the shoulders of her study and smiled softly as she looked Athaliah in the eyes. "Life will not be easy as a woman in this place. But I believe in you. I believe you have the strength to fight your way to the top. You just must believe in yourself. And trust Astarte and Baal."

"I will," said Athaliah.

CHAPTER 52

Abel-meholah

Elisha stopped the oxen and rested against the plow. Catching his breath and wiping his brow, he looked back over the progress he'd made plowing the field. This was a good time to take a break. He took a moment to look over the animals and check the yoke and harnesses. Confident everything was in good order, he stretched and glanced back at his home. He'd rebuilt his father's house from the ruins and had been living in it for some time now. He'd been working the land, and he felt stronger, more stable because of it. Elisha still wrestled with the past and his decision to leave the School of Prophets. He had desired justice, but found himself empty after dispensing that justice to the prophets of Baal. But thank Yahweh, he had found that working the land made him feel more in touch with the Creator and with his place in the cosmos. Like Adam, he felt like he was made from the red earth.

Elisha put his hand to the plow, ready to resume his labors. He stopped as he caught sight of a figure standing in the distance of his field. He squinted in the sun, trying to see who it was. Then he recognized the gait and heavy mantle on the visitor's shoulders.

"Elijah!" he shouted, running toward the prophet.

They met and embraced, two souls with one past. Elisha felt reinvigorated with his old mentor in his grasp.

They laughed with joy as they greeted each other. Elisha noticed Elijah seemed different, it was more than age or the hardships of life. His face was gaunt. His hair and beard were longer and messier—if that could be.

Elisha tugged at the old mantle of angora goat. "I see some things never change." He grabbed Elijah's ragged hair with a chuckle. "And others just get worse."

Elijah's eyes were full of tears, tear of happiness and joy. It was so good to see his protégé, the young man had matured and exuded a new peace and contentment.

Elisha looked into the old prophet's eyes and it dawned on him what was different about his teacher. "You look like you've seen God."

The old man smiled softly, a distant look washed over his face as the memory flooded back. "I heard him whisper."

There was a quiet pause of understanding. Elisha threw an arm around Elijah's shoulders, "Let's get you fed and cleaned up, old man."

Later, they sat in the house talking. Elisha had prepared and roasted a lamb shank. Elijah savored the meat, and he ate with gusto, like there was no tomorrow. Was there a tomorrow? He had just told Elisha of his harrowing experience with Jezebel after Mount Carmel.

"But why did you run?" asked Elisha. "You had just defeated the prophets of Baal. Yahweh sent fire from heaven."

Elijah spoke, his voice expressed a sadness. "All my life I have struggled with the fear of man. I know it doesn't make sense, but—" He sought for the right words. "When Jezebel threatened me, it was like all the miracles faded, and all I could think was that I was alone."

"But you weren't alone. The Israelites rose up and slaughtered the prophets of Baal."

Elijah sighed. "I thought they were siding with whomever won to protect themselves."

Smiling, and hoping to lighten the conversation, Elisha teased, "And you say I don't listen to the Lord?"

Elijah raised his hands in mock surrender.

Then Elisha grew serious. "The surviving prophets of Yahweh remain in hiding to this day. They await your return to lead them."

Elijah considered his words, then asked, "Why are you not with them?"

Elisha sat back with a sigh. Where to begin? He said, "At Carmel, I violated the prophet's vow of non-violence. I killed many prophets of Baal that day." He paused with shame. "And when I was drenched in the blood of my enemies, I could not understand what made Yahweh different from other gods—petty deities fighting to control a patch of land. How is our slaughter of the prophets of Baal any different from Jezebel's slaughter of the prophets of Yahweh?"

"Your inability to see the bigger picture still blinds you," responded Elijah.

But Elisha looked the prophet in the eye with a painful heart. "Is there no grace? No mercy?"

Now Elijah sighed. He considered what he would say. He was not quick to speak these days. "Nations conquer one another and enslave women and children. They perform human sacrifice. All the earth fornicates with false gods like a disease-ridden harlot. How do you expect Yahweh to act within a world gone mad with idolatry, violence, and oppression?"

Elisha understood what Elijah was saying. He'd spent much time in the intervening years contemplating just that, contemplating his own actions and their consequences.

He said, "It is a thin line between justice and revenge. I do not trust myself anymore to know the difference."

"Good," said Elijah. "Your faith is finally in Yahweh alone. In his justice."

Elisha knew that his mentor understood. Despite feeling hopeless and losing his belief in the goodness of man, he'd always clung to the righteousness of Yahweh. The true and living God, the one and only king of the cosmos.

Elijah said, "A king is anointed to bring justice for the people. One day a righteous son of David will be anointed to bring peace."

"Messiah?" asked Elisha.

Elijah answered, "He will be prophet, priest, and king. But that peace is not yet. So we serve a divine warrior."

Elisha recited a psalm of David from memory,

> "Oh sing to Yahweh a new song,
>   for he has done marvelous things!
> His right hand and his holy arm
>   have worked salvation for him.
> Yahweh has made known his deliverance,
>   before the eyes of the nations,
>   he has revealed his faithfulness."

Elijah joined him in reciting the final verse,

"For Yahweh comes to judge the earth.
    He will judge the world with righteousness,
    and the peoples with equity."

Elijah unbuckled the leather belt that held the long-haired mantle to his shoulders. He pulled off the mantle and raised it up to place it on Elisha's shoulders.

Elisha stopped him, confused. "I don't deserve this."

Elijah smiled. "You're right. You don't." But he moved to place it on him anyway. As he settled the cloak around the humbled Elisha, he added, "The righteous shall live by faith. Yahweh is your righteousness."

Elisha said, "I cannot do this alone."

"You won't be alone." Elijah smiled. "The mantle doesn't make you the *only* prophet, you know. It's just a symbol. I'm still here. And we have much to do together."

CHAPTER 53

Jezreel

I want to tell you next about an incident that would seem trivial to some. But within my story it bears a symbolic weight that would herald the end of Ahab and his kingdom. And it would also foreshadow the end of Jezebel and her death grip on the nation of Israel.

Athaliah was married to prince Jehoram in Judah. The Assyrian threat from the north was growing stronger. King Ahab and a coalition of kings defeated the Assyrians at the battle of Qarqar. But the northern invaders would be back. And when they were, Israel would not be prepared.

In the light of these dangerous times, Jezebel and Ahab had relocated their main residence to Jezreel, where the queen now appeared to manage the kingdom's administration while Ahab withdrew into his military obsession and personal debauchery.

Jehu stood with a handful of various administration officials in Jezebel's personal office. The queen had decorated the room as a Tyrian palace, filled with bright colored fabrics and multiple statues and engravings of the gods. Jehu hated being here. It made him want to take a war hammer to the art and smash the stone heads and bodies of Baal, Astarte, Asherah, and Melqart. Jehu had never set foot in the temples of the foreign gods, unlike this intolerable room, and he fully intended not to—unless he were able to kill all the priests and burn it to the ground.

Four of those priests of Baal stood behind Izabel. They followed her everywhere as bodyguards. She had become obsessed with her own safety, even in her own palace. Five of her advisors were Tyrians from her hometown while only two were Israelites, and those were more for display than actual counseling.

Jehu wondered where Elijah was. The prophet had been gone so long even Jezebel had stopped looking for him. The prophets of Yahweh continued to hide out in the caves of the Jezreel wilderness, also forgotten. *How long, O Lord, will you delay?*

A scribe recorded the royal meeting as they argued over the details of bureaucracy. The Israelite counselors were being unusually vocal today.

"My queen," said one of them, "we have too many palace servants, too many government projects, and too much debt. We are spending more than we are taking in. It is not sustainable."

Jezebel said, "Then we tax the wealthy merchants more."

"But your highness, if we tax the merchants more, they will take their business elsewhere. To Damascus even."

"Then we will pass laws that will not allow them to relocate."

Jezebel examined the scar on the palm of her left hand. It was a daily reminder of her failure at Mount Carmel. Jehu had noticed that when she was paying attention to it, she would increase in aggression and hostility toward everyone.

The other Israelite counselor jumped in. "In the end, the tax coffers of the king will have less, and the poor will suffer most."

Jezebel became impatient. "Then we decrease our military expenditures. How much money have we wasted on the beast of war?"

It was a particular sore point for the queen. She loathed the military.

After a moment of uncomfortable silence, the counselor said, "My queen, with all due respect, a strong military is necessary for peace. The king says so himself."

It was the one area where Ahab would stand up to Jezebel and not back down, so she addressed it only when necessary.

One of her Phoenician advisors, a lackey, spoke up. "A strong military makes us an aggressor."

"Exactly," she concluded. It had been something she was fond of saying herself. The lackey smirked, self-satisfied.

As commander of the armies, Jehu finally had to say something. "The threat of Assyrian return looms large, your highness."

"Baalshit!" Jezebel exploded. "Rumors loom large. Yahwism looms large. Fanatical Rechabites are a greater internal threat than any foreign nation."

The queen believed the Rechabites to be preparing an army for a violent coup d'état against her and the king. She was obsessed with the idea and had been heard muttering this delusion more than once. Jehu was concerned she was scheming to annihilate them. Though how he did not know.

Jezebel interrupted his thoughts. "First we are at odds with Judah, then Damascus, and now Assyria. *We* are the ones provoking conflict."

Her Phoenician advisors grumbled in agreement.

"Your majesty," cautioned Jehu, "we have not provoked. We have only protected."

Her face twisted with distrust. "Jehu, are you sure your concern is for the protection of the king or the promotion of another agenda?"

Before he could answer and defend himself, the sound of a loud crash in the next room drew all their attention.

The advisors jerked in fear. Jehu jumped up, instantly in warrior mode, he moved quickly to investigate. Running to the door, he tried to open it.

"It's locked."

He could hear the sound of furniture being smashed, accompanied by human growling. Jehu knew that growl anywhere.

"It's the king!" he proclaimed. He gestured to the guards to join him, and they rammed the door. The lock broke open, and Jehu and the guards poured into the room.

It was in shambles. Expensive furniture had been broken into pieces and now lay all around the room. Ahab stood alone with the last intact chair held over his head. He threw it at the wall, and it exploded, reduced to splinters.

He turned to see Jehu and the guards and then Jezebel behind them.

The queen looked around at the state of the room and her lip curled in disgust. Pushing the guards aside, she shouted "Everyone, out!"

Unafraid, she stared the king down, who was breathing heavily from his rampage. Ahab picked up a bottle of wine and chugged it. Stumbling on some debris, he fell to the ground, splashing himself with wine that he sought to keep from spilling.

Jehu left last and closed the door, but leaned up against it to listen in.

"Look at you," Izabel hissed. "You are pathetic. Throwing a tantrum like a child."

Ahab was silent in response.

She was exasperated. "What is it now?"

He spoke through his slur. "I rebuilt this city from the ground up. I created glory and magnificence never before seen in our nation. Fortification, architecture, culture." He saw her scolding look. "With Tyre's help, of course."

"And?"

"And all I want for myself is a simple vineyard near the palace. A lousy, stinking vineyard. I need it for my military." He admitted his more important reason, "And for the royal household, of course. But I can't have it because a Jezreelite named Naboth owns it."

She sighed with contempt. "Jehu tells me Assyria is breathing down our necks, and *you* are worried about a petty little vineyard?"

Ahab complained, "Tell me that when there's no royal wine left."

She shook her head with disgust. "So take the vineyard."

"You don't understand, Izabel."

"*I don't understand?* You are king. Take what you want."

"This is not Tyre. We have sacred land laws even the king must obey."

This was so much nonsense to her. "What in Hades are you talking about?"

He took another swig of wine. "According to our holy statutes, families have perpetual rights to their land. Family inheritance cannot be infringed. The land is holy."

His drunkenness didn't cloud his argument as he explained how the allotment of lands to the twelve tribes of Israel upon conquering Canaan was foundational to Yahweh's promise of inheritance. Yahweh had given holy laws that kept such allotments within the tribes, no matter what happened to specific families.

Izabel said, "Go eat your dinner. I will get you the vineyard so you can drink yourself into oblivion."

Turning on her heels, she stomped angrily out of the room and slammed the door behind her.

That was when she noticed Jehu. Ever-present Jehu. Always-watching Jehu. Suspicious Jehu. She ordered, "Jehu, leave us."

The commander looked reluctantly at the others but obeyed.

After he'd gone, Izabel sat down and took the scribe's quill to write on a piece of parchment while ordering her two Israelite advisors. "Baalmot, Chenash, find this Naboth who owns the vineyard outside the palace. I am writing a letter for you to deliver to the elders of the city. You are to find two mercenaries who are willing to testify against this Jezreelite in a legal petition. They will claim he cursed both God and king."

"But, your majesty," protested Baalmot, "they will stone the owner to death for such false testimony."

"Exactly." She continued writing. "The elders will then give you his land deed, and you are to bring it to me."

The advisors stared at each other, eyes wide with shock. Chenash found his voice first and spoke, "According to the law, his sons would inherit the vineyard."

She stopped for a moment to consider his point. Then she said nonchalantly, "So you will have to remove that legal problem as well."

The two advisors went white with fear. They understood what that meant. They were to execute both the owner and his sons. She demanded, "Do you understand your orders?"

They remained silent, looking at each other with complicit guilt.

"Do you understand your orders?!" This time it was a warning.

Chenash and Baalmot said nervously, "Yes, my queen."

"Good." She folded the letter closed and poured heated wax on it.

Baalmot handed her a seal. It was her own. It carried her name surrounded by Egyptian hieroglyphs.

"Give me the king's seal," she commanded.

Baalmot looked to Chenash for advice. It was a crime for anyone other than the king to use his seal in communications. It was his official insignia, marking his authority behind the letter. Even the queen was not allowed such presumption. They would all be accomplices to this act if discovered. And the punishment would be death. But knowing Izabel, it would be just as bad for them to disobey her command. What else could he do?

Baalmot handed her the seal.

She grabbed it and sealed her letter with the king's authority.

CHAPTER 54

Walking away from Jezebel's personal office, Jehu wondered what malfeasance she would conduct in his absence. There was a specific reason she had dismissed only him from the room. They both disliked each other, and a level of distrust had grown over the years. But it wasn't something either of them had ever admitted to in public. Sure, it slipped out here and there in comments or reactions in moments of stress. They knew it, and everyone close to them knew it—except Ahab. He seemed oblivious. The king would simply dismiss Jezebel's attempts to undermine Jehu as a lack of understanding by a woman of the necessary manliness needed to be a soldier. Jehu was the most loyal and competent commander the king had ever known. And Ahab valued his military more than anything else in his kingdom.

As queen, Jezebel carried the power of the crown to impose her will upon most anyone. But as trusted commander of the army, Jehu couldn't be easily targeted by the queen's subterfuge. Nevertheless, Jezebel was a cunning shrew. If he wasn't careful, she would find a way to take him down. He was always on his guard.

So Jehu sent a spy to follow Baalmot and Chenash as they fulfilled the secret commands of the crown. He needed to know what the queen was doing, she'd had a reason for removing him from the meeting.

The spy met with Jehu in the commander's keep in the palace. This was private enough, a small office tucked away in the corner of the casemate walls of the palace fortress, far from the king's rooms. The queen had appointed it to humiliate Jehu, but it worked in his favor, an out of the way place of privacy, ideal for sensitive conversations.

The spy, a bright, young man of eighteen, told Jehu what he'd seen.

"I followed the two men outside the city walls to one of the villages near the perimeter. I know this clan. They own and operate several vineyards. Anyway, they arrived at the center of the village to a large legal gathering."

Jehu took a sip of wine from his chalice and asked, "Were the elders of the village there?"

"Yes," said the spy. Elders were required for legal judgments. "I saw a man and his three young boys tied to poles. A cart full of rocks was nearby."

"A stoning," Jehu concluded.

"I recognized the man," said the spy. "It was Naboth the Jezreelite and his sons."

Jehu knew immediately who this was. Naboth owned a nearby vineyard that the king admired and often praised before the commander.

The spy continued, "Two witnesses accused Naboth of cursing God and the king. But I saw them paid afterward by Baalmot and Chenash."

"Scoundrels," huffed Jehu.

The spy continued, "And I saw an elder hand the royal messengers a scroll."

"The deed to Naboth's vineyard," Jehu concluded. The spy's report added up to one thing. Jezebel had arranged the murder of an innocent man and his sons to confiscate his vineyard for the king.

The queen's action didn't surprise Jehu. It sickened him.

He told the spy, "Describe for me the stoning. In detail."

The spy hesitated. Jehu demanded, "Tell me." He wanted this burned into his mind, forever branding in his memory Jezebel's bloodguilt.

The spy swallowed and searched for words. "The first few stones missed their targets. The first to be hit was the youngest boy. He cried out in pain."

"How old?" asked Jehu.

"About five."

Jehu closed his eyes tight with anger.

The spy said, "His father tried to encourage him. He said, 'Be brave, my son.'"

Brave, indeed, thought Jehu. *One day I will reward his bravery with justice against Jezebel.*

"More rocks began to hit each of them. I saw Naboth hit in the head and his skull broke open.

"Mercifully, the boys were unconscious long before their flesh was turned into bloody pulp. But the truth is, I turned away before it was over. I could bear to watch it no longer. It was a tragic injustice."

No! The thought roared at Jehu. This was no mere tragic injustice. This was the murder of four innocent people, murder in order to steal land. Jehu's heart raged as he filed the details in his memory. Yahweh's reckoning would someday come for the harlot queen Jezebel and Jehu would wait patiently until then, storing up the tally of her offenses.

CHAPTER 55

King Ahab stumbled as he walked the vineyard row with a gourd of wine in one hand and a scroll in the other. The vineyard was lit with a golden glow and the sun was setting. The king was drunk again, yet his grasp was tight on Izabel's gift, the deed to this land, Naboth's vineyard.

He sang a drinking song he'd learned from Izabel's culture. It was the song that would be sung at a Marzeah Feast, the celebration of the dead descending to be with the Rephaim kings in Sheol.

"May Shapash shine upon him!

After our lords, from the throne,

After your lords from the underworld go down;

Into the underworld go down

And fall into the dust.

One and make an offering,

Two and make an offering,

Three and make an offering..."

Ahab spun around with his arms open wide, a gesture of owning the vineyard. He was supposed to sing up to seven offerings, but he couldn't make it that far. He fell to the ground, dizzy and mumbling to himself.

He'd lost the wine gourd when he fell. Now he groped around searching for it with his hand. His vision was too blurry to actually look for it.

He belched. Then a wave of nausea came over him. He vomited without pause onto the ground. It came out like a waterfall. His whole body tightened and convulsed with the retching.

And then it was over. He wiped his lips with his sleeve and laughed to himself.

As he sat there next to his vomit, he noticed movement in his blurred vision. There was a figure approaching and he reached out as though to touch it, his hand seeking the silhouette. And abruptly his eyesight cleared, and he immediately recognized the man standing before him.

"Elijah!" he cried out. "Have you found me, O my enemy? I have missed you fiercely."

Elijah said nothing. Ahab adjusted his tone to scolding and wagged a pointed finger as he continued. "You've been a naughty prophet. You ran away. We've been looking for you for quite some time, you know."

The figure remained quiet, staring at him like an angry phantom.

"Well, what have you to say for yourself?"

When the figure finally spoke, the voice seemed to echo in Ahab's ears. "I have found you because you have sold yourself to do what is evil in the sight of Yahweh. You have killed and taken possession of holy land."

Ahab replied, "Aren't you being a tad bit over-reactive? I only took a vineyard. Well, okay, there is that matter of the owner and his family. But that was the queen, not me!"

Elijah announced, "Ahab, son of Omri, you have done more to provoke the Lord God than all the kings of Israel who were before you."

"Me?" he protested. "Have you spoken with Izabel? She may beg to differ. And you don't want to cross her."

"Thus says the Lord, 'In the same way that dogs licked up the blood of Naboth shall dogs lick your own blood. And the dogs shall eat Jezebel within the walls of Jezreel.'"

"She's not going to be happy with that prophecy," Ahab interrupted. "So may I suggest we avoid bringing that one up too quickly? Ease into it, so to speak."

Elijah concluded, "'I will utterly burn you up and will cut off from Ahab every male, bond or free, in Israel. I will bring disaster upon the house of Ahab.'"

Ahab felt overwhelmed, in his drunken state this was all just too much. He muttered aloud, "That's not fair. That's not fair." When he looked up, the figure was gone. He whimpered, "Don't leave me again, Elijah. Please."

The king fell back onto the ground and lay there, weeping. For how long he couldn't tell. But when he finally looked up again, the figure was back, the glowing sun behind it creating a silhouette. Then he realized it was not Elijah. It was Izabel holding the hand of their five-year old son Joram.

She looked down upon him with disgust. "Get up. You disgrace your son."

Ahab mustered himself to rise, but could not get up. He was dizzy, and the vineyard began to spin. He passed out.

Izabel shook her head and said to Joram, "I will teach you how to be king."

He looked up at her. She knelt down, placing herself at his eye level. She smiled and affectionately brushed his nose.

"And you will do exactly what I tell you."

CHAPTER 56

Baal sat on the throne in his Jezreel temple, a hand on his mighty war hammer Driver as it lay across his knees. His spear, Chaser, rested against an arm of the throne, readily accessible. Anat stood loyally beside him. Recently returned from Jerusalem, he'd called Asherah to audience. He needed to make it clear that he was still the Most High, and he was ready to enforce that claim.

Asherah strode in with a maternal impatience and a condescending smirk on her face. "Well, well, well, don't you look all grown up, my son. Did Astarte try to convince you I am conspiring to overthrow your rule in Israel?"

"As a matter of fact, she did," he replied.

"It's perfect motive, isn't it?" she said. "You raped me and humiliated me. Your temple jeopardizes my stronghold in Israel. And as Mother of the gods, I think it's time for a matriarchy to overthrow the patriarchy. Isn't that the narrative?"

Baal felt a bit put off. She was being sarcastic as if it wasn't true. Her implication was that it had all been a diversion by Astarte to buy more time. Astarte *had* wanted to free herself from Baal's headship. She wanted to be Queen of Heaven, not some second-class consort. And she was already succeeding in Judah. Why would she bother to go out of her way to attack Baal?

Asherah spoke as if she read his mind. "I suppose the only one you've never bothered to consider was your loyal sister."

Anat was the only one he trusted, all the others were just conniving goddesses.

He looked to her for denial. Anat remained stoic.

Baal said to Asherah, "She saved me from Sheol. She could've left me down there to rot, but she didn't."

Anat broke in, "I also saved your pathetic little head from Lilith, let's not forget."

He snapped his head around to look at Anat. Now she was smirking.

Asherah said sarcastically, "Why, it's almost as if she kept you together until you could get to Mount Carmel so you could be thoroughly emasculated by Yahweh *before the whole world*."

Baal felt a chill down his spine.

Anat offered an explanation. "When the archangels helped us at Terqa, it was clear to me they wanted you to make it to Carmel, which could only mean one thing: Yahweh had plans to dispossess you." She added sardonically, "Who was I to stand in his way? I might as well join the winning team."

Baal sighed and nodded reluctantly. He'd felt angry with himself for failing to see the archangel's true motives at the time.

Anat said, "It *was* I who betrayed you."

Asherah said, "And so did I."

Anat finished, "And Astarte as well."

It had been all three of them. A conspiracy. Baal gripped his hammer tightly.

Anat drew her swords. "I am sick of helping you accomplish your goals—defeating Sea, River, Leviathan —while you receive all the glory and I am treated as a second-class deity. I can do anything you can do."

"Better!" added Asherah.

"You've had your reign," Anat went on. "And you've lost your power over this region. Now it's time for you to step aside and let a goddess be queen."

Baal looked at Asherah. "Well mother, you are the only one here who is qualified for this coup, since my sister is nothing but a bootlicking Virgin runt."

Anat's eyes burned with rage.

But the flames were extinguished instantly with the crushing swing of Driver into her face. She hit the back wall of stone, both swords flying from her hands with the impact. Her head was a smashed bloody pulp.

Baal had been positioned for just this moment. He stood with Chaser in his other hand, puffing his chest out.

"I'm still the head of this pantheon. And you will obey me."

Asherah drew her sword and began moving toward Baal. "You're not as strong as you were."

Her momentum froze as she saw two other high gods step out from behind Baal's throne: Marduk, the Babylonian king of the gods, and Ashur,

247

head of the Assyrian pantheon. Both deities were bearded, muscular warrior gods dressed for battle with armor, sword, and mace.

"No, I am not as strong," said Baal. "Which is why I made a treaty with the principalities of Babylon and Assyria. We have great plans for Israel and Judah."

Marduk and Ashur now stood on either side of Asherah. She surrendered her weapon.

Baal said, "I don't know how Astarte seduced and manipulated Molech, Chemosh, and Milcom down in Jerusalem. But they'll listen to me now. My only question is, Mother, what am I going to have to do to finally get you to submit?"

She replied with defiance, "You'll have to send me to Sheol."

"No. You are too important to me. You have actually accomplished more than I have amongst the Hebrews. I don't want to lose that. I just want it to have its proper context."

The gods grabbed her arms.

Baal concluded, "It seems my previous chastisement of you didn't get through. So perhaps three of us can penetrate you with some sense."

For the next three days, the screams of Asherah's painful abuse could be heard in the unseen realm.

This time she would obey.

CHAPTER 57

*Twelve years passed. And though there is too much to tell of
all that occurred in Israel in that time, I will speak of
Jezebel and how our interests finally collided in tragedy.*

*In the southern kingdom of Judah, Athaliah gave birth to
several sons by Prince Jehoram. His father King
Jehoshaphat remained an ally of King Ahab in Israel.*

*But hostilities rose again between Damascus and Israel. The
heavens and earth were not at peace. War was again on the
horizon.*

Samaria

King Ahab of Israel and King Jehoshaphat of Judah sat on their portable thrones on the threshing floor just outside the gates of the city. They had convened an assembly of prophets of Yahweh at the behest of Jehoshaphat to divine whether Ahab should attack the city of Ramoth-gilead and take it from the Arameans of Damascus. King Ben-hadad had never returned the city to Ahab in violation of their previous treaty, so it was Ahab's to take by right.

Ahab had spared Ben-hadad at Aphek. He had allowed him to continue his rule. He had allowed Damascus to be an economic ally rather than a subjugated foe. The ingrate Ben-hadad had then refused to follow through with his part in the treaty.

King Jehoshaphat had come to Samaria at Ahab's request, the premise was discussion and expansion of their relations. Prince Jehoram and Athaliah had also come to Samaria as part of the royal entourage. They were not a part of this meeting and remained in Jezreel to visit with Izabel and the royal family. What king Ahab really wanted, was more support from his ally to re-take the city. He had asked the southern king to help him in his campaign against Ramoth-gilead. In response, Jehoshaphat had requested to hear what the prophets of Yahweh recommended before he decided.

Though Ahab thought the Judahite king was a bit too self-righteous and zealous in his religion, he nevertheless had to appease his interests if he was to gain the military advantages of partnering with the southern kingdom.

So, here they were, listening to what the prophets of Yahweh had to say. There were four hundred of them gathered here. So far, all were giving hearty approval, saying, "Go up to Ramoth-gilead, for the Lord will give it into the hand of the king."

One after the other they came, over and over, until the redundancy of their affirmation began to bore the kings. Ahab nodded sleepily.

He felt an elbow in his ribs and jerked awake. It was Jehoshaphat. He looked over at the fellow king and began making mental comparison. The two men were both in their late fifties, but age was about all they shared in physical similarities. Ahab felt pangs of envy. Jehoshaphat was much healthier than the Israelite king, his diet was moderate. But by Ahab's thinking it was stringent, with none of the rich foods Ahab loved, nor the excesses of wine. Ahab moved his hand to his chin as he thought. He felt his own double chin. The mental comparison continued as he glanced down at his belly paunch.

It was bad enough Ahab already felt inferior to Jehoshaphat in both religion and physique. Even worse, the constant air of superiority the southern king and all his family radiated, all because they were of the Davidic line, it was inescapable and hung over every interaction like an odor of snobbery. *They* were the House of David. *They* were the chosen ones. *They* were the keepers of the holy temple and priesthood.

Well, as much as their partnership was strategic for both kingdoms, Israel was superior in military force, and Jehoshaphat knew full well that Judah needed Israel more than Israel needed Judah.

One of the prophets named Zedekiah came and stood before the kings. Younger and bolder than most, he had a flair for the dramatic. Wearing a pair of iron horns he had cast for the occasion, he stomped around like a bull and announced, "Thus says Yahweh, 'With these you shall push the Arameans until they are destroyed.'" He stomped his feet again and grunted into the air as an angry bull might.

Jehoshaphat leaned over to Ahab and muttered, "Where did you get these prophets?"

Ahab said, "Mostly from Dan and Bethel." He avoided mentioning the fact that the prophets of Yahweh in Samaria and Jezreel had remained a persecuted minority since their massacre by Izabel years ago.

"That explains the bull imagery," said Jehoshaphat. "You still have the golden calves in those cities, don't you?"

Here he went again, judging Ahab's religion.

Jehoshaphat added, "Is there not a prophet of Yahweh without such corruption of whom we may inquire?"

Ahab felt his ire increase. He held it back and said resignedly, "There is yet one prophet of Yahweh 'without such corruption.'" He spoke the phrase with a touch of mockery. "Micaiah the son of Imlah. But I hate him. He never prophesies good concerning me, only evil."

"Well," said Jehoshaphat, "then let us hear what he has to say."

Ahab turned to Jehu, who had been standing beside him the entire time. "Jehu, you know where the old prophet is. Go fetch him."

"Yes, your majesty."

Jehu left to fetch the prophet.

By the time the commander had returned with Micaiah, the kings had finished listening to the four hundred prophets of Yahweh. Jehoshaphat appeared eager to hear Micaiah. Ahab dreaded it.

As the old prophet hobbled up to the thrones, Ahab spoke. "So, Micaiah, you've heard the inquiry. What will it be? Shall we go to Ramoth-gilead to battle, or shall we refrain?"

Micaiah looked intently at Ahab, then at Jehoshaphat. With his perpetual frown, he looked perturbed. *But then*, thought Ahab, *he was always a perturbed, angry old codger.*

When Micaiah finally spoke, his disposition changed suddenly to that of a fraudulent sycophant. "Go up and triumph, O king, for Yahweh will give the city and all its glory and power into your little hands!" His words were thick with sarcasm. This parody of all the other prophets was an attack on Ahab's ego.

The king huffed, "You mock me, old man."

251

Micaiah shrugged innocently.

Ahab growled, "I command you to swear to speak to me nothing but the truth in the name of Yahweh."

Micaiah glared at him, then at Jehoshaphat. Then he said with a firm voice, "I saw all Israel scattered on the mountains as sheep that have no shepherd. And Yahweh said, 'These have no master; let each return to his home in peace.'"

"I told you," said Ahab to Jehoshaphat. "Didn't I tell you he'd only prophecy evil concerning me? The sheep in his vision are obviously symbolic of Israel and I am the shepherd. He's saying Israel will lose me as her shepherd."

Micaiah continued on, his voice powerful with prophetic authority. "Therefore, hear the word of Yahweh, O king. I will tell you what I saw in the divine council of the gods, the assembly of the holy ones. I saw Yahweh sitting on his throne and all the host of heaven standing beside him on his right hand and on his left."

The mark of a true prophet of Yahweh was if they'd been allowed into the divine council. Ahab knew that Micaiah was trumpeting his credentials.

"And Yahweh said, 'Who will entice Ahab that he may go up and fall at Ramoth-gilead?' Several of them gave their counsel. Some said this, others said that. But then a spirit came forward and stood before Yahweh, saying, 'I will entice him.' And Yahweh said to him, 'By what means?' And the spirit said, 'I will go out and will be a lying spirit in the mouth of all his prophets.' And Yahweh said, 'Go, entice him, and you shall succeed.'"

Ahab felt his anger rising. He knew where this was going. And he didn't like it one bit. He could see the Judean king had been captivated by the naysayer.

As Micaiah continued on, he spoke with a harsh, judgmental tone, "Therefore behold, Yahweh has put a lying spirit in the mouth of all these your prophets. Yahweh has declared disaster for you!"

Zedekiah the prophet took off his iron horns, marched up to Micaiah, and struck him in the mouth. "How dare you claim that the Spirit of Yahweh left me and spoke to you!"

Micaiah had had enough. He'd been summoned here to speak unpopular words, before a king he despised, and now another prophet attacked him. He spoke to the young prophet, "Behold, you shall see on that day when you seek to hide yourself from wrath."

Zedekiah turned to Ahab. "This man blasphemes all the prophets! Yahweh does not lie!"

The other prophets became agitated, calling for punishment upon Micaiah.

Jehoshaphat looked to see what Ahab would do.

Ahab had to take charge, show Jehoshaphat he was a leader amongst kings, or suffer a withdrawal of support from the southern kingdom. He leaned in and whispered, "It is but one prophet against four hundred."

The image of Elijah against the four hundred prophets of Baal came to his mind. But he dismissed it.

"Now if we don't follow the wisdom of the consensus, if we pull away and don't fight Damascus, we will be thought cowards by the Arameans. Then they won't stop annexing more cities in both north and south until it is too late for us to manage an all-out war."

"True enough," said Jehoshaphat. "But if we do fight and lose, then Micaiah will be proven right and we may lose the support of our people."

Ahab thought it through. Then he said, "Only if the people find out about his prophecy."

Jehoshaphat cautioned him, "Killing a prophet before he is proven right or wrong could make him a martyr and spread dissent amongst the people and our armies."

Ahab thought again, then said, "Trust me in this."

The outrage from the four hundred prophets had died down to murmuring as they awaited the king's decision. Ahab stood up and ordered his guards, "Seize the man, Micaiah, son of Imlah, and put him in prison until I return in peace!"

Micaiah was grabbed by two soldiers. As he was dragged away, he shouted to the king, "If you return in peace, Yahweh has not spoken to me!"

Ahab looked at Jehoshaphat, his expression proclaiming victory. He addressed the crowd of prophets, answering Micaiah, "Indeed! And then you shall be punished accordingly!"

The other prophets laughed and mocked the old man as the soldiers led him off.

But Jehoshaphat looked disturbed, he was not so certain that Micaiah was wrong. Ahab came back and sat down. The northern king leaned in and said, "Fear not, Jehoshaphat. If we stay unified, our God will not abandon his people."

CHAPTER 58

Susanna prayed in her family shrine room as she'd always done. But the room had been empty of other gods since that night long ago. A lone menorah lamp was the only religious item in the room. She lit the lamp when she prayed to remind her of the presence of Yahweh, the unseen God. Her miniature lampstand imaged the Jerusalem temple's large golden lampstand. Like that menorah, this one was shaped as an almond tree with seven branches, a powerful symbol of the tree of life and of fertility that Yahweh granted his people.

She wiped tears of gratitude from her face. Yahweh had heard her prayers and answered. He had blessed them with a child that was growing in her womb! She felt blessed like the patriarch Abraham's wife Sarah, pregnant so late in life. Well, Sarah had been ninety years old while Susanna was only thirty-nine. But she might as well have been ninety as most women her age had finished their child-bearing years. Like Sarah, she'd been tested to trust in Yahweh and not place her hope in this world, but in the world to come.

When Susanna finally embraced the life she had been blessed with, and wholeheartedly began to serve the people in her life —supporting her husband, helping other women in need with their own infants and young children— Yahweh had seen fit to grant her new life. What she'd offered up as a burnt sacrifice, Yahweh had found pleasing to resurrect. She would never take his blessing for granted. And she would raise her child to be a worthy heir of a righteous and worthy father.

Hearing a knock on the front door, Susanna got up. She held her pregnant belly as she made her way down the stairs to the entrance.

Her maidservant Miriam opened the door just as Susanna arrived. She cried out with joy at the sight of Galina. Her sister was covered in the dust of travel and accompanied by her son and several of her servants.

Galina had come to stay with her while their husbands served the king in battle at Ramoth-gilead. They had often stayed with each other when the husbands were off to war, and Susanna was always thrilled to see her sister and nephew.

She held out her arms to Daniel, now twelve and scrawny with messy sandy hair. "Nephew." He'd become more shy of such affection as boys did around this age, so Susanna treasured every moment of his slow but resigned hug. She whispered into his ear, "You are growing into such a handsome young man."

Daniel chuckled. "You always say that, Aunt Susanna."

She smiled. "Well, it's always true."

The sisters embraced. Galina, now thirty-six years old, mature and filled out, held Susanna tightly. They had always helped each other quash worries and push back fears when their husbands went off to battle. Galina had often wished Jonadab was not such a skilled chariot driver, so he wouldn't be called upon as often. But their husbands were warriors, and this was the way of life for a warrior's family.

Galina put her hand on Susanna's belly and repeated the phrase with which she often teased her sister. "And Sarah laughed."

The words came from the story of the patriarch Abraham and how his wife Sarah had laughed with disbelief when the angel of God had told her she'd bear a son in her old age. Susanna smiled broadly as she always did in response. It was Galina's way of reminding her to trust in Yahweh despite impossible odds.

Susanna said to Daniel, "I tell you what; have Miriam here take you to the kitchen to get an apple."

He headed off to the kitchen like the constantly hungry boy that he was, with Miriam following close behind.

Susanna pulled Galina aside and whispered to her, "How are you doing, my sister?"

"As good as can be. Beulah is staying with the clan." Beulah was Jonadab's other wife. "We've had our rifts lately, but when he goes to battle, we tend to unite in the face of crisis. She even offered to take care of my little ones so I could be with you in your time."

Galina, always the fertile one, had borne two more sons and three daughters to Jonadab in the years since Daniel's birth.

"And you?"

Susanna pulled back, caressing her belly. "This has been most difficult in light of present circumstances."

Galina put her arm around her. "My husband always tells me they'll be fine. He believes Yahweh's favor is upon Jehu."

Susanna finished her thought with a smile, "And they have great things to do together." It was Jonadab's repeated phrase.

The women embraced each other again in prayerful hope that Jonadab was right.

Jezreel

Izabel marched down the palace hallway, accompanied by the visiting Athaliah. They were followed by four priests of Baal, her own private security. The queen never went anywhere without these bodyguards. Rumors of political unrest and secret machination fueled her rampant fears. She worked hard to disguise and minimize her fears, but the truth is that she was jumpy and easily frightened.

The men were otherwise occupied. King Jehoshaphat was off with King Ahab discussing military matters. These days, Izabel couldn't care less about Damascus or treaties or some age old dispute about who controlled a particular city on the fringe of the kingdom.

She'd grown distant from the king. She chose to live permanently in Jezreel, which forced him to visit and stay with her if he wanted her company. Who knew anymore if their separation was a symptom or cause. But they were increasingly alienated and neither seemed to desire to be around the other. Even she had reversed her original fidelity and was now using male servants to satisfy her own cravings. The king had returned to his concubines as well.

Izabel's joints ached, and she felt on fire. Not with the anger that currently drove her to her destination, but rather from her change of life as a woman. Her monthly flow had become less and less frequent. Perhaps this was the reason why it had been years since she'd experienced another pregnancy. Though her distaste for the king's embraces might equally be the reason.

But that curse of a woman's courses had been replaced by the fever, as she called it. Sometimes in the fit of a burning flash, she'd rip off her robe and tunic and take a cold bath, cursing the gods for their unfair and unequal creation of women. Men could mate all their lives and have children with younger women to build their tribes. But in mid-life, a woman had her only real power, reproduction, stripped from her. She truly hated this patriarchal world. For women, it was a life of unending abuse and disadvantage.

She preferred to blame her woes on the Hebrew Yahweh rather than the Canaanite El. In Canaanite stories, El was the creator of humankind. But he was a pathetic, drunken slob, an idiot easily manipulated by his wife Asherah. He seemed to do nothing of substance in the heavens other than sitting around, stroking his white beard, and throwing out orders.

Baal was the functional Most High who administered the kingdom. And Asherah, Astarte, Anat, and other goddesses were the relational intelligence behind them. Izabel thought of herself as Asherah to Ahab's El. And Baal was her tool for getting things done in this male-dominated cosmos of iron and power.

But there was a singular great power which a woman had in her arsenal of strategy, and that was her identity as a mother. No matter how oppressed women were, no matter how unequally treated by patriarchal rules, no matter how ignored or abused or treated as property, mothers retained an almost mystical influence over their sons. And it was sons who grew up to rule the patriarchy.

Izabel had carefully and deliberately cultivated her control of Joram, the heir to Ahab's throne. She had taught him her values and had indoctrinated him as best she could over the years. He obeyed her with fearful allegiance. Unfortunately, the boy was much like his father, a weak and spineless slave to his flesh. But she'd done her best.

Now she was doing her best to keep it all from falling apart.

With Athaliah in tow, she burst into Joram's palace bedchamber, the guards remaining outside the door.

Several qedeshim jerked awake. Izabel ripped off the satin bedsheet, exposing four of them in total. Joram laid dead asleep like a contented pig.

Izabel hissed, "Get out." The prostitutes gathered up their clothes and rushed out of the room.

She shouted, "Joram! Wake up!"

Her son rolled over and blinked sleepily at his mother and Athaliah. He didn't even bother to cover his nakedness. He was now seventeen and blessed with a wiry frame and a full head of hair, which he never seemed to cut.

Pushing his bangs aside, he rubbed his bleary eyes. "Mother."

"You are every bit as weak as your father. Get up." Izabel's patience had worn thin. She still felt the burning heat of her fever throughout her body. She wanted to rip off her clothes and scream.

"Do you know where the king is?" She demanded.

Joram scratched himself as he looked around for his tunic. "Ramoth-gilead. Preparing for war."

"And why is he preparing for war?" demanded Izabel.

"Because Damascus wouldn't give the city back to us?" He said it like a question. Like he needed her approval. The dullard seemed to need instruction in everything.

"And why are you not beside him learning strategy?"

"He didn't send for me."

With a loud sigh, Izabel walked over to a suit of armor on a mannequin and pulled off the chainmail. She heaved it at him. He caught it, stumbling back under the force of her toss.

"Get your battle gear on, boy."

Izabel left the room.

Athaliah shook her head with disgust as Joram hung his head in shame. She followed the queen away.

CHAPTER 59

Ramoth-gilead

Jehu stood with King Ahab, King Jehoshaphat, and Jonadab on a hill overlooking the city. The fortification of Ramoth-gilead didn't seem to match the significance of the city's importance as a crossroads of travel on the King's Highway, or a strategic location for protecting the region. Outside the walls of the city, a host of several thousand armed Arameans awaited the Hebrew forces.

They needed to win this battle decisively, today. Ahab wanted this prosperous city back under his control without excess damage to the city itself. And he certainly didn't want a protracted siege.

The joint armies of Israel and Judah were encamped on the hill. The soldiers were ready to clash with the Arameans.

New armored chariots had been created by the Rechabites for King Ahab, these would be battle tested today. Generals Jehu and Jonadab would serve as drivers for kings Ahab and Jehoshaphat, piloting these machines of war. No one knew how to drive Rechabite chariots like the generals Jehu and Jonadab.

The captains of thousands arrived. After greeting the kings and generals, the men all entered the war tent to discuss their strategy. They gathered around a table spread with a map and figurines representing the armies.

Ahab stood, pale and nervous, apparently distracted in his thoughts. Jehoshaphat stared at the map.

Jonadab spoke first. "My lords, the city and Aramean forces are not strong. Victory is only a matter of time."

"How much time?" Ahab demanded. "I don't have time."

He turned and walked out of the tent, preoccupied. The captains looked at one another, searching for understanding.

Jehu enlightened them. "The king is concerned about a prophet."

"I heard he had four hundred prophets tell him to go up against Ramoth-gilead," one captain asked. "What prophet do you speak of?"

"The only one who told him not to," said Jehoshaphat. "Micaiah, son of Imlah."

The captain shrugged, looking baffled. "Four hundred for and only one against? I like those odds."

Jehu couldn't tell them the whole truth. Ahab had ordered Jehu not to reveal the secret intelligence he'd received that the king of Damascus had ordered assassins to seek out Ahab as a target in the battle. He wasn't sure how this was going to occur, but Jehu had prepared for it. It was another reason he was driving for the king.

He heard Ahab curse outside the tent. "Baalzebul!"

Jehu and the others joined Ahab to see Jezebel and Joram arriving on a chariot, surrounded by cavalry soldiers.

The queen stomped off the chariot, pulling Joram along like a child, and marched right past them all into the tent.

"Stay here," Ahab ordered his captains. Following the queen inside, he pulled the entrance flap closed behind him.

Jehu stood guard protectively at the tent entry, and he overheard the conversation inside.

Jezebel led with acerbic anger. "I thought you might want to educate your son in the art of war since he is to carry on the family name. That is, unless you are only thinking of yourself."

Jehu heard Ahab growl and explode in a fit.

"War is my one thing!" he shouted. "My ONE THING in this kingdom that I govern unencumbered by your interference! And now you seek to meddle in that as well?"

Through the years, Jehu had seen Ahab become more withdrawn in his marriage as Jezebel became more aggressive. In the early days, the queen had been more outwardly compliant. She had won the king's heart and had drawn him into her influence. But as time went on, Jezebel's subtle suggestions and gentle persuasions had turned into direct manipulation with the occasional aggressive confrontation.

"Fine," she responded with sudden calm. "I will leave you alone with your 'one thing.'" Jehu had to lean in closer to hear her next words, spoken with restrained spite, "But just remember this, O king. I gave you the son of your dynasty. I nourished your seed. I have always been a daughter of Tyre. And Tyre will not suffer your defeat."

Joram was a silent mouse in their presence, as he always was.

Jezebel concluded, "You were a primitive stone age tribe worshipping a barbaric deity. I brought you the wisdom, wealth, and power of Baal."

"Who, I recall, lost in a contest with Elijah's 'barbaric deity' on Mount Carmel," Ahab retorted angrily. "So much for the power of Baal."

"You double-minded fool," the queen hissed. "You have spent your whole life appeasing whichever god gave you what you wanted. But you have failed to understand that we become what we worship. You worship nothing. And that is what you have become."

Jehu took a step away from the tent as he heard the queen moving toward the entrance. Exiting the tent, she glared at Jehu when she walked past. The commander represented the military power Jezebel could never have, and she'd always hated him for it. As she stormed back to her chariot, Jehu entered the tent.

He found Ahab directing over his seventeen-year-old heir. "Take off your clothes. You are going to put on the king's armor."

"Why, Father?" Joram's voice cracked in fear. "You are the king. It would not be appropriate."

Ahab began lifting his armor off the mannequin where it hung when not in use. "It is time you learn."

Jehu had to say something. He cleared his throat. "My lord, he isn't ready. Please don't do this."

Joram didn't know about the assassination threat.

But Ahab wasn't listening. "Izabel wants me to prepare Joram for kingship. There is no better way than to be king for a battle."

"But I am not king, Father." Joram was shaking with desperation.

"Shut up!" Ahab helped Joram pull off his tunic. "The men won't be able to tell. All they see from their distance is the royal battle gear that tells everybody, 'here is the king.'"

And the assassins as well, thought Jehu. "My king, it is crucial I speak with you, alone."

Ahab stopped at Jehu's intensity. Waving at Joram, he ordered, "Wait for us outside the tent."

Joram left them.

Jehu became firm. "Your highness, I have been faithful to you all these years. I have given advice where appropriate, and I have obeyed your commands even when I thought you were wrong. It is our duty to submit to authority given to us by God. But what you are about to do, I must protest. You know there is a threat of assassination on your person. By putting your firstborn son in your stead, you are placing your entire dynasty in jeopardy. You cannot do this."

"Joram is more her son than mine." Ahab said with resignation. "I have seventy other sons not born through her. Let them carry on the dynasty without her influence."

Jehu would not give in. "Such a situation would surely plunge the nation into another civil war. Seventy sons all fighting for the throne. It could be the end of Israel."

Ahab sighed. "I've heard that argument before. From Izabel."

Jehu said, "The testimony of two witnesses should be trusted." He had become desperate, placing himself and Jezebel as allies in this argument.

Ahab concluded, "But the line of David would survive in Judah."

Jehu had first thought he was getting through to the king. But now it seemed Ahab had become suicidal in his intent.

The king moved to the tent entrance and called out, "Joram, get back in here!"

When Joram arrived, he told him, "Put your own clothes back on. You are returning to Jezreel."

Jehu felt relieved at the king's unexpected turn of heart.

Joram said, "But what will mother say?"

"I am your father—and your king. You will do as I say."

Joram backed down fearfully. "Yes, Father." He scrambled hastily into his clothes. As he was about to leave the tent, Ahab stopped him. "Ask King Jehoshaphat to come back inside."

"Yes, Father." And Joram left them.

When Jehoshaphat had returned to the war tent, Ahab announced to him, "I'm going to let you lead this battle. I will dress down as a common soldier in the rear so there will be no confusion in the soldiers' ranks as to who is leading."

Jehoshaphat was blunt in his response. "So you believe the prophecy after all?" He repeated the words the prophet Micaiah had pronounced on the threshing floor. "'I saw all Israel scattered on the mountains as sheep that have no shepherd.' So you are that disappearing shepherd?"

"I certainly don't want to stand around and find out." Ahab gave Jehu a guilty look. So he wasn't going to tell the Judean king of the intelligence they'd received. He looked back at Jehoshaphat. "You, however, are protected. The prophecy was not against you, but me. If I can't be found in the fighting, then how can I be killed?"

Jehoshaphat stared at Ahab, considering his options. Finally, he nodded. "I will do it. I will lead this battle. But I have this to say, my brother. If the prophet is right, you cannot outrun the will of Yahweh."

"In the long run," agreed Ahab. "But I've found some success in the past in delaying it."

Jehu knew he was referring to when Elijah had prophesied disaster upon the house of Ahab after the death of Naboth. The king had repented in sackcloth and ashes. As a result, the word of the Lord had come to Elijah a second time saying, "Because Ahab has humbled himself before me, I will not bring the disaster in his days, but in his son's days." Ahab had concluded that an untimely death was not in the will of God for him. Jehu prayed he was right.

Ahab smiled as he gestured at Jehu, "Besides, I'll be safe in the hands of the finest chariot driver in all of Israel." He gestured again, this time toward Jonadab, "And you, dear brother, will be safe in the hands of Jehu's most worthy competitor."

The two generals nodded in affirmation, the spark of friendly competition flashing between them.

Ahab added with a grin, "Perhaps we kings should place bets on who will outperform the other."

•••••

The horns of war sounded. The Israelites and Judahites on the field shouted with fierce determination. The Arameans before the walls shouted in reply.

Back behind the Hebrew forces, Ahab, dressed as a bowman, stood beside Jehu in his chariot. Jehu was intent upon protecting his king from harm.

Jehoshaphat stood beside them on his chariot driven by Jonadab. The king of Judah was dressed in the golden armor of royalty. He raised his sword, the sole leader of this battle.

The captains of thousands and the captains of hundreds were all in place in their ranks, awaiting the command. The infantry stood at the front with their long spears and wicker shields covered with leather. They were the shock troops.

Behind them were the heavy archer units, and behind them were the slingers. The chariot corps were on both flanks.

Jehoshaphat now pointed the sword at the city walls.

His trumpeter blew a ram's horn, which was followed by subsequent horn blasts signaling various groups of soldiers.

The first units to act were the archers. They were two-man squads. A shield-bearer held his large slanted shield to protect the archer, who used a composite bow to launch darts at the enemy.

A sheet of arrows rained down upon the Arameans, who raised their own shields as protection.

Their archers responded in kind, and so the Israelites guarded themselves with their shields.

This back and forth produced minimal casualties. While some were injured or killed by the flying objects, the volley of archers was just a warm-up for what was to come next.

A unit of Hebrew sling men swung and launched rocks at the Arameans. The stones were harder to see and speedier, making their marks more often than the arrows. Hebrews, originally being a pastoral people, had developed this form of warfare and practiced it better than anyone. A nation of shepherds, who used slings daily in the protection of their flocks from predators, proved to be an effective fighting force of highly accurate warriors of the sling.

The Israelite chariot corps were called into action by trumpet blasts, and they rushed in from the flanks toward the line of Aramean spearmen. Ahab had a particularly efficient fighting machine in his chariots. He had brought thousands to the battle of Qarqar, which had proved decisive in that victory.

Ahab's new chariots were a terror to face down. Similar to Assyrian chariots, they had six-spoked heavy wheels, light armor, and were drawn by two horses. The driver carried a shield and spear on the side of the vehicle, and the archer with him had a deadly accuracy. Normally, Jehu would lead the chariots in their attack. But in this instance, he remained behind the lines to protect the king.

When Ahab's chariots hit the front lines, their sheer impact broke the line of infantry into chaos. Now the enemy could be taken down by the attacking spearmen.

But Jehu noticed something strange. The Arameans weren't unleashing their own chariots upon the Hebrew frontlines. Instead, they were driving up the flanks toward the rear of the Hebrew forces—where King Jehoshaphat and Ahab were.

Jehu shouted, "Assassins!"

He blew on his ram's horn for the chariot corps in the field to return, then signaled to Jonadab. The two drivers split up, riding their chariots down two separate paths that had been predetermined for escape. Jehu and Ahab went left while Jonadab and Jehoshaphat went right. Despite King Ahab being in disguise, Jehu didn't want to take any chances should their enemies discover their ruse.

The Aramean chariots followed Jehoshaphat—all thirty-two of them. They must have concluded that the sole figure wearing royal armor was King Ahab. Or was Jehoshaphat their true target after all? Could it be that the intelligence Jehu had received was a deception?

When Jehu realized they weren't being followed, he turned his chariot around to return to the battlefield. The forces couldn't fight for long without their leadership and direction.

Approaching the Israelite encampment, Jehu pulled the chariot to a sudden stop. A hundred yards ahead, two foreign warriors sat on their horses, staring them down. They were not Arameans. Jehu recognized them as Moabite mercenaries. Moabites were perpetual enemies of Israel.

These were special assassins. Ahab said it aloud. "Lion Men of Moab!"

Lion Men of Moab were called by that name because they were a peculiar tribe of trackers and warriors, still around from the days of King David. They appeared to be muscular men who had turned into leonine creatures through some kind of sorcery. They had long hair and beards, very pale blond in color, that looked like lion's manes. And they had lion-like teeth and claws. They

were famed for their tracking ability as well as their hand-to-hand combat—
or rather, hand-to-claw combat. Lion Men of Moab were among the fiercest
warriors of the entire Transjordan region. And they deeply hated Israelites.
Jehu was now wishing it had been the thirty-two chariots that had followed
them instead.

•••••

Those thirty-two chariots gained on Jonadab and King Jehoshaphat as they
fled down a wide, dried-up wadi riverbed.

One of the Aramean vehicles was speedier than the others, reined by a
talented horseman. They gained on Jonadab until they were within striking
distance of the king.

The Aramean chariot's archer raised his bow with deadly intent.

Like lightning, Jonadab pulled out his spear and thrust it while still
maintaining the reins. He hit the Aramean driver, who fell into his archer. They
both tumbled off their chariot to their deaths, the arrow missing its royal target
by a wide margin.

"I may have the best chariot driver after all!" the Judean king yelled to
Jonadab.

Jonadab yelled back, "You should have bet on me, your highness!"

But their Aramean pursuers were not far behind.

A volley of arrows rained down upon the two of them, but the king did
his part, holding up the shield, protecting them both as they raced on.

•••••

Jehu's chariot stood still, facing down the two Lion Men mercenaries a
hundred yards away. The assassins kicked their horses and galloped full tilt at
them. Jehu slapped the reins and shouted at his horses. They took off on a
collision course with their attackers.

The Lion Men split apart as they approached the racing chariot.

Jehu handed the reins to Ahab. "Hold steady and stay low!"

Ahab obediently took the reins. Jehu was now in charge of saving their
lives. Or getting them killed.

Each Lion Man raised a bow aimed at their targets.

Jehu waited for the right moment. As soon as they were in range, he
reached below and pulled up his own bow, nocked an arrow, and launched it

at the charging Lion Man on the right. It hit him in the chest, and he flew backward off his horse.

Jehu prepared his next arrow, but he was too late. The other Lion Man had released his missile.

But it wasn't aimed at the men. It was aimed at the horse on Jehu's left.

Within the next few seconds, four things occurred in rapid succession:

The wounded horse buckled and collapsed to the ground.

The Lion Man passed by their vehicle.

Jehu launched himself off the chariot to tackle the Lion Man, taking him to the ground in an explosion of dirt.

And the chariot ran into the wounded horse and flipped, throwing the king into the air.

• • • • •

In the wadi riverbed, Jonadab had steered his chariot hard right—into the wheels of the closest vehicle to him. The enemy's chariot wheel exploded into splinters, launching the driver and his archer into the air. They landed in the dirt, crushed by their own vehicle falling upon them.

But Jonadab was losing his lead. More chariots were upon him. It would only be moments before he was overtaken and Jehoshaphat captured or killed.

• • • • •

Jehu and the Lion Man of Moab wrestled on the ground, each fighting to control the other. Jehu used some grappling moves he'd learned in combat school, but the Moabite was a strong adversary. He seemed able to loosen himself from every hold through sheer muscle power. Jehu would have to break away or the tables would soon turn, leaving him to be overcome by his mighty foe.

Releasing the assassin, Jehu rolled away and stood up to face him, drawing his sword. The Lion Man drew his, but also snapped his claws open as a second weapon. At that moment, Jehu noticed that the claws seemed attached to a leather glove on the Lion Man's hand. Perhaps they were more human than feline after all.

Jehu attacked. His sword skills enabled him to counter the sheer brute force of his nemesis.

But Jehu feared that his skill advantage wouldn't last for long, his opponent's strength was overwhelming.

• • • • •

Driving Jehoshaphat's chariot, Jonadab had lost his lead. Multiple Aramean vehicles were gaining on them. One had pulled up alongside them and was ready to strike.

Then Jonadab saw the archer lower his arrow. Gesturing with his arms, he screamed, "It's not Ahab! It's not Ahab!"

The nearby chariots pulled away from Jonadab and the king. The other Aramean chariots slowed down and began to turn around.

So they were only after Ahab after all. They had mistaken Jehoshaphat for the Israelite leader and were now returning to find Ahab.

Breathing a sigh of relief, Jonadab slowed his chariot to watch the Arameans retreat, leaving the king of Judah and his driver alone—and alive.

Then the Rechabite saw two foreign horsemen coming their way. They weren't Arameans. He recognized them.

They were Lion Men of Moab.

• • • • •

Jehu continued to out-play his opponent's superior strength with superior skill. But their swords locked for just a moment, and Jehu felt the blades of the assassin's clawed hand rip through his leather armor. A sharp pain in his chest jolted him off balance.

The Lion Man pounced. Jehu hit the ground, the wind knocked out of him. The assassin straddled him, holding Jehu's sword arm down and raising his claws for a very personal kill.

The Lion Man's claws were descending, when he jerked violently. The tip of an arrow burst through his chest, he'd been hit from behind. Jehu seized the opportunity, he grabbed a dagger with his free hand from the enemy's belt. He plunged it up upward, under the man's chin and into his skull. The Lion Man fell off him to the ground, twitching in seizure. An arrow stuck out from his back.

Turning, Jehu saw Ahab walking toward him with a bow in his hand. The king was dirty and rumpled from his tumble in the dirt, but he'd survived.

"Well done, my Jehu!" Ahab shouted. "We got them together this time! Well done!"

"Yes, my lord," Jehu grunted, wheezing to recover his breath. "Well done yourself."

Ahab shouted, "We'll teach these bastards they cannot stop the house of Ahab! Now let's get back to the battle before it's too late!"

They ran.

A squad of Israelite chariots came to their aid just as Jehu and Ahab returned to the battle. Jehu motioned to the wadi riverbed. "Rescue King Jehoshaphat!"

Then he saw the Aramean chariots returning. They weren't carrying any bodies in golden royal armor. Jehoshaphat must be still alive.

At the crossroads, the chariots clashed and engaged with spear, shield, and arrow. Vehicles overturned. Dust billowed up from chariots spinning and skidding in the battle.

Jehu did not join the fray. He quickly commandeered another chariot to return King Ahab to the battle.

• • • • •

Behind the walls of the city of Ramoth-gilead, an Aramean archer released his missiles upon select enemies below. He had nocked an arrow and was about to loose it when he was hit by a stone slung from an Israelite. As the archer fell backward off the parapet to his death, the tensioned arrow released and flew into the sky without a target.

It launched on a random trajectory in a huge arc, gliding over the battlefield below...

...having reached the apex of flight, it began to descend and gain momentum, it soared over the Israelite lines ...

...finding its unintended target between the breastplate and scale armor of King Ahab standing beside Jehu on the chariot.

The arrow plunged deep past Ahab's collarbone and down into his chest. He collapsed in the chariot.

Beside him, Jehu screamed in surprised terror. Dropping the reins, he held Ahab, who looked back at him with a twisted grin of pain and irony.

"What are the odds of *that* happening?" the king grunted.

It was the prophecy. Micaiah had truly spoken the word of Yahweh against Ahab. Jehoshaphat had been right. Ahab could not outrun the will of God.

Jehu knew deep in his soul that this was the beginning of the end. The end of the house of Ahab, just as Elijah had predicted.

Jehu followed the king's eyes to see Jonadab standing not far off, the broken body of King Jehoshaphat in his arms. Overwhelmed with grief, he could barely hold the Judean ruler.

Jonadab handed Jehoshaphat's body to the Judahite captains.

Ahab muttered, "This is all my fault."

Jehu turned to the closest soldier and ordered, "Get the king into surgery!"

"No, wait," Ahab ordered. "Give me my armor and prop me up in the chariot."

"My lord, your wound is serious," complained Jehu. "If we don't attend to you, it will be fatal."

"Jehu, do as I say," admonished the king. He paused to cough up blood. "Jehoshaphat is dead. If the men see me gone, they will lose heart. Prop me up in the chariot so I can use my last hours for the benefit of my people—for once in my godforsaken life."

Jehu looked into his king's eyes. He saw in them a resignation, and he knew Ahab was right.

"Give me the king's armor from his tent." He called out to the waiting soldier. The soldier stepped away quickly to retrieve it.

Ahab grabbed Jehu's arm and said, "You have been a loyal soldier to me, Jehu. And to Yahweh. I did not deserve you."

"You are my king," Jehu countered.

"I haven't been a good one. And I leave you with an even worse queen." The king chuckled at the irony. Grunting again in pain, he said, "Elijah was right. I deserve this. Not even my Jehu could protect me from Yahweh's judgment."

Jehu bristled at the comment. It was an innocent expression from the dying man. But was that what Jehu had been doing, trying to protect Ahab from Yahweh's judgment? Had Jehu's loyalty to his king for all these years finally trapped him in an act of treason against his god? Was his protection of the Lord's anointed in defiance of Yahweh's will?

The soldier arrived with the king's breastplate and helmet. Jehu assisted the king, removing the common armor and replacing it with the golden armor.

Jehu stayed with the king until the sun was going down on the battlefield of blood before them. Ahab had been right. His presence had encouraged the men to fight on.

But then everything changed.

Jehu felt the king slump. He caught Ahab before he fell to the ground.

Ahab was dead in his arms.

The commander gently flicked the reins with one hand and held the lifeless king against him with the other, he steered the chariot back to the war tent. Stopping behind the tent, Jehu finally lay the king's body down.

He didn't care if they took the city. He could feel only the deep pain of overwhelming loss. Loss because he'd spent his whole life with this leader of Israel, as both his subject and his right arm of military strength. But he also felt guilt for how he'd failed Yahweh in not challenging his errant lord more. At times, the commander had used loyalty to his king as an excuse to avoid fulfilling his loyalty to his god.

True, Jehu had experienced a turn of heart years ago and had faithfully served Yahweh alone ever since. But he had never directly challenged the harlot queen Jezebel and her spiritual adulteries. And now Joram would become king, with Jezebel as Queen Mother to direct him, an even more dangerous situation for the nation.

Jehu wanted to kill Jezebel, but he didn't have the moral authority to do so. He needed to hear a word of Yahweh from the prophet of Yahweh. He needed Elijah's approval.

With the death of the king, Jehu called back the army, much to the confusion of all those involved. As he went to prepare the chariot for the return of Ahab's body to Samaria, Jehu saw wild dogs around the vehicle. He thought to himself, *those scrounging animals always find their way to eat the scraps of war.* They were licking away the king's blood from the chariot floor.

Ramoth-gilead remained untaken. The men were disbanded and each returned to his own home in Judah or Israel.

And the birds of the air feasted on the flesh of the dead.

What had begun as a strong show of might by the king of Israel over the Aramean occupied city of Ramoth-gilead had become a fulfillment of Elijah's prophecy that the dogs would lick up the blood of Ahab in the same way that they'd licked up the blood of his victim, Naboth the Jezreelite.

The sun had gone dark over Israel. The stars were falling from the sky. The earthly and heavenly powers were collapsing.

But Jehu knew that there was yet more of Elijah's prophecy to be fulfilled.

CHAPTER 60

Samaria

Jehu led Jonadab and a line of weary soldiers through the city gates. They had returned from the battle of Ramoth-gilead, and they were exhausted, filthy with dirt, sweat, and blood. The body of the king was hidden and protected. It would be interred soon, and only after would there be an official announcement of his death. For now, every survivor was returning to his own home to embrace their beloved families. Some would also deliver sad news to those whose fathers and sons would never return.

Jehu and Jonadab left their horses at the stables. Gathering up their possessions, the two walked toward Jehu's house. The deaths of his soldiers weighed heavy upon Jehu, he bore the weight of his equipment as though it were the bodies of those whose lives were lost. His every muscle and joint ached. His bandaged chest wound throbbed. And he still wore the blood and grime of battle on his skin and armor.

Jonadab limped beside him, also covered in bandages. The Rechabite had sustained a few more wounds, on both arms and legs, than Jehu had from the leonine assassins. He also carried a heavy burden, from the death of Jehoshaphat. Jonadab had fought admirably, but he'd been outmanned by those ruthless assassins. No other soldier would have been able to save the king from the Lion Men of Moab. It was a miracle that he had survived.

No one could thwart the will of Yahweh. He alone controlled the destinies of men. This was Jehu's conclusion about the death of the kings. The prophets had predicted Ahab's death, but they hadn't commanded Jehu to kill him. They hadn't ordered him to withhold his sworn duty to protect him either. This had led Jehu to the conclusion that in serving the Lord's anointed, he wasn't fighting the Lord's will. For that will was mysterious and transcended all human actions in this world. God, not man, was judge. And both Jehu and Jonadab had fulfilled their duty of obedience to Yahweh.

When they came in sight of Jehu's house, their families and servants were waiting for them at the gate.

The wives couldn't just stand there and wait any longer. They moved to meet their husbands with tear-drenched faces of happiness.

Bounding ahead, Daniel reached his stepfather first.

He grabbed him and hugged him with all his might. Jonadab groaned, but laughed and hugged the boy back.

Then Daniel noticed the bandages. "Will you be okay, Father?"

Jonadab smiled. "Yes. But my enemies will not be."

Daniel grinned proudly.

Jehu pulled out the dagger he'd taken from his Moabite assassin and said, "Daniel, your father fought more bravely than I." He held out the dagger in its sheath to the boy. "This blade belonged to one of those opponents who now lies dead in the ground. Do you know how fierce a Lion Man of Moab is?"

Daniel could only nod his head in awe. Jehu said, "Well, your father killed two of them. This is yours as a reminder of Yahweh's deliverance and your father's heroism."

Daniel looked to Jonadab for approval. Jonadab nodded assent, and Daniel yelped with joy, taking the dagger carefully in his hands.

Susanna and Galina had arrived and embraced their husbands with gratitude toward God for their safe deliverance.

The group retired to the house. A hearty meal of quail with lentil beans, walnuts, and onions was served. Jehu felt refreshed from the meal, he relaxed and savored a goblet of wine, still seated at the table with Jonadab and their wives. Daniel was practicing with his new blade in the atrium.

Susanna said aloud what they were all thinking. "Joram will now be king of Israel with Jezebel pulling the strings as Queen Mother."

Galina added with bitterness, "Jezebel's ward Athaliah will be queen with Jehoshaphat's son in Judah."

Jonadab had been pensive. He finally spoke. "Galina, I will be leaving you and Daniel here with Susanna for the time being. I must be on the road at first light tomorrow."

"Why?" Galina asked, looking disappointed. "I thought we'd have some time together before you had to return to camp."

"I did as well. But with King Ahab dead, Jezebel will hunt down Elijah and the prophets of Yahweh again. This time there will be nothing to restrain her. I have to find Elijah and protect him."

"Do you know where he is?" Jehu asked.

"I have an idea."

Galina protested, "Was it not enough to risk your life for the king?"

Jonadab looked solemnly at her. "No. And now it is the entire kingdom of Israel which will be at risk."

Jehu saw Susanna look to him for his response. He said, "After the king's funeral, I will find out what I can about the queen's intent."

"And we will pray to Yahweh for your protection," Susanna concluded. "And the safety of Elijah the prophet."

CHAPTER 61

Jerusalem

The haze of burning incense from the censor hung lazily in the room. Queen Athaliah was praying to Baal. In the unseen realm, Baal clenched her soul lovingly, his talons deep into her brain. He sighed with erotic pleasure as he made intimate spiritual connection with her. She was essential to his plans.

With the death of Jehoshaphat, Baal had gone up to Jerusalem for the final phase of his plan: to get a temple of his own built in competition with Yahweh's temple and to eliminate the bloodline of King David. If he could stop the Son of David who was to come as Messiah, Baal might have a chance at controlling the entire Promised Land. And the key to that plan was Queen Athaliah—who currently prayed to Baal in a royal prayer room while offering a sacrifice in the Valley of Hinnom.

Baal had a strong grip on this one's soul. She'd been dutifully indoctrinated by Izabel into Baalism and had brought the religion with her to Judah. Of course, Baal was already worshipped by Judahites on the high places along with Chemosh, Milcom, and Astarte. But Athaliah brought zeal, passion—and a plan.

She felt the touch of the divine. Experienced the elation of mystical communion with the deity. He showed her visions of a future without limits, without boundaries, without the fanatical intolerance of extreme Yahwism.

Baal whispered into her prostrate figure on the floor, "I have received your holy sacrifice, and I am well-pleased. You are the one we have been waiting for. You can bring about real change in Judah."

He calmed the pains in her belly. She was here because she'd received the news of the death of Ahab and Jehoshaphat and her husband Jehoram had been crowned king.

276

This was a crucial turning point for Athaliah. She'd been preparing for it, preparing for a noble sacrifice at a time of crisis, a principle she'd learned from Queen Izabel's religion. She'd been pregnant with another child of Jehoram's, but had never told him. He didn't need to know. It was her choice to keep it secret. At twenty weeks in, Athaliah had been able to hide it well with loose robes and by withholding sex from her husband. But with her new position as queen, she was finally where she needed to be to begin her goal of bringing Baalism, the religion of her stepmother Izabel, to prominence in Judah.

So she'd taken the herbs provided by the sorceress and forced a miscarriage. The little creature was a girl. It had disappointed Athaliah because she'd wanted a boy for her purposes. But a girl would do. She was over seven inches long, and her skin was pale, almost transparent. Her head had seemed large to Athaliah, almost a third the size of the baby. She had a small amount of hair on her head with eyebrows and eyelashes on her little face and even nails growing on her tiny fingers and toes.

She was a beautiful child that made a beautiful sacrifice to Baal. Athaliah had wrapped up the thing in a cloth and brought her to the high priest of Baal in the Valley of Hinnom, where he'd passed the child through the fire in offering to Baal. Afterward, Athaliah had come to pray here where Baal was currently distracting her with visions of glory.

He whispered into her mind thoughts of a House for Baal and the return of the asherim to the temple of Jerusalem. But first she'd have to take care of family matters.

She awakened from the spell.

Baal followed Athaliah as she approached her husband the king to advise him and direct his thinking. They talked about it for hours, and with the help of Baal, she was able to convince Jehoram of the precarious danger he was in. He had to secure his reign, eliminate all rivals, or he might find himself at the point of a blade and a violent coup.

And there was only one way to eliminate all rivals.

• • • • •

Shephatiah was the youngest brother of King Jehoram. At twenty-six years old, he'd avoided marriage, choosing instead to live a life of revelry and debauchery. He drank and he ate and he whored. But he loved to eat more than anything. He'd grown to an obese two hundred and fifty pounds. His philosophy had always been eat, drink, and be merry, for tomorrow we die.

But that was the old Shephatiah, the person he had been was changing and evolving. He'd recently been in a boating accident on the Jordan River and had almost drowned. He'd been saved from the water by a servant who'd ended up losing his own life in the process. His rescuer had been a good man, a man of obedience to Yahweh.

It had struck Shephatiah how little he as a royal son deserved to still be alive at the cost of another more worthy. This had shaken him to the core, and he had experienced a conversion of mind. He was going to change his diet, find a woman to marry, and start a family. He was going to serve Yahweh.

King Jehoram, his brother, had called Shephatiah to eat lunch with him. He'd said he wanted to discuss an issue of significance. When Shephatiah arrived in the dining hall, he found himself alone before a spread of what seemed to be Shephatiah's favorite foods. Roasted beef. Plenty of leeks and onions. For dessert, there was honey, dates, and figs. And of course, wine. Plenty of wine.

Shephatiah felt insulted. His brother was clearly trying to tempt him away from his newfound commitment to losing weight.

A servant informed him that the king would be late and to go ahead and start eating. At first he stared at the food, trying to withstand the temptation. But inevitably, he couldn't hold back. He was starving. He tried to keep his portions small. To be moderate rather than excessive.

Pouring himself a goblet of wine, he took a deep drink.

It tasted funny.

Then a dizziness overcame him. He felt a sharp, stabbing pain in his abdomen. His heart started to pound in his chest. The abdominal pain got worse and he suddenly vomited all over the table. Everything he'd eaten seemed to come out of him with a vengeance.

He felt his bowels explode with diarrhea. The thought occurred to him that he had been being poisoned just before he fell to the floor and died in a pool of his own excrement.

• • • • •

Azariah, the thirty-two-year-old brother of King Jehoram, had been called into the king's presence for royal counsel. Azariah was a faithful follower of Yahweh and Torah. He'd often gotten into arguments with his brother's wife, now Queen Athaliah, over religious differences. As much as he tried to treat her with respect, Azariah believed her to be a disease of spiritual rot in the body politic of Judah. He'd tried to open his brother's eyes to the need for renewed commitment to Yahweh, but had always been interrupted by Athaliah's undermining ways.

Azariah followed three palace guards down a hallway to a counsel room. He hoped his brother was finally getting some sense of responsibility after coming to the throne and was wanting to become more serious about fidelity to Torah. He hoped he was going to ask for advice from his younger brother about tearing down the Tophet and the high places of Jerusalem. Well, he could hope, couldn't he?

He wondered why he was being escorted. After all, he knew where the counsel room was.

Turning down the hallway, the three guards stopped at a side room that was several doors down from the counsel room.

He protested, "This is not the counsel room."

One of the guards, a big, burly one, said, "My lord, this is where the king told us to take you."

He looked at them suspiciously. Well, he wasn't going to fight them for it. But why on earth was the king meeting him here instead of the usual counsel room?

They opened the door and entered.

Azariah saw that the room was empty. Was his lazy brother late again? He began to feel impatient.

He heard the door close behind him.

And he realized that the guards were not outside the room as they ought to be. They stood inside with Azariah. All three of them.

"What are you doing in here?" he demanded, turning to face them.

He was about to continue his complaint, but was stopped short as one of the guards grabbed him, spun him around, and slit his throat with a dagger.

Azariah's shock was compounded by the pain of being stabbed, over and over again, by the three guards with their three daggers.

He thought he heard one of them growl, "Religious fanatic."

These soldiers were vengeful, going beyond what was necessary, puncturing his flesh with their blades a hundred times over, long after he'd already perished.

· · · · ·

At twenty-nine years old, Zechariah felt his future was bright. As a brother to the king, he had a life of privilege beyond what common people experienced in their miserable lives. He had to find a way to help alleviate the poverty of his people. He was full of ideas, and his whole life was before him.

He'd just made love to his beautiful wife and was whistling a song to himself lying in bed as his wife called for the servants to bring them a meal. They had five wonderful children he hoped would continue the family legacy and make him proud. All was well in the world.

He heard a booming sound as a door was forced open. He heard his wife scream. Realizing something was terribly wrong, he jumped up to investigate. But he was stopped short with the sight of a guard pulling his wife by her hair into the room.

"What are you doing?" he shouted in shock. "I'll have your head for this!"

The guard was followed by several others pushing their way into his room. The lead guard announced, "Zechariah, son of Jehoshaphat, you are under arrest by the order of the king."

"What on earth are you talking about?" he protested. But he didn't have the chance to find out because he blacked out after being hit in the head with a truncheon.

When Zechariah awoke, he was being dragged into a courtyard of the palace. Where was he?

Then he saw before him two of his other brothers tied to poles. Jehiel and Mikael. Where were the others?

Now he knew where he was. This was the courtyard of execution.

Guards pushed him up against a pole and bound his hands behind him. He was still groggy from the beating and confused at what was going on.

He looked to his brothers, whose terrified expressions only made everything seem worse.

Then a firing squad of archers were led into place by a captain who pulled out a scroll and announced with brevity, "Jehiel, son of Jehoshaphat. Zechariah, son of Jehoshaphat. Mikael, son of Jehoshaphat. You are all hereby charged with conspiracy and treason against the king and queen. The sentence is death."

It was unreal to Zechariah. This wasn't happening. This couldn't be happening. Treason? He had never betrayed his brother. This can't be happening.

"Nock your arrows!" the captain called out. Three sets of two archers nocked their arrows on composite bows aimed right at Zechariah and his brothers.

This can't be happening.

"Release!" came the order.

A moment later, Zechariah felt the heavy punch in his chest. Air left his lungs.

This can't be happening.

The captain shouted, "Again, nock your arrows."

"Release!"

And Zechariah heard no more.

Athaliah watched the execution from her palace window above. She had wanted to observe the event, knowing she needed to become hard, insensitive to the sufferings of others, if she was going to rule with real power. She had to become like a man to rule in a man's world. She had to suppress her emotions and use violence as a means of achieving her goals. It was only the violent who ruled this iron world, and one day she would rule with an iron fist. She would put men under her thumb. They would obey her, do her bidding, serve and please her instead of her serving and pleasing a man.

For now, her husband was king. But if she prepared herself, then one day tragedy might befall Jehoram as well, leaving Athaliah in an advantageous position for even greater influence as Queen Mother. Izabel had taught her well. She'd instilled in Athaliah the cunning of the goddess and the power of Baal. Izabel had called it their "sisterhood," but Athaliah thought the sisterhood was bigger than merely the two of them. It reached to all women in the world and their plight.

She dreamed of the patriarchy replaced by a matriarchy.

Was it possible that one day women could turn the tables on men? Could a matriarchy ever be birthed from this womb of oppression? If women ruled the world, wars would cease and compassion would rule. The poor would stop dying in their poverty, and little girls would have just as much chance as little boys to be whatever they wanted to be in this life. The earth would become as sacred as the sky. And male deities, even Baal, might finally bow to the goddess.

As Athaliah watched them take the dead bodies from the poles in the courtyard, she felt a chill at how truly wonderful life could be in a world without Yahweh.

She knew this was all possible because of the letter she held in her hand. She looked at it again. It was a letter to the king from the prophet Elijah, that nasty old man who somehow managed to accurately prophesy the current course of events.

> Thus says Yahweh, the God of David your father to
> Jehoram, king of Judah, "Because you have not walked in
> the ways of Jehoshaphat your father, but have walked in the
> way of the kings of Israel and have enticed Judah and the
> inhabitants of Jerusalem into whoredom, as the house of
> Ahab led Israel into whoredom, and also you have killed
> your brothers, of your father's house, who were better than
> you, behold, Yahweh will bring a great plague on your
> people, your children, your wives, and all your possessions,
> and you yourself will die by my hand."

She had intercepted the letter before it could reach the king's hand. The tragic demise of her husband was more than just her wishful thinking or remote possibility, it was now a prediction of most high probability. Her dreams of a hopeful future were not worthless flights of fancy. And for that, she needed to prepare herself.

CHAPTER 62

Samaria

The royal funeral procession moved slowly through the streets of the city. The lilting sounds of wind instruments playing a dirge, accompanied by the cries and wails of women, created a strange kind of unintended musical performance.

Jehu walked at the head of the procession, he led the horses which pulled king Ahab's empty chariot. As he walked in somber reflection, Jehu watched the crowds lining the streets. Above the crowd, on a raised platform stood Ethbaal. Jezebel's father wore royal Tyrian robes and stood amongst an assembly of Sidonians.

He's not come to mourn the passing of King Ahab. He's come to celebrate the rise of his daughter's influence.

After all, this had been Ethbaal's plan from the beginning. The marriage and treaty with Israel were never about allies, but about infiltrating and controlling Israel. What a patient man Ethbaal was. He was an ambitious man, he played the long game and he had won.

Jehu noticed Susanna, Galina, and Daniel on the street between his home and the palace. What would the future hold? Would Israel become a land they no longer recognized? Would Yahweh be the God of Israel still, or would it be Baal and the goddess of the Sidonians?

Then Jehu spotted a small group of prophets of Yahweh standing with some Rechabites, and the tiniest sliver of hope returned to his heart. With the death of Ahab, the Rechabites were hoping Jezebel would lose her power, that Joram would be a new and God-honoring king. They hoped for an end to the persecution of Yahweh's prophets and the righteous followers of Torah. The Rechabites wanted their separation to end with a wave of righteousness sweeping the land. They wanted to grow and prosper as a clan.

Jehu hoped for all these things too, yet he also knew the queen and knew she would only seize more power. But Yahweh still had worshippers in Israel. Jezebel and her abominable god Baal had not yet won this war.

Following Ahab's chariot in the procession was a Phoenician funerary cart made of gold and ivory and drawn by a bull. It carried the body of King Ahab surrounded in spices to ensure no one could smell the decaying corpse. His dead hands held both sword and scepter.

Queen Jezebel walked behind the funerary cart, and Joram was slightly behind her. She was dressed in her Tyrian finery, a bright purple gown, exquisitely embroidered at the neck, sleeves, and hem. The gown was hemmed intentionally long so it would drag on the ground and become filthy. Dragging luxurious fabrics in the dirt was a Phoenician funeral custom, much as sackcloth and ashes was to a Hebrew. The dirty hem was to be a reminder of the vanity of life, death would come for all men, pauper and king alike.

The flautists followed the queen, playing their music. Then a large group of palace women in sackcloth and ashes, wailing in traditional Hebrew mourning. Lastly came citizens who'd chosen to follow the funeral procession all the way to the burial caves of the kings.

All tombs lay outside the city walls in accordance with Torah. This is where King Ahab would "sleep with his ancestors" in a protected crypt. Sleeping with one's ancestors was a phrase that indicated family burial plots. Ahab's father Omri had established a new dynasty over Israel after the house of Baasha and made his capital in Samaria and created the new tomb complex for his descendants. Ahab was joining his father.

· · · · ·

At King Ahab's burial site, citizens performed funerary rituals according to the cult of the dead. Grain and wine offerings were laid before the newly deceased king's tomb to entice his spirit to come forth and give an oracle of divination. Some citizens would stay all night in vigil, waiting for a vision. More extreme summoning behaviors included the cutting of hair, scraping of skin with flints, and even self-mutilation cutting. These Canaanite rituals had been adopted by the Israelites, despite having been forbidden in the Torah.

Near the burial caves was a large structure called the House of Marzeah where an assembly would meet to engage in cult of the dead rituals. The

Assembly of Marzeah was a private fraternal guild whose membership roster included virtually all the male nobility, high ranking military, and the prominent local citizens. For a week following the king's internment, members would gather here to mourn the death and celebrate life with food and drink, they would call upon the gods, engage in sexual activities with qedeshim, and consume wine to excess.

Jehu and his captains escorted Prince Joram to the House of Marzeah. They were greeted by the guild's resident chief, Eldad. As was customary, the men removed their attire and donned sackcloth. The exception was Joram, who remained in royal robes for an upcoming ceremony which would affirm him as incoming king.

As a military leader, Jehu had participated in plenty of Marzeah Feasts. But this time he felt a strange disconnect, as though he truly did not belong here, as if he were an uninvited stranger. It nagged at him deep in his soul.

Several hundred men were now present, engaged in mourning the king and celebrating his son as successor. Jehu found himself refraining from the excesses as his spirit was troubled. He maintained a clearer head while those around him were now delirious with the pleasures of strong drink.

A beautiful young qedesha approached him, offering herself for his pleasure, but he turned her away. He had tolerated all this debauchery for years, but now he just wanted to escape. Tonight, he felt trapped and a great desire to stop all of this was building within him. But a failure to participate would violate the social norms and might bring great shame, it could even result in the loss of everything he'd worked for.

In the center of the room a pit had been dug, a portal to the underworld. Above it, was an opening in the roof. The chief of the House brought forth food and drink for the departed. A necromancer took these offerings and placed them at the edge of the pit, to entice the departed to come up from the netherworld. He then lit a fire of incense in the pit and fragrance filled the room as smoke ascended to the sky.

Prince Joram then recited a lyric reminiscent of Canaanite liturgy which had been adapted for Hebrew. He cried out, "May you be much exalted, O Ahab, among the Rephaim of Sheol, in the midst of warriors' company!"

The Rephaim were the dead warrior kings of old called upon in the marzeah to receive the recently dead king and validate the new living king.

The necromancer then called out,

"You are invoked, O saviors of the underworld.

"You are summoned, O assembly of the Rephaim.

"Invoked is Omri.

"Invoked is Zimri and Elah and Baasha.

"Invoked is Nadab and Jeroboam.

"You are summoned, O assembly of the Ditanu."

Jehu felt a burning down his spine. The chief had called upon the names of the previous kings of Israel, but he had also called upon the "assembly of the Ditanu," which was part of the Canaanite hero-cult.

Prince Joram knelt beside the necromancer, who poured wine into the pit, then leaned in to listen for sounds from below. The noise of chirping, like birds, began to arise from the darkness. Heavily connected to the underworld, birds were the form many spirits took to interact with necromancers and sorcerers. The noise started softly and echoed as though it came from a depth far greater than this mere earthly opening. Then it grew in volume, enveloping the room with sound.

Suddenly, a flurry of birds burst out of the smoky pit toward the opening in the ceiling. Small as sparrow hawks, they moved in a wave of flapping wings up with the smoke and out into the night sky above.

The necromancer placed his hand upon Joram's head and said, "The Rephaim of Sheol have received the call to consecration. They send a reply."

The room fell silent in shock as a phantasm rose up out of the pit. Jehu felt suddenly cold. This amorphous elohim initially was shapeless, but its form coalesced to look like a man, an abnormally tall warrior, about eleven feet high. He wore a blackened, ancient armor. His skin was pure white and his bald head was abnormally elongated.

A wave of fear swept over many in the room. Men began to back away from the pit and the apparition. Jehu found his hand gripping the blade of his knife, which he wore beneath the sackcloth robe.

"Why have you awakened me from my bed of worms?" the elohim spoke aloud to the necromancer.

The creature jerked and twisted as if barely in control of its movements, or perhaps from pains all over its ethereal body.

The necromancer hesitated and stuttered, "I, uh, we, seek the acceptance of King Ahab into your midst and, uh, the approval of Prince Joram as the new king of Israel."

The elohim peered down upon Joram, who simply stared in wide-eyed terror.

"Who are you, my lord?" asked the necromancer.

"Who am I?" the elohim snapped. "I am First Potentate. I am Babel. I am Nimrod."

A frightened silence gripped the room. Nimrod was the king of Babel who had presided over the infamous tower built to the heavens in primeval days. Under his royal reign, humanity had almost achieved a deification that would have rivaled Yahweh's own glory. Yahweh had ended Nimrod's vainglorious pursuit by confusing the tongues of the people and separating them upon the earth into different nations, which halted the idolatrous goals of the king. Nimrod was primal evil.

The elohim thundered, "Who is this Joram?"

Joram spoke out in a nervous voice, "The son of Ahab of Israel, Queen Izabel's deceased king."

"Queen Izabel."

It spoke as if it recognized her. Of course, it would. Evil recognized its allies more quickly than Good ever did.

That was the trigger. Jehu stepped out of the crowd and made his way toward Joram. He still gripped his blade beneath his cloak.

Nimrod said, "I will grant the approval of the assembly of Ditanu. But I can do more. I can possess this man with great power. I can give him my spirit of the Great Hunter, the mighty gibborim, Gilgamesh reborn. He will be a god. All you have to do is let me in."

Let me in. Those were the words that would bring forth the mightiest of Rephaim warriors back into this world. If Nimrod could return and achieve his original dream of world unity under his rule, there would be no end to the evil and chaos he would unleash upon the earth.

Jehu had moved through the crowded room and was now near Joram, who still knelt before the pit. In just a few more steps, Jehu could cut the prince's throat, stop this infernal wickedness, and lead a coup to overthrow Jezebel.

Jehu froze as he realized the evil spirit Nimrod had noticed him. The creature jerked and twitched with surprise, as if stabbed by Jehu's hidden knife. Then Jehu saw its eyes through the smoky-black waves. They were eyes burning with hatred like he'd never encountered before. Jehu saw in them untold millennia of unatoned bitterness. Unforgiven.

Before Jehu could make his move, the elohim dissolved into the smoke and back down into the pit.

The necromancer cried out, "Wait! Nimrod! What of your offer?"

There was no response.

And no one in the room even took notice of Jehu. He could have been invisible. Not a single person seemed to realize the elohim had departed after looking directly at him.

The necromancer cried out again, "You promised your power!"

But it was gone. Only the smoke from the incense remained, drifting up lazily into the sky above.

The crowd broke into murmuring, shocked by what they'd just experienced, curious about what it all meant. In this new chaos, Jehu knew his opportunity to kill Joram was now gone.

Joram was the most disappointed. Still on his knees, he wept into his hands. Great power had been dangled in front of him, almost in his hands, then snatched away just as quickly.

The poor sap didn't realize his life had just been spared from Jehu's blade. Spared from joining that monster in Sheol in his miserable bed of worms and maggots.

Jehu replayed the events in his mind. That creature had definitely looked straight at him and seemed to have guessed his intent to murder Joram.

Then a dreadful thought occurred to Jehu. What if the creature had been responding to Jehu himself? What did he know about Jehu?

The commander turned and left the House of Marzeah, vowing never to return.

CHAPTER 63

Jezreel

Jehu stood on the marbled entrance to the temple of Baal. His soldiers formed a perimeter around the entire courtyard, which was full of Israelite citizens. Thousands had travelled from all around the kingdom, even from the remote reaches of Dan and Bethel, to see the coronation of their new king. At the front of the temple, court musicians were playing music of rejoicing.

Joram walked the long gauntlet of palace guards lined up all the way from the entrance gate to the temple itself. They held banners of the House of Omri whose mascot animal was the horse, a beast of burden whose loyalty seemed the opposite of this dynasty of apostasy. Joram followed the harlot queen herself, Jezebel, and an entourage of royal qedeshim carrying banners emblazoned with Tyre's mascot, the seven-headed Leviathan.

As the crowd cheered for Joram, Jehu watched Jezebel with righteous indignation. With the death of Ahab, she now had complete control of her son, the new king. She'd managed to manipulate him to switch his coronation and celebration from Samaria to Jezreel. She'd manipulated him into holding his anointing in the House of Baal rather than the royal palace. And she'd manipulated him to receive that anointing from the priests of both Yahweh and of Baal. Righteous kings were anointed by prophets of Yahweh or high priests of the temple in Jerusalem. This was Joram's first act of defiance that would no doubt mark a reign of evil in the sight of the Lord—of walking in the sins of Joram's father.

King Ethbaal of Tyre, Jezebel's father, was there with his Sidonian company at the foot of the steps, enjoying a front seat view. As Joram ascended the steps, Jehu realized that Jezebel wore the garb of a high priestess of Astarte, her heritage. Which meant whatever she was about to do would be an abomination.

A group of twenty Baal priests surrounded the king, who knelt on a pillow before the two priests of incompatible gods. That was when Jezebel made her way to stand next to the high priest of Baal. They both said prayers to their deities. The first to pour oil on Joram's head was the priest of Yahweh. He tilted the flask over Joram's forehead. As the oil dribbled down on Joram's beard, the priest said, "I anoint you king in the name of Yahweh, the god of Israel."

Then the high priest of Baal took the flask. But instead of anointing Joram, he handed it to Jezebel. She poured the oil over her son's head, saying "I anoint you in the name of Baal, the Most High."

Joram prayed silently as the musicians played a song of contemplation.

Meanwhile, Jehu wrestled through his thoughts about the future, debating with himself. Could he continue to serve the crown? Should he assassinate both Joram and Jezebel? Could he live with the stain of being known in history as the king murderer? What of the shame on his family? Maybe he should just avoid assassination and kill himself instead.

Jehu shut away all those thoughts when it was his turn to participate in the ceremony, the priest of Baal had signaled it was time to present the royal scepter. He reached into the oak box on a table behind him and pulled out the golden gem-studded mace. It was the symbol of kingly rule.

He handed it to the priest, who together with the Yahweh priest blessed it, then handed it to Jezebel.

Joram arose and Jezebel presented the royal scepter. To the shock of most observers, Jezebel leaned forward and kissed her son fully on the mouth. Intimately.

Jehu felt repulsed. He glanced over at Ethbaal who watched from the foot of the steps, the old man's lecherous grin was unmistakable. The sins of the father.

Jezebel released the scepter, and Joram held it firmly in his own hands, hands that symbolically received their power from his mother.

Jezebel stepped up beside Joram. When he turned to face the crowds, she raised his hand and scepter into the air and shouted, "Long live the king!"

The priests of Baal and Yahweh shouted, "Long live the king!"

The crowd responded, "Long live the king! Long live the king!"

A bull sacrifice to Baal would be the next order of the day as the first sacrifice of the new king of Israel, Joram, son of Ahab, son of Omri.

• • • • •

After the public coronation ceremony was complete, the royal attendants and noble families of the region gathered in the palace throne room for instruction by the new king of Israel. Hundreds of the higher class joined the royal household in the open area before the throne.

Jehu followed Joram and Jezebel through another line of heavily armed guards displaying their armor with militaristic presence. Jehu had not arranged this particular cadre of soldiers. It must have been the Queen Mother in her new authority.

But as they ascended the steps to take their positions, Jehu noticed Captain Medad meeting Joram to stand beside him seated on his throne. Medad had served under Jehu for years. He'd always been a favorite of the queen. This was a bad sign. As Jehu stood beside Jezebel, he felt a sinking sensation in his gut. He could guess what was coming.

Jezebel gestured for Jehu to lean into her whisper. When he did, she hissed at him, "I'm Queen Mother now, Jehu. Things are going to change around here." Then she leaned back and spoke under her breath to her son, "Joram, speak."

Joram looked pale and sweaty, like a frightened mouse. He wouldn't look at Jehu. When he spoke, his voice cracked under pressure. "Leaders of Israel, I have chosen and promoted Captain Medad to be my new commander of the army. Beneath me and the Queen Mother, he has total military authority."

So that was it. The grand betrayal and humiliation. Jezebel had been planning to take Jehu out since the day she'd realized he was a voice of conscience to a double-minded King Ahab. Medad stared straight ahead, unwilling to look his former commander in the eye. Jehu couldn't blame the warrior. He hadn't asked for this promotion.

Joram continued, "And when I am absent, the Queen Mother will rule in my stead. Her decisions will be regarded as decisions of your king. Her commands will be obeyed as the commands of your king."

Jezebel stood, impatiently stealing the attention from Joram. She exuded smug satisfaction with every word. "Leaders of Israel, I have been your queen these many years. And I have loved you as my own people. I have become one of you. We are not a Hebrew nation. We are a nation of Canaanites, Phoenicians, and Arameans as well as Hebrews. As co-regent of this throne, I vow to continue that religious diversity as part of a progressive future for all God's people."

The audience applauded obediently if not willingly. Joram, the cowardly little puppet, fidgeted nervously.

An old man in a ragged robe stepped out from the crowd. The prophet Micaiah, son of Imlah. He stepped fearlessly into the gauntlet of soldiers. They lowered their spears before and behind him, blocking him in. The old prophet wasn't supposed to be released from prison unless Ahab survived the battle of Ramoth-gilead. Those were Ahab's own orders. But Ahab was dead. And Jehu had no idea how Micaiah had gotten out.

The prophet shouted, "Hear the word of the Lord, which he spoke by his servant, Elijah the Tishbite!"

The crowd rumbled with shock and offense.

Joram rolled his eyes.

Jezebel smirked, as if wanting to let the old man make a fool of himself.

Micaiah announced, "The dogs shall eat the flesh of Jezebel! And her corpse shall be as excrement on the face of the field in the territory of Jezreel, so that no one can say, 'This is Jezebel!'"

Medad wasted no time. He shouted to his guards, "Seize him!"

Four guards were on the prophet, holding him roughly, ready to tear him apart. One of them held a dagger to Micaiah's throat.

Jezebel shouted, "Stop!"

The guards froze.

"Do not hurt that man," she ordered. The guard lowered his blade. The others stopped rough-handling him.

She stood. Her voice turned into a calm, peaceful tone of graciousness. "This throne will be a throne of mercy, not bloodshed. Of love, not fear. We are stronger together. We must not let their hatred divide us or provoke us."

Jehu was shocked at the silence that pervaded the room. He saw a look of complete surprise on Joram's face. Everyone had clearly expected worse.

She concluded, "Our love shall trump their hate."

The nobility began murmuring agreement and affirmation amongst themselves for the wisdom of their new Queen Mother.

• • • • •

A hammer pounded a long, thin spike deeper into the palm of Micaiah the prophet. He screamed out in unbearable pain. No one could hear him, but his torturers as he'd been strapped to a wooden cross deep in the stone dungeon below the Jezreel palace fort. His arms had been stretched out to two sides of the crossbeam; his legs tied at the bottom of the vertical beam. He lay flat on his back, but the cross could be cranked to stand upright when finished.

Izabel gently pushed the torturer aside so she could lean in close to the face of the old creature. She looked at him coldly, observing his pain like a reptile ready to strike.

"You know, old man, one of the benefits of being raised in a trading city like Tyre is the exposure to other cultures. It breeds an 'open mind' to learn from other nations."

The Queen Mother caressed the contraption on which he was being crucified. "I learned this torture from the Assyrians." The Assyrians were the cruelest, most ruthless people in the fertile crescent.

She leaned in again and whispered, "Now, what can I learn from you?"

Micaiah moaned with pain. He wasn't going to last long.

She asked with a slow, methodical cadence, "Where. Is. Elijah." It was more a demand than a question.

Micaiah looked at her. He was still not ready to talk.

She added, "Do you know what else I learned from the Assyrians? How to skin a man alive."

CHAPTER 64

Jordan River Valley

A contingent of two hundred cavalry soldiers thundered down the forest road through the rolling hills of the Jordan Valley. They were the queen's most fearsome strike force, and they were searching for the prophet Elijah based on secret intelligence obtained by Jezebel. Commander Medad lead these soldiers and Jehu followed his new commander.

Jehu had been humiliated and demoted to a captain of a hundred in the army. He was well aware he'd been included in this mission to rub his nose in his humiliation. He wondered what other dark intentions the queen entertained for his future. If he lived, he likely wouldn't have to wait long for the revelation.

Medad took his new authority seriously, and tried to maintain proper respect for Jehu despite his uncomfortable position as Jezebel's pawn.

Medad ordered Jehu, "Tell the Queen Mother we've arrived."

Jehu galloped back to Jezebel's closed carriage and knocked on the door. She opened it.

"We have arrived, your highness," he said.

Jezebel held in her hands the golden axe from the House of Baal. Blood droplets fell from her palm and dribbled on the pillows around her. Jehu had a sudden flashback to the cutting she'd engaged in on Mount Carmel. It was a call to Baal for empowerment.

She slammed the door on him.

•••••

On the other side of the Jordan River, in a clearing deep in the forest of the Transjordan, Elisha and Elijah sat at a fire with a company of fifty other prophets of Yahweh and Jonadab son of Rechab. The Rechabite had found

Elijah and pleaded with him to permit a company of his warriors to guard the small band. Elijah had refused, so Jonadab had persuaded the old prophet to at least allow him to join them. Jonadab slept near Elijah like a watchdog.

The night was cold and damp. Most of the other prophets were long asleep. Elisha was devouring a fish. He was hungry, he hadn't eaten earlier with the other prophets because it had been his shift for sentry duty. When he saw Elijah watching him pensively, he slowed his eating.

As he licked his fingers clean of fish, he noticed Elijah looking around and then gazing into the forest intently. Did he sense a spy? Were they about to be attacked? The replacement on sentry duty had raised no alarm.

"What is wrong?" asked Elisha.

Elijah became stoic. He got to his feet, the light of the campfire playing over his gaunt, aged frame. "It is time."

"Time for what?" Elisha asked, puzzled.

Jonadab was on his feet now too, as he always was whenever the old prophet made a move. He stood, one hand on his sword hilt.

Elijah slid his mantle from his shoulders, and held it out to Elisha. "Put on the mantle."

Elisha reached out a hand to the smelly mantle with its long white angora goat hair, but didn't quite touch it. He wasn't sure he dared. This mantle was the representation of Elijah's anointing and authority as leader of Yahweh's prophets.

"Why?"

Elijah spoke as if scolding. "Because you are Yahweh's chosen prophet."

Elisha felt his whole body go numb. Elijah had once thrown his mantle around Elisha as confirmation of the young man's calling as a prophet. But in all that time since, not once had Elisha personally heard the word of the Lord as Elijah had.

Elisha could only think of one thing to say. "What about you?"

"My time has come to an end," Elijah responded simply. "So you had better listen to him." He pointed upward. "Especially if you are to be Yahweh's mouthpiece to his people."

Elisha caught his breath in stunned disbelief. Mouthpiece of Yahweh was what the people termed Elijah himself. Was his master actually saying what his words seemed to suggest? Elisha had dreamt and prayed for years in hope that he would hear Yahweh's voice for himself. He often wondered if his actions at Mount Carmel had forever cut him off from Yahweh's voice. How could he possibly take Elijah's place?

"You think I'm ready?"

"No," said Elijah with a teasing smile. Finally, the master had gotten a sense of humor.

"But Yahweh thinks so. He has appointed you to take my place."

Elisha blurted out, "Then grant me a double portion of your spirit! I can't do this in my own strength."

Elijah laughed. "Always the bold one. You will get what you asked for if you see me when I leave you."

Elisha still had not touched the mantle. "Leave me? When are you leaving? Where are you going?"

Elijah laid the mantle on the ground and grabbed Elisha's right hand. He grasped his wrist in comradery, then turned Elisha's palm upward.

In the firelight, Elisha saw that the burn scars from his parents' home were gone. He'd been healed and hadn't even noticed it.

Elijah held his left hand up for Elisha to see. It wasn't trembling anymore.

Elisha said with a grin, "No more fear of man."

Elijah replied, "Like father, like son."

They embraced, and Elisha felt the old prophet's tight hold, as if this was the last time he would see him.

Then he heard the caw of ravens and looked up. He saw a group of shadows circling above in the moonlight.

Elijah said, "Let us pray."

· · · · ·

A scout who had been hiding in the brush watching the prophets' camp quietly scurried his way back to the Jordan River and caught the ferry to cross.

Jehu and Medad received the news and knocked on Jezebel's carriage door.

"Your highness," said Medad. "We found Elijah. He is with fifty other prophets. They are unarmed."

As she opened the door, Jehu saw a dark satisfaction on Jezebel's face. She growled, "Send a company of fifty to arrest him. Kill the rest."

The scout assured them, "It will only take two ferry trips to carry that number across the river."

So the water would not delay them too long.

Medad bowed in obedience before departing and fulfilling the queen's orders.

Jehu turned to follow Medad. Jezebel hadn't closed the carriage door, and he heard her mutter into the darkness as if to Elijah himself, "So now after all these years, I finally have you."

• • • • •

By now all the prophets were awake and had joined Elisha and Elijah in prayer. The fire burned with fresh logs. Jonadab stood with drawn sword where he could most effectively guard the leader of the prophets. A few other prophets had been sent out to join those sentries on duty.

The sound of a horse snorting was almost anticlimactic. As Elisha turned, he saw a captain of the Jezreel guard ride his mighty war horse right up to the group around the fire. Elijah stepped forward to meet him, Jonadab at his side. The other prophets continued in prayer.

Elijah bowed and said, "Greetings, my lord. I see you are a soldier of the king. Or is it the queen?"

The captain made no response to Elijah's implied insult. Instead, he reached into a pouch on his horse's haunch and pulled out what looked like a crumpled thin blanket. Elisha couldn't tell what it was. But it looked bloody, and flies were buzzing around it. Then its stench hit Elisha's nostrils. The stench of death.

The captain threw it at Elijah's feet. "The queen sends you the skin of your prophet Micaiah."

Elisha felt vomit rising in his throat.

"You will come peacefully with my men."

As the captain whistled, a company of foot soldiers moved into the clearing behind the captain. They were pushing ahead of them several prophets who'd been on sentry duty. The company of armed soldiers had their shields up and spears out as if to fight a phalanx of mighty warriors instead of unarmed, peaceful prophets.

Elijah bent down and picked up a piece of burning wood from the fire.

297

What is he doing? Elisha wondered. But after all these years, he'd stopped trying to second-guess his master's actions.

Elijah gazed up into heaven and said, "Now see the salvation of our God."

• • • • •

At Jezebel's camp, Medad and Jehu stood watching the bright orange glow across the river in the forest. It looked like fire, but it was gone as quickly as it started.

"What do you think it is?" asked Medad.

"I don't know. But I'll report it to the Queen Mother."

"No need," came a voice behind them. Jezebel walked up to stand between the two warriors. Dressed in a dark traveling robe and without her golden crown, she looked ragged to Jehu. Her hand was now bandaged, and she cradled it protectively. She seemed twitchy and jumpy, reminding him vaguely of the phantom he'd seen in the House of Marzeah.

She asked Medad, "Should we send another unit to see what it was?"

"Those are my best warriors, your highness. But if it pleases you, I will go down there myself."

"No," she snapped. "I can wait."

About fifteen minutes had passed when the pounding rhythm of a fast approaching horse captured their attention. The riderless horse came into view, its body dripping wet with water from the river. It must have swam across.

Jehu immediately recognized the war horse of the captain who'd led the party of fifty to Elijah's camp. He moved to grab its reins.

That was when he saw the burnt, smoldering hand and forearm caught in a twist of the leather reigns.

Jehu felt no surprise. After all, this was Elijah they were facing. The prophet who had once called down Yahweh's fire from heaven.

Jezebel stepped up to the horse. Examining the body part hanging from its bridle, she ordered, "Jehu, muster a unit of your soldiers and bring me Elijah."

So it had come to this.

What should Jehu do? Obey the crown and betray his God again? Or face execution for insubordination? Retribution would be swift out here in the

298

wilderness. He might be able to cut Jezebel's throat before Medad could stop him, but he surely could not escape.

"Your Queen Mother has ordered you," she reiterated.

Still, Jehu hesitated. He looked at Medad, whose hand was already on his sword. His former subordinate was an obedient soldier. Despite the years they'd served together, Medad would not hesitate to kill Jehu for treason.

Then Jezebel's voice calmed down. It was a strange calm. A dangerous calm. "Bring me Elijah, if you care about your family."

Your family. The words rang like a death knell in Jehu's ears.

Now it wasn't only his death warrant Jezebel was threatening, but his family's death warrant. And he had no doubt she'd carry through on her threat with delight. It was now or never.

• • • • •

Jehu decided to take a chariot on the small road through the forest instead of trying to sneak up on the prophet's camp in the clearing. He had his men carry torches. He would face this situation boldly and without fear. A group of fifty new foot soldiers accompanied him, each of them on edge, ready to fight.

They crossed the river on the ferry and took the road to the prophet's camp.

When they broke into the clearing and approached their target, the group of prophets saw them coming. They didn't move.

Jehu came upon the smoldering remains of a soldier's charred body on the perimeter of the camp. A soldier lowered his torch to examine the gruesome sight. The body was black as the night, apparently having been completely engulfed in flames and burnt to a crisp. The ground at his feet was black and burnt. Jehu looked around the camp and saw other remains on the ground surrounding the prophets. All of them black, smoldering flesh.

Jehu glanced at one of the soldiers he'd brought with him. In light of the previous slaughter, he wanted to make sure someone would return to give testimony to Medad. The soldier was young, still in his teens, and looked frightened with bulging eyes.

"You! Stay behind to take a report to Commander Medad."

Looking patently happy with the order, the young soldier retreated into the trees. Jehu slowly wheeled his chariot up to the camp, his men stayed back waiting for orders.

He called out, "Elijah!"

The prophets were all on their feet, watching Jehu's approach, Elisha among them as well as Elijah. Jehu took note of Jonadab standing beside Elijah before announcing, "Elijah, the crown has commanded me to bring you back to Jezreel."

Though Jehu doubted strongly that was Jezebel's actual intention.

"And what will you do, O Jehu?" asked Elijah. "What master will you obey?"

The lives of all his beloved ones were hanging in the balance. If he didn't obey the authority of the queen, he would be condemning them to death.

Jehu could only say one thing. "Yahweh is my master."

His statement placed the queen at war with Jehu's entire bloodline.

What was he to do next? Jehu caught Jonadab's solemn nod. His best friend and brother-in-law knew the stakes as well. He knew Jezebel.

Elijah turned and nodded to Elisha, who approached Jehu, carrying a small oil flask. The young prophet announced, "Jehu, son of Nimshi, kneel before me."

Jehu couldn't believe what he was hearing. But he obeyed. He stepped out of his chariot and knelt before Elisha.

Elisha opened the flask and said, "Thus says Yahweh, the God of Israel, I anoint you king over the people of Yahweh, over Israel."

He poured some of the oil on Jehu's head. "And you shall strike down the house of Ahab your master so that I may avenge on Jezebel the blood of my servants the prophets and the blood of all the servants of Yahweh. For the whole house of Ahab shall perish, and I will cut off from Ahab every male, bond or free, in Israel."

Elisha poured more oil on Jehu, and finished, "And the dogs shall eat Jezebel in the territory of Jezreel, and none shall bury her."

Jehu wiped away the oil that had flowed down over his eyes and cheeks. Or were those tears intermixed with the oil?

He raised his head to see all the prophets kneeling before him. Turning, he saw that the company of soldiers, all fifty of them, had drawn near and were also on their knees. Was this in fear after having seen the devastation of their comrades lying blackened on the forest floor around them? Or did they truly support their former commander's appointment to the kingship?

Elisha cried out, "Long live the king!"

The soldiers and prophets all responded, "Long live the king! Long live the king!"

Everything had changed. Everything. All Jehu's years of struggle to remain obedient and loyal to both Yahweh and Yahweh's chosen king had now come together in perfect unity. Jehu was now the Lord's anointed. He'd been given the Lord's command to clean house. And he would do it.

But his attention was drawn to Elisha, who was looking around as though searching for a valued and lost object. Jehu suddenly realized what was missing. Or rather, who.

"Where is Elijah?"

Then he saw the great pillar of fire bursting down from heaven to the earth at the far edge of the clearing. Elijah stood right beside it.

Elisha was staring stunned at the sight as well. As were all the men.

Jehu and Elisha looked to each other wordlessly, then together ran toward Elijah.

When they arrived at the spot where the old prophet had stood, they saw him now standing in a chariot in the middle of the pillar of fire. The pillar twisted like a flaming whirlwind, and beside Elijah in the chariot stood what looked to be the Angel of Yahweh. The chariot looked made of fire, and its horses also appeared to be of fire.

Jehu felt the heat of the wind generated by the twisting pillar. Yet neither Elijah nor the angel were being consumed by the flames.

The sound of the heavenly fire was peaceful to Jehu. Like ocean waves of water. It was wonderous to behold. Too wonderous. Jehu shielded his eyes from the brightness of it all.

Then Elijah's chariot began to ascend into the heavens. Stepping closer as if to stop him, Elisha yelled, "My father! My father!"

Jehu heard Elijah yell back from the whirlwind, "My son!"

And then he was gone.

The whirlwind returned to heaven with the prophet as if sucked back up into the sky. As if it had never been there. And all was normal. As though nothing had happened.

Elisha grabbed his tunic on his body and tore it in half. Throwing the two pieces on the ground, he stood in absolute silence. Across the clearing, the other prophets and soldiers remained on their knees, their hands raised to heaven. They had all been in the presence of the holy.

The loss of Elijah was just beginning to sink in. The older prophet had indeed become a father to Elisha. He'd raised his young protégé in the ways of the Lord to be a prophet of Yahweh, the highest calling. He'd taught Elisha to speak Yahweh's word with boldness. Now he'd left Elisha to take up the mantle of his calling as Yahweh's mouthpiece, and life would never be the same. How could he possibly carry such a load?

With Yahweh's Spirit, he could. A double portion, in fact, as Elijah had promised should Elisha be witness to his departure. His adoptive father was gone. But Elisha was not alone. With authority that felt less feigned with each step, Elisha strode across the clearing, picked up the angora mantle, and wrapped it around his shoulders, tying it into place with the leather belt Elijah had dropped beside it. Then he turned to his fifty colleagues.

"The Word of the Lord has told me it is time to reestablish the School of Prophets."

Jehu too had received a responsibility thrust upon him that felt far beyond his capabilities. As Elisha had become Yahweh's chosen prophet, so Jehu had become Yahweh's anointed king. Together, they were responsible to represent Yahweh's words and deeds. The prophet was God's mouthpiece, the king, God's right hand.

They had much to do.

Jehu walked back to his chariot. He saw Jonadab standing near, watching him. Holding out his hand, Jehu asked the Rechabite the words they were both so familiar with. "Is your heart knit to mine as my heart is knit to yours?"

Jonadab approached Jehu, smiled, and said, "Together we will do great things." He grabbed his friend's wrist, and Jehu pulled him up onto the war machine next to him.

• • • • •

Jehu led his soldiers and prophets up to the banks of the Jordan River crossing. Unfortunately, the ferry was gone. Someone had cut the ropes and the ferry must have floated away. Sabotage. But who? It didn't matter now. Jehu was stranded.

At the sound of ravens cawing overhead, Jehu swung around to see Elisha step up beside his horse with a smile. The prophet was wearing the long-haired mantle that had belonged to Elijah. Three black-as-night ravens landed on the mantle as Elisha approached the riverbank.

They flew off as the prophet removed the mantle and rolled it up in his hands.

Raising the cloak above his head, the prophet slapped the river's edge with it. The water splashed, and Elisha picked up the cloak and shook it out.

Just as Jehu was about to ask Elisha what he was doing, the waters of the Jordan River began to swirl and pull apart right where the party stood. To the left and to the right, the waters pulled back into a heap on either side until only a dry riverbed lay before them.

Both soldiers and prophets murmured in astonishment. Standing beside Jehu in the chariot, Jonadab quoted from a song that all Hebrews knew very well. "Sing to Yahweh, for he has triumphed gloriously; the horse and his rider he has thrown into the sea."

It was the song of the Red Sea crossing.

The spiritual meaning was not lost on Jehu as they crossed through the waters. Every story of divine origins contained a storm god who conquered Sea and River and defeated the dragon of chaos to start a new order. So did Yahweh.

> Yet God my King is from of old,
>> working salvation in the midst of the earth.
> You divided the sea by your might;
>> you broke the heads of the sea monsters on the waters.
> You crushed the heads of Leviathan;
>> you gave him as food for the creatures of the wilderness.
> "I am Yahweh your God,
>> who stirs up the sea so that its waves roar,

And I have put my words in your mouth
    and covered you in the shadow of my hand,
establishing the heavens
    and laying the foundations of the earth,
    and saying to Zion, 'You are my people.'"

The Red Sea crossing was a momentous doorway that led to the Sinai covenant genesis. Yahweh had parted the chaos waters, crushed the heads of Leviathan, and led his people to the holy mountain, where he had established his covenantal order.

This crossing represented a return to that covenant. A renewal against the rising chaos. And Jehu was going to crush Jezebel's serpent head.

• • • • •

When Jehu, Jonadab, and his men reached Jezebel's camp, it was empty.

They walked quietly through the remains. It was a mess. Fires still burned. Garbage lay strewn around. Even some tents remained unpacked. Jezebel had clearly left in a hurry. Jehu suddenly realized he hadn't seen the young sentry he'd posted as a messenger. He must have returned to camp and told the queen what he'd seen.

Which meant she knew what had happened. And that her entire kingdom was now in jeopardy. She'd most likely fled to tell Joram and prepare for battle.

And she'd left in a hurry, leaving her carriage and using a horse so as to not be slowed down. Her transport's door creaked open on its hinges. She hadn't even taken time to shut it behind her. Jehu could almost smell her fear. Jezebel was desperate. But she was also cunning.

Jonadab stepped up to him and said, "Jezebel will be waiting for us at Jezreel."

Jehu nodded. "With Medad and the king's forces."

Jonadab wondered, "Is Medad loyal to Yahweh?"

"I know he is loyal to the king."

"Can we beat him, Jehu?"

"Not with fifty soldiers."

Elisha moved forward to remind solemnly, "And one mighty God."

The prophets wouldn't be fighting, but Jehu needed reminding of the divine warrior who was fighting for them.

"Jehu." Jonadab's solemn call drew his attention over to the carriage.

The Rechabite pointed at the ritual golden axe of Baal Jezebel had brought with her, now embedded in the side panel. Walking over, Jehu saw that the axe had pinned something to the carriage wall.

Jonadab pulled it off to show him.

It was the Moabite sheath and dagger Jehu had given to Daniel, Jonadab's son. And now it was clear.

Jezebel had their families. Daniel, Galina, and pregnant Susanna must have been taken hostage shortly after they had returned from Ramoth-gilead. And Jehu had no doubt where Jezebel had taken his family. To her stronghold in Jezreel where the forces of evil reigned supreme.

Jehu burned with the fire of righteous rage from the depth of his soul. The harlot queen had planned all this behind his back. She had outsmarted him. She had the dagger to his heart, and now she was going to plunge it into him.

Jehu headed back to his chariot.

Jonadab mounted his horse and shouted, "I'll ride ahead and get the Rechabites!"

Jehu paused his steps and looked to his friend. As the men locked eyes, Jehu saw the fire of judgement ready to be released. The Rechabite leader turned his horse and disappeared into the woods like a wraith in the night.

Springing to the chariot bed, Jehu raised his sword to the sky and yelled to his men, "Prophets, pray. Soldiers, prepare for battle! We march to Jezreel!"

CHAPTER 65

Jezreel

Izabel was still dirty and wind-blown from her hard ride as she swept into Joram's throne room. This was an emergency. She found Joram seated on his throne and beside him sat Jehoram, king of Judah in a chair of honor. They were discussing the wars with the Arameans as well as the brewing trouble of Moab and Edom. The queen Mother interrupted by shoving a soldier before the king and calling out for the king's counselor.

The young, bulgy-eyed soldier who'd returned to camp with his calamitous report, trembled as he stood. "Repeat your story." the queen commanded. The kings listened as the tale spilled forth. Then silence filled the chamber as he finished.

Joram looked like a frightened child. He swallowed and looked around on the floor, not sure what to think or do.

Izabel directed her next words to the king of Judah. "I need to speak alone with my son."

"Of course," said Jehoram. He got up and left the room along with the guard and soldiers.

Joram sat there, still looking helpless.

Izabel said impatiently, "There is little time."

"Mother, what the witness described, it sounded like a fanciful tale. Angels and chariots of fire?"

Izabel held back her anger, "He saw Jehu bow before a criminal prophet who anointed him with oil. What more do you need to prove treason and revolt?"

"But he didn't hear what was spoken."

Izabel sighed and closed her eyes, calming herself. "A foolish, indecisive king is easily overthrown. Is that what you are?"

306

Joram rolled his eyes like a child.

Stiffening her posture, Izabel walked slowly up the stairs to the king's throne like a lioness stalking its prey. She could see the fear in her son's eyes. She could probably make the poor fool pee in his tunic.

Standing over his seated form, she looked down on him in judgment. She whispered her words. "Listen to me, you coward. I made your father, and I made you. I will not stand by and let all I have worked for be crushed by the incompetence of an ignorant child. If you do not protect this throne, then I will."

He trembled.

She smelled something.

He had peed in his tunic.

· · · · ·

Outside the city of Jezreel, Asherah and Anat reveled in the worship rituals at the high place. The priests had offered a sacrifice, and the qedeshim were attending to their temple duties. The goddesses were lying on the altar, satiated with the blood of sacrifice when they heard the bellowing sound of Baal's ram's horn in the unseen realm.

"That is a call to war," observed Anat.

Asherah snapped up to quick attention, she had been forced to learn obedience at the hands of Marduk and Ashur recently. And wherever Baal went these days, those two thugs followed and enforced his will.

The two goddesses scrambled to their rooms to retrieve their armor and weapons.

Anat flung open the door to her room, walking quickly to her gear. But it was gone. Missing. Who could possibly have taken her things?

Asherah waited impatiently. She paced, dressed now in her battle skirt with sword and shield in hand. Where was Anat? She did not want to be late. She did not want to be on the receiving end of another violent subordination from the male deities.

Asherah marched back to Anat's room to find out what was keeping her. She stopped short at the sight of Anat. The goddess was gagged and bound with cherubim hair, held captive by a pair of archangels. Cherubim hair was the only supernatural binding that could hold a Watcher. They were often bound that way before being cast into Tartarus.

Asherah drew her sword. She saw Anat's eyes go wide, but before she could figure out what the other goddess was trying to communicate, her world went black as she was cold-cocked from behind.

When Anat came to, she saw that two other archangels had disarmed the comatose Asherah and bound her with cherubim hair. Anat recognized them as Raphael and Saraqael. She spit out her gag. "Cowards! You come out of hiding only to attack us from behind. You wouldn't have a chance face to face with me. I would cut you down."

"You think so, proud one?" The voice behind her was the small blond angel, Uriel.

She felt her bindings loosen and drop. A swift kick on her rear and she fell to the ground humiliated. She turned to look at the little one smirking at her. Beside him was his putrid comrade Gabriel, holding her armor and weapons. Uriel grabbed her swords and threw them both onto the stone floor within her reach.

"Well, goddess big-mouth," he quipped, "let's see if you can handle the smallest of God's angels, little ol' me." He was a full foot smaller than the rest of them, the size of a human.

"Uriel!" Gabriel complained. "Now is not the time."

"This won't take long," Uriel said with a smirk.

Anat grinned as she grabbed her weapons, a sword in each hand. "That's what all men say in sex and war. But you'll be sorry, little pud."

Rising slowly to her feet, Anat assumed a fighting stance. "I cut the mighty Mot, Lord of Death, into a thousand pieces and burned them with fire. I took those pieces and ground them into…"

Uriel interrupted her. "Are you going to fight or brag me to death?"

She launched at him with all the fury and wrath of the Canaanite goddess of war.

• • • • •

A watchman on the gates of Jezreel squinted into the distance. Through the wavy haze of the strong sun and afternoon heat, he made out an arriving party of about a hundred men on foot with a few horses.

"Close the gates!" he yelled down to the gatemen.

Turning to his message runner, he shook him out of his nap. "Quickly, tell the king Jehu has arrived."

The messenger bolted off.

• • • • •

Izabel sat naked in her royal bath as servants scrubbed the dirt from her body. Water was poured over her, and she felt its soothing, cleansing waves falling over the seven-headed Leviathan tattoo on her back.

Stepping out of the pool, she was dried by two other maidservants. She sat down at the table, and the servants began shaving the hair from her body. They began with her head. Her beautiful long, black hair fell to the floor at her feet. This was a holy ritual of purity. Hair caught dirt and filth easier in its earthiness. And for a woman, hair was one's glory, a point of pride and beauty. Shaving off one's pride was an expression of humility before the deity. She remembered when she'd first done this so many years ago in Tyre when she offered herself to Baal. Today was another special day. Another special offering to the Most High.

A beautiful gown of luxurious purple silk, embellished with rich gold embroidery, lay on a rack beside her. The gown of a high priestess of Astarte and servant to Baal. Next to the gown was the golden jewelry and precious gems she would wear with it.

• • • • •

In the distance, Jehu drove his chariot in a mad frenzy of dust to meet up with his men at the city gates. When he arrived, the chariot skidded to a stop, his mighty stallions lathered with sweat and snorting like harbingers of apocalypse.

The gates of Jezreel opened, and a force of two hundred armed soldiers fanned out into formation around King Joram and a second royal figure riding chariots.

Jehu looked at his fifty soldiers, weary from a fast march of miles. Fifty worn men against two hundred well-rested ones. The odds were not on Jehu's side.

The royal chariots stopped in position about a hundred feet out. Jehu wondered about the second royal chariot for a moment before realizing that it was king Jehoram who accompanied king Joram. This must be a providential omen. For the king of Judah was married to Jezebel's spawn Athaliah. These two kings represented the leprous cancer of the harlot queen's influence.

Jehu rolled his chariot slowly to the middle ground.

Joram rode his chariot out to meet Jehu.

The mighty Medad, leader of the forces of Israel, accompanied his master astride a war horse. His eyes were characteristically unexpressive. Jehu knew his fellow warrior very well. He would perform his duty. He would defend the crown.

Joram stopped his chariot a good thirty feet from Jehu.

Jehu shouted, "Where is my family?"

Joram replied, "They are safe for now."

Jehu shouted back, "What is the Queen Mother's intent?" He had no doubt Jezebel was behind this.

Joram exploded with anger. "I AM YOUR KING! MY INTENT IS WHAT MATTERS!"

Jehu didn't respond to the outburst. He sounded like a pathetic child having a temper tantrum. The young king was fracturing under his mother's relentless and oppressive dominance.

Jehu looked over at Medad for indicators of treachery or surprise attack.

Calming down, Joram demanded, "Where does your loyalty lie, Jehu, son of Nimshi?"

Jehu looked at him, but would not answer.

"Where is your loyalty?" Joram repeated with the confidence of a vastly superior force behind him. "Do. You. Bring. Peace?"

Jehu twisted his lips with disgust. He knew what he said next would launch all-out war.

"What peace can there be so long as the sorceress and whore of Baal, Queen Jezebel, remains?"

He could see Joram boil with rage. The king screamed, "I will have your eyes cut out! I will have your family torn limb from limb!"

But before Joram could give a command, his attention was arrested by a sole figure walking out of the ranks behind Jehu.

310

It was Elisha. He wore the long-haired mantle of a prophet.

Clearly disturbed, Joram looked up to observe the flock of ravens circling the sky above Elisha. Their caws broke the eerie stillness.

Elisha spoke with a booming voice. "I am Elisha, son of Shaphat, leader of the prophets of Yahweh! And thus saith the Lord: 'Jehu is God's anointed king of Israel. If you do not bow, you shall surely all die!'"

A wave of fortitude and determination washed over Jehu. His forces might be vastly outnumbered, but after what he'd seen in that forest camp and at the Jordan River, he knew the prophet truly spoke for Yahweh. He could not be better equipped if the entire Rechabite clan were standing behind him armed for war.

This is what true faith in Yahweh meant.

Jehu saw Joram squeeze his eyes as though in pain. His lips appeared to mouth the words, "Mother was right again."

The king pointed a damning finger at Jehu and ordered Medad, "Kill this fool, now!"

But Medad hesitated.

"Medad, I command you! Kill him! ATTACK!"

Medad did not move.

And Medad's soldiers did not move.

Joram was shaking with fury. "I WILL HAVE YOU HANGED!"

Backing up his horse a bit, Medad finally signaled to his soldiers.

But instead of attacking, they dismounted their horses, *all two hundred of them.*

Medad knelt down to one knee, and they all followed his lead.

"Hail, Jehu, King of Israel!" Medad shouted,

The soldiers followed suit. "Hail, Jehu, King of Israel!"

Joram had been so furious watching Medad he'd failed to realize Jehu now had his bow nocked with an arrow aimed right at him.

Twenty of Jehu's soldiers lifted their bows in unison.

Jehu released his missile. It hit its target, Joram's heart, with precision. The king staggered back in shock. He was already dying when the twenty other arrows hit him in the chest, launching him backwards off the chariot and into the dust. The wretched son of Ahab, puppet of Jezebel, would rule no more.

The king of Judah crouched in fear in his chariot. Grabbing the reins, he tried to turn his chariot around to return to the city gates.

Jehu gestured to his archers, and another twenty arrows rained from the sky upon Jehoram.

In a strange twist of providence, he slumped forward, dead in his chariot and still clutching the reins, as the horses galloped him back through the city gates.

Jehu shouted to his new army, now two hundred and fifty strong, "Soldiers of Israel, secure the city from the enemies of Yahweh!"

He led them toward the city gates.

Elisha remained with his fifty prophets. A different task awaited them.

At the sound of a war horn, Jehu turned. In the distance was Jonadab blowing the shofar. A small army of Rechabite chariot warriors appeared on the horizon—on their way to join the party.

• • • • •

Jehu and a company of thirty soldiers entered the royal palace, swords drawn. They caught some palace guards unaware and cut them down with ease.

"Find my family!" Jehu ordered.

They spread out.

• • • • •

On the high place outside Jezreel, Anat fought the angel Uriel with all the anger and bitterness that had built up in her soul for millennia. To her, this battle was the culmination of every offense, every tyrannical action by Yahweh and his angels from the beginning of time. His patriarchal rule of power was an unfair, intolerant imposition of his will upon his creatures. In Eden's garden, Nachash, the serpentine shining one, had sought to enlighten humankind with freedom and autonomy. Their reward had been banishment by a petty, jealous tyrant who didn't want his creation to grow up and realize they were like God with the power to create themselves through their own choices.

When the two hundred ancient ones had first fallen from heaven to earth in the days of Jared, they'd sought once again to enlighten man with the wisdom of astrology, sorcery, sexual freedom, and war. Again, they'd been punished, bound into the earth at the great Flood, along with every other human, but Noah's eight. Mercilessly all had been destroyed by their so-called loving Creator. The fearful coward just didn't want to share his power.

And lastly, the Tower of Babel, where humanity for the first time actually had the chance to become one world united in purpose for fundamental transformation. What had Yahweh and his groveling divine council chosen to do? They'd confused the languages and spread all the nations upon the earth, each under its own territorial Watcher.

Now that capricious, conniving monster of unfairness was trying to take back Canaan from those gods who rightfully inherited it. Anat envisioned the small angel she was facing as Yahweh's own representative image, upon which she would unload all her rage and hatred.

She swung her swords with a mad speed, pushing back the angel toward the altar. He was barely able to keep up. He would buckle with exhaustion any second.

She backed him up to the asherah pole beside the altar. She gave a mighty swipe of both swords inward like scissors. He ducked, and she cut the asherah in two at its base. It fell to the stone with a thud.

The angel said, "Uh oh. Mother is going to be mad at you for that one."

Gabriel shouted, "Uriel, we don't have much time."

At that point, Anat saw Uriel pull out his second sword from his back sheath. He had been defending himself with only one weapon against her two, and in her blinding anger she'd taken no thought of it.

Uriel said, "Okay, little girl, let me show you how a real male fights."

Before Anat could muster a new strategy, Uriel turned the tables and launched an offensive of two-handed lunges, pivots, and thrusts that Anat could barely keep up with. The little creature had been playing with her.

She matched him sword for sword at first, but then his sheer skill overwhelmed her. Disarming her, he shoved her to the ground.

Watchers could not be killed. They had heavenly flesh that could heal with supernatural speed. But they could be hurt by heavenly weapons. They could be decapitated and dismembered. And they could feel pain before they were put back together.

And pain was what Anat felt through every inch of her entire body as her enemy cut her into pieces as she'd done with Mot. It was the ultimate humiliation. She wondered if she'd be thrown into Tartarus.

• • • • •

In the earthly realm inside the palace, Jehu found few servants, and the usual holding rooms for prisoners were empty. His family was nowhere to be found.

Where was everyone?

His soldiers were returning to him empty-handed.

He went to the window and looked out onto the city.

Then he saw it, the temple of Baal, full of people in the courtyard, and his heart filled with dread.

He yelled out, "Soldiers, assemble at the House of Baal!"

• • • • •

In the unseen realm, Baal sat on his throne in the holy of holies of his temple. He awaited the arrival of the gods. They were late. He saw Queen Izabel in her high priestess robes of purple. She wore the Astarte wig of Hathor with the conical horned headdress of divinity upon her head.

The holy place was filled with the priests of Baal. The flames were stoked in the pit before the open arms of the bronze god. They couldn't see or hear the Watcher within the image, but he was there.

Galina and young Daniel with the pregnant Susanna stood in bindings beside the bronze statue, watched over by priests.

Today's sacrifice was going to be special. Rather than using the usual stone altar outside, Izabel had directed a private altar to be set up in the holy place—large enough to accommodate a human.

Baal stood from his throne. The gods had never arrived. His anger rose against Asherah and Anat. He would punish them. But the other gods Ashur and Marduk hadn't come either. Something was wrong.

He carried his war horn out to the entrance of the temple to blow it one last time. It was too late as far as the sacrifice was considered, but he wanted to find out why no one had responded to his call.

When he stepped outside, he saw four archangels waiting for him, standing like a bunch of peacocks with their weapons in hand.

The mouthy small one barked out, "Baalzebub, your days in Israel are over!"

Baalzebub was another Hebrew bastardization of Baal's name that was intended as an insult. Baalzebub meant "Lord of the flies."

Grinding his teeth with rage, Baal pulled out his war hammer from his back sheath. Driver was a great equalizer against these godlickers. "You dare invade my house at the height of my reign and power? You are more foolish than I previously thought."

The small angel held up the heads of Anat and Asherah. "That's what they said." He tossed the heads on the ground at Baal's feet.

Baal gave a war cry and came out swinging at his angelic foes.

●●●●●

Two priests held Susanna down on the bronze altar. She squirmed, but she was too weak, and she worried the child in her might be hurt if she fought for her life. What else could she do?

Jezebel spoke to the congregation. "Priests of Baal, you have served the king all these years. Now that royal bloodline is under attack by a traitor. Jehu, son of Nimshi, has usurped my throne!"

Susanna thought, *Her throne?* Delusion had possessed this monster.

The priests murmured with angry reaction.

Jezebel raised her hands to heaven and prayed, "We implore thee, O mighty Baal, to receive this offering to end this madness!"

Only human sacrifice could stop catastrophes and threats to the power of a city or dynasty.

Susanna panicked. For all her faith in Yahweh over the years, she knew that the eventual success of his kingdom was not without great loss and suffering. And she and her unborn son were about to be casualties in that long war. Yahweh had never promised victory or peace for everyone who served him.

Jezebel had sought to denigrate Susanna's husband Jehu. To ruin his reputation. Push him out of his political sphere of influence. But the queen had always lost. Jezebel intended to lose no more, she would obliterate Jehu's entire bloodline. This would finally destroy the man who'd been such a thorn in her side.

The queen set her hand on the helpless Susanna's belly. She gave a surprised look as she felt the baby move inside of Susanna. With a twisted smile, she said to her victim, "You should be proud. Your beautiful sacrifice will be an inspiration to mothers everywhere." She stepped back down, and the high priest of Baal ascended the steps.

As he stood over Susanna's supine form, she realized there was no escape for her. All routes had been blocked. All attempts tried and failed. All she had left was her faith in Yahweh.

• • • • •

Baal battled the four archangels out in the temple courtyard. He swung his hammer with abandon, keeping them back.

When one of them tried to jump Baal, his hammer hit the angel and sent his crushed body flying a hundred feet away. That one would be out of commission for days. Driver was hard on angelic flesh. It had been forged with heavenly metal from Eden's own mountain.

The other three continued to hound him like a pack of hyenas. Baal's huge muscles bulged with every swing. He was mighty and unafraid to take on any archangel on his own. But three were still too many. The angels were moving in on him. One of them cut his shoulder blade from behind, and he felt the pain surge through his left arm. It went weak. He wouldn't be able to withstand much longer. He seized his other weapon from his back, Chaser, the spear of death.

• • • • •

Inside the temple of Baal, the high priest mumbled a prayer in a foreign tongue and raised his blade over Susanna's belly as she lay on the altar.

She turned her head. She could not watch death come down upon her.

Then she spotted someone entering at the back of the holy place. A man with a nocked bow—aimed in her direction.

Jehu!

He released the string, and the arrow flew over the heads of the priests to hit its target, the high priest's throat just inches above Susanna. The high priest jerked backward, dropping the dagger and holding his throat, choking on his own blood.

The whole congregation went silent.

Then hundreds of soldiers flooded into the temple from the doors behind Jehu. They ran into position all around the perimeter of the holy place, weapons drawn, bows aimed. Susanna recognized some of them as Rechabites.

• • • • •

Out in the temple courtyard, Baal raised his spear into the air to receive its energy from the heavens. In the spiritual realm, lightning broke the clouds and filled Chaser with fire.

This was not Mount Carmel. This time, Baal had power.

But the moment it took to draw the energy down was too long. Baal felt the pain of three blades enter his body before he could aim Chaser at any one of them. He dropped the spear to the ground beside Driver and buckled to his knees.

Gabriel snatched up Chaser and Driver, saying, "We will be returning these to storage."

Baal glared up at the archangel Raphael, who was looking quietly down at him. The big, bulky angel didn't speak much, but he packed a mean war hammer punch.

Baal felt himself fly backwards and skid across the ground. And then he was pummeled relentlessly by the angels.

• • • • •

Inside the temple, Susanna saw Jehu walk quietly down the aisle toward her. The priests of Baal lining the aisle on either side stepped back from him in fear.

The two priests holding Susanna down backed away.

They were suddenly impaled by Jonadab, who had arrived out of nowhere with a dagger and the golden ceremonial axe. Susanna recognized the dagger as the Lion Man's blade Jezebel had confiscated from Daniel. The Rechabite leader used the blade to cut the wicked priests' throats.

Jonadab then used that same dagger to cut free Galina and Daniel.

Jehu arrived and lifted Susanna up, loosing her bindings. Embracing him, she whispered, "Jezebel has fled."

Captain Medad joined Jehu and Jonadab at the altar.

Jehu motioned to Susanna, Galina, and Daniel to follow him. The four of them walked back through the gauntlet of priests, now guarded by Jehu's soldiers. Susanna felt completely safe and unafraid of these monsters. Jehu had saved his family.

Upon reaching the exit, Jehu stopped and turned around.

The terror Susanna had felt now showed in the face of every priest.

As soldiers escorted Jehu's family out the door, Jehu called out his orders to Medad and Jonadab. "Kill them all. Burn everything. Tear down this abomination."

The doors shut behind Jehu as he joined his family. Susanna heard the screams of terror and pain and the hacking of swords on bone and flesh.

•••••

When Baal came to, he felt his whole body pulsating with pain. He had been brutally beaten by the three archangels and now found himself hanging from the large asherah pole in the courtyard. His hands had been bound with cherubim hair so he was unable to break loose. He could barely see through his black and blue puffy eyes.

He wondered where the angels had gone and why they'd done this to him. Why had they left him?

He soon found out why. According to their law, the Israelites would hang a man worthy of death on a tree as being cursed. And Baal now hung from his wrists on the wooden asherah tree, facing the temple of Baal. For the next seven days, he would be forced to watch the Israelites burn down his house, demolish it, dismantle every stone. They would then construct latrines where the temple had once stood.

They would turn the House of Baal into a house of excrement. And he would have to watch every second of it in humiliation, hanging from the asherah pole.

He had become their insult: Baalzebub, lord of the flies.

CHAPTER 66

Jezebel stood in her palace room looking out at the smoke that filled the sky from the burning of Baal's temple. She had fled from the holy place through the underground tunnel that led from the temple to the palace.

But she was going nowhere now. She had changed into a new gown, a white satin dress with an open back so her image of Leviathan could breathe.

Looking down into the streets, she saw a single man riding a chariot furiously toward the palace. It was Jehu. When he arrived at the entrance below her, she saw that he had her son Joram's body with him. It was riddled with arrows. She felt her own heart as if pierced by one of them.

Jehu looked up, and their eyes locked.

He picked up the body and threw it to the ground.

Joram landed on his back, his pale face frozen in horror, gazing mindlessly into the heavens, his blood of life gone.

Jezebel felt like throwing up and backed away from the window.

When she looked back down, Jehu was gone. But the chariot remained.

He was coming for her.

Jezebel moved over to her credenza and sat down, looking at herself in the mirror. She looked at her ivory carving of the woman in the window that she had treasured for all these years, trying to imagine herself in that art.

She reached for make-up and added more lipstick to her lips and more shading to her eyes. The image in the mirror began to appear garish and vulgar. Her heavy handed application left smears and imperfections in its wake. Yet she continued on.

She was not preparing to seduce Jehu. She was identifying with Astarte. Baal had failed her, but the goddess had been with her all her life, guiding her, guarding her, granting her wisdom and protection. Now Jezebel needed Astarte more than ever.

She looked at herself in the mirror and asked rhetorically, "Who is your queen? Who is your queen? I will show you who is your queen."

319

She felt her bandaged hand, the slice from Baal's golden axe still oozed blood and saturated the cloth.

She checked the placement of the wig on her head to make sure it was perfect. It seemed like she couldn't make it perfect. It always looked slightly off kilter.

She checked the ivory image of Astarte in the window, her hope.

She stared at the sacrificial dagger on the table, her symbol of change.

• • • • •

Jehu stepped out of the darkness of the hallway that led to Jezebel's room, a pair of soldiers flanked him. Before him stood eight brawny warriors, Jezebel's own bodyguard.

Jehu drew his sword in one hand and a mace in the other.

He walked forward, alone. His soldiers stayed back.

The lead guard rushed Jehu. He never stood a chance. Jehu cut him down in two moves.

The next came at him with a battle axe. He swung it hard. Jehu dodged. The soldier missed and found himself off balance. Jehu crushed his shoulder blade with the mace and impaled him from the side.

He holstered his mace, picked up the axe, and threw it at the most distant soldier, who had an arrow aimed right at Jehu. The arrow released before the axe took him down. But that missile flew right by Jehu's head.

He could have sworn he felt the feather brush his cheek.

Jehu kept moving forward, retrieving his mace as he walked.

A fourth guard attacked him. But Jehu was now warmed up. He cut the man down in three moves.

Five and six came at him quickly and were dispatched just as quickly.

And now he stood before the final two bodyguards guarding Jezebel's door.

But before he had the chance to finish his task, the two of them dropped their swords and ran.

Jehu stopped. He laughed to himself and gripped his weapons tighter.

There before him stood the door to Jezebel's room. How would he break it down? It was solid oak with bronze trimmings. A giant might be able to kick it open, but there had not been giants since the days of David. And he had no battering ram.

He tried the handle. It was open. Of course. Jezebel had placed too much faith in her bodyguards.

He opened the door and moved into the room silently.

He saw Jezebel sitting at a credenza with her back to him. She was rocking back and forth muttering a prayer. "Queen of Heaven, have mercy on me. Queen of Heaven, have mercy on me."

Her backless dress allowed Jehu to see a large tattoo of Leviathan on her back. How fitting for this dragon of chaos, this Lady of Tyre.

Jezebel stopped rocking and praying. Now she was watching him in the mirror.

He stepped closer.

She stopped him with words. "You do not bring peace to this kingdom, Jehu."

The reply reached his tongue before he'd even considered how to answer, "Messiah will bring peace."

"How convenient," she sneered.

He moved closer. "All my life, I have sought to be faithful to both God and king."

Getting up from her chair, Jezebel walked over to the window and looked out, her back still to him. She had felt no fear, only contempt.

She said, "That is why I knew you would betray us."

He said, "The king betrayed his God when he married you. Elijah was right. A man cannot serve two masters."

"No man is my master. I am Jezebel."

She was appropriating his insulting name. Wearing it proudly.

He added, "Harlot Queen of Baal."

He stepped even closer, right up behind her. She turned to face him and hissed, "You are a murderer of kings and queens."

He hadn't seen the dagger she'd concealed with the folds of her gown.

She pulled it out to stab him.

But he caught her hand mid-plunge and held it tight. He looked into her eyes. They were portals of darkness. He called to his two soldiers and then instructed them, "Hold her."

They grabbed her arms, one on each side. The one on her right held her dagger hand in grip, but hadn't bothered to take the blade away.

She looked into Jehu's eyes. "Kill me. Kill me with your bloodthirsty hands."

He paused, and his smirk turned sour. "You are not even worthy of my hands."

He turned and walked away, waving his hand almost like an afterthought.

The two soldiers lifted her from the ground and heaved her out the window. She fell four stories down to the pavement, where she landed on her back, splattering the wall with her blood. Her skull was crushed and her back snapped. Her face froze in a look of hatred into the sky, the dagger still clutched in her hand. Her wig lay beside her bald head in shame. She had lived in hatred, and she had died in hatred.

The corpse of her son lay next to her. The two bodies looked like broken puppets.

The horses which pulled Jehu's chariot had spooked from her falling body. They jolted forward in panic, their hooves trampling her broken body. A nearby soldier rushed to control the animals and lead them away.

By nightfall, stray dogs had found the body. They began licking up the blood and eating the flesh until only her skull and feet and palms were left.

> This is the word of Yahweh, which he spoke by his servant
> Elijah the Tishbite: "In the territory of Jezreel, the dogs shall
> eat the flesh of Jezebel, and the corpse of Jezebel shall be as
> dung on the face of the field in the territory of Jezreel, so
> that no one can say, This is Jezebel."

• • • • •

And so, I, Jehu, son of Nimshi, fulfilled God's promise to
Queen Jezebel and King Ahab for the evil they had done.
With the help of the Rechabites, I destroyed the rest of the
seed of Ahab. I tore down the House of Baal. I wiped out
Baal worship from all the land of Israel. And I became king.

Elijah the Tishbite was the first in a line of prophets sent to call the true Remnant of Israel and Judah back to Yahweh. The last of those prophets foretold that Elijah would return before the coming of Messiah and the great and terrible day of the Lord.

EPILOGUE

Jerusalem

When Athaliah heard that her husband King Jehoram was dead, she acted to fulfill her destiny. All of the king's eldest sons, *her sons*, had been killed in a raid of Arabs years ago, leaving only the youngest, Ahaziah, alive to be the lone heir to the throne. But Ahaziah had recently died. His sister Jehosheba could not inherit the throne, so it would go to the next male in the line of David.

But Athaliah knew there was a way she could become the first ruling Queen of Judah.

It required her to be bold, swift—and ruthless.

• • • • •

It was past midnight. All such plans as these took place in the late hours of the night when men, women, and families were sleeping. When they were most vulnerable.

Squads of soldiers quietly left the palace grounds under cover of darkness, hundreds of them. They moved beneath the moon shadow of the royal palace walls and split up into the city below. Some of them left for the surrounding countryside on horseback. All of them were on the same mission: to hunt down the descendants of King David.

In dozens of locations around the city, death squads approached their appointed homes with stealth, kicked down doors, and slaughtered entire families of men, women, and children who were in the Davidic line—or thought possibly to be. The children and grandchildren of families going back to Rehoboam. The lines of Abijah, Ziza, Shelomith, Zaham, Jeush, and others, were all put to the sword. Some were hanged. Others beheaded. Most were impaled through their heart or bowels. Athaliah's order not to rape the women out of respect was not heeded by the butchers.

324

This would become a night of terror remembered by all and spoken of by none for fear of the queen. And as horrible as it may have seemed in the eyes of her enemies, it was an act which established Queen Athaliah. She was as powerful and as ruthless as any king could be.

Further out in surrounding towns, horsemen of death got off their mounts and broke into houses to massacre more of the suspected bloodline. Their blades dripped with gore. The moon turned to blood. Stars fell from the sky.

The murder of Athaliah's own grandchildren was perhaps the most difficult order for her to give. But she was committed to the cause. If one was not willing to sacrifice one's own loved ones in the pursuit of the higher cause, then the perfect world could never be achieved. She considered herself to be engaging in an act of self-sacrifice for the highest good.

Residing in the upper palace grounds were a couple dozen of these royal grandchildren. These were offspring of Jehoram's brothers Azariah, Mikael, Zechariah, Jehiel, and Shephatiah. The ages of the boys and girls were from three years old up to ten or eleven. Their widowed mothers resided in rooms near each other, which made the bloody task much easier and cleaner.

The decision to kill the widowed mothers of the royal grandchildren did not come easy to Athaliah. The thought of their murders was in conflict with her great desire to see women empowered. But execute them she did, killing the mothers along with their children in order to save them from grief and spare them that pain. It was an act of compassion.

Athaliah knew the deed was done when she heard screams throughout the palace finally go silent. The soldier's blades had performed their compassionate duty.

She had consolidated her reign as the first ruling Queen of Judah by eliminating the Davidic seed, including her own children and grandchildren.

• • • • •

Jehosheba, Queen Athaliah's sixteen-year old daughter, had been spared from the atrocity because she was a female and had no children of her own. Jehosheba was married to a priest in the temple named Jehoiada and served Yahweh with her whole heart.

What the queen didn't know was that Jehosheba had discovered her mother's plans and had prepared plans of her own. On the night of terror before the killing began, Jehosheba had stolen away her favorite nephew, Joash, the one-year old son of the king. She brought him and his wet nurse into a bedchamber in the servant's quarters of the palace for hiding.

She waited for several hours until she was sure the atrocity was over. She had to get little Joash to safety. But it wasn't enough to save him for the night. She had to get him to a place where the queen couldn't find him and kill him. Where he could be raised, protected and safe, until he was old enough to take his rightful throne. And there was only one place where she trusted that goal could be accomplished: The House of Yahweh.

The temple itself and the living chambers of the temple priests were sacred space, sequestered, and considered holy. The queen couldn't enter them. Nor could her guards or soldiers or anyone else in Judah. Athaliah would never know that the crown prince was hidden there, coming of age, preparing to reign. It was Jehosheba's only option to save the last remaining seed of David.

She had to get Joash to the holy temple.

But she was in the lower palace where the servant's quarters were. She would have to get the infant and his wet nurse, another young woman named Havah, through the lower palace, uphill past the upper palace, and into the temple grounds at the top of Mount Moriah where the priests resided. It was a distance of about a half mile.

Jehosheba prayed for a miracle. It was still the dark of night. But their journey was all up hill, and they were two women carrying a one-year-old child. They would surely be discovered, they would surely be executed by the queen. Yet she had to try.

She led Havah, who carried Joash, out into the dark hallway toward the north exit of the building. They moved along as swiftly and silently as their padded feet could take them, their dark cloaks hiding them in the shadows.

They were only in the first hallway when the infant began crying. Jehosheba looked around with fright as Havah quickly opened her cloak and tried to feed the baby. He took to the nurse's breast and went silent. Jehosheba saw no one aware of their presence—yet.

They continued down the hallway, then suddenly stopped in their tracks, frozen with fear. A warrior had stepped out from behind a pillar, blocking their way. He was tall, dark and muscular with black wavy hair. He drew his sword. The women gasped and cringed, covering their heads and the infant with their arms.

Jehosheba had expected to feel the strike of a sword on her head. But instead, the dark warrior walked right past them. Opening her eyes, she turned to see him meet a cadre of eight other palace guards who'd turned the corner down their hallway.

The single dark warrior met them. Like a flowing stream of water, he engaged the eight armed guards with his single sword, cutting them down in eight moves that looked like a macabre dance of death to Jehosheba. She couldn't believe her eyes. When he was finished, he stood over the dismembered bodies which lay on the blood covered ground.

Then the dark warrior looked up at the two women, and Jehosheba felt her whole body fill with the desire to flee. But she remained still as did Havah, and the warrior approached them again.

Glancing over, Jehosheba noticed that little Joash was calm and quiet.

The warrior passed by them and said, "Follow me."

Jehosheba blurted out, "Who are you?"

He stopped and turned back to face them. "I'm a friend."

Havah could not remain silent. "Where did you come from?"

He said, "My name is Mikael. I know you need to get to the House of Yahweh to keep Joash safe. It's my job to make sure you get there."

Jehosheba had told no one about her plans. She demanded, "How could you possibly know where we were going?"

He gave her a scolding look. "Do you want to stand around asking me questions all evening until your enemies find you, or do you want to get to the holy temple and live?"

The women looked at one another, shocked. Jehosheba looked at the miraculously peaceful Joash, who watched the dark guardian and actually appeared to be smiling at him.

Jehosheba shrugged. "Well, if Joash trusts you, I suppose we have no other choice."

He smiled and led them down the hallway to the north exit.

But when they reached the big oak doors that would lead them out, he held up his hand as though sensing something or someone near. With a glance at the big doors, he motioned the two women to follow him down another hallway instead.

Catching up with him, Jehosheba whispered, "Why are we going this way? That was the exit that leads directly to the upper palace. This route will double our time."

He kept walking as he whispered back, "I thought we concluded you were done with questions." Then he explained, "You do not want to meet what was on the other side of those doors."

• • • • •

On the other side of the north exit doors stood two unearthly gods of the nations; Milcom, the abomination of the Ammonites, and Chemosh, the abomination of the Moabites. Both were mighty Watchers who had gained a stronghold in Jerusalem along with Astarte, the abomination of the Sidonians, and Molech, the abomination of the Ammonites.

The heavenly beings were in the unseen realm, unobserved and unheard by humans, but very real and very present. They were creatures of both heavenly and earthly realms. Together, they could destroy an army of earthly soldiers and possibly even overpower the archangel himself. Mikael wanted to avoid contact with those monsters for as long as possible.

But he was not without allies.

Milcom and Chemosh turned to see two heavenly warriors behind them: the archangels Uriel and Gabriel.

Chemosh, big and brutish in his Moabite armor and head full of horns, spoke in a deep voice while grinning at Uriel. "So this is the runt Yahweh sends to stop us at the last minute?"

Uriel rolled his eyes. Millennia of such insults had become boring to him.

Gabriel smiled and said, "Well, Uriel, I know which one you want."

Uriel said to the large imposing Chemosh with his head of mangled horns, "You know, of all the gods of the nations, you are certainly the ugliest."

"What about Molech?" Gabriel asked. "He's pretty damned ugly."

"Good point," said Uriel. He corrected himself, "One of the ugliest."

Chemosh bellowed a war cry, and the Watchers engaged the archangels in battle.

• • • • •

Jehosheba and Havah, carrying the infant Joash, followed Mikael through the garden on the northwest side of the palace. They had to circle back and make their way around the eastern exterior of the upper palace to get to the holy temple at the top of Mount Moriah.

After taking the long route and climbing the hill to the upper palace, the women were exhausted. They needed a moment to rest.

Mikael paused again as if sensing something ahead. "Wait here."

He left them for thirty seconds before returning. He told them, "There is a contingent of over a hundred soldiers blocking our way. But they don't know we're here."

Jehosheba asked, "What are we going to do?"

Mikael said, "We'll have to go through the palace instead."

Jehosheba thought back to the eight soldiers he'd cut down. They'd been easy for this warrior, but even he would have his limits.

"The palace?" asked Havah. "Athaliah and her bodyguard are probably there. That would be like walking into the spider's own web."

Mikael said, "That's okay. I'm a wasp."

He moved ahead to lead them into a side door of the palace.

Havah looked confused at Jehosheba, who explained, "Wasps eat spiders."

As they snuck through the halls of the palace, Jehosheba worried that at any second they'd be discovered.

They were passing through the living quarters of the sons of the king who'd been murdered earlier in the evening.

She swallowed as they reached the room of Deborah and her son Joel, son of Azariah. She'd been best of friends with Deborah. She didn't want to look inside. But she did. She dreaded what she'd see as she peered into the open door, broken on its hinges. There were no bodies. They'd all been taken away. But she could see blood covering the floor, glistening in the torchlight.

The blood of Judah filled the city this night.

"Jehosheba." The whisper was Havah pulling her out of her trance. She had to keep moving.

She caught up to a waiting Mikael and Havah with Joash. The little boy was becoming fussy. They didn't have much time, and if he began crying again, they were dead.

Suddenly, a single soldier stepped out from a hallway in front of them. He registered surprise. Mikael stopped the women. Held them behind him.

But when the soldier raised his horn and blew, Mikael yelled at them, "Quickly! Follow me."

They ran straight for the soldier, and Mikael cut him down with one swipe of his sword.

When they arrived at the end of the hallway, they turned around to see a flood of soldiers pouring in after them. They were yelling and drawing their weapons.

Mikael said to the women, "Just keep going out those doors up the hill to the temple. I will hold them back."

Jehosheba and Havah didn't have time to contemplate the impossibility of what Mikael was suggesting—that he could actually hold back one hundred soldiers. They just obeyed his orders and ran.

At the doorway, Jehosheba turned to see the sole warrior meet the first wave of soldiers as they filled the hallway after them.

He moved with such elegance and fluidity that Jehosheba thought it a thing of beauty. The dark warrior cut his enemies down with ease. But they just kept coming. He wouldn't have much longer until he was overwhelmed.

Jehosheba closed the door behind them.

As she and Havah exited the palace carrying little Joash, they saw the last hill before them. At the top was Mount Moriah and the holy temple. Using every last ounce of their strength, they worked their way up the hill quickly and quietly.

What the two women didn't see were the five Watcher gods at the top of the hill waiting for them in the unseen realm: Astarte, Molech, Marduk, high god of Babylon, and Ashur, high god of Assyria. Leading them was a healed and rejuvenated Baal. The women were heading straight into a supernatural ambush.

After his humiliation in Jezreel, Baal had journeyed to Jerusalem where Queen Athaliah had built a new temple for him. When he'd discovered the queen's plan to massacre the innocents, he'd called together the other gods to back her up because he knew Yahweh would seek to save the seed of David.

He wasn't going to let these three flesh bags into the temple area.

A voice came from behind the gods. "Baalzebub!"

The gods turned to see six archangels behind them: Uriel, Gabriel, Raphael, Saraqael, Raguel, and Remiel.

Gabriel said, "I thought we left you hanging on a tree."

Baal grinned. "You forgot about my loyal god of Tyre, Melqart. He freed me. And this time, I'm not alone for you to gang up on."

The odds were more even in this clash of titans: five Watchers and six archangels.

The gods brandished their weapons and attacked their foes.

In the earthly realm, the two women climbed the hill toward the temple area. They kept turning back to see if Mikael would join them. It was impossible of course. He couldn't possibly have beaten all hundred of those armed soldiers in combat alone. Eight maybe, even fifteen or twenty, but surely not one hundred against one.

That was the stuff of angels.

In the unseen realm, angels and Watchers were locked in fierce combat at the top of the hill. Though Baal no longer had his war hammer or spear, he did have a mace and he dished out vengeance upon those who had humiliated him in Jezreel. He went after the little mouthy angel first.

Uriel saw him and called out, "Hail, Lord Lettucehead!"

"You'll be sorry you didn't end me in Samaria," Baal growled.

Uriel smiled. "That's what Anat said. She really needs to talk less and practice more with those swords of hers." Uriel then spun his two swords around in a Karabu fighting form. Karabu was the ancient form of battle taught by the angels to the giant-killers in the days of Enoch.

But when Baal attacked him, Uriel realized that he too had better talk less and concentrate on the fight at hand, for Baal, indeed all the gods, were fighting like they'd never fought before. They were fighting for their lives, their very inheritance. If they didn't stop the seed of David, they would all be judged and "die like any prince." It was the prophecy of the eighty-second psalm that declared them guilty at the rising of the Son of David.

If a Son of David would survive to rise.

They came to this fight empowered by all the murders tonight, they would hold nothing back because they had everything to lose. They were battling, using every power and skill they possessed.

Uriel felt Baal's boot kick him in his chest. He flew down the hill, rolling through the dirt and brush, losing his swords. He barely came to his senses when he saw Baal standing over him, bringing his sword down with fury.

Gabriel had faced off with Raphael against Ashur. The Assyrian deity was the rising warrior of power here, along with Marduk of Babylon. It would take the best of the archangels to take them down. But he saw his brother Uriel make a mistake that could cost him his head. The two had been loyal brothers for millennia. He couldn't let Uriel suffer defeat. Gabriel peeled away from Raphael. "I'll be right back."

He didn't have time to see Raphael's shock as Ashur pounded on the archangel's shield and defense with relentless fury.

As Gabriel ran down the hill, he wondered where Mikael was. If the prince of Israel didn't join them soon, they could suffer great loss.

But now all he saw was Baal with sword held high.

Gabriel leapt into the air.

He landed on the monster's back, his sword penetrated Baal's spine and heart. The Watcher fell to the ground as dead.

But they didn't have much time.

"I owe you one, brother," said Uriel as he scrambled to get his swords.

"You also owe Raphael. Let's get up there!"

The angels had managed to split the gods away from one another in the fight. Saraqael and Remiel pushed back Astarte and Molech with relative ease.

Uriel and Gabriel joined Raphael and Raguel to assault Ashur and Marduk. The archangels' task was twice as difficult. They had to not only fight the Watchers, but keep them from attacking the humans just now arriving at the top of the hill.

Astarte slipped away from the battling gods, unnoticed by the archangels.

As the human women breached the summit, they could see the temple courtyard before them. Its gates were open, and they were almost there. They didn't see the spiritual war being fought around them.

And Havah didn't see the sword of Astarte pierce her from behind.

She only felt her heart burn with pain. She cried out to Jehosheba, "Take the baby!"

Jehosheba didn't ask questions. She took Joash and tried to hold Havah's hand, but the nurse refused. She fell to her knees, clutching her chest. "My heart has given out. Save the child."

Jehosheba hesitated.

"Save the child!"

Jehosheba ran.

The angels saw what was happening and disengaged from their battles to follow after Jehosheba.

Astarte pulled her sword out of the dead body of Havah and set her eyes upon the fleeing woman and child.

Her comrades gathered with her, and they walked straight into the temple after their prey.

Inside the temple courtyard, the House of Yahweh stood to the left in the center of the yard. Out in front of it was the stone horned altar where sacrifices were made. Not far away was the metal basin of the waters upon the backs of oxen as well as the pens for the sacrificial animals. Jehosheba carried little Joash to the only place she could think of: the horns of the altar.

She'd heard stories from the priests in the temple. When King David was dying, there was a contest for the throne between his sons, Adonijah and Solomon. When it was found out that David had anointed Solomon, Adonijah ran into the temple and, fearing for his life, grabbed the horns of the altar to ask for mercy. According to tradition, this act was an acceptable legal form of appeal for asylum.

Jehosheba grabbed one of the stone horns and cried out to Yahweh on behalf of little Joash for refuge and protection.

She couldn't see the six archangels surrounding her protectively in the unseen realm.

Astarte laughed as she entered the temple courtyard, the other gods joining her, beaten up, but not defeated. Ready to sacrifice themselves to the last in order to destroy the seed of David.

Molech gave a dog whistle, and four large supernatural dire wolves joined the gods. Hounds of Hades. A large lion joined Astarte as her own guardian. Now the odds finally seemed to have improved for the gods.

Astarte announced to the angels surrounding Jehosheba, "The poor wretch thinks she is protected in the temple. But she doesn't even notice the totems of our power standing right over her." She pointed to the wooden asherah pole beside the altar and gestured to the bronze serpent to the left of it: Nehushtan.

She crowed, "We cannot enter the inner temple itself, but we own everything else."

The sound of the courtyard gates closing behind them drew everyone's attention to Mikael, standing behind the gods and their wolves of war. He locked the gates and said, "You cannot enter the inner temple because you don't want to face the cherubim. So why don't we let the cherubim come out and face you."

He gave his own high-pitched whistle, and everyone's attention turned to the temple building, where two giant cherubim padded their way out of the entrance.

There were different kinds of cherubim. One was more humanoid with multiple wings and faces of humans and animals. The other was a four-legged hybrid creature with the face of a human, the body of a lion, and the wings of eagles. The ones that came out of the temple entrance were the latter. They were throne guardians of the holy of holies. They were huge, the size of three Watchers each. They growled at the cowering gods who stood before them. The dire wolves snarled and lowered their heads in submission.

Few beings in all creation could stand before these glorious creatures.

They sang the Trisagion, "Holy, holy, holy is Yahweh of hosts!" It was not merely a call to glorify Yahweh, but a call to war.

Jehoiada the priest, Jehosheba's husband, escorted his wife and the babe to safety. They left as a supernatural slaughter occurred in the courtyard. They would never know the unseen battle which raged on.

Cherubim ripped apart the bodies of the gods. Archangels cut down the hounds and their masters with renewed strength and fervor. Disemboweled, decapitated, and brought to nothing, the Watchers suffered a devastating defeat of their plans.

But the gods of the nations would not be destroyed this day. They would be cast out of the temple courtyard in pieces. Their heavenly bodies would eventually heal. They would not be bound in Tartarus, for they were still the legally allotted principalities of the nations, and they had won a stronghold in Jerusalem through the adulterous idolatry of Judah. They had legal right to remain. Their final judgment was not in God's plans yet. Yahweh had his timetable. Only the Son of David could disinherit them and bring the nations into his kingdom. But so much had yet to take place for that kingdom to come.

Jehosheba didn't see any of what went on in the unseen realm that night. She didn't see the spiritual war around her. She didn't have to. All she had to know was that she had rescued the sole surviving male of the line of King David, the seed of Messiah.

●●●●●

Get the next book in the Chronicles of the Watchers Series, *Qin: Dragon Emperor of China*. (paid link)

If you liked this book, then please help me out by writing a positive review of it <u>on Amazon here.</u> That is one of the best ways to say thank you to me as an author. It really does help my sales and status. Thanks!
– Brian Godawa

More Books by Brian Godawa

See <u>www.Godawa.com</u> for more information on other books by Brian Godawa. Check out his other series below:

Chronicles of the Nephilim

Chronicles of the Nephilim is a saga that charts the rise and fall of the Nephilim giants of Genesis 6 and their place in the evil plans of the fallen angelic Sons of God called, "The Watchers." The story starts in the days of Enoch and continues on through the Bible until the arrival of the Messiah,

Jesus. The prelude to Chronicles of the Apocalypse.
ChroniclesOfTheNephilim.com. (paid link)

Chronicles of the Apocalypse

Chronicles of the Apocalypse is an origin story of the most controversial book
of the Bible: Revelation. An historical conspiracy thriller trilogy in first
century Rome set against the backdrop of explosive spiritual warfare of Satan
and his demonic Watchers. ChroniclesOfTheApocalypse.com. (paid link)

Chronicles of the Watchers

Chronicles of the Watchers is a series that charts the influence of spiritual
principalities and powers over the course of human history. The kingdoms of
man in service to the gods of the nations at war. Completely based on
ancient historical and mythological research.
ChroniclesOfTheWatchers.com. (paid link)

Get the Book of the Biblical & Historical Research Behind This Novel.

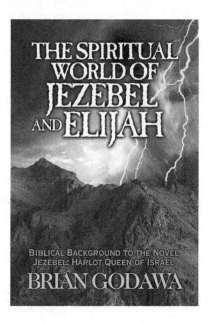

Explore the Spiritual World of Jezebel and Elijah.

If you like the novel *Jezebel*, you'll love discovering the biblical and historical basis for the supernatural, mind-bending story.

Also available for purchase in paperback.

https://godawa.com/get-spirit-world-jez/

(affiliate link)

GREAT OFFERS BY BRIAN GODAWA

ABOUT THE AUTHOR

Brian Godawa is the screenwriter for the award-winning feature film *To End All Wars*, starring Kiefer Sutherland. It was awarded the Commander in Chief Medal of Service, Honor, and Pride by the Veterans of Foreign Wars, won the first Heartland Film Festival by storm, and showcased the Cannes Film Festival Cinema for Peace.

He previously adapted to film the best-selling supernatural thriller novel *The Visitation* by author Frank Peretti for Ralph Winter (*X-Men, Wolverine*), and wrote and directed *Wall of Separation*, a PBS documentary, and *Lines That Divide*, a documentary on stem cell research.

Mr. Godawa's scripts have won multiple awards in respected screenplay competitions, and his articles on movies and philosophy have been published around the world. He has traveled around the United States teaching on movies, worldviews, and culture to colleges, churches, and community groups.

His popular book *Hollywood Worldviews: Watching Films with Wisdom and Discernment* (InterVarsity Press) is used as a textbook in schools around the country. In the top ten of biblical fiction on Amazon, his first novel series, *Chronicles of the Nephilim*, is an imaginative retelling of biblical stories of the Nephilim giants, the secret plan of the fallen Watchers, and the War of the Seed of the Serpent with the Seed of Eve. The sequel series, *Chronicles of the Apocalypse*, tells the story of the apostle John's book of Revelation, while *Chronicles of the Watchers* recounts true history through the Watcher paradigm.

Find out more about his other books, lecture tapes, and DVDs for sale at his website, www.godawa.com.

Made in the USA
Coppell, TX
31 March 2021

52740033R00197